NEW HOPE F[illegible] THE CLARKS FACTORY GIRLS

MAY ELLIS

B

First published in Great Britain in 2025 by Boldwood Books Ltd.

Cover Design by Colin Thomas

Cover Images: Colin Thomas and Shutterstock

A CIP catalogue record for this book is available from the British Library.

Paperback ISBN 978-1-83633-913-7

Large Print ISBN 978-1-83633-912-0

Hardback ISBN 978-1-83633-911-3

Ebook ISBN 978-1-83633-914-4

Kindle ISBN 978-1-83633-915-1

Audio CD ISBN 978-1-83633-906-9

MP3 CD ISBN 978-1-83633-907-6

Digital audio download ISBN 978-1-83633-908-3

This book is printed on certified sustainable paper. Boldwood Books is dedicated to putting sustainability at the heart of our business. For more information please visit https://www.boldwoodbooks.com/about-us/sustainability/

Boldwood Books Ltd, 23 Bowerdean Street, London, SW6 3TN

www.boldwoodbooks.com

This book is dedicated to everyone who has ever worked for C & J Clark Ltd whose headquarters are in Street, Somerset. The shoe company celebrates its bicentenary in 2025, having grown from its humble beginnings in 1825 to become a global brand. Long may it continue.

1

JUNE 1917

The hammering on the front door woke both Kate Davis and her landlady, Betty Searle, from their deep sleep. The two of them met outside their bedroom doors, each pulling on dressing gowns over their nightclothes.

'Whoever can it be, making such a racket at this time of the night?' grumbled the older woman as the noise, which had ceased for a moment, started up again.

'I peeped out of my window, Auntie,' said Kate. 'It's some young lad.' She'd looked because she'd been afraid it was her pa, drunk and belligerent as usual, come to cause more embarrassment to her. 'Do you want me to go down and tell him to go away?'

Auntie Betty tightened the belt of her dressing gown and shook her head. 'We'll both go down and see him off. Come on, lass. The sooner we shut him up, the quicker we can get back to our beauty sleep.'

She led the way down the stairs in the dark, then stopped to light a lamp before flinging the door open. The lad who had been hammering on it staggered, nearly falling through the doorway before he was able to catch himself and step back.

'You'd better have a jolly good excuse to be rousing folks at this time of the night, young man, or I'll box your ears,' she said. 'What on earth are you thinking?'

The lad gulped at the two women's fierce expressions. 'Sorry, missus, but the constable sent me. Reggie Davis's house is on fire. He said you should come straight away.'

'Oh my word!' gasped Kate. 'What on earth has he done now?'

'It's a proper blaze, it is,' said the lad. 'The whole street is awake and trying to put the flames out, else it spreads to the other cottages. You'd better come quick.'

When Kate would have rushed out the door after the lad, Auntie Betty grabbed her arm to stop her. 'Go on and tell them she's coming,' she told the lad. 'But she'll not be running through the village in her nightgown.'

The lad nodded and ran off as she shut the door and turned to Kate. 'Are you all right, lass? Because you don't have to go, you know. Reggie Davis has long since lost any right to expect any consideration from you.'

Kate agreed. He had been a cruel father who had become worse when her dear ma had died. The woman he'd moved into the family home shortly after – referred to by Kate and her friends as the Floozy – had been even worse, attacking and mistreating Kate and even encouraging her horrible children to do the same. Kate had been forced to endure it until her older brothers had heard about it and rescued her. She'd lived with Auntie Betty – her ma's oldest friend – ever since, but that hadn't stopped Pa and the Floozy and their wild offspring from abusing her in the streets if she wasn't quick enough to get out of their paths.

'I know, Auntie,' she said. 'But the constable sent the lad to get me. I should go round, shouldn't I? And he is my pa, whether he deserves the title or not.'

She sighed and nodded. 'You're right, lass. But I'll not let you go on your own. Let's get dressed and we'll go together.'

* * *

The village of Street seemed eerily quiet as they made their way from their home in The Mead to the Davis family home in Silver Road. As they got closer to their destination, however, they began to hear the shouts of people and the roar of the fire. They could see the glow in the sky before they turned into the road.

Kate groaned as she saw the crowd of people around her father's house, which was an inferno. It was rented from Clarks, where she and her pa worked. She wondered how he'd talk his way out of this one. It was a miracle he still had any work after he'd been sacked last year for being drunk at his station in the Clicking Room. He'd ruined a perfectly good hide of leather, which was already in short supply on account of the war. This was the last in a long line of mistakes he'd made while in his cups. He'd been out of work for a couple of months before he managed to persuade Clarks to take him back on rather than let him end up in the workhouse, although that fate was no more than he deserved, in Kate's opinion. How he'd talked his way back into Clarks, she'd never know. She supposed it was because of the chronic shortage of labour as so many young men were away fighting in the trenches. But they didn't trust him with a skilled job any more, so he spent his days doing menial tasks like sweeping the yards, cleaning windows and ferrying goods between the different departments on a hand cart. Kate suspected he was pilfering things from the factory because she couldn't see how his reduced earnings could pay the bills and still leave anything over for his beloved cider. She knew that he was still drinking, because some people delighted in telling her about the fights he got into at the Street Inn. And now the house he rented from their employers – where Kate and her siblings had been born, and their beloved ma had died – was ablaze.

Smoke and flames poured from the windows, lighting up the area around the building. People were passing buckets of water hand to hand in an effort to quench the flames. The village fire engine had arrived and the firefighters were aiming their hoses at the building, but it was clear that the Davis home was beyond help.

Kate stood on the edge of the crowd, watching, as the man in charge directed the firefighters to dampen down the neighbouring buildings in an effort to save them. Auntie Betty put an arm around her. All of Kate's old neighbours were out on the street, everyone doing what they could to help fight the fire.

'Where is he?' she asked. 'I can't see Pa anywhere.'

'He'll be around somewhere, lass,' said Betty. 'Although I wouldn't put it past him and that floozy to have run off rather than face the consequences of their drunken foolishness.'

A woman standing next to them shook her head. 'They're still in there,' she said, pointing to the blazing house. 'I'm sorry, Katie lass. But I don't think anyone has come out.'

Betty gasped as Kate felt a chill run down her from head to toe. 'Are you sure?' she asked. 'I mean, were they even there? They could've been out carousing for all anyone knows.' They often left the children on their own, she knew. The chill in her body got worse, even as she felt the heat from the flames on her face. She disliked those children almost as much as she loathed their mother; they were little beasts who'd made her life a misery. They had a newborn as well. Kate hadn't seen it, but she'd heard it was a boy. But she would never wish them dead. If Pa and the Floozy had run off and left the little ones inside, there was no hope for them. She didn't want this sort of fate for the children, no matter what.

The woman shook her head again, unable to look Kate in the eye. 'I heard screaming and your pa shouting. I thought they were just having another fight – lord knows they have 'em regular enough. But then we smelt the smoke. I'm sorry, lass. By the time we came out to see, the fire was too fierce for anyone to go in there to get 'em out.'

Kate closed her eyes. Even the wickedest folk didn't deserve to die like this. Yet she couldn't believe it to be true. She felt sure they would all appear once the excitement died down, unharmed and the same as ever. Maybe this would be a good thing for them – show them the error of their ways. Lord knows, those children deserved better.

'Should I go round and tell Ada and Vi?' she asked Auntie Betty. Her sisters-in-law both lived around the corner in Goswell Road. Their husbands – Kate's brothers – were both away in the trenches. None of them would be concerned about the fate of the adult occupants of the Davis family home, but she felt they should know.

The older woman shook her head. 'Leave them be, lass. They've got their babies to think of so they won't be able to rush round here. Chances are someone has already knocked on their doors like that lad did for us. We'll go and let them know what's what when we know for sure.'

Kate nodded. Clearly, Betty was thinking the same as she was, expecting the family to appear like phoenixes out of the ashes. They would have an excuse for how the fire had started –

all lies, of course. Someone else would be blamed, even though every decent soul in the village knew Pa and the Floozy lied about everything. She took a deep breath. No matter. Whether Pa and his second family were alive or dead, it was nothing to her. She could only hope that, with the house reduced to ashes, they would finally leave Street, never to return.

'I feel like I should be doing something,' Kate murmured as people moved around, hauling water or helping to rescue furniture and belongings from the neighbouring houses in case the fire spread along the terrace. 'But I don't know what.' She felt strangely lethargic, as though she were in a dream, that none of this was real, even though the air was full of choking smoke that made her chest tight, and her skirt and shoes were damp from the water that had slopped from buckets as people rushed past them.

'There are plenty doing their best. There's nothing for you to do, love. I think you'd be best getting over to that constable over there.' A stern-faced police officer was surveying the scene, making notes and asking questions of the people standing around him. 'I reckon he's the one who sent the lad for you. Best find out what he's wanting.'

'When did you last see your pa?' he asked after she approached him and identified herself.

She shrugged. 'Weeks ago,' she said. 'Even then, we didn't talk.' In truth, she made sure to stay well away from anywhere he might be. 'I've not lived here in over a year.'

'She lodges with me because he mistreated her so,' said Auntie Betty, who remained steadfast by her side. 'And that man carried on attacking her even then. He was locked up for a few weeks for setting about her in front of witnesses a while back – you'll have it in your records.'

Kate shivered as she remembered the day when Pa had

grabbed her by her hair in the high street, demanding her purse and telling her he was taking her home to be his skivvy again. She'd been rescued by her friend Jeannie's brother Peter, who'd given her attacker a black eye before the constable had arrived and taken him off to gaol.

The constable nodded, his expression grim. 'We know Reggie Davis well enough, ma'am.'

'Is… is he dead?' asked Kate.

He shrugged. 'No one knows for sure, lass. But if he's in there, he will be,' he said. 'Neighbours reported hearing shouts, but they might have escaped. No one's seen him, though. Nor the rest of them. There's no point in looking for him until first light, and even then, I reckon we should search what's left of the house for bodies first. No point in wasting our time looking for a ghost, is there?'

Kate closed her eyes and nodded. She crossed her arms over her chest, trying to dispel the odd feeling of cold dread that shook her body even as the heat from the blazing cottage scorched her cheek.

Someone caught the constable's attention and he strode off to deal with whatever it as they were telling him. Auntie's arm came round her shoulders again and she leaned into the older woman.

'All right, Katie, love?' she asked gently.

'I don't know,' she whispered. 'If I wish him dead, does that make me as wicked as him? Will I go to hell?'

'Ah, come here, lass.' Betty turned and pulled Kate into a hug. She patted Kate's hair as she buried her face in her landlady's shoulder. 'You're not wicked. You've been treated so ill by that man, it's only natural you should want him gone from your life. Don't fret now. Dead or alive, I reckon he's gone too far this time. He'll not be welcome around these parts again, that's for sure.'

'But we don't even know if he started the fire. It could have been any of them, couldn't it?'

'Maybe,' Betty conceded. 'But don't you remember the time he knocked over a lamp once and set fire to your ma's best curtains? He was in his cups then, the fool. It was only her quick actions that prevented him burning down the house then. I'm not saying he did it deliberately, but Reggie Davis is a danger to himself and others when he's drunk.'

Kate couldn't argue with that. He was always a sour old beggar, but when he'd had his fill of cider, he turned nasty, lashing out on a whim. Kate had taken many a slap from him for just being in the same room. She wished she could remember just one instance of her pa being kind or making her feel like he cared for anyone but himself, but she couldn't think of a single one. It made her heart ache.

They stayed there through what was left of the night, joining the lines passing buckets hand to hand. At first, Kate had expected someone to tell her to get away, that her family had done enough damage, but no one did. She didn't know whether it was because they knew it wasn't her fault and she genuinely wanted to help, or because they were simply too heart-sore and weary of the fight to save the homes to care who was there to help.

She watched in horror as the roof of the cottage collapsed and the homes on either side began to burn in earnest. She cried then, her heart breaking for the people who had been good neighbours to her and Ma and then had to put up with the disgusting behaviour of Pa, the Floozy and their children. She didn't know how this fire had started, but these good people didn't deserve to lose their homes like this. Everything they'd worked for all their lives turned to ashes because of whatever had happened in her pa's cottage. She had never been more ashamed to be Reggie Davis's daughter.

As dawn rose, the fire was at last brought under control. Three cottages were destroyed. Others were damaged by smoke and water.

'We should leave, lass,' said Auntie Betty, wiping her forehead. She looked so tired that Kate immediately felt guilty that she hadn't insisted the older woman had gone home to rest.

'You go, Auntie. I can't,' she said.

'There's nothing more you can do, lass. We've got a half-day shift starting in a few hours,' she reminded her. It was Saturday. 'They'll still be expecting us at the factory. We'll need to work, then we can rest this afternoon.'

'But...' She sighed. She was bone-tired and wanted nothing more than to wash off the smoke clinging to her skin, hair and clothes. But she shook her head again. 'I have to stay. To see if... I need to know if they're in there.'

She looked at Kate, her gaze a mix of love and pity. 'All right, lass. Stay if you must. I'll let your supervisor know what's happened in case you don't manage to get there in time to clock in.'

'I'll get into trouble, won't I, if I miss work?' she said, torn between waiting to see if the cottage was where her pa had met his end, and not missing her shift. She only had herself to rely on and her wages weren't that good, even though she did better these days on piecework. Lads her age earned more, even if they weren't as skilled. It wasn't fair, but regardless of that, she couldn't afford to miss even a half-shift.

Auntie Betty shook her head. 'Don't fret, lass. Bad as he proved to be, he's still your pa. If you need to stay, I'll speak to personnel and make sure you don't suffer on account of it.' She ran a weary hand down her face. 'But I've reached my limit, lass, so I'll take myself home and rest awhile. I'll go round to your sisters-in-law on the way and let them know what's happened and that you're still here.'

Kate nodded. 'Tell them not to worry. Their little ones come first, not him.'

* * *

Vi arrived half an hour later, having left her children with Ada. She rushed over to Kate, who stepped back, holding her hands in front of her when she would have hugged her. 'Don't, Vi. I'm all sooty and filthy.'

Vi grabbed her hands, her anxious gaze running over Kate. 'I don't care about that! Are you all right? I heard the commotion in the night but I had no idea what it was and didn't want to leave the babies to find out. I didn't know what was going on until Betty Searle knocked.' She looked at the still smouldering ruins of the cottages and gasped. 'Oh my word, what has that devil done now?'

Kate shrugged, too tired to say anything.

'What's he done?' asked a man standing nearby. It was their neighbour, Mr Harding, someone that Kate had known all her life. His arms were around his weeping wife. His children sat on the ground, still in their nightclothes, soot-laden blankets around their shoulders, staring at their ruined home. 'I'll tell you what he's done. That fool has gone too blooming far, that's what. It wasn't enough that he made our lives a misery with his drinking and carousing and fighting all day and night. No, he had to burn down my damned cottage, that's what! Look at it! Fifty years my family's lived there – my grandpa got the tenancy when he was an outworker, then my pa took over when he married my ma, then me and the missus took over when they passed. Fifty years! Gone!'

'I'm so sorry,' said Kate, her tears overflowing again.

The man turned on her. 'Sorry doesn't put a roof over my head, Kate Davis. Sorry doesn't give me back what that pa of yours has taken from me and my family. I hope he rots in hell!'

'So do we,' said Vi, her voice tight as she stepped forward to stand between Kate and the angry man. 'Believe me, we've no love for Reggie Davis. You've no idea what he's put this family through, especially Kate. But none of this is her fault.' She waved an arm towards the ruined buildings. 'She doesn't even live here any more, hasn't for months.'

'Vi, it's all right,' Kate said wearily. 'Don't argue with him, please.' She moved around Vi and approached him. 'I'm so sorry,' she said again. 'I tried to help. We all did. If there's anything I can do...'

The man's wife put her hand up to his cheek, stopping him when he would have started to shout again. 'Don't, love,' she said through her tears. 'She's right. It's not Kate's fault. It was that woman. She drove the lass from her own home and now... oh, God!' she sobbed. 'What are we going to do?'

Kate closed her eyes, shame flooding her as the woman fell against her husband, weeping. She felt so helpless in the face of their despair. That her own pa was no doubt responsible, whether it was a deliberate act or an accident, was almost too much to bear. She'd spent so long trying to drag herself out from under his influence, to get people to see her as a person in her own right – a good person who worked hard and respected others – but now she would be back to square one. She was Reggie Davis's daughter and after this, no one was ever going to forget it.

A shout from nearer the ruins caught everyone's attention.

Grim-faced firemen came out of the ruined building. Everyone who remained outside the burnt cottages froze as they waited to hear the latest news.

One of them spoke to the weary-looking constable. He asked a couple of questions which had the fireman shaking his head. With a sigh, he turned, his gaze catching Kate's.

'A woman, two children and an infant have died here. But there's no sign of Reggie Davis,' he announced.

Kate felt as though her heart had stopped. She couldn't breathe as he went on. 'It's therefore safe to assume that he is a fugitive and likely responsible for the deaths of these souls.'

'Oh dear God,' muttered Vi. 'Now he's gone and killed them, the stupid, horrible man. He'll hang for sure.'

Kate hung her head and closed her eyes, willing her lungs to work again. She pulled in a painful breath, shame flooding her. She was only grateful her poor, dear Ma wasn't here to witness this. She wouldn't let herself think about the relief flooding her at the knowledge that the Floozy was dead and couldn't torment her ever again. That woman had been so cruel to Kate, nearly choking her to death once – if Jeannie hadn't been there, she would have been dead for sure. But she couldn't help feeling sick to her stomach that those little ones had suffered such a fate. They hadn't deserved that any more than they'd deserved such terrible parents.

'Where is he?' someone shouted. 'We'll hunt him down, the murdering so-and-so. He's got to pay for all of this.'

Kate didn't look up. She knew that, like her, they were more angry about the destruction of the homes than the death of the Floozy, who with Pa, had made their lives a misery, but to cause the death of such young ones was beyond the pale. The children had been unpopular as well, but she knew these good people would acknowledge that they were under their mother's bad influence. None of them would wish them such a terrible death. She felt a pang of regret that the baby, born just a few months ago, would never have the chance to experience life. It had been too young to have been corrupted by the rest of its family yet – a true innocent. She couldn't mourn Pa and the Floozy, if he had indeed perished in the fire, although that added a new level of shame on her heart. As a God-fearing person, she should have been able to forgive them for their ill-treatment of her. But she couldn't. The wounds they had inflicted on her body and mind were too deep and too raw.

'Where on earth could he have gone?' whispered Vi. 'He's got no friends round here.'

Fear filled Kate. 'What if he's gone to Ada's? Or Auntie Betty's? Should we go and make sure they're all right?' The idea that Pa might harm more women and children terrified her.

Another shout came from the back of the cottages. 'We've got him!'

Men ran towards the noise.

'Phew!' said Vi, resting her hand over her heart. 'Thank goodness for that. I was ready to run home and grab my biggest skillet to hit him with if he'd got anywhere near my little ones. Looks like I won't end up having his blood on my hands after all. Shame.'

Kate put a hand over her mouth, trying to stifle the hysterical laugh that escaped. 'I was going to grab one of those bricks from the rubble pile.'

'That'd do the trick,' her sister-in-law agreed, her tone matter of fact, as though they were talking about the best way to remove a stain. 'But thankfully, we won't be called upon to do violence. The constables can sort him out.'

They watched as Reggie was dragged forward. He was pale and looked confused. Dried blood matted his hair. His clothes were scorched and his hands were red and blistered. He didn't try to fight off his captors, nor did he seem to notice the destruction around him.

'He was passed out in the outhouse,' said one of the men who was holding him up. 'Looks like he crawled there.' He pointed to the mud and grime on Pa's trousers.

'Drunk as usual!' spat one of the women in the crowd. 'Crawled there like the filthy worm he is. I hope they hang him high.'

'Wha?' Pa looked up and seemed to notice the people standing there for the first time. 'Wha's gone on?'

The silence that greeted his question chilled Kate. She couldn't look at him. Had he been so drunk he hadn't known he'd killed the Floozy and their children? Or was this all the Floozy's fault? Lord knows, Kate had learned the painful lesson that the woman was capable of anything.

'You're coming with us, Reggie. You'll be going before the magistrate as soon as we can arrange it.'

Reggie shook his head as though trying to clear it. 'What you talking about? I ain't done nothing.'

At the jeers of some of the crowd, he looked around, noting at last the destruction of his and his neighbours' homes.

'What the hell? Who did this?' he demanded.

'You did, you drunken fool,' screamed one woman. 'You killed your own family and nearly killed us in our beds.'

Kate cringed as he began to protest, declaring he didn't know what they were talking about, trying to get out of taking responsibility for his actions as usual. It didn't matter to his neighbours if he'd done it deliberately or by accident – or if it was even his fault at all – he'd caused enough trouble for all of them for too long. She turned away, unable to bear it.

'I've got to get to work,' she said.

Vi put a hand on her arm to stop her. 'Betty's telling Mr Briars what's been going on. They won't be expecting you in today.'

Kate shrugged, her gaze on the sodden ground. 'I've no excuse, have I? He's still alive. Even if he was dead, I don't believe it would be reason enough for me to miss work in the circumstances. I'd better get on.' She kissed Vi's cheek, urging her to go on home to her babies. She didn't look back at Pa, who was being man-handled by the constables. The crowd jeered and shouted at him as they dragged him away.

2

On Saturday afternoon, Jeannie was in the bedroom she shared with her ma when her sister-in-law Louisa knocked and came in.

'Are you all right, love?' she asked.

Jeannie looked up from the book she was reading and nodded. 'I just wanted some time on my own. It's not often I can be in here alone, with Ma spending so much time in bed.' A combination of depression and arthritis kept Mrs Musgrove bed-bound a lot of the time. 'But she's feeling all right today and the twins helped her downstairs. She's enjoying sitting out in the garden this afternoon. She feels better in the sunshine.'

Louisa sat on the bed beside her. 'Then is it the news about Reggie Davis and the Floozy that's upset you? Because it sounds like the rest of the village is rejoicing.' She pulled a face. 'It's horrible about the little ones, though.'

She shook her head, looking down at her hands on her lap. 'No. I can understand why folk would be glad that awful woman is gone, even though I know I shouldn't judge – that's up to the Almighty. But I don't want to think about the rest of it – those children dying and their neighbours losing their homes. It's going to be hard for Kate, with people saying her pa could be a murderer, isn't it?'

'Mmm,' Louisa agreed. 'So long as no one tries to imply that Kate is anything like him and the Floozy, because I'll soon put them right if they do. She suffered more than anyone at their hands. None of this is her fault.'

'I know. We'll all support her, no matter what.'

Kate, Jeannie and Louisa had been friends since they'd started school together and looked out for each other through everything that happened in their lives. Since the war had begun three years ago, they'd all been through difficult times.

Louisa stroked her sister-in-law's hair. 'But if that's not what's driven you inside on a summer's afternoon, what has?'

Jeannie looked away, her gaze catching sight of Lucas – Jeannie's brother and Louisa's husband – and his friend Tom standing outside in the back garden. She closed her eyes briefly before she looked back at her friend. Louisa glanced out of the window, suddenly understanding.

'Ah. You're avoiding Tom, aren't you?'

'No,' she denied, lifting her chin.

Louisa raised her eyebrows but didn't say anything.

Jeannie blew out a breath, her shoulders slumping. 'All right, so I am. I just don't see why he needs to come round here so much. It... it's hard, you know?' Her cheeks grew pink under her friend's scrutiny.

Louisa put an arm around her shoulders. 'I know, love. But now more people know about him being an amputee, he keeps getting asked to make other appliances for people like that false leg he modified for himself, and the splint he made to help Lucas with his injured arm. You know Lucas and Peter are helping him. If it's any consolation, I think it's just as hard for him being here. You know he's mighty fond of you.'

She shrugged. 'And much good it does us, with him having a wife already.' When Tom had first come to work at Clarks from his home town in Northampton, Jeannie had been wary of him. He'd come to her rescue after she'd fought off a drunken attack from a lad called Sid Lambert. She'd been ashamed that he'd seen her like that, and a little scared by Tom's blazing emotions when he'd looked at her. But as time had gone by, she'd got to know Tom and found him to be a lovely chap. She'd begun to have high hopes that he might return her feelings, only to have her dreams dashed when he confessed to her that, although he was indeed very fond of her, he could do nothing about it because he was already married. That his bride had chosen to be unfaithful to him while he was away fighting and was now living with his cousin as husband and wife was irrelevant as far as the law was concerned. Tom was legally tied to the woman, which meant Jeannie couldn't be with him. She'd not live in sin with any man; she just couldn't do it. It would break her ma's heart. Not that he'd asked her; Tom respected her too much for that. It still hurt, though.

'Oh, Jeannie. I know it's hard, but there's nothing to stop the two of you being friends, is there? We all need friends, don't we?'

She nodded, sighing. 'I suppose. But sometimes, it just gets too much to bear, you know? It's so hard trying to keep things friendly with lads. I thought I could get along with Cyril next door, but since I told him I didn't want to be his sweetheart, he's been a bit standoffish. I think I might have hurt his feelings.'

Louisa scoffed. 'He'll live, the toffee-nosed twit,' she said. 'Just because he's a teacher, doesn't mean Cyril's any better than any of us. I'm glad you didn't go out with him, Jeannie. He's no fun and spends all his time telling people what to do. He'd make your life a misery, love.' She squeezed Jeannie, leaning closer to whisper in her ear. 'And he's not nearly as handsome as Tom, is he?'

She couldn't deny it. Cyril definitely wasn't as handsome as Tom. Cyril, who was lodging next door with his grandpa while he taught at the local Board School, was pale and skinny on account of his asthma. Whereas Tom, a former soldier, was an engineer at Clarks, and was tall, strong and full of life, despite having lost his foot and part of his leg in battle. He didn't dwell on his loss though, but simply got on with life as best he could.

It seemed as though Cyril liked to demonstrate his superior intellect at every opportunity, such as when she hadn't read a book he mentioned when they chatted over the garden fence. It made her cross, because she read plenty of books from the library in the Crispin Hall – just not the same ones as Cyril. She liked uplifting stories that made her feel better in these difficult times, whereas he favoured Greek mythology and other such serious tomes. She found them depressing, full of unpronounceable names and gods changing into animals and the like. They just confused her, making her feel stupid.

Tom never made her feel inferior, just sad. They'd shared one beautiful kiss and he'd told her that if he was free, he'd want to be her sweetheart. But he was too honourable to lead her on, knowing he wouldn't be able to wed her.

'I went off Cyril when he mocked Tom for his limp,' she said.

'What?' Louisa sat up straighter. 'When was this?'

'A while ago,' she said. 'I meant to tell you, but I forgot. But don't worry, I put him straight. I told him, our Tom's a war hero. He's making the best of things and helping others, never making excuses or feeling sorry for himself. There's at least half a dozen men around here that Tom and Lucas have helped now, so no one has any right to criticise Tom for limping, or Lucas for having a weak arm after being injured fighting for king and country, especially not someone who hasn't fought for anything.'

Tom had kept the true extent of his injury secret when he'd first come to Street, but eventually it had come out and, thanks to his skill at creating things to help other men returning injured from the battlefield, word had spread. Most people respected him for it, but clearly Cyril didn't appreciate Tom's talents.

'Oh my, what did he say?'

She shrugged. 'He started spluttering about his asthma and that he was doing important work, shaping young minds. I told him fine, but that didn't give him the right to mock war heroes or to act like he was any better than they were.' She didn't mention he'd frightened the life out of her, making her think she'd set him off with an asthma attack when he'd started gasping for air after she told him off.

Jeannie sighed again. These days she was polite to him on account of his grandpa being their next-door neighbour, but that didn't mean she wanted Cyril to be a close friend. She'd settle for being polite to each other, but he could barely manage that.

'The more I hear about that man, the less impressed I am by him,' Louisa said. 'He might not be as sneaky as his cousin Douglas, but he's no catch, is he?'

Douglas had been Jeannie's sweetheart a while back, but she'd discovered he was only interested in her so that he could worm his way into the Quakers and pretend he was a pacifist to avoid conscription. He'd been so convincing that Jeannie had believed him when he'd declared he loved her and was becoming a Quaker Friend like her and her family. But he had shown his true colours at a dance at Crispin Hall. She'd found him in a corner, kissing Doris, Sid Lambert's sister, in a way that wasn't decent. She'd thrown some drinks over them and Douglas hadn't been able to avoid conscription when it came into effect in

1916 because everyone had known about his deception. She hadn't seen or heard anything of him since, other than to hear he was fighting in the trenches.

She pulled a face. 'I know. But he lives next door, and I rather like old Mr Baker, even if he is a bit grumpy. He gives us a lot of advice about our kitchen garden – we didn't produce half as much as we do now until he started helping us. He'll not be happy if I'm rude to this grandson, not after the fuss with Douglas as well.'

Louisa shook her head. 'You don't have to be rude, just keep your distance from Cyril. But I still think you should give Tom a chance to be your friend. You've always got on with him pretty well, haven't you? That's why I can't understand why you're hiding up here today.'

Jeannie grimaced. 'You're right. I suppose I am hiding. It's just that I've had another letter from Michael.'

'The conscientious objector you've been corresponding with?'

She nodded. Both she and Kate had been writing to young men locked up for refusing to take up arms on account of their pacifist beliefs. 'Even while he's in gaol, he's managed to get himself engaged.'

Louisa frowned. 'Really? How?'

'It seems the daughter of a family friend lives near the prison and has been visiting him as well as writing to him. They've fallen in love and she's agreed to marry him when he finishes his sentence.'

'Goodness. Well, it just goes to show that you can find love in the most unlikely places, can't you?'

Jeannie smiled. She was happy for Michael and his young lady, but that didn't mean that she expected such a happy ending for herself. She believed she had found love – at least, she was fairly sure that it was love that she felt for Tom. But, with him being legally wed to another woman, albeit an unfaithful one... Jeannie tried not to think on it too much because she couldn't see how they could ever be together.

'I know you're trying to help,' she said. 'But can we not talk about my marriage prospects right now?'

Louisa gave her a sympathetic smile. 'All right. I just want you to be happy with a good man.'

'Like you are, you mean?' She nudged her shoulder. 'Who'd've thought it, eh? You and Lucas make a good match.'

Louisa laughed. 'We do, don't we? I never thought I'd ever be happy again after Mattie was killed. But... well, me and Lucas understand each other's grief and that's brought us closer together.' She glanced out of the window, where her husband and his friend were deep in discussion over some sort of contraption outside the open shed door. 'I'm happier than I expected, thanks to him. He's a good man and I'm so lucky he took a chance on me.'

Jeannie knew that it wasn't a great love match for Louisa because she'd witnessed the romance between Louisa and Mattie Searle, Betty's youngest son. They had been set to wed, but her pa had said no on account of Mattie being a Quaker. Mattie had enlisted and been killed in France, leaving poor Lou heartbroken and pregnant. She had run away to live with Mattie's brother, who was married to Kate's sister Peg. Once the baby was born, she'd had to leave him in their care, knowing they would love him as their own as her own parents had refused to countenance her returning home with an illegitimate child. She had never been the same, but Lucas had been a good friend to her, on account of Mattie being his oldest and closest friend.

Then Louisa's pa had died and her ma had sold their house

and moved to Exeter to run a boarding house. When Louisa had refused to go, she'd been cut off without a penny.

So Lucas had stepped in and he and Louisa were married last October. Jeannie had been thrilled that her friend was now her sister-in-law, but she knew that Louisa's heart would always belong to Mattie. It worried her sometimes that Lucas would get his heart broken, but Jeannie couldn't deny that their marriage seemed to be working well. Both of them seemed happy enough, so maybe she should stop worrying about them.

'I don't know about that,' said Jeannie. 'I think he's the lucky one, and so am I. I'm so glad you married Lucas. You're the best sister a girl could have.'

'Aw, bless you. So are you. I've always wanted a sister.' She wrinkled her nose. 'I'm still not sure about having younger brothers, though. The twins are a bit of a challenge, aren't they?'

Jeannie laughed. 'That they are. Well, John is. Peter seems to be growing up at last. He's not as obsessed with football as John since he started his apprenticeship in the mechanic's department. At least John is more content now he's gone to work for Ada Davis's pa at the haulage company. He never was happy at Clarks.' She stood up. 'Anyway, let's go and see if there's any elderflower cordial left, shall we? It's too hot for tea.'

As they went downstairs, Jeannie hesitated. 'Do you think Kate's all right? Should we go round and see her?'

Louisa shook her head. 'Not yet. She'll be sleeping, having been up most of the night. Anyway, Auntie Betty's there at home with her. We can either pop round this evening, or wait and ask Auntie how she is when we see her at the meeting tomorrow.' Louisa had left the Anglican church and joined the Quakers when she and Lucas had married. Kate had attended some meetings with Betty Searle when she'd first started lodging with her, but had decided to go back to Holy Trinity after her brother

George enlisted, so that she could accompany her sister-in-law Ada and help her with her two small children at services.

Jeannie couldn't imagine what poor Kate was going through now. If her pa was convicted of murdering the Floozy and her children, as well as burning down three cottages owned by the Clarks, the chances were he'd be facing the gallows. She felt sick at the thought of it. She couldn't imagine how Kate must be feeling.

'All right,' she said. 'We can pop round later. If she's still resting, we can see her tomorrow.'

In the kitchen, Louisa made up a jug of elderflower cordial and put it on a tray with some tumblers. 'There's some sponge cake in the pantry,' said Jeannie.

'Lovely,' Louisa smiled as she picked up the tray. 'I'll take these outside. You follow along with the cake.'

Jeannie took her time, collecting the cake, a knife and some small plates. She was still nervous about seeing Tom. She always had such a bittersweet feeling when he was around these days – happy to see him, but disappointed and frustrated that nothing would ever come of it. It was like a physical pain sometimes, and she didn't know how long she could bear it. But she knew she'd rather see him and feel the pain than not see him at all, so she took a deep breath and found a tray to carry everything outside.

But before she could pick it up, the back door opened and Tom stepped inside.

'Jeannie.' He nodded at her.

Jeannie nodded back, feeling her cheeks warm. She wondered briefly whether her gaze was as hungry on him as his seemed to be on her before she blinked and looked away. 'I'm just bringing out the cake,' she said. 'It's only a sponge, but it's got to be eaten.'

'Louisa said. I came to carry the tray for you.'

'It's all right, I can manage,' she said, smiling despite herself at the thought that he wanted to help her. Her brothers were more inclined to let her get on with it.

'I know,' he said, smiling back at her. 'But I wanted an excuse to talk to you. How are you?'

Her blush deepened. 'I'm fine, thank you. A bit worried about Kate, though. Did you hear about the fire?'

He nodded, his expression coming sombre. 'It's a terrible thing. The talk at the factory this morning was that Reggie Davis is sure to swing for it.'

She flinched. 'I have no love for that man and of course he should be punished if he set the fire. But I can't rejoice in anyone facing execution. And I dread to think what it would do to Kate. She's already convinced everyone thinks badly of her because of who her pa is.'

He frowned. 'But Kate's nothing like him,' he said, earning him an approving glance from Jeannie.

'Of course she isn't. She's just like her ma, who was a lovely woman. None of the family are like Reggie. He spent more time in the Street Inn than with his children.'

They were silent for a moment, each lost in their thoughts.

A burst of laughter from the garden brought them back to the present. Jeannie sighed, looking at the tray she'd set on the table when he'd come in. 'Well, I'd better get this out to them or they'll be complaining.'

'Right,' he nodded. 'Let me take it. You get the door.'

He came closer and smiled at her, his eyes warm. She smiled back, forgetting herself as she enjoyed this moment. Then she remembered herself and she took a deep breath. No matter how lovely it was in Tom's company, she could never expect any more than this. She should stop acting like a daft girl with a crush and get on with her life. She took a step back and walked around him to open the door.

‘Come on then,’ she said, sounding far more cheerful than she felt. ‘They’ll be complaining if we take much longer.’

‘We’d better stuff ’em with cake quick, then. They can’t complain while they’re eating. It’s bad manners.’

They were both chuckling as they went outside.

This is enough, Jeannie told herself silently. *His friendship is better than nothing.* She knew that it was true, but she couldn’t get rid of the painful knot in her stomach at the thought.

3

Over the next month or so, Kate avoided going out in public, other than to go to work and to church on a Sunday. She couldn't bear to face the hostility towards Reggie Davis that rumbled through the village of Street.

'No one's blaming you, Kate,' Jeannie told her one dinner time when Kate insisted on sitting in a corner away from everyone in the canteen.

'I know,' she sighed. 'But it doesn't stop me feeling guilty by association.' It wasn't even the fact that the police had charged Pa with murdering the Floozy and the children after finding evidence of arson. No, it was the destruction of the homes of the neighbouring families that left people so angry and Kate feeling so ashamed and so terribly sorry for the families who had lost everything. She rubbed her eyes. It had been hard to sleep these past weeks. 'I've been keeping myself busy, though,' she said. 'Auntie's been helping me, knitting and sewing new clothes for the families who lost all theirs in the fire. It's the least I can do.'

Louisa smiled at her. 'That's a lovely thing to do. I think a lot of folks are doing things like that – giving them furniture and household goods as well as clothes and food. And of course, Clarks have rehoused them.'

Kate nodded, keeping her head down, not wanting to catch anyone's eye. It had taken a couple of weeks before her friends had been able to persuade her to even come to the canteen. She hadn't spent any money on food there, though. She'd brought her own, so that she could spend all her spare pennies on things for the families her father had made homeless. 'I heard,' she said. 'But it's hard to start again with nothing, isn't it? I wish I could do more for them.'

'Kate, love. You've got to stop feeling so responsible for this. It's your pa's fault. Not yours.'

She sighed. 'That's what Auntie Betty and my sisters-in-law say. It's hard, though, you know?' She glanced up at them. 'I'm so angry with him. He didn't just ruin his own life, but all his neighbours' as well. They didn't deserve that. And then I start thinking horrible things about Pa. I'm really wicked. I keep wishing he'd died as well, and that makes me feel as though I'm as bad as he is.'

The friends immediately enveloped her in a hug. 'No, you're not,' said Louisa in a fierce whisper. 'He's a wicked person; you're definitely not. He made you suffer so much. It's only natural you'd want to be free of him for good. I can't imagine how you must be feeling at the prospect of a trial.'

'She's right, Kate,' said Jeannie, her voice soft and gentle.

She hugged her friends back, grateful for their unconditional support. No one had been unkind to her face in the past few weeks, but she'd seen people staring at her and others turning away to avoid speaking to her. Even worse had been the looks of pity; she couldn't bear those.

'I'm going back to work,' she said. 'I know it's early, but I'm trying to get my numbers up to earn a bit more. I've nearly got enough to buy one of the families some slippers for their children.'

'We'll come with you and donate a few pennies as well,' said Jeannie.

Louisa nodded. 'Yes, we'll help.'

'You don't need to,' said Kate.

'We know,' said Jeannie. 'But we want to. Even Ma has sent them some chutneys and some of our preserved goods to help them set up their pantries again. The whole village is doing what they can for the families, Kate. You mustn't feel as though the whole burden is on your shoulders.'

* * *

When Kate got home later that day, she was exhausted. She only hoped she could sleep tonight.

She had just filled the kettle when she heard Auntie Betty at the front door.

'Kate, love, are you there?' she called out.

'Yes, Auntie. I'm just putting the kettle on. Do you want me to peel some potatoes for our supper?'

'Not just yet, lass. You've got a visitor,' said her landlady from the doorway.

Kate turned around to see a constable standing behind the older woman. 'Oh!' She took a calming breath. 'Can I offer you a cuppa, officer?'

He shook his head. 'No thanks, Miss Davis. I'll not stay long. But there's been a development in the case. We thought you should be informed.'

For a moment, she thought her pa might be dead. The mix of hope and guilt was so strong that it took her breath away and she put a hand to her chest. 'What is it?'

'Come and sit down, lass,' said Auntie Betty gently. 'Whatever it is, I'm sure it's nothing for you to worry about, is it, Constable?' She levelled a look at the policeman, as though daring him to contradict her.

He waited for Kate and Betty to sit at the table, then he took a seat opposite them. He cleared his throat. 'That's right, ma'am. Nothing for Miss Davis to worry about. But we've had some information that shines a new light on the crime.'

When he paused, Betty tutted. 'Well come on, lad, what is it? Don't leave the poor lass in suspense.'

He cast an apologetic look towards Kate, who could hardly breathe for wondering what this was all about. 'Do you remember when we found your pa?' he asked. 'His head was bleeding.'

She nodded.

'Well, we thought he'd banged his head when he passed out in the outhouse. But the surgeon who patched him up said he'd taken a blow to the back of the head, even though he'd been found laid out on his front. At the time, we assumed he'd fallen, hit the back of his head, then tried to get up again and fallen forward.'

'And what did Reggie have to say about that?' asked Auntie Betty.

The constable frowned. 'He swears he can't remember. Not the fight the neighbours heard, the fire, or how he ended up in the outhouse.'

'He was drunk, he must have been,' said Kate, feeling the familiar disgust as she remembered how he'd lose days and days of his memories when he was drinking heavily.

'Without a doubt,' he said. 'He stank of cider when we picked him up. So we could only assume he had committed the murders and the arson and either genuinely didn't remember or chose to pretend he didn't.'

The women nodded, both lost in their memories of times when Reggie Davis chose not to remember things he'd said or done.

'Anyhow, his head injuries and the burns he sustained to his hands and chest have been serious enough to keep him in the hospital wing of Yeovil Gaol. The doctor there says he's not fit to stand trial yet – reckons the blow to his head has caused some brain damage.'

'Brain damage?' asked Kate. 'What does that mean?'

The officer shrugged. 'We're not sure at this stage. He might genuinely have lost his memory, or he might still be pretending in an effort to avoid justice. But he's not himself. He's prone to episodes of incoherence when he doesn't make any sense at all. Other times, he's been so agitated, the staff have had to restrain him.'

'He always was a tricky customer,' said Betty, looking put out. 'I wouldn't be surprised if he was putting on an act to save his sorry carcass.'

'Quite,' agreed the officer. 'However, this morning, we got a communication via Glastonbury police station from the authorities looking for a man named Walter Longstaff.'

Kate frowned. 'Who is he? I don't know any Longstaff. Do you, Auntie?'

She shook her head. 'Not a name I'm familiar with around here. What's that got to do with Reggie's case?'

The constable sighed. 'It seems he's a seaman who has deserted. We believe he was married to one Beryl Longstaff – the woman who died in the fire along with her children.'

Kate gasped. 'The Floozy's husband?' She covered her mouth with her hand. 'Sorry, I shouldn't...'

He shook his head. 'Don't worry, we've heard her called that and worse by plenty of other people over the past few weeks and we had a number of complaints about the behaviour of her and those littluns prior to their deaths. She was well known to our colleagues in Glastonbury as well.'

'Of course she was, the rotten strumpet,' muttered Auntie Betty. 'I know we shouldn't speak ill of the dead, but honestly, officer, that woman...' She shook her head.

'Yes, well...' He looked as though he wanted to agree with her again, but he cleared his throat once more and carried on. 'The reason we're now interested in finding this man is because he jumped ship in Bristol a couple of days before the fire and hasn't been seen since. He was on shore leave, meant to be heading back out to sea as soon as the tides were right. His merchant ship has been working the supply lines for our troops. His ship left without him, so he's now classified as a deserter and a fugitive. The authorities want him found. His captain questioned some of his crewmates to try and ascertain where he might have gone and one of them said he'd told him he was going to sort out his missus once and for all.'

'Oh my,' said Betty. 'I remember he got in a fight with them the last time he showed up, but we never knew his name.'

'That's right, ma'am. The magistrate let him off light, given that he'd returned from sea to discover his wife had taken up with Reggie Davis in his absence.'

'All the while still taking her husband's hard-earned wages,' Betty added, shaking her head.

'And pretending her children were his,' said Kate, her eyes filling with tears. 'When it was obvious to anyone who saw them that they were Pa's. That poor man... she fooled him for years while Pa cheated on my blesséd ma.'

The policeman sighed. 'It's a rotten situation, that's for sure.

He'd have been better off turning his back on it all and starting a new life for himself. But, if this sailor is right, it seems that Longstaff planned to come to Street to confront his wife again.'

Kate frowned. 'Do you think that was what all the shouting was about on the night of the fire?'

He nodded, looking grim. 'It's possible. It would explain how your pa got a wound on the back of his head if he was trying to get away from this man. But unless we can find him, we might never know.'

Kate stood up, too agitated to sit still. 'So, let me get this right. You're saying Pa might not be guilty of murder or arson? He might be one of the victims of this Longstaff fellow?'

'It's a theory we have to explore,' he said carefully.

'But if you don't find him, you could still try and convict my pa and hang him as a murderer?' She put her hands to her temples. Would this nightmare never end?

He cleared his throat again. 'We've been ordered to re-examine the evidence, even if we can't locate Longstaff.'

Kate looked at him. She was so confused. Part of her hated Pa so much, she wished him dead. She wanted to wash her hands of him and leave him to rot. Yet, another part – the part of her that had been loved and nurtured by her sweet mother and now by Auntie Betty – knew that, if he was innocent, she would feel it her duty to fight in his corner to make sure that he wasn't punished for something he hadn't actually done. Oh, he had done plenty for which he *should* be punished, she knew. But no one deserved to hang for another man's crime. She rubbed at the pain blooming in her chest, wishing with all her heart that her pa had been a different man – one who could have loved his wife and children and done his best for them.

'So what happens now?' asked Betty.

'Longstaff is a wanted man. If he shows his face in Somerset, he'll be arrested and interrogated. In the meantime, Reggie Davis is still too sick to shed more light on what happened or to stand trial. His mind may never recover from whatever happened to him on the night of the fire. To be honest, the doctor thinks his drinking has added to the damage to his brain as well as his liver. He's not a well man. They've suggested removing him to the asylum at Wells for the time being, where he'll be kept under lock and key and receive appropriate treatment. If he shows any improvement, we might be able to get a bit more information out of him. Even if he's innocent, he's a witness to what really happened.'

'You're not letting him go, are you?' Kate asked, suddenly afraid. Despite all the shame she was feeling, she had at least felt safe from having to face him. She didn't want to think about what it would mean to her life if Pa was set free.

He shook his head. 'He's in no fit state to be let out into the world, miss. He's either a victim – in which case, he could help us to bring the perpetrator to justice while receiving the treatment he needs to improve his health – or he's guilty of murder and arson and will face justice in the proper manner. But, from what the doctor tells us, the asylum is the best place for him. Even innocent, he'll not be leaving there for a good long time, if ever.'

4

Life went on in Street as summer brought sunshine and the odd shower that nurtured the orchards and the flourishing kitchen gardens. The girls worked hard at the factory and at home.

Reggie Davis had been moved to the asylum. Folk in Street were still convinced of his guilt, even though the police had issued a statement that Walter Longstaff was being sought in connection with the murder of his wife and her children. Louisa didn't care whether it was Reggie or this Longstaff fellow who had done the deed, so long as Kate wasn't drawn any further into it. Their friends and families agreed with her.

The Floozy and her children's bodies had been given a pauper's burial on account of no one claiming them, not even the Floozy's mother in Glastonbury, who remained silent and aloof from the scandal. No one who knew her daughter could blame the woman. No one went to the funeral.

Now it was a sunny evening at the beginning of August and Louisa worked alone on the vegetable patch in the Musgroves' garden. She was weeding around the carrots and swedes. She'd been doing a little each evening after supper and the whole of the kitchen garden was looking smart and weed-free.

'You don't need to do that every day,' said Lucas as he came out of the kitchen door with a mug of tea.

'I enjoy it,' she said, straightening up and rubbing her belly. 'Is that for me?' She nodded at the drink.

'It is.' He handed it over with a smile and a wink. 'Got to keep the workers happy. I'll just pop back and get mine.'

She took a sip of her tea and watched him over the rim of the cup. His words were a stark reminder that his injured right arm still wasn't strong enough for him to be able to hold more than one hot cup of liquid without a risk of it slipping from his grasp. She remembered when she'd gone to visit him in hospital after he'd been brought back from the trenches. His right hand had been completely useless then – he hadn't even felt it when she'd held it. At least now he had some feeling in his fingers and, thanks to a leather and metal splint Tom had made for him, he could use his hand a little. While she hated that he was maimed like this, she was also grateful that his injuries meant his time in the trenches was over and he was home safe. It was the same for Tom. He might limp along on his false leg, but he was safe like Lucas.

Not like Mattie. She closed her eyes, wrapping both her hands around the warm mug as she thought about the lad she'd loved and lost.

'You all right, Louisa?' asked Lucas.

She opened her eyes and tried to smile. 'I'm fine. More tired than I thought, I guess. I'm glad it's the factory shut-down next week. Seven days to lie in and not have to worry about work.' She sighed.

He studied her face, his hazel eyes warm. 'You look sad. Is it Mattie?'

She swallowed on the lump in her throat and nodded. 'Sorry. But his ma is going to visit Will and Peg in Lincolnshire again during the shut-down. It made me think about Mattie and the baby. He's a toddler now, growing so fast.'

He came closer, shaking his head. 'Don't apologise,' he said softly. 'I think about Mattie as well. He was important to both of us. We'll never forget him, and if I'd known in time that you were expecting, I'd have married you then so that you could've kept his son. But you did what was best for the baby, and Mattie wouldn't want you to be sad, Louisa.'

She blinked against sudden tears. 'I know.' She sniffed. 'I don't know what's wrong with me. One minute, I'm fine, then I remember and feel bad that I'm carrying on with my life when he...'

Lucas put an arm around her and gently guided her down the path towards the end of the garden, away from the kitchen window where his ma and sister would no doubt be watching. 'It's the same for me. It's all right.'

'It's not,' she said on a sob. 'It's not fair on you. You're my husband.'

He kissed her temple. He did that a lot. It was the closest they ever got to being a real married couple. That made Louisa feel even more guilty.

'Louisa, don't fret, love.' He turned her so that she was looking out over the apple orchards that filled the land behind their garden.

She took a deep breath, trying to calm herself. She was grateful her face couldn't be seen from the house. She did her best to play the happy wife, and on the whole, she was content. But she was constantly aware of her mother-in-law's concerned scrutiny, especially at certain times of the month.

'I'm sorry,' she said. 'It's just that my monthlies have started and your ma was so disappointed.' She scrubbed at her face, wiping her tears away, not caring if she was transferring mud from her hands to her cheeks. 'I feel so awful every month, knowing she's hoping we'll give her a grandchild when we maybe never will.'

He sighed and held her closer and she leant into him. 'It doesn't matter,' he said, stroking her hair. 'I'll speak to her. Ask her to be less obvious about it.'

She shook her head. 'No, don't, please. She means well. Don't upset her.'

'I don't want you upset,' he said. 'It's not fair on you.'

She sighed and buried her face in his chest. 'It's not fair on you, either. Maybe you shouldn't have married me. I'm sorry.'

Lucas put his hands on her shoulders and pulled her away from his chest so that he could look into her eyes. 'Listen to me, Louisa. I do not regret it and I don't expect I ever will. I know we married to save you from having to move to Exeter with your ma after your pa died, and that's probably not the best reason to get wed. But we get along well enough, you and me, don't we?'

She nodded. 'We do, but—'

He put a finger to her lips. 'No buts, Louisa. Now, I know it's difficult when you get your monthlies, love. I'll try and persuade Ma to mind her business and not make you feel worse.'

'She just wants us to have a baby,' she said, her tears welling again. 'And then when Kate said Auntie Betty was going to see Peg and Will again during the factory break, I realised she'll see little Mattie while I can't.' Her breath caught on a sob as the real reason for her distress burst out of her. 'How am I going to bear it when they move back to Street, Lucas?'

'Aw, come here.' He pulled her into a hug and let her cry.

As she wept quietly, Louisa couldn't help but feel fortunate that Lucas understood her pain. After Mattie's death, she'd realised that she was carrying his child and her parents had determined that she should go and stay with her aunt in Exeter until the baby was born in secret. Their plan was that the child would be given up for adoption and Louisa would come home and carry on with her life as though nothing had happened. Horrified, Louisa had confided in Kate, whose sister Peg was married to Mattie's brother Will. The couple were childless after three years of marriage. They offered to help Louisa run away. She lived with them in Lincolnshire. It was there that baby Mattie had been born and where Louisa had left her son in the loving hands of her lover's brother and sister-in-law. Better that than losing him to strangers who might not love him as much as his own kin.

Lucas knew all this, as did Jeannie and Kate. But no one outside of their small circle of friends in Street did, including Mattie and Will's ma, Betty. All she knew was that her son and daughter-in-law were bringing up her grandchild. She had no idea that the child was actually the baby of the son she had lost.

Louisa was aware that, once this awful war was finally over, Will's job at a tank factory in Lincoln would end and the couple would return to Street with little Mattie. Part of her longed for the day when she could see her darling baby again, but another part of her dreaded it, because she would never be able to claim him as her own. She would have to watch him grow from afar, playing the role of a doting godmother.

'I don't know how I'll be able to survive it, Lucas,' she whispered. 'Maybe I should've moved to Exeter like my ma wanted.'

'Nonsense,' he said, his voice low and fierce. 'You'd have hated it. Look, who knows when this war will be over? It could be years yet, at this rate.'

'But now the Americans have allied themselves to us, they say it will be over sooner rather than later.'

Lucas snorted. 'Maybe. But it seems like the Allies are just supplying more cannon fodder to the trenches. It hasn't stopped the Hun, has it? We've had more of our ships sunk, and they killed civilians in those air attacks on London.'

She shivered. 'You can't think we're going to lose.'

He sighed. 'I'm not saying that. I'm just frustrated because, after everything we've been through, there's still no end in sight. But that's not what we were talking about, is it? Staying here in Street was the right thing to do, and I think deep down, you'll be happy to see little Mattie and know he's well cared for. You know how much Peg and Will love him, don't you?'

She nodded. Little Matthew was seventeen months now. Peg sent her regular letters, keeping her informed of the child's progress. She knew when he'd got his first tooth and that he loved to blow bubbles and that he had started crawling at nine months. 'He's walking now, did I tell you? Peg says he'll be off and running soon, just like our Mattie. He never could stay still, could he?'

Lucas chuckled. 'No he couldn't. Any excuse to run rather than walk.'

Louisa's smile was bittersweet. It was good to be able to talk to Lucas about all this. He understood. They had been life-long friends and Lucas had loved Mattie as much as she had. She hadn't realised until Lucas had asked her to marry that Lucas's feelings for Mattie were far more than friendship. Mattie had been the love of Lucas's life, just as he'd been for Louisa. It was their shared grief that had brought her and Lucas together after they'd got the news of Mattie's death.

He stroked her hair again. 'Look, I know it's going to be hard, love. But, well...' He paused, his cheeks going red as she gazed up at him. 'I've said it before and I know you might not want to consider it, but maybe we should think about...' He gulped.

'Maybe if you and I had a baby, then it might not be quite so painful when they bring little Mattie home to Street. It would stop Ma embarrassing you every month as well. We both know she doesn't mean to, but it's so obvious she wants to be a grandma; it's embarrassing me as well.' He gave her a lopsided grin. 'But I'm not going to force you into anything. It has to be your decision, Louisa. We can carry on as we are; it's no odds to me. I told you when I asked you to marry me that I wouldn't expect that of you. I just want you to be happy, so would Mattie.'

Neither of them heard the kitchen door open. It was only when Jeannie was halfway down the garden path that they noticed her.

'What are you two up to?' she called. 'You don't need to be canoodling out here; you've got your own room for that.' She giggled.

'Mind your own business,' grumbled Lucas. 'You're embarrassing Louisa.'

She'd buried her head in his chest and was busy wiping away the evidence of her tears.

Jeannie, being a soft-hearted lass she was, immediately apologised. 'Sorry, Lou. I didn't mean to.'

'It's all right,' she said, raising her head and smiling at Jeannie. 'I've just got to put away the hoe and I'll be in.'

Lucas hooked the tea mugs off of the wall where they'd left them and handed them to his sister. 'Here, take those in and I'll help Lou. We'll be in in a minute.'

Jeannie nodded and took them from him. 'All right.' She turned away, then turned back again. 'Oh! I meant to say, the reason I came out is that John's just got back from work and he said they were doing a delivery in Glastonbury and someone said the Floozy's husband has been apprehended.'

'What? Really?'

She nodded. 'Apparently, he's been living as a vagrant, poaching and stealing food. Someone caught him trying to steal eggs and bashed him with a shovel, knocked him out cold. The constables have got him now. John says they think he might well have been the one to set that fire. It looks likes Reggie Davis is innocent after all.'

She turned and disappeared into the kitchen.

'Well, that's a turn up for the books,' said Lucas, scratching his chin as Louisa put the hoe back into the shed and secured the door. 'Let's hope for Kate's sake, Reggie doesn't come back here.'

'I know,' said Louisa. 'Maybe we should go round and tell her.'

He shook his head. 'The constables will, I'm sure. They've been keeping her informed, haven't they? You can see her in the morning at the factory.'

She nodded. 'All right. I confess, I'm feeling a bit weary now.' But as she glanced at the house, she hesitated.

He held out a hand and she took it. 'You all right now, love? We can stay out here a bit longer if you want.'

She gave him a tired smile and shook her head. 'It's all right. I'm sorry to be such a moaning Minnie. Thank you for listening and being so sweet about it.'

'Any time, love. Any time.' He gave her hand a gentle squeeze.

When he turned to walk back up the path, she pulled at his hand and stopped him. 'Lucas,' she said. 'Do you really mean it, about us having a baby?'

His cheeks warmed again. 'Yes. If it will help you.'

She studied his face, her heart hammering. He wasn't Mattie, but he was a handsome man. She knew his heart had been buried with Mattie, as had hers. So for him to be willing to make this false marriage of theirs real filled her with gratitude.

But... would she be able to bear letting another man touch

her in the way that Mattie had? Even when she'd agreed to this marriage with Lucas, she hadn't thought she ever could and she'd told him so. He'd understood, because he'd loved Mattie as more than just a friend – a secret that only she knew. She'd never expected him to offer to give her a baby.

Yet... in the months since they'd married, they had gone to their marriage bed every night like polite strangers, each turning their back and clinging to the edge of the mattress in order to avoid encroaching on the other's space. But, without fail, they had awoken in the middle of the mattress in each other's arms. They had both been mortified at first, but after the first few times, they had laughed about it together and she had grown more relaxed in his company. His sweet gestures of affection when they were in company no longer embarrassed her, and – even now when there was no one around – she liked it when he hugged her. Would it really be so awful to be intimate with Lucas? He was her lawful husband, after all, and she felt safe and comfortable with him, knowing that he was privy to all of her secrets, and she to his. Lucas would never knowingly hurt her and she had vowed to be a good wife to him.

She had no complaints. She was happier than she expected to be most of the time. But sometimes, her grief got the better of her, especially when her dear, kind mother-in-law tried to persuade her that she would soon conceive. Then, she would be overwhelmed by the loss of her first-born son, as well as the guilt she felt at deceiving Mrs Musgrove. That Lucas was willing to overcome his own feelings in order to give her another baby to fill the aching void in her heart was more than she felt she deserved. But, even though she would never forget the child she had had to give away, she knew that she had an abundance of love to give to another child. And it would make Lucas's ma so happy to have a grandchild.

She nodded, looking away, suddenly shy. 'Thank you, Lucas. I think it might. If you're sure.'

He didn't respond until she finally glanced back at him. When their gazes met, he gave her the sweetest, shyest smile she'd ever seen. 'I'm sure if you're sure, Louisa. I want you to be happy, and I think you'll be a wonderful mother.'

She laughed and put a hand on his broad chest. 'Don't be so nice to me, Lucas Musgrove, or you'll have me blubbing all over you again!'

He grinned. 'All right, wife. I'll make sure to be a bit sterner from now on.' He winked, so she knew he was teasing. 'Now come on, let's go in before someone else comes out to find out what we're up to.'

5

Jeannie knocked on the door of Mrs Searle's cottage in The Mead. Moments later, it opened a crack and Kate peered out.

'Oh, Jeannie, love. It's you. Come in.' She opened the door wider to let her friend enter. 'Where's Lou?'

'She's gone for a walk with Lucas,' she said, sighing. 'Ma says they need more time alone together.'

Kate frowned. 'Whatever for?'

Jeannie rolled her eyes, even as her cheeks warmed. 'What do you think for? It's nearly ten months since their wedding. Ma's desperate for them to produce her first grandchild.'

'Oh!' Kate pulled a face. 'I can't imagine Louisa and your brother doing *that*, especially not while they're out on a walk.' She fanned her own red cheeks. 'But I suppose it's naïve of us to think they never do it. They are married, after all.'

'I know, but... well, she was my friend before she had anything to do with Lucas. I don't see why she can't still spend time with me. It's not like we can talk much at work, is it? I thought that now she's living at our house and she's my sister-in-law, we'd be able to do more together.' Jeannie knew she was sounding like a whining child, but she was jealous of the time Lucas spent with Louisa. She sighed again. 'I'm being unreasonable, aren't I?'

Kate chuckled. 'You are a bit, love.' She linked arms with Jeannie and urged her towards the kitchen. 'But if I'll do as your second-favourite friend, we can do something and try to forget about what those two might be up to.'

'Oh no, Kate, I didn't mean it like that. You're just as good a friend to me as Louisa is, you know that, don't you?'

Kate grinned at her worried expression. 'Of course I do, you daft thing. I'm just teasing.'

Jeannie's shoulders dropped as she released a relieved breath. 'Oh, you! You had me worried there. I thought I'd really upset you.'

'Ha! It'd take more than that to upset me. Now, how do you feel about writing to a new conscientious objector? Only Gerald tells me there's some new chaps arrived at Wormwood Scrubs who would appreciate some letters.'

Jeannie pulled out a chair from the table and sat down. 'Yes, all right,' she said. 'That Michael I was writing to is getting married when he gets out next month. I don't suppose his bride will appreciate him corresponding with single women if he gets rearrested.'

'Huh. *When* he gets rearrested, you mean,' said Kate as she sat next to her. 'I hope his bride is prepared for that. Look at poor Gerald. He'd been home with his mother for less than a week after his first prison term last year and the recruitment officer knocked on his door again.' That time, he got a six-month sentence when he once again refused to take up arms, and after his release earlier this year, the same thing happened again, only his third term was for nine months. He's already been told that the next time his term would be for at least a year, if not longer.

Kate had been writing to him from the time she'd heard about his plight from Auntie Betty, who was Gerald's mother's cousin. She had met him and his mother at the home of Mr and Mrs Clothier, who had been campaigning for better treatment of conscientious objectors, following his first release from prison. They were good friends now and she wished she could do more to help him. But what could a factory girl do to change the minds of the men tasked with trying these cases? It was all so unfair. Gerald had been one of the first volunteers to join an ambulance unit back in 1914 and he'd spent over a year in France, doing what he could to save lives. But it had all got too much and he'd come home, even more sure of his Quaker and pacifist beliefs. When conscription had been introduced in 1916, he had taken a job in a market garden rather than enlist, but his local tribunal had refused to grant him exemption from conscription and he had been sent to prison when he would not take up arms.

Jeannie had joined Kate in writing to these young men in order to offer moral support. She'd corresponded with a few of them, although none had developed into a firm friendship like Kate and Gerald's. 'Did I tell you? I got a letter from one lad's ma, thanking me for writing to him.'

'No, you didn't mention it. Which lad was that?'

'Jacob. He... I don't know... he seemed very unhappy. I felt sorry for him and tried to cheer him up. But then he stopped writing.' She sighed. 'His mother said he contracted TB in the prison, so now he's in a sanatorium. She's hopeful he'll get better, but I don't know. It's not usual for someone to survive it, is it?'

Kate shook her head. 'I don't think so. Poor lad. And what a choice, eh? Go to France and face death in the trenches, or to prison and catch a disease that might kill you anyway. Are you going to carry on writing to him?'

'I offered. I'm waiting for his ma to let me know if that's what he wants. At least, with the damage to his lungs, he'd be rejected by the army now anyway. Not much consolation for him or his family, but at least he won't go back to prison. But I'm happy to write to one of Gerald's new friends anyhow.'

Kate nodded. 'Right, thanks. I'll find his letter in a minute and get you a name.' She paused. 'I wanted to talk to you about something else. You know Walter Longstaff, the Floozy's husband, has been arrested? Well, it seems he confessed to setting the fire. Which means Pa's innocent.'

'Oh lord, Kate. Does that mean he's going to be set free?'

'I hope not!' she said. 'The constable who came to tell me said Pa's still not fit to be released from the asylum. He said that Longstaff told them he'd hit Pa round the back of his head with a poker. The doctors say it's affected his mind and he should remain where he is.'

'Well,' said Jeannie. 'It's awful that he was attacked, but I can't say I'm sorry that he's locked up in the asylum where he can't hurt you, Kate.'

'I know. I can't tell you how relieved I was about that. I mean, where would he go if they let him out? He's got no home and none of the family would take him in after the way he's treated all of us. But can you imagine the fuss he'd make, just to shame us in front of everyone in Street?'

Jeannie rested her elbows on the table and her chin in her hands. 'Mmm, and I doubt if he'd be able to get a job, not now. Who would work with him after everything that's happened?'

Kate sighed and mirrored Jeannie's stance. 'I don't want him ever to come back to Street and I know Vi and Ada feel the same.' Her sisters-in-law were adamant that he deserved to remain incarcerated, even if he wasn't guilty of arson or murder. The man had been horrible to his whole family for long enough that none of them wanted anything to do with him. 'Yet...'

'What?' Jeannie asked.

She blew out a breath. 'It's just... I keep thinking about Ma and how she never judged anyone, not even Pa when he was treating her so shabby. If he'd been guilty of those awful crimes, I would have felt that God and the law were the best judges and I could've turned my back on him and left him to face the consequences of his actions. But now they say he's innocent and I'm starting to think that Ma would've wanted me to do something.'

Jeannie frowned. 'I don't understand. What can you do? It's not like he's going to treat you any better or be grateful for anything you do for him.'

'I know.' She grimaced. 'But think about it, Jeannie. If he's been left with a permanent injury even though he didn't do the terrible things everyone thought he did that night...' She sighed again. 'I just think Ma's up in heaven looking down at me and shaking her head with disappointment because I'm doing nothing. I mean, it's not very Christian of me, is it?'

'Kate.' Jeannie reached for her friend's hand and squeezed it. 'Listen to me. The fact that you're even thinking like that shows that you're a good person and I know your ma will be proud of you. But... you can't possibly take responsibility for your pa. He nearly killed you with his violence and neglect last time. If his mind's gone, he could be even worse.'

'I know that, too,' she said. 'Don't worry, I'm definitely *not* Christian enough to want to make that kind of sacrifice. I vowed I'd never let Pa control my life again, and I won't change my mind about that. I'm not that daft!'

'So what are you saying?' Jeannie asked, still confused.

Kate closed her eyes and was silent for a few moments. Eventually, she opened her eyes and spoke, her voice sounding scratchy and uncertain. 'I think I need to go and see him.'

'In the asylum?' Jeannie looked horrified.

She nodded.

'But what if he attacks you again?'

She shook her head. 'I'm sure I wouldn't be left alone with him. And if what the constable says is true, it doesn't sound like he's capable of fighting these days. I can't explain it, Jeannie, but I just need to go and see for myself. Otherwise I'll feel like I've let Ma down again.'

Jeannie sat back and this time, it was her who blew out a breath. 'All right,' she said. 'I think I understand. What does Auntie Betty say about this?'

Kate shrugged. 'She's in Lincolnshire so I haven't had a chance to tell her yet. And if I'm going to go, it'll have to be this week while the factory's shut for the summer break. I'm not going to lose wages by missing a shift for him.'

'That's understandable. But if you think you're going to that place on your own, you've got another think coming, Kate Davis. If you won't wait for Auntie to get back, then I'm coming with you.'

6

Kate, Jeannie and Louisa got off the bus in Wells two days later and walked the rest of the way to the imposing building that now housed Reggie Davis. Kate swallowed hard when she stood before the sign that declared the place to be the *Somerset & Bath Pauper Lunatic Asylum*.

'Are you sure about this, Kate?' asked Louisa, touching her arm. She'd refused to countenance her friends making this visit without her. 'No one will think anything of it if you decide you don't want to go in there.'

'She's right,' said Jeannie as she stood on the other side of Kate, peering up at the building. 'You don't owe your pa anything, love.'

Now that she was here, Kate's courage was draining away. While she might be fierce and independent most of the time, her pa always reduced her to a shaking wreck. She'd thought he couldn't affect her now, not with him being locked up in here. He couldn't hurt her any more. He might not even recognise her, what with his head injury. But if he did, would he want her to be there? She was almost ready to agree with her friends and turn around, but the memory of her dear mother held her still.

'I have to go in,' she said, straightening her shoulders and lifting her chin. 'I owe it to Ma.'

Jeannie and Louisa exchanged a glance, then both nodded. 'We thought you'd say that,' said Lou.

'Although I'm sure she'd understand if you couldn't do it,' said Jeannie. 'But if you're going in, then so are we. You shouldn't have to do this on your own.'

Kate looked from one friend to another, grateful for their strength as they stood by her side. 'Thank you. You have no idea how much this means to me. You're the best friends a girl could ever ask for.' She blinked away the tears that threatened to fall as she smiled at them.

'Aw, don't cry, love,' said Jeannie, gently touching her cheek. 'Come on, let's get this over with. Then maybe, if we've got time and you feel like it, we can have a wander around Wells before we get the bus back. Maybe we can light a candle for your ma in the cathedral.'

Kate nodded and took a deep breath. 'All right. I'm ready.' She huffed. 'Well, as ready as I'll ever be.'

* * *

Even though she'd sent a letter confirming that she was coming, it took a little while for them to be shown to a meeting room and for Reggie Davis to be brought in, flanked by two burly attendants.

As they urged him into a seat on the other side of the table at which the girls were sitting, Kate studied her pa, noting that he'd lost weight and that his skin was a pale yellow, apart from odd patches on his hands and the side of his neck, which were a livid pink where his burns were still healing. His hair had been shaved, leaving a rough stubble which was growing through white rather than his previously dark locks. When he turned to look at one of his guards, she could see the jagged scar of the wound at the back of his head left by the blow he'd received from Walter Longstaff that had been meant to kill him. It had been roughly stitched and no hair grew around it. How he'd survived the attack and been able to crawl out of the house to the sanctuary of the outhouse, she would never know.

He didn't fight against the men, but rather did as they bid him, which surprised Kate. Reggie hated being told what to do; he had always been in trouble with the foremen at the Clarks factory. Maybe it had been the blow to his head that made him more manageable now, although Kate didn't trust it. It was just as likely that he was behaving because he was getting three square meals a day and a roof over his head without having to pay for it. She watched him carefully, ready to take flight should he suddenly attack.

When he was settled, he finally looked at her, his rheumy eyes showing no emotion.

'Hallo, Pa,' she said, hoping that she was managing to keep her expression clear and her voice firm and confident. It would never do to show any weakness. 'How are you?'

For a moment, she caught the flash of anger in his expression, but then his eyes shifted to side and he adopted a confused demeanour.

'Who's this?' he asked, his voice shaky as though his vocal chords had rusted over. He looked up at one of the men standing over him. 'Are these my new nurses?'

'No pretty young nurses for you, Reggie,' he said, his expression stern. 'Not with your record. No, this is your daughter and her friends, come to see if we're treating you right.'

Kate wanted to protest. She would never presume to criticise the work of the staff at the asylum. She imagined they faced challenges every day that she was glad not to have to face herself. Rather, she'd come to make sure Pa was locked up securely so that she could feel safe, and maybe to see whether there was any chance that the attack he'd suffered and the loss of the Floozy and their children might in some way have changed him for the better. After all, they said that near-death experiences could change a man – show him the error of his ways and give him the chance to repent in this life rather than face the fires of hell in the next. But, before she could open her mouth to say anything, she looked at the attendant and noticed that his eyes were brimming with humour. She relaxed a little, realising he was teasing. She sent him a grateful smile before turning her attention back to her pa.

He studied her, his face slack as though he wasn't in full control of his senses. But his eyes told a different story and she felt a chill run down her spine. He knew exactly who she was, and he didn't appreciate her or her friends being here. But he was playing a game. She glanced back at the attendants and realised that they knew it and were on their guard. It made her feel safer, knowing they weren't fooled by him.

'That's right,' she said, raising her chin and holding his gaze. 'I heard you're recovering well and I wanted to see for myself.'

Again, that flash of anger. She felt Lou's hand squeeze her leg under the table as Jeannie coughed to cover the gasp she'd made at the sight of it.

Pa shrugged, his face still slack, his sharp gaze not leaving hers. 'They said a bad man tried to kill me,' he said. 'Took my woman and children, he did.' He looked around, as though trying to gather his wandering thoughts, blinking rapidly against non-existent tears. 'My poor loves,' he whimpered theatrically.

Kate gritted her teeth, wanting to call him out. It didn't suit him, playing the imbecile or the grieving man, when his eyes showed his usual cunning. *His poor loves* indeed! He'd never shown those children – or any of the rest of his family for that matter – an ounce of affection. As for the Floozy, he had displayed nothing but the lust that blinded him whenever she had pouted and pushed her bosom towards him.

'We're sorry for your loss, Mr Davis,' said Jeannie, her voice gentle.

Kate didn't dare look at her. Surely Jeannie didn't believe this performance? Again, Louisa squeezed her thigh as though she'd read her thoughts and agreed with her.

He ignored Jeannie and turned his attention back to Kate. 'Have you come to take me home? I'm innocent, you know. They can't keep me in prison.'

She shook her head. 'You're not in prison, Pa. You're in hospital. They're helping you get better.'

'But I want to go home,' he whined, sounding just like his dead son.

The reminder of that little beast, who'd delighted in tormenting her and encouraging his ma to make Kate's life a misery, hardened her heart. A part of her felt wicked for thinking ill of the dead, but another was angry to be reminded of those painful and humiliating times. She hadn't deserved any of it. 'You don't have a home to go to any more, Pa. It burnt down, along with the neighbours' cottages. If you don't stay here, you'll have to go to the workhouse until you can find a job that'll pay your rent. But you won't be able to go back to the house in Silver Road. It's gone.'

He smirked at her, keeping his expression hidden from his guards. 'I could come and live with you. My dear daughter, who's come to visit me with her friends.'

'We thought Kate would appreciate our company,' said Louisa.

He turned his gaze towards her, his apparent confusion dropping away from him in an instant, putting all three girls on guard. 'I'll bet your ma wouldn't like it if she knew you were here, would she, Louisa Clements?' None of them bothered to remind him that she was Louisa Musgrove now. 'And what about your pa? His princess, slumming it at the asylum.' He rubbed his hands together as he cackled, sounding truly mad. 'He'll be turning in his grave, won't he?'

Louisa sat back, looking down her nose at him. Kate admired how she showed no weakness to Pa. 'Probably,' she said. 'But I'm a married woman now and not answerable to them. Even if I were, they'd both understand that I'm here for Kate, not for you.'

Pa growled and leant forward. The attendants immediately put their hands on his shoulders, holding him back.

'Calm down now, Reggie. You be polite to these young ladies, or we'll take you back to your room.'

He grunted and looked away from the girls. 'I don't know why they're here. I ain't some zoo animal. If they wanna see a real lunatic, they should come and see young Stan Jackson. Off his rocker, he is.'

Kate was suddenly alert. 'Stan's here?'

''Course he is. I've seen that old cow of a mother of his visiting regular, looking down her nose at me like that one.' He pointed at Louisa. 'Sodding foremen. Their kin think they're too good for ordinary folk.'

Kate had had enough. She stood up. 'We'll go then and leave you in peace. I just wanted to see if you were all right.'

Her friends rose as well. Louisa picked up the basket she'd placed on the floor beside her. Reggie eyed it, his eyes lighting. He nodded towards it.

'What did you bring me?' he demanded. 'You can't visit a sick man without bringing something to make him feel better. Go on, hand it over.' He held out a hand.

Kate closed her eyes, mortified by his ill-manners and the greed that shone from his beady eyes. 'Pa,' she sighed. Would she always be ashamed of him?

Louisa placed the basket on the table. 'You're right,' she said. 'We did bring something.' She put a hand in and brought out a green bottle. She had just reached in again to get the fruit cake that went with it, when Pa moved so fast, his guards couldn't stop him from grabbing the bottle. 'Cider! I knew you wouldn't let me down,' he crowed, holding it against his chest and stroking it, a genuine smile on his face.

'Oh, no, Mr Davis,' said Jeannie with an earnest smile. 'We couldn't bring alcohol. No, this is some of my ma's best elder-flower cordial. We thought you'd find it refreshing with a nice piece of cake.'

Reggie stilled, frowning. 'What?' He pulled the stopper out and sniffed the contents. 'Bloody elderflower?' he roared, causing Jeannie to take a step back even though the sturdy table separated them. 'Cake?' He peered at it as Louisa put it on the tabletop.

Jeannie squealed and covered her head with her arms when he lifted the bottle by its neck, the contents spilling over him as he raised it above his head as though to throw it. Kate and Louisa both stepped towards Jeannie to protect her, but the attendants were quicker. One grabbed Reggie's arm and the bottle to stop him throwing it, while the other got him in a headlock, pulling him backwards and twisting him off balance so that within seconds, he was face down on the floor, yelling blue murder as the men held him down.

The girls stood there, watching with horrified fascination.

The guards didn't seem bothered by Reggie's rage and held him easily. One even managed to wrestle the bottle from his grasp and hold it out for Louisa to take. He smiled and winked at her as she retrieved it and returned it to the table.

'Calm down now, Reggie,' he said. 'You're making a spectacle of yourself in front of these nice young ladies. If you don't want their thoughtful gifts, I'm sure someone will.'

'We should go,' said Kate, wanting nothing more than to leave here and never come back.

'Go on, get out of here!' shouted her pa, his voice muffled as his face was pushed into the stone floor. 'What did you come here for, anyway? To gloat? Brought your holier-than-thou friends to see me in my cage, eh? What the hell are you doing, bringing me bloody *elderflower*? You're no daughter of mine. I want cider! Don't you dare show your face here again without bringing me some.'

'Come on now, you know we don't allow alcohol, Reggie,' he was told. 'Besides, the doctor says your liver can't take any more of it.'

'I'd rather die in me cups than stay locked up here when I've done nothing to deserve it. A man's entitled to his cider.'

Kate looked at her friends, nodding towards the door. She couldn't speak, she was so ashamed. The others followed her silently. One man held Reggie down and gave them a respectful nod. The other got up and escorted them out of the room.

'I'm sorry,' Kate said to him as they walked through the corridors.

'Don't fret, lass,' he said kindly. 'We're used to outbursts like that. He's docile a lot of the time, but he keeps trying to get people to supply him with cider and has become violent when we tell him this is a temperance establishment. It's clear he's in the thrall of alcohol and the doctors aren't inclined to let him out to continue down that path of destruction. They say his liver is so riddled with disease, he's unlikely to ever be well enough to leave now. He's not long for this world, I reckon.'

They said nothing until they were well away from the asylum.

'Are you all right, Kate?' asked Jeannie.

She shrugged. What could she say? That she was relieved by the news that Pa was likely dying? How wicked was she to be thinking like that? But then she remembered how horrible Pa had been when the alcohol got the better of him and how it had led to her dear Ma's awful, untimely death because all his money had gone on cider rather than medicines to relieve her suffering, and she couldn't be sorry for how she felt now.

'I thought it went as well as could be expected,' said Louisa. 'Don't you?'

Kate grimaced. 'I should have gone on my own. You didn't need to see that.'

'Nonsense,' said Louisa. 'We wouldn't have let you do that. It's not as though we're surprised. We've seen your pa acting a lot worse than that, haven't we? At least this time, there were some men there to stop him hurting anyone.'

Louisa put a hand over her mouth as a giggle escaped. 'His face when he realised it was elderflower; it was a picture.'

Jeannie giggled as well. 'I know! He wasn't very happy, was he? I thought he was going to smash it over my head. But I didn't have time to be scared before they had him on the floor.'

Kate carried on walking, just wanting to get as far away from him as possible.

'He'll be smelling of elderflower now, since he spilt half of it over himself,' said Louisa. 'That'll make him furious won't it, Kate?'

The image of Pa sniffing his sleeve and flying into another

rage finally cracked the wall of shame she'd felt growing around her. It wasn't her fault that he had acted like that. He was being true to form. It was nothing to do with her. 'That it will,' she said, her grin growing as she thought about it. 'And it serves him right.'

By the time they reached the bus stop, all three of them were laughing hard, as though they'd been out for a fun afternoon rather than facing a nasty, raging Reggie Davis at the asylum.

What none of them mentioned was his revelation that Stan Jackson was so close to home. Just the mention of the lad's name made Kate think about her former sweetheart, Stan's brother Ted. She'd heard little of him since he'd enlisted shortly after the Jacksons had lost their eldest son, Albert, at Ypres and poor Stan had been driven mad by the experience of seeing his brother killed. It had simply broken him. For some reason, it had never occurred to her that he had been brought back to Somerset, but she was glad because at least it meant his ma and pa could visit him. She just hoped their visits were more pleasant than the one she'd just been through.

'I've done my duty,' she announced as they sat on the bus back to Street. 'I'll not go back there again.'

'Good,' said Louisa.

Jeannie nodded and patted her hand. 'You did the right thing and he didn't appreciate it,' she said. 'You can put it all behind you now.'

She hoped so. She really, really hoped so.

7

Louisa blinked. It was a bright day for October and the sun was shining straight through the high windows of the Machine Room at the Clarks shoe factory, into her eyes. The sharp light made her head throb in time with the hum of the machinery that vibrated through her body, as did the high-pitched chatter of her workmates around her. She felt ill. The smells of the machine oil and leather and stale air that pervaded the vast room, and the racket created by three hundred women and girls, all working at their sewing machines, were overwhelming her this morning.

Louisa was usually a fast, accurate worker, hardly ever making silly mistakes. But today, she couldn't concentrate. The noise and the smells and the dust from the cotton were conspiring together against her, making her light-headed. She could feel the throbbing vibrations of the machinery through her feet and her hands, adding to her nausea. Her hands weren't as quick as they usually were and she had narrowly missed piercing her fingers with the swift, sharp machine needle more than once in the past hour. It left her shaky and ready to weep.

The last time she'd felt like this was the day she'd realised she was carrying Mattie's baby. As the thought occurred to her, she gasped and slapped a hand over her mouth. *Could I be...?*

Since August, she and Lucas had been making love. It had been awkward at first, neither of them knowing how they should act. Both of them had felt as though they were betraying Mattie and they had shared tears the first time, even when they agreed that Mattie wouldn't have blamed them, that he would have wanted them to be happy. With patience, things had got better. They learned each other's bodies and what pleased them so that being a real wife to Lucas had become a pleasure. She thought Lucas was surprised at how much he had come to enjoy their congress as well. It seemed that, even though he had loved Mattie with a forbidden passion that was never realised, he was still able to find pleasure in her woman's body. Louisa didn't doubt that, had he had the chance, he would have loved Mattie's body just as thoroughly as he loved hers. But maybe now he would be content with her rather than wishing he was with a man. It was something that had worried Louisa when he had first confessed his secret to her, but now she felt more confident that she could satisfy him and not lose him to a forbidden love one day. He assured her that Mattie had been the only man for him and he had no desire for another. She hoped so. Especially if this nausea that was building in her was what she thought it was.

'You all right, Lou?' asked Kate when she didn't move, her mind awhirl.

She glanced at her friend, dropping her hand and taking a deep breath as she tried to give her a reassuring smile. The smell of machine oil filled her head and her stomach lurched. Kate's eyes widened as Louisa surged to her feet.

'I'm going to be sick!' she cried as she ran for the privy.

She made it just in time, emptying her stomach with painful retches. It seemed to go on forever, even after she was sure there was nothing left inside her. When the tremors finally eased, she leaned her head against the cubicle wall trying to catch her breath.

Could I be...?

It was just like this last time, but she'd been keeping track of her monthlies, as had her mother-in-law. She'd had a bleed a couple of weeks ago, so surely she couldn't be expecting. Although now she thought of it, it had been much lighter than usual.

She flushed the toilet and blew her nose before leaving the cubicle. She rinsed her mouth and washed her hands, aware of her pale reflection in the mirror over the sink, unwilling to look at it. She knew she would see the pain of past memories there. There would be hope there as well – something she didn't dare let herself feel, not yet.

Back at her machine, she was grateful that a cloud now obscured the sun. After rushing off like that without permission, she needed to get on and catch up before Mr Briars complained.

'Are you all right, Lou?' Jeannie asked this time, her brow creased with concern.

She gave her a shaky smile. 'I was sick. Must've been something I ate.'

'But you had the same porridge as me this morning, and I'm all right.'

Louisa shrugged. 'I know. I don't know what caused it, maybe something I ate yesterday. But I feel fine now and I'd better get on before I'm in trouble.'

She bent her head to her machine and worked furiously until dinner time, all the time aware of the curious glances her friends sent her way. She focused her attention on the liners she was stitching, trying her best not to think about the reason why she'd been sick. But through the whole morning, the thought kept running around in her head. *Could I be...?*

She felt fine until she entered the staff canteen. She raised her hand to wave at Lucas, who was there waiting for her at their usual table. As she and her friends walked towards him, she was aware of the aroma of fish in the air. It was Friday, and there was smoked haddock on the menu. She wasn't intending to eat it as they'd brought their own sandwiches as usual, but even the smell of it made her stomach churn. By the time she reached her husband, he was frowning.

'What's wrong?' he asked as he stood to greet her. 'Are you ill? You're mighty pale, love.'

She shook her head, intending to say she was fine, when Kate spoke up.

'She was sick this morning.'

Lucas's gaze sharpened on her. 'Maybe you should go home,' he said.

'No, it was hours ago. I'm feeling all right now,' she insisted. But even as she spoke, someone walked past her with a plate of hot food and the smells of smoked haddock and boiled cabbage filled her nostrils. She gasped and turned her head away. She couldn't be sick again; there was nothing left in her stomach, yet she felt the bile rising. 'I just need to eat my sandwich to settle my belly,' she said, trying to give Lucas a reassuring smile.

'Louisa.' He stepped forward.

He might have said something else; she saw his lips move, but she didn't hear it. There was a loud buzzing in her head and she felt dizzy. Black spots swirled in her vision until she couldn't see Lucas any more. She took a step forward and reached out a hand towards him, but before she could touch him, everything went black.

* * *

She was vaguely aware of being carried, but didn't really come back to her senses until she was laid on a bed in the Ambulance Room. When she realised she was on the same bed where her pa had been examined after his heart attack, she tried to rise.

'Don't, love. Stay still.'

Lucas had a hand on her shoulder as he looked down on her with a concerned frown so like Jeannie's expression this morning that she wanted to laugh even as she opened her mouth to argue with him.

'Quite right too,' said a female voice on the other side of her. 'You're not to move until I've examined you.' The nurse came to stand beside the bed. 'We can't have people fainting on the machines.'

'I was in the canteen,' said Louisa. She frowned and looked up at Lucas. 'Is that what happened? Did I faint?'

Lucas nodded. 'You did. So let the nurse take a look at you.'

'I'm all right,' she insisted. 'I just need my dinner.'

The nurse frowned as she took Louisa's pulse. 'Your husband tells me you were sick this morning. Are you expecting?'

She shook her head as Lucas's eyes widened. 'I had my monthlies just a couple of weeks ago. I can't be.'

'Mmm. Was it heavy?'

Louisa felt her cheeks redden. She did not want to be having this kind of conversation while her husband was listening. Seeing her embarrassment, the nurse took pity on her and suggested that Lucas wait outside. He looked reluctant, but gave in under the older woman's fierce stare. Once he had closed the door behind him, she turned back to her patient and pinned her with that same stare.

'So, my dear. Was it the same as usual this month?'

Louisa shook her head.

'Or heavier or lighter?'

She sighed. 'Lighter, and it only lasted a day or so.'

The nurse nodded and checked her blood pressure without comment. She then asked a slew of questions about Louisa's health and her symptoms this morning, making notes on her clipboard. When she asked whether her breasts were sore, Louisa felt sure her pulse and blood pressure must be going through the roof as she looked away, unable to have this conversation face to face with this relative stranger.

She hadn't thought about it, but now that she did, her breasts felt uncomfortable, as though they were tight within her clothes. *Like they did when I carried little Mattie.*

She nodded, her mind spinning. *Could I be?*

'In that case, my dear, I think there's every chance that you're expecting.'

Her heart skipped a beat. 'But... my monthlies.'

The woman patted her shoulder, her smile reassuring. 'Some women have bleeds all through their pregnancy. So long as it's light and there's no clots in it, there's probably no danger of miscarriage. But you must take care, just in case. No heavy lifting or overdoing things. See a doctor in a month or so. It's early days yet. I suggest your husband takes you home now and you rest for the remainder of the day. I'll inform both your foremen.'

Louisa sat up on the bed and swung her feet round while the nurse went outside to talk to Lucas. As the two of them spoke in low tones just outside the open doorway, her hands crept towards her belly.

Another baby. Not to replace little Mattie; that wasn't possible. But a new child, Lucas's son or daughter. A new start. Someone to give all the love she wasn't able to bestow upon her first-born child.

Lucas came into the room looking as shocked as she felt. Her eyes filled with tears as he kissed her forehead. He was a good man. He'd been her friend, her saviour, and now he was her lover and the father of her new baby.

'All right, love?' he asked softly as the nurse busied herself on the other side of the room. 'Looks like we're going to be a ma and pa soon.'

'She said we won't be sure until we see a doctor in a few weeks. It might still be a tummy upset.'

His gaze was warm and concerned. 'But you don't think so, do you? Kate and Jeannie said you fainted last time too.' He kissed her hair. 'I reckon we should assume that you are expecting until we know one way or the other, don't you?'

She nodded and sniffed, blinking away her tears. One spilled out onto her cheek and he gently wiped it away.

'Thank you, Lucas,' she whispered.

He smiled. 'Thank you, Louisa. You've made me happier than I ever expected to be.'

'That's how I feel as well,' she told him.

'Let's get you home. I expect Ma and Jeannie will be spoiling you rotten from now on.'

8

October gave way to November. The nights were drawing in and it got colder. Louisa didn't faint again, but she continued to be sick at least once a day. The doctor confirmed that she was indeed expecting and that the baby was due in May. Jeannie was thrilled for her and her brother, even while she was embarrassed every time she thought about what the two of them had had to do in order to make a baby.

She wondered whether she would ever have a husband and child of her own. She hoped so, but when she couldn't help herself comparing every lad she encountered with Tom, she felt as though she'd never find anyone to spend her life with.

As 1917 slowly came to an end, the war continued with no resolution in sight. Everyone had been sure that America joining the Allies would tip the balance, but reports from the front were full of tales of ever more casualties on both sides. Some men and boys returned to Street injured. Other families were informed that their menfolk would never return. The latest news Jeannie had heard from Mr Baker was that his grandson Douglas had been left blinded by a gas attack. She was reflecting on this as she was making pastry in the kitchen on a Saturday afternoon, so when there was a knock at the door, she sighed and took her time answering.

She was wiping her hands on a cloth as she opened it to find Tom in the process of turning away.

'Oh, Tom!' she said, immediately flustered. 'I'm sorry, I was elbow-deep in flour. Lucas and Louisa are out for a walk. She wanted to visit her pa's grave on his birthday, and the twins are at their football match.'

He turned back slowly and she noticed the suitcase in his hand.

'Are you going away?' she asked, putting a hand to her throat, suddenly afraid.

He nodded. 'My mother's ill. There was a letter waiting for me when I got home today. Father says I need to come home to see her. I've been round to see my foreman. I'm taking some unpaid leave.' He paused for a moment, looking up and down the road. 'Can I come in, Jeannie?'

Unable to say anything, she simply nodded and stepped back so that he could enter. He brought his case with him, putting it beside the front door. She closed the door and stood looking at him. He seemed tired, probably worried about his ma. She couldn't imagine being so far from home and getting news like that.

'Do... do you have time for a cuppa?'

He shook his head. 'No. I've only got a few minutes. I need to get to the station. It's going to take me a few trains to get to Northampton. I'll probably not make it today. Might have to stop in London overnight. I just didn't want to leave without telling you.'

She nodded again, glad he had, but not sure if he meant her specifically, or her family in general. 'I'll tell the others. I'm not sure when they'll be home. You might see Lucas and Louisa along the high street as you go.'

'Thanks. But it was you I was more worried about,' he said, stepping closer. 'I will be coming back, Jeannie. I promise.'

She couldn't look away from him as he touched her cheek.

'I've been doing a lot of thinking these past months,' he went on. 'I was intending to speak to you soon, but this news about Mother has thrown me and I didn't want to go away without making myself clear.' He took a deep breath and stepped closer. 'Is your ma home?'

'No,' she said, her voice feeling strained. 'She's next door talking to Mr Baker. His grandson Douglas has been blinded in a gas attack. He's upset and Ma took a pot of soup round to make sure he's eating properly.'

Tom frowned. 'Didn't you walk out with Douglas a while back?'

She felt her cheeks warm. 'Yes. He's the one who kissed another girl at the Crispin Hall dance when he was supposed to be with me.'

The side of his mouth rose in a half-smile. 'The one you drenched in dandelion and burdock?'

She closed her eyes, embarrassed that he remembered. 'I'm never going to live that down, am I?'

He chuckled. 'I think you should be proud. Everyone knows that they can't mess with Jeannie Musgrove.'

She huffed out a reluctant laugh. 'Between that and me defending myself against Sid Lambert, you mean? I know I've got a reputation that puts off most lads these days.'

'Good. If you standing up for yourself puts them off, they don't deserve you.'

She shrugged, not knowing what to say. She just wanted to

stand there, his hand against her cheek, basking in the warmth of his regard, even though she knew it was wrong.

'Jeannie,' he said softly. 'I'm intending to see my wife while I'm in Northampton. As soon as I've seen my mother, I'm going to track her down.'

She stiffened and took a step back. 'You're going back to her?' She felt as though her heart was breaking into a thousand pieces. Not being able to be with Tom was hard enough, but the thought that he might leave Street and return to his unfaithful wife was more than she could bear.

'No,' he said firmly, moving forward again to reduce the distance between them. 'I'm done with her forever, Jeannie. I'm intending to tell her that I'm going to save every penny I can to pay for a divorce from her. It might take a while, but I will be free of her one day. I can't carry on living in this awful purgatory, unable to declare to the whole world that I love you, Jeannie.'

For a moment, she couldn't breathe. She stared at him, her mouth dropping open. 'You love me?' she asked, her eyes filling with tears.

'I do,' he said, resting his forehead against hers.

She let out a shaky breath. 'Oh Tom, I love you, too.'

He pulled her into his arms and she rested her head against his chest, her heart full to bursting. 'Thank God,' he said. 'I don't know what I would've done if you didn't feel the same. What I felt for her isn't nearly as strong as my feelings for you, love. I'm more sorry than you'll ever know that I haven't sorted this out before now.'

'But... divorce is expensive, isn't it?'

'That it is,' he sighed. 'I'll try to persuade my cousin to chip in as well so that he can make an honest woman of her, although I doubt he'll have the money. So I'll save up, as quick as I can.

You're worth it, Jeannie. I just hope you'll be willing to wait for however long it takes.'

She clung to him, knowing that she would wait for him until the end of time, now that she knew he loved her. 'I will, my love. I promise. I don't want anyone else.'

He lifted her chin so that he could look at her. 'It might take years, you know?'

'I know. But you're worth it.' She smiled, echoing his sentiment.

He smiled back, relief lightening his gaze. 'Can I kiss you?'

'Yes please,' she said.

It was the best kiss she had ever had and it left her clinging to him and wanting more. Eventually, though, Tom sighed and lifted his head.

'I need to go. I don't want to leave you, but my mother...'

She touched a finger to his lips, stopping him. 'It's all right. You need to go to her. I hope she gets better. I'm sure seeing you will help her. She must miss you terribly.'

He nodded and reluctantly stepped away from her to retrieve his suitcase.

'When will you be back?' she asked.

'I'm not sure. Probably in a week, depending on how everything goes.'

She nodded. 'Safe journey.'

'I don't know if I'll have time to write to you, but I'll be thinking of you every day.'

'It's all right.' She smiled. 'I'll be thinking of you too. But you must spend what time you can with your ma, and then you'll have the other business to deal with.'

He nodded. 'I'm so glad I met you, Jeannie. You make my life worth living.'

'Oh, don't you go being so sweet and nice to me, Tom, or I'll be weeping all over you. You can't travel all that way with a damp shirt now, can you? Just make sure you come back to me when you can, all right?'

'I will, Jeannie. I promise. And one day, I'll be able to tell the world how much you mean to me.'

After the front door closed behind him, she sank onto the nearest armchair, hugging herself as she went over everything they had said and done over the past few minutes. She could barely believe it had happened. For months after he'd told her about his wife, Jeannie had been keeping her distance from him, finding it too hard to be around him. But now Tom had told her he loved her so much, he was prepared to do whatever he needed to be free of his unfaithful wife so that he could be with her.

The thought made her wildly happy and desperately frightened at the same time. What if, when he saw his wife, he changed his mind? After all, he must have loved her once, otherwise he wouldn't have married her in the first place. What if, when he confronted her, his love for his wife overwhelmed him again? She knew that Tom felt things deeply and he was an honourable man. What if the woman repented of her affair and begged him to take her back? He might bring her back to Street with him to make a fresh start with her... or he might choose to stay in Northampton where the rest of his family were. Either scenario would break Jeannie's heart.

He was clearly concerned about his poor ma as well. What if he didn't want to leave his parents and his sisters again? He hadn't seen them since he'd moved to Street a couple of years ago. Maybe they would convince him to stay in Northampton for good. Then what would Jeannie do? She couldn't leave Ma, and Louisa was having Lucas's baby, and then there was Kate, who needed her friends after all the trouble her pa had caused, and the twins still needed to be kept in line and...

She covered her face with her hands. She had to stop this. Tom loved her. She loved him. She needed to keep faith with him. He said he would be back and that he wanted to be with her. Remembering his kisses and caresses, she began to feel calmer.

Before she could get herself into any more of a state over it, she got up and went back into the kitchen. She'd been halfway through making pastry for a rabbit pie. The filling was cooked and cooling in a pot on the windowsill. Ma would be back in a moment and would wonder why on earth it wasn't in the oven yet.

She set to work, only realising she'd been kissing and cuddling Tom while she still wore her flour-covered apron. She only hoped she hadn't sent him on his way with white dust all over his overcoat! She giggled as she realised that both of them had been so wrapped up in each other that they hadn't noticed.

When Ma came back from next door, Jeannie was smiling as she slid the pie into the oven.

9

Kate got back from church at about the same time that Auntie Betty returned home from her Friends' meeting.

'Ooh, it's cold,' she said, rubbing her hands together. 'I'll get the kettle on.'

'Good idea, lass. I can't believe it's December already. Another year nearly over.'

'I know,' said Kate as she filled the kettle and set it on the range. She opened the firebox door to check that there was plenty of coal. She added a few pieces from the skuttle and used the poker to spread them over the glowing embers. They were using a lot more coal now to keep the cottage warm. She longed for spring, when the bitter winds would ease and they could look forward to more sunshine to warm their blood. 'It'll be our fourth Christmas at war. So much for them telling us it would all be over by Christmas back in 1914.' She closed the firebox door and turned to Betty. 'Will it ever end, Auntie? It feels like we'll always be at war.'

The older woman sank onto a chair at the kitchen table.

'Who knows, lass? I pray every day for peace; that's all we can do.'

Kate joined her at the table. 'I know.' She sighed. 'I do as well. I'm just getting so tired of it all. Did you hear the government is planning to order all restaurants and canteens to go meatless at least two days a week? There's so many shortages.'

'We've been lucky so far,' she replied. 'Living here in Somerset, it's easier to get fresh produce. I think it's harder in the cities where folk don't have big gardens and everything has to be shipped in.' Betty maintained a kitchen garden that kept the two of them and some of their neighbours in fresh vegetables and soft fruits in return for the occasional chicken or rabbit and fresh eggs, although most eggs were collected and sent to the local depot to be distributed to hospitals where they were needed to help feed wounded soldiers and sailors. The scheme of Eggs for Wounded Soldiers and Sailors, of which Queen Alexandra was patron, had helped the government to collect up to a million eggs a week from around the country, and no one begrudged it. People got behind it, and many even wrote little messages of support and encouragement on the eggs – 'eggograms' they called them, much to Kate's amusement – to cheer along the men during their recovery.

Kate helped where she could in Betty's vegetable patch and was learning to love gardening. But, apart from a few hardy crops like Brussel sprouts, winter cabbage and parsnips, there wasn't much growing in the garden right now. They would rely on the bottled, pickled and dried produce they'd prepared through the abundant months.

'Ada says the haulage company is suffering; they're short of drivers with all the men being conscripted. She said there'll be restrictions on motor fuel for non-essential journeys soon as well.'

'We must make the best of it,' said Betty. 'After all, whatever we're suffering is nothing compared to what our menfolk are facing, is it?'

Kate nodded, knowing from her expression that Auntie was thinking about her sons – poor Mattie, who was never coming home, and Will, stuck in Lincolnshire working in a factory, making tanks for the duration of the war.

'I just want it to be over, Auntie. I'm so tired of it all. In Gerald's last letter, he said that if peace isn't declared before his release in January, he'll likely be sentenced a whole year next time.'

Auntie Betty shook her head and sighed. 'I know. My poor cousin misses him something awful. That lad should never have been put in gaol in the first place.'

'Speaking of which, Katie love, she's asked me if I'd join her in Bristol for Christmas while the factory's shut.'

'That'll be a nice break for you,' said Kate, trying to dispel her gloom. 'I know you get on well with Gerald's ma, and you'll both be missing your sons this year.'

The older woman nodded, but looked uncertain. 'I haven't said I would yet. I was thinking of asking her if you could come with me. You shouldn't be on your own at Christmas.'

Kate smiled. 'That's kind of you, but there's not need. Ada and Vi have both asked me. I haven't said yes to them yet on account of thinking you would be on your own. I was going to ask if I could bring you with me. I know you'd be welcome.'

'Well, aren't we a fine pair?' Betty chuckled. 'In that case, you must go to your sisters-in-law for the holiday, and I'll tell Ethel I'll be happy to visit her.'

Kate got up and made the tea while her landlady brought a pot of leftover stew in from the pantry and placed it in the oven to warm through for their dinner. They often made larger meals that would stretch over more than one day. It saved them both a lot of work when they had plenty of other things to be getting on with.

'Ada's a bit worried, actually,' said Kate, feeling again the dread in the pit of her stomach as she remembered what she had told her. 'She hasn't heard from George when she was expecting to. Fred told Vi in his last letter that George was moved to a different platoon and was transferred away from Fred's position. He doesn't know where he is.' She sighed. 'I've tried to tell her no news is good news, but... well, you know how it is. At least if it was the worst news, she'd have been told, wouldn't she?'

'Oh, my word. Why didn't you say, love? Is there anything I can do?'

'Just pray for him, Auntie. Like you said, that's all any of us can do.'

She hated this uncertainty and hoped more than anything that Ada would get some good news from George soon. The thought that he might never come home filled her with dread. What would become of Ada and the children? If they didn't hear something soon, it was going to be a miserable Christmas. It was bad enough that her brothers were both away fighting, but their letters had kept the family going.

Auntie Betty nodded. 'He's already in my prayers along with all the menfolk away from home, lass, but I'll be sure to hold him up in the light and ask the Lord to bring some good news to Ada.' She looked tired and sad. Kate wondered if maybe she shouldn't have said anything. Any news of local lads being killed or injured always brought back awful memories for Betty. But Kate knew she would want to be told about anything that happened to the Davis brothers. She had been Ma's best friend most of her life, just like Jeannie and Louisa were Kate's. She regarded all of Ma's children as family – and she supposed that they *were* family on account of their sister Peg's marriage to Will.

They laid the table and sat down for their dinner in silence. Once they had eaten, the older woman rallied.

'Right,' she said. 'Let's think of something more cheerful, shall we? How's Louisa getting along? I saw her at the meeting this morning but I didn't get a chance to speak to her. She's looking well. Is she still being sick?'

Kate smiled. 'No, she seems to be over that now she's a few months along. She's even got a little bump, did you notice?'

Auntie nodded.

'Mrs Musgrove is pleased as punch,' Kate went on. 'Lou says she's spoiling her rotten, which is making her feel guilty because she's feeling so much better now the sickness has worn off.'

She paused, reluctant to say too much. As far as Auntie Betty was concerned, this was Louisa's first pregnancy, but of course it wasn't. Her first born – Mattie's son – was being brought up by Will and Peg as their own. He was Betty's grandson, but she had no idea that Peg hadn't given birth to him. She wished she could tell her; she was sure Betty wouldn't mind – the babe was her blood regardless – but it wasn't her secret to share. She'd promised Peg, Will and Louisa that she wouldn't breathe a word.

'I expect Jeannie's excited about being an auntie,' said the older woman, unaware of Kate's thoughts.

Kate grinned. 'That she is. She's so happy about it.'

That wasn't the only thing that made Jeannie happy these days. She'd sworn her and Louisa to secrecy (although, of course, Lou would be telling Lucas), but after Tom's visit to Northampton a few weeks ago, he'd been working hard to save enough money to pay for a divorce from his unfaithful wife. Kate had a feeling it would take an awful long time before he had enough money, even though he was on a good wage as an engineer at Clarks. She didn't know anyone who had ever ended their marriage; most working folks made their bed and had to lie on it. Apparently, if a man could prove that his wife had committed adultery, and he could afford to pay for a solicitor and a barrister, then he would be granted a divorce from her by the courts. But it was horribly expensive, therefore out of reach for most ordinary folk.

Although, she supposed that the war might change things. No doubt a lot of men might be returning from war when it finally ended to find their wives had found someone else in their absence. There could be plenty of men wanting to be free of their cheating women and there would be pressure on the government to change the law.

She also suspected a lot of women would have become accustomed to being without their husbands and might not relish the idea of them coming home to lord it over them again after they'd enjoyed the freedom of making their own decisions and earning their own money. But it was Jeannie she was thinking about. She hoped that her friend didn't end up disappointed if it proved harder than Tom thought to gain his freedom.

He must think an awful lot of Jeannie to be considering it. What worried Kate was that the court proceedings could be reported in the newspapers. Tom might love Jeannie, but the scandal would be horrible for her.

'We must knit some things for the baby,' said Auntie Betty, drawing Kate's attention back to their conversation. 'It will make a nice change from socks and balaclavas for soldiers.'

'It will,' said Kate. 'I found a lovely pattern for a crib blanket I thought I'd try. But I might need you to help me as it looks a bit complicated. I've nearly finished some gloves and a hat for Gerald for Christmas – he says it's bitterly cold in the prison exercise yard, yet he persists in going out there whenever he's offered the opportunity, if only to see the sky and breathe in some fresh air.'

Auntie Betty sighed. 'I know. His ma is hoping to send him some warmer clothes and maybe even some blankets. But she's not sure whether the prison authorities will let him have any of them. Sometimes, they're fair, but other times, they treat the conscientious objectors so ill, it breaks my heart.'

Kate got up and put some water on the range to heat up so that she could wash their dishes. She felt so out of sorts, she couldn't sit still for long. She fretted about Gerald and his fellow prisoners, suffering for their beliefs. But at least they were relatively safe, even though Jeannie had told her about at least one lad whose health had suffered permanently because of his treatment in prison. They didn't think the poor lad would see another year, and even if he did, he was unlikely to ever get home but rather he'd see out his days in a sanatorium. Then there was the worry about George. It had brought up all sorts of feelings about both of her brothers and, though she tried not to think about him, she couldn't help but wonder whether her one-time sweetheart, Ted Jackson, was safe as well. It was so hard when there was no news. She just wanted everyone she cared about to be safe.

'I've heard folk say that this revolution in Russia is making it harder for the Allies,' said Auntie. 'With the Eastern Front being weakened by mutinies, the Hun might be able to defeat them easily. Then they'll throw all their might against the Western Front.' She sighed and bit her lip, concern making her look older than her years. 'I'm too old to be learning German.'

'We can't be thinking like that, Auntie,' she said, leaning against the sink. 'We have to have faith that we'll win. You never know, they might rush off to conquer the Russians and it would leave our boys in a stronger position to win back France and

Belgium and force the Huns to surrender. Those Russian soldiers might be mutinying, but I'll bet they don't want to be talking German any more than we do. Even if they're not fighting for the Tsar any more, they're fighting for freedom for their families, aren't they? They won't want to kowtow to the Kaiser now, will they? No, I reckon that will spur them on to fight even harder if push comes to shove. It might prove to be the downfall of the Kaiser in the end.'

Auntie Betty regarded her with curiosity. 'Is that what you think?'

Kate shrugged, feeling a bit foolish. 'I've been listening to the men when they talk about these things after church, and I read the newspapers when I get the chance. I know that it's a worry that the Russian people have imprisoned the Tsar and his family and there seems to be no real leadership there at the moment. But we have to have faith in their men at the front. The Russians' revolution is about freedom, not giving in to the Hun. With so many countries fighting on our side, we have to believe that we'll win one day. I can't bear to think otherwise.' She grimaced. 'And I'll not be learning German, that's for sure. If they come here and want to talk to me, they'll have to speak as we do.'

Betty laughed, even though her gaze was sad. 'Oh Kate, love. You're so fierce. Do you think if the Allies win, our men will speak to their prisoners in German? Of course they won't. Whoever wins, the defeated people will have to bow down to them.'

Kate blew out a breath. 'Then we'd better pray extra hard that this rotten war goes in our favour.'

'That we should, lass. That we should.'

* * *

Kate went round to Ada's after work finished early on Christmas Eve. She was going to stay the night and was excited about seeing the children open their presents on Christmas morning. In her bag, she had her best Sunday dress to wear, plus the small presents she'd made for both her sisters-in-law and her niece and nephews.

But when Ada opened the door, all thoughts of the coming festivities flew out of Kate's mind as she saw her tear-stained face. 'What's wrong? Is it George?' she asked, hardly wanting to know the answer.

Ada's eyes filled with tears as she nodded. 'Don't fret, he's not dead,' she said, trying to give her what Kate assumed was a reassuring smile, but failing miserably. 'He's safe now, thank God.'

Kate followed her into the cottage. 'I don't understand,' she said. 'Is he injured?'

'Not as far as I know.' Ada raised her hands. 'Probably not. But he's been taken prisoner,' she said on a sob. 'They've carted him off to Germany. Oh Kate! When will I ever see him again? What if the Hun win and they never let him go?'

Kate pulled her sister-in-law into a hug. 'Hush now, don't fret so, love.' She held Ada as she sobbed, her mind whirling. 'We've got to look on the bright side. He's not on the battlefield any more, which is good, isn't it? No more bullets or bombs or gas attacks. No chance of freezing to death in the mud. As a prisoner of war, he'll be looked after. It's the law, isn't it? Every side has to take care of their prisoners. He'll be fed and housed, even if he's feeling angry about having been captured.'

'I know, but...'

'No buts now,' she said. In truth, Kate wanted to weep along with Ada. She was torn between profound relief that her brother was safe and despair at the knowledge that he was now a hostage of fortune until this horrible war was over. But she had to stay strong for Ada and the children. 'He's safe and we know where he is. The war can't go on forever, and the government keeps saying we're winning, so we have to have faith that they're not lying to us. George will be home before we know it, and when he does, it'll be like all our Christmases coming at once.'

Ada sniffed and nodded. 'I suppose so,' she said. 'It's better than hearing that he's injured or worse. When I saw the postman with the letter, I nearly died; I could barely bring myself to take it. But you're right, Kate. At least we should get him home in one piece at the end of the war. Although when that'll be is anyone's guess.' Her tears overflowed again. 'I just miss him so much.'

'I know, love. We all do. But he won't want us spoiling the children's Christmas with our tears, will he?' She wiped Ada's tears with gentle fingers. 'Come on, now. You put the kettle on while I go and see where little George and Catherine are. They're mighty quiet, so they're bound to be up to mischief.'

In fact, both of the little ones were napping together, snuggled up on the settee in the parlour, worn out no doubt by the excitement of Christmas. Kate smiled as she kissed them both and left them to their dreams while she went into the kitchen, determined to cheer poor Ada up.

10

The Christmas season was a quiet time for all the girls. The ongoing war, with news of bombardments, gas attacks and casualties in the mud and cold of the trenches left them all unwilling to celebrate the holiday. Rather than indulge themselves, they helped put together gift parcels that were sent for soldiers and prisoners of war abroad as well as prisoners of conscience at home.

At least Ada had heard news of George, so the family knew he was safe, but that didn't stop them all fretting about Fred and everyone else they knew for whom the battle raged on.

As 1918 began, shortages of materials at the factory and shortages of goods in the shops meant that prices went up and everyone had to be careful with their pennies. The twins' seventeenth birthday in mid-January was greeted with mixed feelings as far as the Musgrove family were concerned.

'I hope the cake we made is all right,' said Louisa. It was a simple fruit cake, made without eggs. They had sent smaller versions of the same cake in their gift parcels at Christmas – the recipe was known as Trench Cake. 'I know the twins prefer a nice sponge, but with all the restrictions on things like sugar and eggs, we couldn't manage it, could we?'

'Don't fret,' said Jeannie. 'They'll eat what they're given, birthday or not. And anyway, with the extra cocoa and spices we added, it'll be a tasty one.'

They were planning a tea on the Sunday afternoon, when everyone would be at home. Ma had agreed that the boys could ask some friends to join the family. John had invited a couple of his pals from the football club and Peter had asked Tom, which wasn't a surprise, and Kate, which was.

'Why would he ask Kate?' Lucas said to Louisa and Jeannie. 'I mean, she'd likely come anyway because she's your friend.' He shook his head. 'I thought he'd bring along another lad from the club or one of the other apprentices.'

Louisa smirked. 'You must have noticed he's sweet on her,' she said. 'Ever since he gave Reggie Davis a black eye for attacking Kate in the High Street, he blushes whenever he sees her.'

Jeannie smiled. 'I've noticed him gazing at her with puppy dog eyes when he doesn't think anyone's watching.'

'What? Like you and Tom do?' Lucas laughed.

'Oh you.' She blushed, smacking his arm.

He scratched his chin. 'He hasn't got a chance with Kate, has he?'

Louisa and Jeannie both shook their heads. 'Kate's not interested in any lad,' said Louisa. 'Especially not one so much younger. She's twenty now. I know Peter's more sensible than John these days, but he's got a lot of growing up to do before Kate would give him the time of day.'

'Not that she'd be cruel to him,' said Jeannie. 'She's grateful for what Peter and Tom did that time when her pa grabbed her.' They had rescued Kate and held Reggie Davis until the constables had arrived and taken him off to gaol. That was the last time Kate had had anything to do with the man until he'd been injured in the fire. Now that he was being held indefinitely in the local asylum, Kate was finally free of him. 'But I agree with you, Lucas. She's not interested in Peter as a sweetheart.'

'Let's face it,' said Louisa. 'Kate's been saying she doesn't want any man ever since Ted went away.'

'Mmm,' said Lucas. 'But what about that one she met at the Clothiers' last year?'

'Oh, that's Gerald, one of her pen pals,' said Jeannie. 'They're friends, that's all. She did worry that he might grow feelings for her, but since they met, she's sure he doesn't think of her like that. She says he's far too well-educated for the likes of her.'

'But if they liked each other, it shouldn't matter who was more educated,' said Louisa. 'And he doesn't lord it over her just because he's better read.'

'Not like Cyril next door,' muttered Jeannie with a grimace. These days. he didn't go out of his way to talk to her, which suited Jeannie just fine.

'Exactly. Anyway, Kate is happy to be friends with anyone who treats her with respect, which Gerald does. But our Peter is on a hiding to nothing if he's carrying a torch for her,' said Louisa. 'Maybe you should have a quiet word with him, Lucas.'

He pulled a face. 'Maybe. I suppose I can try and save him from being humiliated.'

'But not today, eh?' said Jeannie. 'It's his birthday.'

The gathering was cheerful and the twins were in good spirits. The birthday meal was modest but tasty and served with plenty of hot tea. Louisa could see that Jeannie was happy because Tom was there, although the two of them continued to act as though they were just friends rather than sweethearts.

'We can't do anything else,' she had told her friends. 'I talked it over with Ma. If he's serious about getting a divorce, we can't let people think that we're as bad as his wife, can we? He has to be above that kind of behaviour.' So there was no hand holding, no kissing – at least not in public – and no walking out alone together.

Louisa wondered how they could bear it, being so close yet unable to declare their feelings to the world. It reminded her of when she and Mattie had to keep quiet about their relationship in the face her parents' objections. It had been exciting for a while, but in the end, it had been horrible. She only hoped it didn't take as long as they thought it might for Tom to be free of his unfaithful wife. Jeannie deserved some happiness. But at this rate, she could be old and grey before he was free to marry her.

'I've got an announcement,' said John, standing up and puffing out his chest. 'Now I'm seventeen, I'm getting my driving licence. I've saved up the five bob I need to pay for it and I'll be popping down the Post Office to get it in my dinner break on Monday. The boss says he'll let me learn on the small delivery van first but if I do well, I'll be moving on to drive the bigger lorries soon enough.'

'Oh my,' said Mrs Musgrove, putting a hand to her throat. 'You will be careful, won't you, John? I do worry so about you on those vehicles.'

Louisa thought John was going to scoff at his ma, but he caught Lucas's warning glance and he rearranged his expression before he turned to her.

'Of course I will, Ma. I know what's what. Don't you fret.'

His mother nodded and stood, collecting up plates and cups.

'All right, son. So long as you keep safe. I'm proud of you for working so hard now you've found a job you like.' She smiled at his twin. 'And you, Peter. You're doing well, learning to be an engineer. All of my children are doing so well and soon I'll have a grandchild to love as well. I'm a lucky woman.'

Jeannie stood up and took the plates from her ma. 'You certainly are, with both a daughter and daughter-in-law to help with the tidying up while all these lads have a good old gossip. You rest up now, Ma.' She grinned as Mrs Musgrove laughed and sat down at the table again.

'I'll help too,' said Kate. 'All this talk about motors and machines is worse than when they're rabbiting on about football.'

'Go on then, lads,' said Louisa, joining her friends. 'Take yourselves off into the parlour and leave us in peace... unless you want to do the washing up?' She raised her eyebrows and then laughed when the twins and their friends all moved quickly to leave the room. Lucas and Tom chuckled and shook their heads before following behind, leaving the three girls and Mrs Musgrove to restore order in the kitchen.

'You sit down with Mrs Musgrove, Lou,' said Kate. 'Me and Jeannie will wash up this lot soon enough. Then we'll have another cuppa, eh?'

The older woman smiled her thanks and urged Louisa to join her.

'I can help,' Louisa protested.

'You can put the dishes away after Kate dries,' said Jeannie.

Mrs Musgrove rubbed her temples.

'Are you all right?' Louisa asked her. 'Has this afternoon worn you out?'

Her mother-in-law looked up and smiled. 'I am a little tired,' she admitted. 'But it's good to see the twins happy. They've not been the easiest to live with as they've grown up, have they?'

'No,' said Jeannie as she began scrubbing cups. 'They were little beasts when Lucas was away. But they seem to be growing up at long last.'

Her ma's smile slipped. 'I just wish this war would end. They'll be eighteen next birthday. I don't think I could bear it if Peter and John get called up.'

None of the girls spoke. They knew all too well the pressure on young men to answer the call to arms, regardless of their Quaker and pacifist beliefs. Both Mattie and Lucas had given in and paid the price. None of them could imagine either of the twins having the strength of conviction to face the ordeal of a gaol sentence rather than accept conscription like Gerald had. Nor did they mention to Mrs Musgrove the rumours that the government might change the age for conscription for all men to between seventeen and fifty-one if the war continued for much longer. Soon there would be no men left.

A burst of laughter came from the parlour.

'Well, they're happy enough right now, Ma,' said Jeannie. 'Let's not fret about anything today. It will have to end sooner or later. I'm sure we're doing better now we've got the Americans on our side.'

'The Hun don't know where to turn,' said Kate. 'We've more chance of defeating them now than ever.'

Mrs Musgrove sighed, her shoulders slumping. 'I hope you're right, girls.'

Louisa touched her mother-in-law's arm. 'Why don't you go and have a lie down, Mrs M? We'll finish tidying in here and the lads are entertaining themselves.'

'I think I will,' she said, getting to her feet. She winced as she straightened her back. Louisa hovered over her as she left the kitchen. Lucas looked up when his ma opened the door. He rose and held out his arm for her and escorted her up the stairs.

* * *

The twins went out with their friends for a kickabout, even though it was already dark at four o'clock. The girls joined Lucas and Tom in the parlour, enjoying the warmth from the fireplace. As Louisa sat next to Lucas on the sofa, he smiled and put an arm around her shoulders, kissing her hair as she snuggled close. She sighed, feeling that familiar feeling of contentment tinged with guilt. It was getting easier to focus on the warmth of her husband's affection, but she didn't think she'd ever forget Mattie or get over the feeling that she shouldn't be happy without him. She was only thankful that Lucas understood and didn't resent it. When she'd confessed it to him, he'd admitted that he felt the same. That had helped. She'd realised she wasn't alone.

Tom was sitting in one of the two armchairs. He rose, offering it to Jeannie with a smile. She blushed as she sat down while Kate took the other chair. Once she was settled, Tom perched on the arm of the chair, resting his hand on the back of it.

Kate rolled her eyes and waved a hand at her friends. 'If you lot are all going to get all lovey-dovey, I'll take myself home.' She shuddered. 'There's far too much of that going on around here these days.'

Jeannie put her hands to her burning cheeks. 'Kate! We are not *lovey-dovey*.'

Louisa giggled as both lads smirked. 'Yes we are,' she said. 'You can't deny it, Jeannie.'

'We can't... we mustn't,' she protested, looking helplessly at Tom, who shrugged.

Kate tutted, still looking miffed, although her eyes were sparkling with mirth. 'Then you'll have to stop looking at him, because you give yourself away every time you glance in his direction.'

'Is that right?' asked Tom, looking pleased even as Jeannie groaned and covered her face.

Lucas laughed. 'You're so easy to tease, Jeannie. Let her be, Kate. It doesn't matter if they're looking all *lovey-dovey* here. We'll not be gossiping about it to anyone else.'

'You're just as bad, Lucas Musgrove,' said Kate.

He shrugged. 'So what? I'm allowed. A man can look fondly at his wife. In fact, I'd say it's required.' He winked at Louisa and she giggled again, enjoying the feeling of his arm around her shoulders and his body pressed against her side.

A fluttering in her belly made her gasp and look down, her focus on her womb.

'What is it?' Lucas asked, immediately concerned.

She shook her head and gave him a shaky smile. 'The baby moved.' She took his good hand and laid it over her bump. 'It's the first time I've noticed it.'

Everyone was silent as Lucas talked softly. 'Come on, little one. Say hello to your pa, eh?'

Nothing seemed to happen for a few moments, but then Lucas gasped and Louisa smiled. 'Did you feel that?' she asked.

He nodded, his mouth open, his gaze filled with shock and wonder. 'Oh my word, Lou. Can you believe it? There's a brand-new life growing in there.' He shook his head before kissing her temple. 'We are so blessed.'

She felt quite tearful at his heartfelt words. 'That we are,' she said.

Jeannie sniffed and Kate sighed before she stood up. 'On that note, I'm definitely going,' she announced. 'I'm happy for you, but I'm not sure I can stomach the idea of something growing and wriggling inside you.'

'What, like a tapeworm, you mean?' asked Tom with a grin.

Kate burst out laughing. 'Exactly!'

Louisa laughed along with the others. 'I do not have a tapeworm,' she said. 'At least I hope it's not.' She looked at her growing belly and pulled a face.

Kate took her leave and Tom made a comment about having to make a move soon.

'No,' said Louisa after she closed the front door behind Kate. 'Don't rush off, Tom. Me and Lucas are going to make some more tea, so you and Jeannie can get as lovey-dovey as you want for the next ten minutes.' She grinned as Lucas chuckled.

In the kitchen, Lucas shook his head. 'I'm not sure how I feel about my sister canoodling in the parlour,' he said.

'She's not a child any more, Lucas, and she deserves some happiness, doesn't she?'

He scratched his cheek. 'I suppose so. But she's still my sister. It's hard to imagine someone fancying her.'

'Oh, you,' she scolded as she put the kettle on the range. 'She's a lovely girl and any lad would be lucky to have her. Surely you'd rather she was with Tom than with anyone else?'

He grimaced. 'He's definitely a better man than either of the Baker lads or that buffoon Sid Lambert, so I suppose so. But he's still married, isn't he? What if he can never afford a divorce?'

She sat and put her elbows on the table, resting her chin on her hands. 'Have you talked to him about it?'

'I have. He swears he'll do it. He's saving every penny he can, working overtime when it's offered. But every month, another soldier comes home without a limb or with some other problem, and folk ask Tom to help him. Sometimes, people give him materials to use. But if they don't, he won't see any man left without a decent prosthetic or splint, so he has to spend his own money to get the right stuff. At this rate, he's going to take years to be free to marry Jeannie.'

'Mmm.' Louisa frowned. 'I wonder...'

'What?'

'The folks Tom's helping are locals, aren't they? Probably worked at Clarks before they joined up?'

'Either they did, or someone in their family does,' agreed Lucas.

She nodded. 'Then I think someone needs to speak to management – point out that Tom's been helping everyone for no reward and often at his own expense. I reckon Clarks will find a way to cover his costs, don't you?'

His face lit up. 'Of course! Why didn't we think of that before?'

'Do you think Tom would mind? He's proud. He might not like us asking for a handout for him.'

'But it's not for him, is it? It's to help him help others. I'll talk to my foreman tomorrow. He's already mentioned how impressed he was with my splint and how it's helped me increase production. I'll bet the management would be happy to fund Tom's projects if it helps men work better.' He kissed her gently on the lips. 'Clever girl for thinking of it. We can't have our Jeannie waiting until she's old and past it before she can get wed, can we?'

* * *

In the parlour, Tom and Jeannie sat on the settee, enjoying a quiet moment in each other's arms.

'I love cuddling up with you,' she sighed.

He kissed her hair. 'Me too. I just wish we didn't have to

sneak around to do it. It doesn't sit right with me. Neither of us has done anything wrong.'

'I know, I don't like it either. But that solicitor you spoke to was clear, wasn't he? Just because your missus is doing wrong, it doesn't mean you can as well. The courts won't look favourably on you if we're not careful.'

Tom grumbled a little, but conceded she was right. Ever since he'd returned from Northampton, he'd been impatient to see an end to his marriage. He was sure the scandal had contributed to his mother's illness, yet his cousin and his wife continued to carry on as though they were a married couple for the whole community to see. The upset and strain had resulted in Tom's ma suffering from a stomach ulcer. He'd given his parents some money so that she could get some treatment. Then he had gone round and confronted his missus. She had been embarrassed and guilty, but it was clear her loyalty now lay with his cousin, who had been called up to fight in France. It was just as well he wasn't home, because Tom would have wanted to punch him on the nose. As it was, he'd wanted to pick something up and smash it against the wall. Maybe it had been the thought of gentle Jeannie and how she hated violence that had held him back. In the end, he had been able to have a calm conversation with her and got her agreement that they wouldn't fight him if he managed to get his application for a divorce into the courts.

Now all he had to do was get together enough money to pay for it. After his conversation with a solicitor just before Christmas, he knew he had a long way to go. It would be quicker if he didn't spend so much money on materials for his projects, but he knew how the men he was helping struggled and he had to do all he could to alleviate their suffering. It wouldn't sit well on his conscience if he stopped doing that work in order to use the money for his divorce. He prayed every day that somehow he could find the funds he needed and that Jeannie would understand if it took longer than they wanted.

'We'll be careful, love,' he said. 'I promise. And one day, I'll be proud to tell the world that you're mine.'

He just hoped that Jeannie meant it when she said she'd wait for him. If she lost patience and chose a man who was free to marry her, he wouldn't blame her, but it would break his heart.

11

Spring came with the news that allied forces were suffering, as typhoid and influenza decimated the men in the trenches. In March, they heard that Kate's brother Fred's company had been the victims of a mustard gas attack.

'Vi got a letter from one of his comrades,' Kate told her friends when they arrived at the Machine Room. 'The gas blinded poor Fred at first, but the chap who wrote to her said not to worry as he'd seen a lot of chaps like this after an attack and most of them got their sight back.' She frowned, remembering that Douglas Baker had been reported blind after an attack. No one had heard whether he'd regained his sight. 'I hope he's not just saying that to stop Vi from fretting. It would be just like Fred to get someone to write that.'

'Oh lord,' said Jeannie, almost in tears. 'I hope he's all right. I can't imagine...'

'Me neither,' said Kate. 'We just have to hope for the best. But at least Fred's safely away from the front line now. They said the gas has burnt his lungs as well, so the fighting's over for him.

With any luck, he'll be home soon.' She paused and took a shaky breath. 'Let's hope he'll recover and he can get back to his old life with Vi and the children.' She didn't want to think about her brother being blind and unable to breathe properly. He didn't deserve that. No soldier did. They were just doing what they were told by generals who stayed nice and safe well behind the lines. It wasn't fair.

Louisa stroked her arm. 'I'm so sorry, Kate. We'll all pray for him and the others who were hurt with him. It's inhuman. How can people do that to other folk?'

Kate shrugged. 'The Hun started it, but I heard that our side has been attacking them with gas as well now. Tit for tat.'

Jeannie sniffed, blinking hard. 'And what good would that do? Just kill and maim more lads.' She closed her eyes and shook her head. 'It has to stop soon; we can't go on like this, can we? And if the twins have to go, it will kill Ma. She's already fretting and it always affects her health.'

Louisa nodded, rubbing her round belly. 'I know. I think it's only the prospect of this little one making an appearance that's keeping her going.'

Glad of a distraction, Kate put a hand on her friend's growing bump. 'I don't understand why you're still working,' she said. 'You're what, nearly seven months along now?'

Louisa nodded.

'And we can see how you're struggling to get up and down the stairs to the Machine Room now, and you're looking so tired this week. I'm surprised Lucas hasn't put his foot down and made you stop. You need to rest and put your feet up before baby arrives. Lord knows, you'll be busy enough once he or she gets here.' In normal times, women gave up work when they married and were at home throughout their pregnancies. But with so many men away, more married women needed to step up to fill the jobs, so

Louisa wasn't the only one who was working while she was expecting, even though it was frowned upon.

She pulled a face. 'I know. Lucas is on at me about it as well. But... he understands I need to work this week at least. If I stay at home, I'll probably give in and weep. And then Mrs Musgrove will want to know what's wrong and I can't bear to tell her.'

Kate closed her eyes, remembering the letter she'd had from Peg a couple of days ago. 'Of course,' she said gently. 'It's little Mattie's second birthday, isn't it?'

Jeannie groaned as Louisa nodded, her expression downcast. 'Oh, Lou!'

Louisa took a deep breath and raised her chin. 'I've promised Lucas I'll put my notice in on Saturday and stop next week. I know it's time. My belly's so huge, I can't see my feet and I'm scared of losing my footing on those stone stairs.'

'You mustn't try and go up and down on your own,' said Jeannie. 'I promised Lucas I'd help you.'

Louisa smiled at her, even though the air of sadness still surrounded her. 'Thanks, Jeannie. Although I'd squash you like a fly if I fell on top of you. Just look at me. I'm enormous.'

'We'd both catch you,' said Kate. 'Though it might be better if we were to stop you from falling in the first place. I don't relish the prospect of being as flat as a pancake if you land on me.' She grinned.

'Oh, you.' Louisa laughed and pushed her away. 'Stop it. You're supposed to tell me I'm not that big and that I'm simply blooming.'

'Watch it,' said Jeannie. 'Mr Briars is coming.'

They all turned to their machines before the foreman reached them.

'And you're right, Louisa,' said Jeannie as they began sewing. 'You're not that big and you *are* blooming.'

As Kate settled into work, her mind wandered to Fred and his family. She'd heard such awful things about mustard gas: how it burnt the skin and seared the lungs. She couldn't imagine the pain her poor brother was going through.

Her sight blurred as tears welled. She blinked them away, focusing back on her work, making sure she didn't make any mistakes that would cost her in wasted thread. If Fred's blindness proved to be permanent, or if his lungs were so bad that he couldn't work, she'd have to help him and Vi with what money she could spare. Even if she had to go hungry herself, she wouldn't let their sweet children suffer.

She did wonder about trying to get a transfer to a job in the offices. People often commented on how clear and neat her handwriting was. If she could learn book-keeping or shorthand and typewriting, she might be able to earn more. Her wages in the Machine Room weren't bad, and because she was fast and accurate, she did well on piecework. Once she was twenty-one, which was soon, she'd be on full wages at last, so she'd have a bit more in her pay packet. But her prospects for advancement were limited. Some women were deputies to the foremen, like Auntie Betty was. But only Miss Florrie Bond, the woman who Auntie worked for in the Trimmings Department had reached the same level as Mr Briars. But she'd heard that even at foreman level, Miss Bond earned a lot less than the male foremen, which was really unfair. Given that there were now more women than men working at Clarks, Kate couldn't see why they didn't have more of them running their own departments and earning the same as any man who did the same job. After all, Miss Alice Clark was a director and in overall charge of several departments, so it was clear that Clarks knew women were as capable as men, wasn't it?

It occurred to her that if she could join the pen pushers in the offices, the work wouldn't be so physically taxing, either. She still might not end up with any sort of authority, but she'd be better off.

She'd been thinking about it for a while, but now, with the news about Fred, she thought it was time to do something about it. She'd speak to Auntie tonight and see what she said.

12

A month later, Jeannie arrived in the Machine Room five minutes before their shift was due to start, her coat damp from the April shower that she'd run through to get to the factory. She wasn't complaining about the rain, though. It would encourage the vegetables they'd planted to grow and with luck would mean good crops. With prices rising and shortages of so many foodstuffs, it was important to be able to grow their own fruit and veg.

She just hoped that it wasn't so wet in the trenches. Now that Russia had withdrawn from the war, the German forces were focusing their fire power on the Western Front and the Allies were under immense pressure and they didn't need more mud to add to their woes. It worried Jeannie that things weren't going well, even though the government insisted that the Allies had beaten the Hun in the air thanks to the flying aces who were dominating the skies, and that the current offensive was their last gasp. She prayed they were right.

It was strange, coming to work without Louisa. Her sister-in-law had been at home for three weeks now and Jeannie was still getting used to it. A new girl was sitting at the end of their bench of three now. She was pleasant enough and worked hard, but it wasn't the same. Jeannie missed Louisa at work, although she knew she should be grateful that she saw her every day at home, not like when she'd moved away to Lincolnshire before she had little Mattie. And she *was* grateful. She'd always wanted a sister and that it was one of her best friends was a blessing. But she knew that everything was changing, with the baby coming in just over a month now. Lucas and Ma hovered over Lou, who was tired and bored. She spent her days with her feet up at Ma's insistence, with just a few books from the Crispin Hall library and her sketch books to keep her busy. She'd given up on knitting and sewing, because between Ma, Jeannie, Kate and Auntie Betty, she had so many baby clothes and blankets that she was sure the child would grow out of them before it had a chance to wear them all.

Jeannie sighed as she thought about Louisa and Lucas. She couldn't help but feel jealous of their happiness, and that made her feel ashamed because she didn't begrudge them it. She couldn't help it, though, because she'd like nothing better than to be married and with a baby on the way. But, even if Tom worked all hours to earn enough money to rid himself of his faithless wife, it would be years before he could afford a divorce, if ever. Jeannie was beginning to think she'd be too old to have children by the time they were finally able to wed. She tried to stay positive, knowing that he loved her. But it was hard to be patient when Louisa was having her second baby and Jeannie had no idea when she could even tell people that she was courting, let alone settled and married.

Kate rushed in with a minute to spare and sat down with a huff, pulling Jeannie out of her gloomy thoughts. 'Made it! I was sure I was going to be late, but I got a letter from Gerald and had to read it.' She pulled a face. 'It was a small envelope, written in pencil, so I knew he'd been arrested again.'

'Oh no,' Jeannie sighed. 'Didn't he get home just a week or so ago?'

She nodded, looking miserable. 'He served nine months last time. He reckons he'll get a whole year now. He's worried about his poor ma. Auntie says she's living on a small income from her late husband's estate and with Gerald being away and unable to work, it's a struggle with the price of everything going up. It makes me so cross. It's bad enough what they're doing to Gerald. But why should a poor widow suffer like this, just because her son is a man of honour and principle?'

'I'm sure she'd rather suffer than have her son forced to fight after everything he's been through.'

Kate sighed. 'I know. I think Auntie would have her come and live with her to make her life a little easier, but she doesn't have the room, not with me there. Maybe I should leave so she doesn't feel like she's letting Ethel down.'

Jeannie was horrified. 'No, Kate! I'm sure Auntie Betty wouldn't want you to move. Where would you go?'

Her friend shrugged.

'And I'm sure Gerald's ma will want to stay in her own house, if she can, so that there's somewhere for Gerald to come home to. Please don't do anything silly. I'm sure they wouldn't want you to sacrifice your home, even if it is for the kindest of reasons.'

Mr Briars appeared in front of them, making her jump. Jeannie hadn't even noticed him approach. 'You're not paid to gossip, ladies. Get to work.'

'Sorry, sir,' she said, putting her head down and getting on with it. Kate muttered her own apology and focused on her machine.

They carried on their conversation in the canteen at dinner time. Kate was working herself up into quite a lather.

'I can't wait until I'm thirty,' she announced.

'What?' Jeannie was astonished. 'You're barely twenty-one. How can you be wishing away so many years of your life?'

'I know, but now that parliament has granted the vote to women over thirty, the powers that be will have to start listening to women if they want their votes, won't they? If I was thirty, I could write to our MP and the minister in charge of prisons and even the Prime Minister to complain about Gerald's treatment and his ma's struggles they'd have to at least take my views into account. But any letters I send now will be ignored because I'm not old enough to vote, so they can ignore me with impunity. Just like women have been ignored since time immemorial.'

Jeannie frowned. 'How would he know your age?' she asked.

That gave Kate pause. 'I don't know. I expect he'll instruct his secretary to check before he decides whether to read it. He won't bother wasting time with someone who can't vote yet. But that's beside the point.' She glared at Jeannie and huffed again. 'Times are changing, Jeannie, you mark my words. With so many men dying in this damned war, us women will have a bigger part to play in society from now on. Why, one day, a woman might even run the whole country. Wouldn't that be a wonderful thing? We've more sense than those warmongering men. We'd have stopped this war years ago.'

Jeannie frowned. 'I don't know about that. I hope we would be able to stop it, but it's the men who are fighting, isn't they? Many of them would say they're doing it to protect their women and children. And our enemies are all governed by men. Would they even agree to negotiate with women?' She shook her head. 'I hate to say it, but I think they'd be even worse, intent on defeating us and putting us back in our place.'

'What? Suppressed and enslaved again?' Kate looked like she'd swallowed a lemon. 'Well, I won't put up with it, I can tell you. After what Pa put me through, I'll answer to no man, thank you very much.'

Jeannie regarded her thoughtfully. She had a feeling that there was one man who she'd answer to, but he was long gone and probably never to return from what he'd told Kate when he left. It was on the tip of her tongue to mention Ted, but the arrival of Tom at their table drove every other thought from her mind. She smiled at him as her cheeks warmed as usual. She knew they needed to be discreet, but she couldn't help glowing whenever their eyes met. She was sure everyone who saw them together would know that they were more than friends. Sometimes, she despaired that they could ever be able to declare themselves. It was all taking so long, but she was determined to present a cheerful face to him and the world.

But the moment she saw his expression, she sat up straight. 'What's wrong?' she asked before she even bothered to greet him.

He sat down next to her, giving Kate a brief nod before turning his attention to Jeannie. 'I've had some news,' he said. 'I can't believe it.'

She frowned, confused by his expression. He seemed to be in pain, but his eyes were burning with an emotion she couldn't quite recognise. It looked like relief.

He pulled a letter from his pocket. 'This arrived just as I was leaving for work this morning. I wanted to find you earlier, but I missed you before the shift started and for once, I didn't have any excuse to come to the Machine Room.' He put it down in front of her. She saw that it was postmarked Northampton and sat back a little, almost afraid to touch it.

'Is your ma all right? You said she was getting better.'

'She's fine,' he said. 'So's my pa. The letter's from her. It's about…' He glanced around and put a hand to his mouth to stop others lip reading if they were so inclined. 'It's about my wife.'

Jeannie felt the air in her lungs still. She stared at the letter. What on earth was it about?

'Read it, please,' he said, nudging it towards her. 'It's important.'

So many thoughts ran through her mind in just a moment. *Is his wife refusing to agree to a divorce? Has she asked his ma to write on her behalf to ask for a reconciliation? Would he consider it? Is he going to leave me and return to Northampton? How would I live without him?* His expression was so strange that she couldn't work out whether this letter contained good news for her and Tom, or bad.

'Come on, Jeannie,' said Kate. 'Don't keep us in suspense, love. What does it say?'

She looked at Tom as she reached out and picked it up. *Better to know than to sit here like a scared ninny*, she thought.

He nodded, as though he'd read her thoughts. 'Go on, love,' he said softly.

She began to read.

My Dearest Son,

I'm not sure how you'll take this news. I know you've been in hell since she ran off like that, but I'm writing to tell you that you're finally free of that strumpet. The lord has heard our prayers and decided you've suffered enough. I got the news this morning and knew I had to write to tell you straight away. She was in town shopping on her own. It seems she was distracted by something or someone and fell, right into the path of a tram.

Jeannie gasped and put a hand to her mouth. She glanced up

at Tom. He nodded again, his face sombre now. She took a deep breath and turned her gaze back to the letter.

She didn't stand a chance – it hit her and sent her flying through the air. She landed on her head on the cobbled street and was dead before anyone could reach her. There was nothing they could do.

'Oh my lord,' said Jeannie, her voice shaking. 'How awful,' she whispered.

'What it is?' asked Kate. 'Jeannie, are you all right?'

She looked at her friend, blinking. She was so shocked, she didn't know what to say or do. Kate turned to Tom.

'What have you done to her, Tom?' she demanded. 'What on earth is this about? She looks like she's about to faint.'

Tom ignored Kate and put an arm around Jeannie's shoulder and she leaned into him, for once not caring if anyone saw them.

'Is it true?' she asked, still unable to believe it.

'It is, love. She's dead.'

Kate gasped. 'Who's dead?'

Finally noticing her, Tom took the letter out of Jeannie's trembling hand and handed it to Kate. Jeannie was aware of Kate exclaiming quietly as she read it, but she only had eyes for Tom.

'You realise what this means?' he asked quietly. 'I'm free of her. I'm free to be with you.' He paused. 'If you'll have me, that is.'

Her eyes filled with tears.

'Don't cry, love,' he said, pulling a clean handkerchief out of his pocket. 'There now, don't be upset. If you don't want me, I'll understand. I know I've put you through enough these past months.'

She took it and wiped at her face. 'It's not that,' she said. 'Of course I want to be with you. It's just… I'm sorry someone had to die so that we can be together.' She took a deep breath, trying to calm down. How could she feel so relieved, so happy, when… 'What about her child? It'll grow up without its ma.'

Tom closed his eyes for a moment, his expression so sad. 'I didn't wish her dead,' he said softly, 'and I'm as sorry as you about the little one. But my mother-in-law will take care of the child, I'm sure. She's a good woman with a big heart. So's my aunt, who's the other grandma. And, God willing, my cousin will be back from France one of these days. They say the tide is turning in the war and we're close to winning. The child will be loved, I'm sure.' He smiled gently at her. 'You know, I should've expected such a reaction from you, Jeannie. You always care about others, don't you? That's why I love you.'

Kate touched her arm. 'That's why we all love you, Jeannie,' she agreed. 'But you mustn't fret.' She held up the letter. 'No one wished this fate on her but it sounds like it was quick and she didn't suffer. She probably didn't even realise she was in danger.' As she handed it back to Tom, she glanced around. 'But I have to say, you're both in danger of causing a scandal right here in the canteen if you don't get your hands off each other. There's plenty of gossips watching, not that it's any of their business. But maybe you should keep your hands to yourselves until you can be in private, eh?'

Jeannie looked up and noticed nearly every pair of eyes in the canteen were trained on her and Tom. With a sharp intake of breath, she sat up straight, putting a few inches between them. 'Oh my,' she said as her cheeks warmed. 'Whatever will people think?'

Tom chuckled. 'Who cares?' he asked. 'They'll know soon enough that you're my sweetheart. But I don't want to embarrass you, love.' He stood up and looked down at her, his heart in his gaze. 'Are you going to be all right? I'm sorry to give you such a shock, but I've been itching to find you and tell you since the moment I read Ma's letter. This changes everything, doesn't it?'

She gave him a shaky smile. 'It does.' It was still sinking in. Her whole body was trembling with suppressed emotions. She could feel pure joy growing within her, even while she felt so terribly sorry for a life cut short and a child left motherless.

'Can I walk you home after our shift?'

She nodded again. He smiled at her as though there wasn't another soul around and her joy expanded.

Kate stood as well as the hooter rang out. 'Right, we'd best get back to work.' She waved a hand in front of her face. 'Goodness! I think you'd better wed her soon, Tom, before you two burst into flames.' She laughed out loud as Tom blushed and Jeannie squeaked and covered her hot face with her hands. 'It's no good trying to hide now, Jeannie Musgrove. And there's no reason for you to either, is there?' She smiled at them. 'I'm happy for you both,' she said softly.

'Thank you,' said Tom, dipping his head in acknowledgement. 'Appreciate it. See you later, Jeannie.' He leaned towards her as though he was going to kiss her cheek, but a cough from Kate brought him up short and he looked around, his expression sheepish as Kate chuckled. 'I'll wait at the bottom of the stairs,' he told Jeannie before he departed.

Jeannie watched him go in a daze and let Kate lead her back to the Machine Room. Tom was free and he still wanted her. She might just get the Happy Ever After she'd dreamt of after all.

But it worried her that her happiness, her freedom to love Tom, was gained at the expense of his first wife's life.

13

The cherry and plum blossom in April gave way to apple blossom in May and the weather improved. Kitchen gardens began to thrive and folk hoped that the news from the front – of victories and gains by the Allies – would mean that peace would soon come. No one wanted their lads to have to face another winter in the trenches.

Louisa sat in the garden, enjoying the sunshine with her mother-in-law. 'It's so nice to have some warm weather, isn't it? The garden is coming to life again and the orchards are looking beautiful. I can't say I've taken much notice before, but now I'm not working all day at the factory, I feel lucky to see it.'

'We are lucky, lass, living in this fine county. I can't imagine being anywhere else. How your ma is coping in Exeter, I'll never know. I've only been there once, and it was far too busy for me.'

Louisa smiled. 'I think it suits her, having her lodgers to look after and being in charge of her own destiny. It's not like Street. I get the impression she felt a bit constrained here, what with Pa being a foreman. She always acted as though she were on show, and I think she found it difficult, worrying about what people would think.' She sighed, missing the mother she'd had when she was little. Her ma had become difficult as Louisa had grown up and proven to have a mind of her own, and then turned into a monster when Louisa had fallen pregnant with Mattie's child out of wedlock. But of course, her mother-in-law had no idea about all of that and Louisa hoped she never would.

Strangely, her own ma had softened a little since Louisa's marriage, even though she'd been dead set against it at first. Perhaps it was easier for her to reconcile the fact that her daughter had married a Quaker now that Mrs Clements lived in Exeter, away from the tensions about that she'd felt when she had lived in Street. They had managed to maintain a civil correspondence, especially since she had told her ma that she was expecting. It seemed that she was content to become a grandmother now that her daughter was safely married – something that in turns angered and saddened Louisa. In their letters, Louisa had learned about the property her ma had bought next door to her sister and how the two women worked together, running them as boarding houses. The tenants were respectable gentlemen who paid their rent on time and appreciated their landladies' housekeeping skills. Louisa was glad that her ma seemed to be thriving as an independent woman. She only wished her pa could have lived longer, but there was nothing anyone could do about that, and it occurred to her that she wouldn't be married with a child due any time now if Pa had survived his heart attack because she probably wouldn't have ended up rushing to marry Lucas to avoid being dragged off to live in Exeter. So perhaps everything happened for a reason.

The baby shifted inside her and Louisa groaned. 'Oh my word, this little one is a right fidget today.' She rubbed the side of her belly, feeling a knee or a foot poking at her. 'But the trouble is, there's not a lot of room left in there, so every time the child moves, it hurts. I hope baby comes soon, or I'm sure I'll burst.'

Mrs Musgrove smiled. 'Aw, I don't suppose it will be long now, lass. It looked to me when I saw you this morning that the babe has dropped a little. Of course, it might still be a week or two.' She paused. 'Are you worried about it? The labour, I mean.'

Louisa took a deep breath. 'A bit,' she confessed. Not because she didn't know what to expect, but rather the thought of the pain of childbirth, which was wrapped up in the awful memories of having to give her first-born child away so soon after experiencing all that agony bringing him into the world. 'But I was with Peg in Lincolnshire when little Matthew was born, so I know what it will be like.'

Mrs Musgrove gave her a sympathetic look, no doubt thinking she'd been a witness to the birth rather than the one producing the child. Louisa could imagine that the older woman thought she was scared by what she'd seen rather than what she'd gone through. She patted her hand.

'Well, don't you fret, love. I'll be here, and I've had four of my own. I reckon I know what's what when it comes to birthing a child. I promise I'll see you right. It's a shame your own ma can't be here, but I'll try to make it up to you, lass.'

Louisa felt herself well up. She'd been tearful a lot through this pregnancy – sometimes with happy tears, but other times with grief and loss – of her first child and both of her parents. 'Thank you,' she said, guilt choking her. 'I'm glad you'll be there. I think my ma would be here if she could, but it's difficult for her to get away with her boarding house being full.' She didn't mention that she wasn't sure if she would have wanted her ma there when she gave birth this time. The hurt from last time was still there, deep inside her.

In the silence that followed, they heard the clock on the tower at the factory chime the hour.

'Goodness, time's getting on,' said her mother-in-law as she stood, slow and stiff. 'I'd better get on with that mutton pie I promised everyone for supper. They'll all be hungry when their shifts end.'

'I'll help,' Louisa called after her. 'Shall I make the pastry? I can't sit around doing nothing. I'd rather keep busy.'

As she stood, she felt a sudden gush of liquid between her legs. She gasped, looking down to see a puddle form on the ground while at the same time her womb clenched.

Mrs Musgrove looked around at the noise she made. 'What it is?'

'My waters,' said Louisa. She looked up, at once excited and afraid. 'I think it's time.'

* * *

At the end of her shift, Jeannie walked the length of the high street on Tom's arm, all the time chatting. She loved this part of the day, spending time with him without having to worry what people thought. He was a single man again (not that anyone else in Street had known about his first wife) and free to court her, and now everyone knew that Jeannie was his sweetheart. As they walked, they talked about their days and about the latest project Tom and Lucas were working on – a false hand and forearm to replace one lost by a local man in the trenches.

'I've got the arm shaped to fit his stump,' he said. 'The straps are attached so he can wear it comfortably. Now me, Peter and Lucas are looking at how we can add on attachments.'

'What do you mean?' she asked. She couldn't imagine.

'Well, there's a shaped hand that he can wear with a glove so it isn't obvious that it's not a real one,' he told her. 'But we've made it detachable, using a screw device that can hold a number of difference attachments so that then he can also have a hook, and one that can grasp things, plus something to skewer or cut if that will be useful to him. We're trying to think of all the things he might need to do and provide him with the tools to do it that he can just attach to this false arm.'

Jeannie felt her chest swell with pride. 'You're so clever, Tom. And so thoughtful, helping people like this.'

He looked pleased, but he shrugged. 'I've been blessed with a good brain and if I can make life easier for an injured soldier, then I'll do what I can.'

Jeannie smiled up at him and squeezed his arm. 'I'm so proud of you,' she said. She really was. He was making life better for people, and she felt a little bad because she was beginning to fret about whether, if Tom was to meet the demand for his special prosthetics and splints out of his own pocket, could he afford a wife and family as well? Not that she could say this to him. They'd only just heard about his wife's death and at least now everyone could know they were together. She was being selfish, wanting more when he was working so hard for everybody's sakes, and more than a little ridiculous considering she was still a young woman with plenty of time to have a family. But, although they were sweethearts now, which was lovely, Jeannie wanted more. She wanted marriage and babies and a home of her own and she didn't want to wait.

A groan came from behind them. She turned her head to see Lucas and Peter approaching.

'They're canoodling again,' complained Peter, his cheeks red. 'In the middle of the street.'

'Mind your business,' Jeannie scolded him. 'We're not doing anything wrong.'

'It's not just you,' he said. 'Lucas and Louisa are always smiling and touching.'

Lucas laughed and messed Peter's hair. 'You're just jealous. Me and Tom have found our women. It's about time you got yourself a sweetheart, then you wouldn't be worrying about us.'

Peter opened his mouth to reply, but a shout caught their attention. The four of them looked around to see John running towards them.

'Lucas! You've got to come, quick!'

'What's the panic?' he asked, frowning.

'I just got home and Ma sent me to come and get you. Lou was screaming blue murder. Ma says the baby's coming.'

Jeannie gasped as Lucas went deathly pale.

'Really?' he asked. 'Right now? You're not playing a joke on me, are you?'

John shook his head, breathing heavily. 'I wouldn't. I swear. I thought someone was killing her, but Ma said to get you and not waste any time.'

Before he'd even finished, Lucas was running towards the house, the twins following behind as swiftly as they could.

Jeannie turned to Tom. 'I need to go.'

He nodded. 'Of course. I'll leave you to it.' He kissed her cheek. 'Hope it goes well.'

'Me too,' she said, biting her lip. She'd heard about the pain of labour, but she'd never thought about it for herself and her friends, even though she knew Lou had been through it before. 'See you tomorrow.'

She took off, running after her brothers. She was going to be an auntie!

* * *

Ruby Mary Musgrove came into the world kicking and screaming at just after ten o'clock that evening. The twins had had to make do with bread and cheese for their supper while Jeannie and her mother attended to Louisa and Lucas paced the floor of the parlour, his gaze on the ceiling, as though he could take away his wife's pain and deliver their child safely through his sheer will.

When he heard the babe's cries, he wasn't ashamed to cry. When Jeannie came down the stairs, looking tired and a little shocked, he grabbed her shoulders.

'Is Louisa all right?' he demanded.

She nodded and smiled as she wiped his cheeks. 'She is, and so's your daughter. I've just come down to get some more warm water so Ma can wash them both.'

He stilled for a moment. 'A daughter?'

Her smile got wider. 'She's perfect, Lucas. So beautiful. Lou did so well.'

He looked up the stairs. 'Can I go up?'

'Well, Ma said you should wait until they're cleaned up. But if you want to carry the water up...'

He didn't need telling twice. There had been a couple of kettles warming on the range for the last couple of hours. He grabbed them both and took the stairs two at a time.

* * *

Lucas paused for a moment outside the bedroom door, taking a deep breath. He was about to meet his and Louisa's daughter. His life was never going to be the same. In the middle of the maelstrom of relief and joy in his heart, Lucas felt the familiar guilt that he was here, husband to Louisa and father in a family that should by rights have been Mattie's. He raised his eyes to heaven and sent up a prayer that Mattie would bless them and help him be a good husband and father. He'd never have been in this position if Mattie were still here. But Mattie was never coming home, and he renewed his vow to his dead friend that he would do everything in his power to make Louisa happy.

A feeling of warmth stole over him as he stood there and in his mind's eye, he saw Mattie smiling at him. It would be all right.

He tapped on the door with his elbow. 'Ma? I've brought the kettles.'

His ma opened the door, giving him a beaming smile. 'I thought you'd be up here. Your pa was the same. Couldn't wait.' She stepped back. 'Come and meet your daughter, son.'

He entered, his gaze going straight to Louisa on the bed. She looked tired but happy. 'All right, love?' he asked gently as he put the kettles on the dresser for his ma to deal with.

She nodded. 'She's perfect, Lucas,' she said as she lifted the tiny, wrapped bundle in her arms towards him.

He sat on the edge of the bed and looked upon his child for the first time. She was small and fragile-looking, her skin pink and her face a little scrunched up. She didn't have much hair, but it looked from the little tufts there were that she was going to be a blonde like her mother. He reached out and touched the baby's cheek. He was amazed by how soft it felt. At his touch, she opened her eyes and gazed at him, frowning slightly as though trying to focus on this strange person regarding her. A wave of love swept over him as he met her gaze.

'Hello, little miss. I'm your pa,' he whispered. When he could bear to look away, he shifted his gaze to Louisa. 'Thank you,' he said and kissed her forehead.

Louisa smiled through her exhaustion. 'Thank *you*, Lucas,' she replied.

He'd forgotten that Ma was still in the room until she spoke.

'Lucas, love, can you hold the baby while I help Louisa clean up? We had enough water for the little one, but your dear wife will be glad of a wash, I'm sure. Sit in the rocking chair, son and I'll pass her to you.'

He'd moved the old rocker into the bedroom a week ago at Ma's suggestion. With the bed, the crib and a dresser, there wasn't much room for anything else. Lucas took the swaddled child carefully in his arms. Ma showed him how to support her head and kissed his forehead before turning back to Louisa. The child began to fret a little so he held her closer and began to rock gently. He whispered soothing words, telling her about her grandma and her aunt and uncles who were going to love her so much, and she began to settle. He stroked her cheek and the child moved her head, finding his finger and locking onto it, sucking hard.

'She'll be hungry,' said Ma, smiling at him. 'Come on Louisa, love. Let's get you cleaned up and the sheets changed, then we can see if she'll take the breast.'

Lucas felt his cheeks warm at his mother's words. It was daft. He'd touched and kissed his wife's breasts. But the thought of Louisa feeding his child with them seemed unreal. As was the thought that his own ma had done this with him and all her babies.

'Now, my dear,' Ma continued, touching Louisa's cheek. 'I know Lucas is your husband, but if you'd rather he wasn't in the room while we do this, I can chase him out. All you have to do is say. Most husbands wait outside until all this has been dealt with.' She sent him a meaningful look. 'But he was obviously so impatient to see you and meet the babe. You mustn't worry if you want him gone for a bit longer.'

Lucas glared at his ma, but then realised that Louisa might be embarrassed for him to witness such personal ministrations so soon after giving birth. He looked at her, shame-faced. 'Sorry, love. Do you want me to go?'

She shook her head. 'No, it's all right. You stay there and talk to our daughter. Just don't look.' She gave him a rueful look as she pulled at the sheet that covered her. 'I think I'm a bit of a mess.'

He smiled. 'You're beautiful,' he said, causing her cheeks to redden. To save his wife further embarrassment, he turned his attention to his daughter. 'And you're beautiful, too, aren't you? Your ma is so clever, birthing you. I swear you're going to be as smart and pretty as she is and I'm going to have to chase all the lads off.'

Louisa giggled. 'We won't have to worry about lads coming calling for a while,' she said.

'You need to give the babe a name first,' said Ma, laughing along with Louisa as she kept busy, washing her quickly and helping Louisa into a fresh nightgown. 'Have you decided?'

Lucas looked up. 'You tell her what we decided, Lou.'

Louisa gave her mother-in-law a shy smile. 'She's Ruby Mary, after her Nanna Musgrove and her Nanna Clements.'

Mrs Musgrove put a hand over her heart and blinked back tears. 'Oh my. Are you sure?'

They both nodded. 'Of course we are, Ma,' said Lucas.

She didn't say anything as she helped Louisa back into the clean bed. 'Come now, bring little Ruby over here. It's time for her first feed.'

Lucas brought her to his wife and looked away as the women did what they needed to do. When he glanced back, Ruby was suckling greedily at Louisa's breast, her tiny hand clutching at it as though to make sure her mother didn't take away her sustenance.

Ma sighed happily as she draped a piece of clean muslin over Lou's exposed skin, covering the baby's head as well. Ruby didn't seem to notice, so intent was she on feeding.

'Ah, Louisa, love, you're a natural. She's doing so well; she'll be growing like topsy before you know it.' She patted her shoulder. 'You've been lucky. I know it was painful, but that was a short labour for a first baby, and now she's feeding so well.' She tipped her head at her son. 'This one took two full days to come out and then it took me a while to get the hang of it while he wanted feeding almost constantly. No wonder he's such a big man now.'

'The twins are taller than me,' grumbled Lucas, his cheeks warming.

'I know,' said Ma. 'They were worse than you, even though they were so tiny when they were born. Only my Jeannie was an easy baby. She was so content, bless her. Let's hope young Ruby is the same as her auntie, eh?' She smiled and touched the baby's head. 'I'll leave you alone for a bit to get to know your daughter. No doubt Jeannie will want to come up and say a proper hello to her niece, but I'll keep her away as long as I can, then I'll send her up with a nice cup of sweet tea for you Louisa, and maybe a sandwich. You need to keep up your strength.'

'Thanks, Ma,' said Lucas.

'My pleasure, son.' She smiled, although she was beginning to look tired. She gathered up the dirty washing and the empty bowls and left the room. Lucas heard her calling down for the others to come and get it all so she didn't have to carry it down the stairs.

The two of them were silent, watching Ruby feed. Louisa had moved the muslin away when they were alone, wanting to see the baby.

'I can't believe she's here,' she said softly. She sighed. 'Your ma was so kind; I'm glad she was here. But I was terrified she'd realise this wasn't my first time. I don't think I could bear it if she found out and thought badly of me.'

Lucas stroked her hair. 'She didn't realise, I'm sure. But even if she did, you don't need to worry because she wouldn't judge you harshly. She thinks the world of you.'

'And I love her,' said Louisa, her eyes filling with tears. 'She's been kinder to me than my own ma. She's a saint, your ma. A true saint.'

14

Kate placed the posy of summer flowers in the stone jar next to her ma's grave. 'There you go, Ma. Some sweet-smelling blooms for you to enjoy. It's July the twentieth. Happy birthday,' she said softly. She'd wiped down the gravestone and tidied up around the grave, wishing that Ma was still here to really appreciate the flowers and enjoy her special day. These were her favourite flowers. They'd grown some together in the garden at Silver Road, but they were all gone now. The cottages that had burnt down had been demolished and replaced with new dwellings, not that any member of the Davis family would have been allowed to go back there. Her pa had seen to it with his awful behaviour that no one would have wanted them for neighbours again.

'Fred's coming home this week, Ma,' she continued, sitting on the grass by the grave. 'They said his lungs are damaged, so he can't fight any more. But Vi's hopeful that he'll be all right. Clarks have said his old job is waiting when he's ready to go back to work.' She sighed. 'We just need George home as well, but that won't happen until this war is over.' *And then only if we win,* she thought. She didn't want to think about what would happen to him if the Allies were defeated. 'They say it shouldn't be much longer now. Our lads are pushing their lines back every day, if the papers are to be believed, so God willing, it'll be over soon. I'm going into the church in a minute to light a candle for you and both of them.'

In the silence that followed, she closed her eyes and tipped her head back, enjoying the July sunshine. It had been a strange few months, with Lou having little Ruby back in May, and Jeannie officially courting Tom now. Both of her friends were happy and she was pleased for them, really she was. But their contentment made her feel her own loneliness all the more.

As was usual when she felt like this, an image of Ted's laughing eyes came to mind and the ache in her heart increased. Since the brief report she'd had of him from his father about a year ago, she'd heard nothing more. She didn't know if he was alive or dead and it hurt to feel so cut off from him. He'd been her rock when Ma had died. She didn't think she'd have survived it without him. His going away so abruptly had left a gaping wound inside her that still hadn't healed.

The churchyard gate opened with a squeak and Kate opened her eyes to see Peter Musgrove enter and walk towards her. He gave her a shy smile and sat beside her on the grass.

'Afternoon, Kate,' he said. 'Jeannie mentioned it was your ma's birthday, so I thought you might be here.'

She nodded, wondering why he would bother. 'Thank you, yes, it is. I wanted to bring some of her favourite flowers.'

He nodded, studying the gravestone. 'My pa's stone is smaller than this, with just his name and the dates he was born and died.'

'I know,' she said. 'The stones in the Friends' graveyard at the

Meeting House are all the same, aren't they? Even the grandest families have simple stones like that.'

'That's right. In heaven, we're all equal before God. There's no money, no status. We're all God's children.'

She smiled. 'That's good to know. I just hope I make it to heaven and don't end up in hell with the Floozy. I'm pretty sure Pa's heading in that direction when he goes.'

He frowned. 'You won't be with them. You're nothing like those monsters.'

'Thank you, Peter.' She bowed her head. 'That's very kind of you to say so. But no one's perfect. I thought so ill of them and those children, and I'm still glad she's gone, that I'm sure God will think I'm as wicked as they were for thinking like that.'

He shook his head. 'After the way they treated you, anyone would think the same. That doesn't make you wicked; it makes you human.'

She sighed. 'But maybe I should be trying to forgive them?'

'I don't see why you need to. It's God that needs to do that. He's our only judge. All we can do is try to follow the right path in our lifetime.'

She tilted her head to one side and regarded him thoughtfully.

'What?' he asked, noticing her scrutiny. His cheeks turned pink and he looked away.

'Nothing,' she said. 'I'm just impressed by your wisdom. You don't normally talk like this when John's around, do you?'

He shrugged, not looking at her. 'He doesn't take anything serious, except playing football and wanting to drive the biggest lorries.'

'So I heard. Ada says he's doing well, but he's too young to be given the responsibility for more than a small van right now. He's got to learn to walk before he can run.'

'That's what everyone tells him, but he's too cocky by far.'

She chuckled. 'There wasn't much difference between the two of you not so long ago. I thought you two were joined at the hip and shared the same brain.'

He grimaced. 'It's hard when you're a twin,' he said. 'Everyone expects us to be identical in every way. But it's not turning out like that, not since I started my apprenticeship. I realised before he did that we wanted different things.'

That was Tom's influence. He'd encouraged Peter and put in a good word for him at Clarks. He'd also engaged both Peter and Lucas to help him with his prosthetics projects, something that both of the brothers enjoyed. John hadn't been interested in any of it.

Before she could say anything, Peter let out a huge yawn. He covered his mouth, his pink cheeks getting even warmer. 'Sorry,' he mumbled behind his hand. 'Ruby wakes us up a lot.'

Kate frowned. 'I thought Lou said she's settling and sleeping better.'

'She is. It used to be every couple of hours. Now she goes for about four hours before she starts screaming again. I barely get any decent sleep these days, but you should see Lucas. He's got permanent bags under his eyes. He's starting to look like an old man.'

She laughed. 'I suppose at least Lou gets the chance for a nap in the day when the babe is asleep. I hadn't thought about how hard it is for new fathers, having to get up and go to work after a broken night.'

'*And* new uncles,' he pointed out.

That made her laugh again. 'You'll live. Just wait until you've got your own babies.'

'That's a long way off. I've got to finish my apprenticeship.'

'But there's no reason why you couldn't have a sweetheart in the meantime, is there? A lad like you must have plenty of lasses chasing after him.'

He huffed out a breath. 'Most of 'em are just plain daft – giggling and preening. I want a woman I can talk to, who won't complain when I'm working or studying hard to better myself.' He paused, finally looking her in the eye again. 'Someone like you, Kate.'

Her heart sank. She liked Peter well enough; he was growing up into a very nice young man. But he wasn't for her.

'Peter,' she began gently. 'I'm three years older than you.'

'I don't care about that,' he said. 'So you're Jeannie's age. So what? It's not like you're Ma's age, is it? And the older we get, the smaller the gap is between us.'

She chuckled and shook her head. 'No, I suppose so, but...'

'I've got good prospects,' he went on before she could think of what to say. 'Once I've finished my apprenticeship, I'll be on damned good money – plenty to support a wife and children. And I've proved I can protect you, haven't I? I floored your pa and saved you from him before anyone else even thought to stop him, didn't I?'

'You did, Peter, and I'll always be grateful to you for that. But... I'm sorry, but I've no plans to wed, so I don't intend to waste your time by letting you think there's a chance. You've heard me say this before, I'm sure. After everything I went through with my pa, I'll never let another man have any power over me. I'm in charge of my own destiny now, and that's how I like it and how I intend for things to stay.'

'I wouldn't treat you ill like he did,' he said, his gaze and tone both earnest.

'Of course you wouldn't,' she said immediately. 'I know you're not like that. You're a good lad. But, well, how would your pals react if they thought you had no control over your own woman? Because I'm set on my path, Peter. I'm going to be learning shorthand and typing and book-keeping in evening classes come September. Then I'll find myself an office job, have a proper career. I'll earn my own money and make my own decisions.'

'But... what about when you have babies like Louisa? You won't be able to work then.'

She sighed and ran a hand down her face. 'I don't see me being a mother.'

'Don't you want children?'

Of course she did; she loved little ones. She doted on her niece and nephews and was already a regular visitor at the Musgrove house to have cuddles with little Ruby. But that would mean she had to give up her freedom to a man and, after what she'd been through with Pa, and then with being left by Ted, she couldn't bring herself to trust another man ever again.

She raised her chin and gave Peter a cool look. 'I don't need to be a mother. I'll enjoy my niece and nephews and my friends' children in years to come. But I won't be tied down.'

'But you could change your mind. I wouldn't tie you down, Kate. I respect you.'

Kate closed her eyes. She didn't want to hurt him, but she had to make him see that he didn't have a chance with her. As far as she was concerned, he was Jeannie's little brother (all right, not so little, but still far too young for her).

'Truth be told,' she said, resigned to admitting her humiliation, 'I might have thought about marriage a while back. I was ready to give my heart to someone, but he didn't want it and he let me down something cruel. I don't want to hurt you, Peter, but he's the only one I ever considered marrying.'

'I'd never let you down, Kate.'

'I know you wouldn't want to. But it's not right, don't you see? I thought the world of Ted, but he didn't feel the same as me and he let me down and broke my heart. I like you, Peter, but as a friend, not as a sweetheart or a husband. It would never be enough for you, and you should never just settle for less than full commitment from the woman you give your heart to. I'm not the one for you. But there'll be a lass out there who will love you to bits and once you find her, you'll be a happy man.'

'I really like you, Kate.'

She smiled and touched his arm. 'I like you, too. I want to be your friend. I just can't be your sweetheart.'

His shoulders slumped as he finally accepted the truth of it. He sighed and looked away from her. He was silent for a moment, staring out across the graveyard. She waited, not wanting to make things worse. Eventually, he glanced back at her.

'Are you really going to evening classes?'

She nodded, relieved that he had changed the subject. 'I am. With Louisa gone and Jeannie dreaming about getting wed, I don't want to stay in the Machine Room on my own, thank you very much. I reckon learning office skills will help me get a good job, with better pay.' She grinned. 'It will be quieter in an office as well, and I won't smell of machine oil all the time.'

'I quite like that smell,' he mused. 'Which is probably just as well, given that I'm going to be an engineer.'

'It is.' She smiled. 'Nothing wrong with a manly engineer smelling of machine oil. It's not such a nice scent on a lass, though.'

He nodded, a half-smile on his lips. 'I wouldn't mind.' He took a deep breath and ran a hand through his hair. 'But if an office job – a career – is what you want, Kate, then I wish you well. I know what it's like to have a dream. I just hope you'll still be my friend when you're a fancy office lady.'

'Oh, go on with you.' She poked him in the ribs as she laughed. 'Me, fancy? Can you imagine? No, I expect I'll be the frumpy little spinster in the back office that everyone's scared of. But I reckon that will suit me, so that's what I'm aiming for.' She nudged his shoulder with her own. 'I'll be seeing you in your boilersuit, rushing across the yard to the next emergency with your toolkit after some lad or lass have messed up their machines. You'll be the saviour of the Machine Room, like Tom is now. All the lasses will be making a play for you, especially now Tom's spoken for with Jeannie.'

He chuckled, his cheeks red again, before he sobered a little. 'If you ever change your mind, Kate, will you let me know?'

'I won't change my mind, Peter. I'm sorry.'

She watched him get up and walk away, realising that she'd spoken the truth. She wouldn't marry, not just because she was wary of giving any man power over her, but also because her heart still belonged to Ted, who didn't want it.

She walked home with a heavy heart. Much as she denied it to everyone else, she had never really got over the way Ted had left, cutting himself off from her and their friends so completely. It had hurt so much. They had shared everything, been the best of friends as well as sweethearts, right up until the moment he'd turned away from her. Even all this time later, there was so much she wanted to say to him, to share with him. She would often find herself thinking, *Oh, I must tell Ted about that!* before she remembered that she couldn't do that any more.

By the time she got home, Kate felt an overwhelming urge to reconnect with him in some way. So she took out her writing paper and started to write to Ted, telling him everything that was in her heart. By the time she finished, she felt exhausted, but lighter in spirit. Ted might never see this letter, she realised, but at least she had been able to release everything that had been building up inside her. She folded the papers and slid them into an envelope. She couldn't send it; she had no idea where he was. Instead, she simply wrote his name on it, sealed it, and put it into her bag, where it would stay as a reminder to her that she had only herself to rely upon.

15

The late summer campaigns seemed to be a turning point in the war. The Allies were pushing the Hun back towards Germany. It was slow going, but everyone was optimistic that things were finally going the right way. There was a feeling of hopefulness in the air that Jeannie hadn't felt for a long time. She hardly dared to hope that it would all be over soon and that the twins wouldn't get called up when they turned eighteen in January. No one in the Musgrove household talked about it in front of Ma, because mention of the war continuing that long drove her to despair.

The family and friends celebrated Louisa's twenty-first birthday in the first week of September. Ruby was coming up to four months old now and had learned that if she smiled at someone, they smiled back at her. She was a joy to everyone; even the twins were taken with her, pulling faces to make her laugh, although she became cranky a week after Louisa's birthday, grizzling and drooling. Nothing would comfort her except when she was chewing on someone's fingers.

'She's teething,' said Mrs Musgrove as the baby gnawed on

her finger as the family gathered round the kitchen table for dinner on Saturday. 'Look, you can feel her first teeth at the front, just under her skin. Poor little love.' She kissed the baby's rosy cheek. 'And poor Ma and Pa. She'll be waking you up at all hours again while she's cutting them. We'll have to get some soothing balm for her gums; that might help.'

Louisa yawned. 'Let's hope it helps. She hardly settled at all last night and she's not much happier now.'

'And what about the poor uncles?' grumbled John, rubbing his eyes. 'We've got a match this afternoon. We haven't had a decent night's sleep all week. We need our rest if we're going to be fit for the game.'

Jeannie rolled her eyes. 'Oh stop whining,' she said. 'The poor love's in pain and all you can think about is a stupid game.'

He looked outraged. 'It's not *just* a game. This is an important match. We need to win.'

'Why?' she asked. 'Will it earn you some money? Or get you a promotion at work?' She gave him a sideways glance. 'Or is it that you're trying to impress that lass Tom told me was cheering you on from the touchline last Saturday?'

John puffed out his chest. 'I can't help it if lasses like to watch me play.' He grinned. 'But it spurs a man on when a pretty one is paying attention.'

Peter rolled his eyes. 'She might be pretty, but she hasn't got a brain. You'll soon get bored with that one.'

John's grin widened. 'I'm not looking for conversation.'

'Just as well,' said Lucas. 'The words that come out of your mouth are daft enough to put off any sensible lass.'

John sneered as even his ma joined in the laughter. 'Well, I'll not be tying myself down with a wife and baby for a long time yet. I'm going to have some fun before I have to put up with all this. So, while you and your missus try and settle Ruby down, I'm going to have a nice *quiet* lie down for half an hour before I have to get ready for the match.' He got up, leaving his dishes on the table, and clumped up the stairs to his room.

Tutting, Jeannie stood, gathered up John's dishes with her own and took them to the sink. The others helped and the table was soon cleared and the dishes washed. Jeannie left them to dry on the draining board and went into the parlour. Ma had also gone up for a nap and Peter was sorting out his football kit. Louisa and Lucas sat on the sofa with a fractious Ruby.

'Here, give her here,' she said, holding out her arms. 'You two look exhausted. Get yourselves upstairs for a nap while I have cuddles with her.' She took the child from Louisa, who gave her a grateful smile.

'Are you sure?' she asked. 'We can always take her up with us.'

Jeannie shook her head. 'No, you go and rest. Me and Ruby will be just fine, won't we sweetheart?' She nuzzled the baby's red cheek. 'Auntie Jeannie doesn't mind if you want to grizzle a bit. I'd grizzle n'all if I had horrible teeth cutting through my gums.'

'Come on, love,' said Lucas, standing and holding out a hand to his wife. 'She'll be fine with Jeannie.'

As they went upstairs, Jeannie smiled and sat down on the sofa, enjoying the warmth of the baby in her arms. She treasured the times she could spend with her niece on her own. Before she was born, Jeannie had been in two minds about how she would feel about the baby, because at the time, she had been stuck in that awful situation where Tom had been tied to his unfaithful wife. But then, just before Ruby was born, fate had intervened and he was now free. God willing, Jeannie hoped she could now look forward to a life with Tom, and maybe some babies of her own one day, so she welcomed the chance to practice her mothering skills on her niece.

She rocked Ruby, singing softly to her until she eventually fell into an exhausted sleep in her arms. Jeannie relaxed and closed her eyes, and began to doze.

* * *

Tom raised his hand to knock on the Musgrove family's front door, but before he made contact, it opened and the twins came out.

'Hey, Tom, are you coming to the match with us?' asked John.

He shook his head. 'Not today. I need to see Jeannie. Is she in?'

Peter nodded his head towards the interior of the cottage. 'She's snoring on the settee with the baby.'

John snorted. 'They're all snoring. Ruby's been keeping us all up. We'll be lucky to get through the match without dozing off.'

Tom laughed. 'You'll be all right. The fresh air will keep you awake. Good luck.'

They rushed off and Tom entered the house. As he expected, it was silent. He found her in the parlour, the baby sprawled on her chest, both of them asleep. He stood watching them for a moment, his heart swelling with love for Jeannie.

One day, it could be *his* child sleeping on her like that. He'd never thought much about having a family before, even when he'd first married. His sisters had so many children between them and were always so tired and busy, that he'd regarded parenthood as a hard and thankless job. Yet the thought of Jeannie bearing his child filled him with warmth and hope. She would be a wonderful mother.

Careful not to wake her or the baby, he sat down next to her, gently putting an arm around her shoulders. She sighed but didn't wake. Instead, she turned her head to rest it against his shoulder as though it was the most natural thing in the world. He smiled and kissed her hair and settled down to wait for her to wake up.

* * *

Jeannie became aware of the heat surrounding her as she awoke. Little Ruby was still slumbering on her chest, but she also felt warmth against her cheek and her left side and something was stroking her right shoulder. She took a deep breath before she opened her eyes, inhaling the scent of Tom's tweed jacket, so that by the time she looked at him, she was smiling.

'This is a nice surprise,' she said softly, mindful of the sleeping child.

He kissed her temple. 'It's good to know you don't snore,' he said, keeping his voice low. 'The twins said you did.'

She huffed. 'Those boys, honestly. They'll say anything to embarrass me.'

He chuckled. 'But you do make these sweet little snuffling noises as you wake up,' he said.

'I do not,' she protested in a fierce whisper, then she giggled when she saw his amusement.

The baby shifted in her arms and sighed, but carried on sleeping.

'She's exhausted, the poor love,' said Jeannie, stroking her back. 'Ma says she's cutting her first teeth, so we've got months of this to look forward to. I sent Lou and Lucas up for a nap; they looked that worn out, I thought they were going to fall asleep in their food at dinner time.'

'You're a good sister,' he said, kissing her cheek. 'And you'll be a natural mother one day.'

Jeannie blushed. 'Thank you.' She didn't know what else to say. She would have liked to have said something brave like *and will you be a good father to my babies?* But she didn't have the nerve. Despite having declared their love for each other and being sweethearts for months now, he'd made no definite declaration about their future, even though he sometimes hinted at it. She couldn't help wondering whether, with his wife now gone, he might one day decide to return to his family in Northampton. After all, he still hadn't proposed. Maybe he'd decided against it?

'Now what's caused that shadow to pass across your face?' he asked, lifting her chin with his finger so that he could gaze into her eyes.

Jeannie blinked, wanting to look away. 'Nothing. It's just...'

'You know you can tell me anything that's on your mind, don't you?' he said when she hesitated.

She sighed and nodded. 'I just don't want you to think I'm too forward.'

He smiled. 'Not you, Jeannie. Now, come on. Out with it. What's on your mind?'

She shrugged. 'All right. I'm thinking that you might go back to Northampton one day, and then what would happen to me? To us? Because I can't leave Ma; you know that, don't you?'

He gave her a light kiss. 'I'm not going back there, Jeannie. Why would I when you're here? In fact, that's why I came round today. I've got something to tell you.'

Her smile was radiant with relief that he hadn't taken offence and thought she was pushing for a declaration. She really wasn't, *although one would be nice*, she thought. 'Oh, good. So what is it?'

The baby shifted again, and they both froze until she settled.

'You know I was working extra hours and saving hard to pay for a divorce?' he whispered.

She nodded. 'Yes.'

'Well, even though I've been paying for materials for my projects, I've managed to put by a nice little nest egg that I don't have to use to buy my freedom now. And, on top of that, when I went to Northampton to see my ma when she was ill, she passed on a gift that my grandfather had wanted me to have as the only grandson in her family. It was fifty pounds.'

Jeannie's eyes widened. 'Oh my, that's a lot of money.' It was more than a year's wages for a girl like her.

He nodded. 'Grandpa owned a busy ironmongers and sold it at the start of the war. He made a pretty penny from it and has a good income from the proceeds. When I was injured, he told Ma he wanted to give me some money, but decided it was better to wait and see what happened in case my missus decided she wanted to try and get her hands on it. It's only now that he felt able to pass it on.'

Not for the first time, Jeannie felt a pang about Tom's late wife. She never wished anyone dead, so she felt guilty that she was so relieved that the woman was no longer alive to make life difficult for Tom.

'And on top of that, I've got a sponsor for my projects.'

He explained that he had been approached on behalf of an anonymous benefactor who had heard about his work for injured soldiers. 'Now, when I'm asked to help someone, funds are available to help me get the materials I need. I still won't get paid for this work, nor do I want to. It's my way of giving thanks for having survived, you know?'

She nodded, her heart swelling with pride and love for him. He was such a good man, satisfied to be able to help folk.

'I'm sure it's someone in the Clark family,' said Jeannie. 'It would be just like them to want to help but not take any credit for it. You hear rumours about how they help folk in need, but no one ever officially confirms it. But I know for a fact they helped Ma after Pa died in the accident. We could've ended up in the poor house, but they made sure we didn't. That's why I'm happy to work at Clarks. They're good people and they care about their workers.'

He nodded. 'I don't know for sure, of course. But I think you might be right. Whoever it is, I'm grateful for them. Now I can make these prosthetics and splints without worrying about finding the money for the materials. Which means that with that money from Grandad and my savings, I've a good stake, so I've just been round to look at a house in Cranhill Road. It's three bedrooms, a good, solid house, with a decent garden and a brick shed out back that I can use to work on my projects. It's been hard, trying to build prosthetics and splints without a proper workshop.' He only had one room at his lodgings in Wilfred Street, so he had to rely on friends like the Musgroves letting him use their sheds when he needed to.

'That's wonderful, Tom. So you'll be renting it?'

He shook his head. 'Not renting, Jeannie. I'm going to buy it. I'm set to spend the rest of my days here in Street, and I know you've had trouble believing that. Do you reckon you'll accept it now I'm investing in a property?'

She searched his expression, hardly daring to believe it. 'You're really staying? For good?'

He smiled and nodded. 'For good,' he confirmed. 'I'm hoping that you'll agree to be my wife and come and live there with me. I want to be wherever you are, Jeannie, love. If you don't like the house in Cranhill Road, we can look around and find something that suits you better.'

She squealed, forgetting herself, and the baby startled awake.

As the child began to cry, Jeannie laughed. 'Goodness, Tom, now look what we've done! I thought proposals were supposed to be romantic and we've managed to rouse Ruby and make her cry.'

As she soothed the baby, he grinned and kissed her cheek. 'I know I should have taken you for a walk in the garden and got down on one knee and made a pretty speech, but I couldn't wait. I'm sure little Ruby won't mind that she was here. It's a story we can tell her when she's grown and we're an old married couple. If you're going to have me, that is.' He raised his eyebrows and tilted his head to the side. 'You haven't actually said if it's what you want yet.'

'Of course it is,' she said, raising her voice above Ruby's protests.

There was a clatter on the stairs as Louisa came down in response to her baby's cries, but Jeannie was too busy kissing Tom to notice until her sister-in-law spoke.

'Um, I expect she's hungry,' she said. 'Shall I take her now, Jeannie?'

The couple sprang apart. Tom laughed at Jeannie's hot cheeks.

'Oh! I'm sorry, Lou. She's only just woken up,' she said, handing the baby to her mother.

They stood up and Tom pulled her close again. He grinned. 'We've got news,' he said.

Louisa raised her eyebrows as she jiggled the baby up and down. 'Which is?' she asked.

'I'm buying a house,' he said. 'In Cranhill Road. And we're getting married.'

Jeannie squealed again, so full of joy that she thought she might burst.

Louisa beamed at them. 'It's about time!' she declared. 'I'm so happy for you both.'

The baby's increasing wails brought Lucas down the stairs. 'Whatever's going on? Is she ill?'

'No,' Louisa assured him with a laugh. 'She's just hungry, but we've been distracted by the news. Tom's proposed.'

'And I've said yes,' said Jeannie, clinging to him.

'I'll pop up to our room and feed this little one,' said Louisa. 'Then I'll come back down and we can celebrate. Lucas, love, why don't you put the kettle on? I expect your ma will be down in a minute with all this racket.'

As Louisa disappeared upstairs, Lucas shook Tom's hand and kissed his sister's cheek. 'I can't say I'm surprised,' he said. 'We've been expecting this for a while now.'

Tom looked bashful. 'I wanted to get properly settled in the village before I asked her. But now I've seen a house in Cranhill Road and I'm thinking of putting in an offer on it.'

'You're going to buy, not rent?' Lucas looked impressed.

He nodded. 'I've managed to save a good amount, even with paying for my projects, and now I've been offered sponsorship to cover those costs. Then my grandpa gave me some money, so I'm in a position to pay a decent deposit. I'll need a mortgage, but I can afford it and still provide for Jeannie and any children we have. It means we'll own it free and clear one day.'

Lucas whistled. 'Those places in Cranhill Road are a couple of hundred pounds, aren't they?'

'They are. I want the best for my Jeannie,' he said, smiling down at her.

Mrs Musgrove appeared at the top of the stairs. 'Is everything all right?' she asked. 'Louisa says you've got something to tell me.'

'We're getting married, Ma!' Jeannie burst out. 'I'm so happy.'

'Oh, my dear sweet girl.' She put her hands to her mouth as her eyes welled with tears. 'That's wonderful news.'

Lucas jogged up the stairs and offered Ma a hand to help her down. When she reached her daughter, she pulled her into a hug. She looked over Jeannie's shoulder at Tom and put out a hand towards him. He took it and held it in both of his.

'I hope that's all right, Mrs Musgrove? I realise I should have asked your permission first.'

'Nonsense,' the older woman replied. 'It's between you and Jeannie; it's her decision. However, I confess I'm delighted because I've been hoping for this for a long time. Welcome to the family, Tom.'

16

While Kate was delighted for Jeannie and Tom, she couldn't help feeling a bit left out now that both of her dear friends were spoken for. She was relieved that she'd made the decision to take evening classes when they started up after the summer. While the other girls were busy with their beaus, Kate kept busy with her classes. It had been a long time since she had done any studying, so it was hard going at first.

There was an interesting mix of people there, none of whom she knew well. They seemed quite nice, but she was so busy trying to keep up with all the learning that she didn't really spend a lot of time chatting to them, although she had an interesting time talking to one older woman who had joined Miss Alice Clark and the Suffragists on the six-week-long suffrage pilgrimage to London back in 1913. Kate wished she had been able to join the movement and gone on the pilgrimage, but she had been too young and her pa would have forbidden her from going.

She wouldn't admit it to Jeannie and Louisa, but she was a bit intimidated by some of the other fellow students – young women who had stayed on at school until they were sixteen and whose fathers were professionals. They would likely become personal secretaries and marry men like their fathers one day. She didn't have anything in common with girls like that. But she persisted, not least because she had paid good money to take the course, and by the end of October, she was doing well with her lessons and felt less inferior to her fellow students.

She still saw Jeannie at work, and her and Louisa out of it, although she sometimes felt like a right gooseberry when Lucas and Tom were around. She didn't know why it seemed more acute since Jeannie's engagement, because the five of them had often spent time together before that. But now the talk was more and more about marriage and babies and houses, leaving Kate feeling as though she had nothing to say. Those things weren't in her future. She worried that sometime soon, her friends would leave her behind, although she knew they wouldn't mean to abandon her. It was just that the focus of their lives was changing.

As the nights drew in and the weather turned colder at the end of October, the news that everyone was waiting for came from the front. The Allies had the Hun on the run after four long years of fighting. In early November, the ringing of church bells across the land brought the people onto the streets to celebrate the news that Germany had surrendered. The conflict would officially cease at the eleventh hour on the eleventh day of the eleventh month.

'Oh thank the lord,' said Jeannie when everyone spilled out of the factory after the news was announced. 'The twins won't have to fight.' She wiped away her tears of relief. 'Ma's been really fretting these past few weeks, thinking they would be dragged off to enlist. Now she can rest easy.'

'And we'll get George back from the prisoner of war camp,'

said Kate. 'And about time, too. Maybe when he gets home, Fred will be able to let go of some of his feelings of guilt and get better.'

Jeannie frowned. 'What do you mean?'

Kate shrugged. 'Since he's been home, he's been feeling guilty that he's here and poor George is incarcerated by the enemy in a foreign country. We're all sure it's keeping him from getting back to his old self, even though we keep telling him there's nothing he could have done.'

'That's awful,' she said.

'But not uncommon,' she pointed out. 'Both Lucas and Tom have their moments as well, don't they?'

Jeannie nodded.

'I think this war has changed everyone,' she went on. 'Not just because of the lads who'll never come home, but because of what the survivors went through.'

The two of them stood on the sidelines, watching as people danced and laughed and cheered. Kate could understand their relief, but she also felt for the people suffering the aftermath of the conflict. For a lot of people, the conflict would live on in their hearts and minds. With so many men killed and even more coming home after years of hell in the trenches, how could they ever think that life would be the same again? *But that doesn't mean it won't be a good life.*

Louisa ran up to them. 'Isn't it wonderful news?' she said. 'Mr Baker knocked on the door to tell us. I had to come and see for myself. Your ma's watching Ruby while she's napping.'

Kate took her friends' hands in hers. 'Come on,' she said. 'Why are we standing here, watching everyone else having fun? We should celebrate. We won! The war is over. We've got peace at last!' Her voice grew until she was shouting the last words.

Folk around her cheered and Kate raised her face to the sky and laughed with sheer relief.

Someone had produced a fiddle and was playing a lively jig. The friends joined the dance. Kate felt lighter than she had for years. A little way along the road, she spotted Mrs Jackson clinging to her husband as she sobbed. For a moment, Kate's heart seemed to stop as she wondered whether her tears were for Ted. It would be a cruel god who would let a mother lose all three of her sons. But then the older woman raised her head and gave her husband a beatific smile, joy making her look quite beautiful. His answering smile and the kiss he bestowed on his wife, right there in the middle of the high street, relieved the fear in Kate's heart. When Mr Jackson looked over and caught her eye above Mrs Jackson's head, he smiled and nodded as if to say, *He's safe.* Kate felt tears well as she smiled back at him. That was all she wanted: for Ted to be alive and well, even if he didn't want anything to do with her. It would be enough, she assured herself, even as she felt the now familiar feeling of loneliness when Lucas and Tom arrived and claimed Louisa and Jeannie for a dance.

The party in the high street went on for a while, with more instruments being pressed into service. Some folk shared jugs of cider, and the mood got livelier.

Louisa and Lucas left quite soon, wanting to get back to Ruby and Mrs Musgrove. Jeannie pulled Tom away from the crowds when he began limping – no doubt due to his trying to dance on his prosthetic – leaving Kate alone among the crowd.

Rather than stand there like a lemon, she made her way to Goswell Road where her brother Fred sat on a kitchen chair outside his front door while her sisters-in-law and niece and nephews were doing their own victory dance in the street with their neighbours. Kate kissed him on the cheek and sat on the step next to him.

'It's over at last,' she said.

'Thank God,' said Fred, his voice still raspy from the effects of the mustard gas attack that had sent him home. 'We just need George home now.'

She nodded. 'That we do. And Peg and Will can come back as well.'

As she said it, she realised what that would mean for Louisa. After more than two and a half years, she would finally see her little boy again. Kate wondered whether her friend would be able to bear the pain of it.

17

FRANCE, NOVEMBER 1918

It was over. Germany had surrendered. He had survived.

He leaned against the wall and watched as his comrades celebrated. He supposed he should join them, drinking and singing and carousing, their hearts full of joy and relief. He would in a minute. But first he wanted to remember the ones who hadn't made it this far. Too many of them had fallen or been taken, such unnecessary loss of life, so cruelly cut short, that he found it hard to share the others' joy.

'Eh, Bouledogue!' called a voice from across the square. 'Why aren't you drinking?'

He'd been given a code name when he'd been sent here. But he'd only used that to gain access to the networks he was to work with and to send secret communications back to his controllers. His comrades had soon named him *Bouledogue*. To them, he was the British Bulldog, the stubborn man who managed to stay alive – and who managed to keep most of his comrades alive as well. *Most of them.* It was the ones he hadn't managed to save that preyed on his mind at this moment.

He shrugged as the man who he knew only as *Serpente*

approached. 'Maybe because you're hogging all the good stuff,' he replied in French. He couldn't remember the last time he'd spoken in English.

His comrade laughed and handed him an open bottle of fine cognac. He took it and raised it to his lips. He drank, letting the spirit warm his belly.

'Mmm, that's good,' he said, handing the bottle back.

'Liberated from the stores of the local German governor,' his friend told him. 'The bastard had stolen from the best cellars in the region.' Serpente spat on the floor. 'May he rot in hell.'

'Are you heading home?' he asked him.

Serpente shrugged – that over-exaggerated gesture so natural to the French, but which the Englishman had had to learn in order to survive. 'What is the point? My village was destroyed, my family are all gone. No. I'm going to Canada. They speak French there. You should come with me, my friend.'

He shook his head. 'I need to go home.'

After losing one son to a bullet and another to the madness of shell shock, his parents needed him back in Somerset.

Serpente nodded, suddenly sober. 'You are fortunate, my friend. Your home and family wait for you. You can go back and maybe marry a sweet girl and forget all about us.'

He closed his eyes, the vision of the sweet girl he'd left behind filling his mind. He'd told no one here about her. His Kate. Only he knew how fierce and brave and strong she was. Only he knew how cruel he had been to her. And only Kate knew whether she would be able to forgive him.

18

December was cold and bleak but spirits were high as the first men began to return home from the front. It would take months to get them all back to Britain, of course, and some soldiers would remain in the army of occupation to keep the peace in Europe as the shift in power took effect. Most of those would be regulars rather than conscripts. But the fact that war was over meant that everyone in Street was determined to celebrate this Christmas.

Just a week before the holiday, Kate received a message from the asylum informing her that her pa was gravely ill. So, on Saturday afternoon, Kate and Fred took the bus and went to see him.

'I'll not believe it until I see for myself,' said Fred. 'That old rogue could be pulling the wool over their eyes, couldn't he? He'll be making sure he doesn't have to work for his keep, I'll wager. Playing the invalid and enjoying three square meals a day.'

'Probably,' said Kate. 'I'm sure he was playing up when I went to see him last time. Even when he was acting confused and pathetic, his eyes told a different story. He knew exactly what he was doing.'

But when they were granted entry to the infirmary, it was clear that Reggie Davis was a very sick man. He'd lost so much weight, he was barely recognisable. He looked so frail and insignificant as he lay in bed, his skin a bright yellow against the stark white bedsheets. For a moment, Kate felt a fierce satisfaction that this once vital man should be so reduced after the pain he'd caused so many people, not least her poor dear ma.

'Christ,' said Fred, visibly shocked. 'Is he already dead?'

The ward orderly shook his head. 'No, he's just sleeping. We don't think he's got long, but you should be able to speak to him if he wakes. Even if he doesn't, he can probably hear you, so if you want to say anything...'

Kate sat down and stared at her pa. She didn't want to talk. She feared that if she did, all the years of hurt would come rushing out of her mouth and she'd never be able to stop or take it back, and then she'd feel ashamed for the rest of her life because she knew that Ma in heaven would be looking down on her, disappointed that she wouldn't – couldn't – forgive her father, even on his death bed.

Fred seemed to feel the same, because he sat beside her in grim silence for a while. They watched as the old man's chest rose and fell, each breath causing his lungs to rattle. It reminded Kate so much of the sound of Ma's breathing in her last hours that she wanted to weep. Not for him – never for him – but for Ma. She was so lonely without her, even with the loving friendship of Auntie Betty.

When she would have suggested they give up and go, Reggie coughed, waking himself up. He turned jaundiced eyes towards his visitors and frowned as he recognised them.

'Come to gloat, have you?' he asked. 'Well get it over with. I ain't got long and I want to go in peace.' He coughed again, the effort of speaking weakening him.

'Not gloating,' said Fred. 'You're not worth the effort. I can't speak for Kate, but I've come to make sure you're finally doing us a favour and dying.'

Kate gasped at the cruelty in her brother's words, but Reggie just laughed, coughing again and grimacing in pain.

'Where's the rest of 'em?' he demanded. 'I thought you'd all be here, ready to dance on me grave.'

'George is being repatriated from Germany,' said Kate. 'And Peg will be moving back from Lincolnshire in the New Year.'

He closed his eyes. 'I'll be gone by then. No matter. It's not like they'll be weeping over me, is it? None of you will.'

'Why would we?' asked Fred, his voice low and angry. 'You've never shown an ounce of care for any of us. You get back what you give out, old man. You treated us with contempt and that's all we can feel for you now, especially after the way you let that damned Floozy mistreat our Kate.'

Reggie opened his eyes again and glared at Kate. He looked like a devil, with his jaundiced skin and the whites of his eyes such a bright yellow, edged round with red, that he barely looked human any more. She had to fight to remain still and calm when her instincts were to move away from him.

'You were all pathetic, but you was the worst,' he snarled at her. 'Don't expect an apology. If that's what you came for, you can bugger off, the pair of you.'

She breathed out, feeling her fear fade, to be replaced by acceptance. He was never going to change, not even now when he was about to face his maker. Kate had had enough. She stood up.

'Come on, Fred,' she said. 'You heard him. There's no point in staying here. Let him die alone.' She spared a final glance at her father. 'It's no more than he deserves.'

As she turned away, Reggie spoke again. 'Saw that lad of yours,' he said. 'Looks like someone shot him. Come to see his brother, he did.' He cackled, producing another round of coughing as Kate turned back to him, her senses alert.

'What lad?' she asked.

'You know,' he gasped between coughs. 'That lanky kid. Caught him with you on my settee.'

Kate felt the blood drain from her head and she swayed. Fred grabbed her arm, preventing her from falling.

'Go and ask mad Stan,' said Reggie, his face twisted in a cruel smirk. 'Ask him who shot your Ted.'

'You're lying,' she said, suddenly angry. He was cruel enough to say something like that just to upset her.

'When I'm looking death in the eye? Why would I lie? Someone got him good.'

'Leave her alone,' said Fred, almost carrying Kate away from the bed as she began to shake. 'For the love of God, man, can't you ever do a decent thing even at the end your life?'

The old man began to laugh. 'What's God ever done for me, eh?' he shouted after them as they walked the length of the ward. 'I'll see you in hell, you ungrateful brats.'

The orderly rushed forward as Reggie's coughing wracked his body again and he began to vomit over the bedclothes. Neither Kate nor Fred looked back as they exited the ward.

They paused in the corridor outside. Fred's breathing was laboured and Kate was still trembling, her heart beating so fast, she was sure it was about to burst out of her chest.

'Are you all right?' she asked her brother as she stepped away from his grasp, worried about his damaged lungs.

He bent at the waist, his hands on his knees as he caught his breath. He nodded. 'Yeah,' he said eventually. 'What about you?'

She wrapped her arms around her body. 'I don't know what to think. He was lying, wasn't he? He must have been lying?'

Fred slowly stood, his breathing a little easier, although still raspy. 'Sit down for a bit.' He indicated some chairs along the wall. 'I'm going to see the matron. See what she says.' He ran a hand down his face. 'I want to know how long the old bastard has got left as well. So help me God, I'm tempted to go back in there and put my hands round his scrawny neck and help him into the next world, but I've got a family who needs me, so I won't give in.' He barked out a bitter laugh. 'That would please him no end, wouldn't it? Seeing me swing for putting us all out of our misery.'

Kate touched his clenched fist. 'He's not worth it, Fred. He's really not.'

'I know, love. Don't worry.' He took another shaky breath. 'Sit. I'll talk to someone, then we can go.' He paused and turned back to her. 'I'm going to tell them he's to be buried in the hospital graveyard with the other lunatics, all right? He's not worthy to lay anywhere near Ma.'

She nodded, too overwhelmed to say anything. She knew there would be no gravestone for Reggie Davis. None of them wanted to mark where he lay. It wasn't as though they would visit his grave.

Fred walked down the corridor in search of the matron and Kate sank back in the chair, resting her head against the wall and closing her eyes.

She shouldn't have been surprised by her pa's cruelty. He delighted in playing with her emotions, keeping her on edge. Why, just because he was dying, did she think he'd be any different? Of course he hadn't seen Ted, she was sure. He just wanted to upset her, make her worry all over again about where Ted was and whether he was safe. She shouldn't believe a word of it. Ted was probably miles away from here, not even in the country, and even if he was, he'd already said he wouldn't ever come back here, didn't he?

Fred was gone for a while, but Kate didn't fret. She simply waited, too exhausted to worry. She couldn't hear anything from the ward either, but the doors and walls were thick, so even if Reggie had been yelling his head off, she might not have heard anything. It occurred to her that she need never see that man again, whether he lived or died. The relief that thought brought was palpable. It brought a small smile to her lips as she sent a prayer of thanks that she was free of him at last.

A door opened further along the corridor. She wondered if it was Fred coming back for her and she sighed, trying to summon up the energy for the walk to the bus stop. She opened her eyes and glanced in the direction in which her brother had gone, but the hallway was empty. Frowning, she turned in the other direction to see two men standing with their backs to her, talking quietly. She must have made a sound, because they turned to face her.

For the second time in less than half an hour, Kate felt her heart go wild. She recognised them. She stood abruptly, too shocked to pay any heed to the dizziness her sudden movement caused, or her bag falling, the contents spilling across the floor at her feet.

'Kate?'

She knew that voice, but it couldn't be true. She must be having a hallucination. Reggie's madness had infected her mind and made her see things. She shook her head, trying to rid herself of the sound and vision.

The men approached, wearing identical expressions of concern.

'Hello, lass,' said the older man. 'Are you all right? Have you been to see your pa?'

'M... Mr Jackson?' she stammered, barely able to get the words out.

He reached forward and touched her arm. She flinched, not expecting to feel it if he were a figment of her imagination.

'Steady now, lass. Come on, sit down. You look like you've had a shock.'

He guided her back to her seat and she sank into it, her confused gaze on the young man at his side.

'Ted?' she whispered.

He nodded, smiling gently. 'Hello, Kate. Long time no see.'

Kate pulled in shaky breath, her hand covering her mouth as she took in the sling holding his arm against his chest. 'Oh God, you *have* been shot! I thought he was lying.'

He frowned and shook his head. 'Not shot,' he said. 'I dislocated my shoulder in a motorcycle accident a couple of days ago.' He sat in the chair next to hers. 'Don't worry, love. I'm all right. It earned me some leave, so I came to see how Stan and my folks are.'

Mr Jackson cleared his throat. 'I'd better pop back in and see your ma, son,' he said. 'You keep young Kate company for a bit.'

Kate was barely aware of him leaving them alone in the corridor. All her attention was on Ted. She reached out a shaking hand and touched his cheek. 'I thought I was seeing things. That I'd gone mad.'

He reached up and held her hand against his face. 'I'm real, Kate. You're not mad, I promise.'

She was silent, staring at him, feeling his touch, the flex of his jaw under her fingers, barely daring to breathe in case he disappeared again.

'So,' he said. 'I heard your pa was in here.'

'He's dying,' she blurted out. 'Everyone thought he was a murderer but he wasn't.'

He nodded. She didn't know whether he knew the whole story or if he was just humouring her. She was so confused, she couldn't think straight. 'I thought I'd never see you again,' she whispered. 'I can't believe you're here.'

His grave expression softened. 'It's good to see you,' he said softly.

'You said you wouldn't come back.'

He shrugged. 'I had to.'

Another door opened and she heard her brother's voice.

'Fred's coming,' she said. 'He was gassed.'

Ted winced. 'Bad luck. Bloody awful stuff that.'

'And George was captured. We're waiting for him to come home from Germany.'

He nodded. 'I'm glad he's coming home.'

'And what about you?' she asked, fearful of his answer. 'Are you coming home? Because you told me you wouldn't and I've tried to get on without you.'

He dropped his gaze and sighed. 'There's stuff I need to explain to you, Kate. But now's not the time. Can I come and see you in a few days?'

Fred was still talking to someone by the open door. She couldn't hear what he was saying, and she didn't care. She'd made her peace and let go of the hurt and fear of her pa while she'd been sitting here waiting for her brother. All her attention now was on Ted, the man who'd walked away from her suddenly and then reappeared in her life so unexpectedly today. Could she bear to hope, when he could well walk away from her again?

He looked up again, capturing her gaze, and she felt all the hurt and confusion that she'd felt on that long-ago evening when he'd rejected her; she remembered the loneliness she'd endured in his absence, the uncertainty of never knowing whether he was alive or dead, and she was overwhelmed with fear.

'No,' she said, shaking her head. She pulled her hand away from him. 'I don't think so.' She couldn't go through that again. She'd promised herself she'd be content to know that he was alive and well, and now she did. It was enough. *It had to be enough.*

She stood up, scrambling to grab her things from the floor and shoving them back into her bag. 'I'm glad you're all right, Ted. But I've got to go. Bye.'

Without waiting for him to respond, she ran. Away from Ted. Towards the reassuring presence of her brother.

She didn't need a man. She was strong and was making a life for herself. That was what she kept telling herself as the bus trundled back to Street, away from the only man she'd ever loved.

It was only as she put her purse back into her bag after paying her fare that she realised that the letter she'd written to Ted and kept in there was missing.

* * *

As Kate and her brother walked away, not looking back, Ted sighed and sank back down onto the chair. He put his head in his hands, feeling unutterably weary. He supposed he'd deserved that after the way he'd left Kate when he'd enlisted, but it still hurt.

Another door opened and he knew his ma and pa would be looking for him, ready to go home. *Home.* He'd dreamt of it so many times over the years and always Kate had been there, ready to welcome him back. What a fool he'd been to think it would be that easy. He sighed and opened his eyes as he heard his parents' footsteps getting closer.

A flash of white caught his gaze and he saw that someone had dropped an envelope on the floor under the chair where Kate had been sitting. He reached down and picked it up, his heart racing when he saw his name on it, written in Kate's handwriting. He didn't have time to think before they reached him, so he slipped it into his pocket. It had obviously fallen out of Kate's bag. It was a little ragged around the edges, so it had been there for a while, he thought. Maybe he should chase after her and return it to her. That would be the honourable thing to do.

But 'honourable' was the last thing he'd been since he'd left Street, so maybe he should keep it and read it? After all, it was clearly meant for him, even if there was no address. Kate might have had it with her ready to give to him if ever she saw him... or she might have never intended for him to read it. He didn't know. But now that he had it in his possession, he knew that he wouldn't be able to stop himself from opening that envelope. He might regret it, but he knew he would regret it more if he never found out what Kate had written in this letter that she had probably never expected to be able to deliver.

'Ted?'

He looked up to see his parents looking at him with concern. They had been treating him with kid gloves from the moment he'd arrived home so unexpectedly. He understood their fears and hopes. After all, Albert was dead and Stan was never going to be the same again. He was the only one left whole – in body anyway. He might not be as damaged as poor Stan, but he knew without doubt that he wasn't the same lad who had left Street to fight. He had wounds that went deep but that he hoped no one would ever see, especially not Ma and Pa. Or Kate.

'Ready to go home, lad?' asked his pa.

He nodded. 'Yes,' he said. He offered his ma his good arm. 'Let's go home.'

Today, he needed to concentrate on his family. He could see that his years away had taken their toll on his parents and he needed to reassure them that he was all right. They deserved that after everything they'd suffered.

But soon, he would read Kate's letter. If it told him that she really didn't want him back, he would try and accept that. But... if it didn't say that, and her unguarded reaction to the sight of him was anything to go by... then he would make sure that he did see Kate again and that they could talk. She needed to know the truth. He owed that to her and to himself.

19

Christmas 1918, the first in peacetime after four long years of war, was joyful in the Musgrove and Davis families, especially when George arrived home on Christmas Eve, a year to the day after they'd heard that he'd been taken prisoner. He'd lost a lot of weight and his head had been shaved, but his joy at seeing his wife and children shone through.

'Just our Peg to get home now,' said Fred. 'Then we'll be right.'

Reggie Davis had died three days after their visit to him. None of the family had gone to his funeral. He would not be mourned.

'I can't wait to see Peg's little lad,' said Vi, reminding Kate of the dilemma Louisa would soon face. 'It will be good for him to meet his cousins.'

'I wrote to her,' said Ada. 'The cottage three doors up from ours is coming up for rent as the old couple who live there are moving to Yeovil to be near their daughter. She said they're going to try for it. Then we'll all be on the same road.'

Kate smiled. 'The little ones will be in and out of the houses all the time, won't they? You'll never be able to keep track of them.' She liked the idea of all of her family being so close together, although it emphasised her feeling of isolation as she was the only one who wouldn't be there. But she mustn't think like that, because she was only a few minutes' walk away. She was happy at Auntie Betty's and she was alone by choice. She wouldn't feel sorry for herself.

She took her leave of the family in the early evening. Auntie Betty was spending the holiday with her cousin Ethel – Gerald's ma – in Bristol, so Kate wasn't in any rush to go home to an empty cottage. She'd promised to pop round to the Musgroves, who welcomed her with as much cheer as her own relatives.

'Come on in,' said Jeannie, giving her a hug. 'Have you had a good day? We've had a fine time. Ruby's first Christmas has been a good one.'

'Our first in peace for so long,' said Mrs Musgrove. 'I thank God every day that he has spared my boys. Let's pray that there'll never be another war like it.'

Kate accepted a glass of warm spiced apple juice and joined the family in the parlour. Ruby was sitting without assistance now and she waved her arms and smiled at Kate when she saw her.

'Aw, look at you,' Kate cooed. 'Getting prettier every day. Your pa will have to fight the lads off with a stick, won't he?' The baby had her mother's blue eyes and blonde curls.

Louisa laughed as Lucas groaned. 'Don't remind him,' she said. 'He's already fretting about it.'

'Can we talk about something else?' asked Lucas.

'All right,' said Kate. 'Now that Christmas is over, we've got to think about the New Year. What's in store for us in 1919, eh?'

'We'll be eighteen in a couple of weeks,' declared John.

'Yes,' said Jeannie. 'And thanks to the armistice, you can enjoy your lives without fear of ending up in the trenches.'

Her ma put her hands together, giving thanks again.

'Amen to that. Mrs M,' said Kate. 'So, the next big event will be Jeannie and Tom's wedding. Are you all set?'

The twins groaned and, complaining, took themselves off to their bedrooms. 'We're sick of hearing about it. The sooner it's over, the better,' said John.

The others laughed at their rapid departure. 'So,' said Kate. 'How are the plans going?'

'We're all set for Easter in April,' said Jeannie. 'Then we'll have a few days while the factory's shut over the Holy Weekend.'

Kate frowned. 'I don't understand why you need to wait. Once Tom proposed, I thought you'd be rushing to get wed.'

'There's no rush,' said Jeannie. 'We've got our whole lives to look forward to. But Tom's folks can't get here before Easter. They need the long weekend to travel here and back to Northampton.'

'And I've been working on the house,' said Tom. 'It needed decorating and we've had to furnish it. I'm living there now, but there's still a few jobs to do before it's good enough for me to bring my bride home.' He smiled at Jeannie, who blushed prettily.

The conversation turned to what Jeannie was going to wear, which prompted Lucas and Tom to go off to the house in Cranhill Road to check on some project they were working on together.

'Bring Ruby into the kitchen for me, Louisa, love,' said Mrs Musgrove, standing up. 'I'll give her a bath in the sink, then she'll be ready for her feed before bedtime.'

While the two of them got the baby's bath time organised, Jeannie and Kate chatted about their day.

'How's George?' Jeannie asked.

'Not bad,' said Kate, her tone hesitant. 'I mean, he's laughing and joking like he always does, but... it was a shock seeing him. He's lost so much weight; they must have kept them on starvation rations. And all of the men sent back were so full of lice and such that they shaved their hair and had to douse them in chemicals to get rid of them before they could let them come home.'

'That sounds horrible. Poor George. But Ada will soon feed him up, and his hair will grow out before you know it.'

'I know.' She nodded. 'It was just a shock to see him like that. Anyway, we've been teasing him all day about him needing to wear a woolly hat to cover his baldness or he'll scare the children.'

They were chuckling when Louisa came back. They told her about George's changed appearance and how he'd taken the family's teasing with good grace.

'He'll be back at work in the New Year, although Ada's saying she'll carry on working at the haulage company to keep an eye on him for a while. She doesn't want him overdoing it. It's bad enough that Fred's pushing himself so much since he got back to work.'

'Are his lungs still bad?' asked Louisa.

'They are,' Kate confirmed. 'He's back in the Clicking Room, but they've had to put a stool by his bench so he can rest when he needs to. His productivity is lower than before, but we've told him it's early days. He'll soon get back up to speed. In the meantime, Clarks and his new foreman are supporting him, like they are with all the other men who have come back injured.'

Louisa looked down at her hands and Kate felt bad about mentioning the Clicking Room and the new foreman. Before Fred had gone away to fight, his foreman there had been Louisa's pa. He'd died of a heart attack midway through the war.

'So, Jeannie,' Kate went on. 'Tom's preparing your love nest, is he?'

Jeannie giggled and covered her cheeks with her hands. 'Stop it! Love nest indeed!'

Kate raised her eyebrows and winked at Louisa, who smiled at her teasing. 'I don't know what else you'd call it,' she said. 'I mean, the man has bought you a house and now he's painting and decorating so it's fit for his true love.'

'It is lovely,' said Jeannie, a dreamy expression on her face. 'I'm so lucky.'

'It's no more than you deserve,' said Louisa.

'Quite right, too,' agreed Kate.

'And judging by the frequency that we catch the two of you canoodling,' Louisa grinned, 'it will soon be filled with babies.'

Jeannie gasped at her sister-in-law's words. 'We do not... well, not much... Oh, Lou, don't! You make me sound like a terrible person. Like I'm like... like Doris Lambert.'

Kate laughed out loud at Jeannie's outrage. 'Don't be daft. We know you're nothing like that strumpet. She'd canoodle with anyone. You've only got eyes for Tom, and that's as it should be.'

'I'm only teasing, Jeannie,' said Louisa. 'I don't mean anything by it. I love seeing you so happy, and I can't wait for you to have a baby so that Ruby will have a cousin.'

Kate stifled a sigh. 'If you two are going to start talking about babies, then I'm off. I'll go home and contemplate my future as the spinster auntie of half the kiddies in Street. I've a feeling that Vi is expecting again, although she hasn't said anything yet, and no doubt Ada will get broody again now that George is home. With you two having babies as well, I'm going to have to find ways to entertain myself while you're all busy being mothers.'

'Aw, don't go yet, Kate,' said Louisa. 'We want to know how

you're getting on. You've told us about your family, but what about you?'

She shrugged. 'My evening classes are going well. It took me a while to get used to the typewriter keyboard, but I managed to buy myself a second-hand typewriter, so I've been practising every day. The shorthand's a bit tricky, but I'm getting there.'

'And the book-keeping?' asked Jeannie.

She tilted her head to one side. 'Mmm. It's all right, I suppose. I'm okay with numbers, but it's a bit boring. That said, if I can get a job in accounts, I'll take it. With Jeannie packing in work when she weds, I don't want to stay in the Machine Room on my own.'

The others shared a glance.

'What?' asked Kate.

Jeannie shrugged, but Louisa turned to Kate with a determined expression. 'If a better job is what you want, then you should go after it. But... I know you said you turned Ted down when you saw him, and we understand why—'

Kate held up a hand. 'Hold on, what has Ted got to do with anything?'

Before they could tell her, Mrs Musgrove called Louisa from the kitchen. 'We're all done, love. Can you come and get her?'

As Ruby had grown and become more wriggly, Mrs Musgrove had been nervous about carrying the child in case she lost her footing and fell. Louisa jumped up and went to get her daughter, so Kate turned to Jeannie.

'What was she talking about, Jeannie? And don't say you don't know because I could see the two of you looking at each other. Something's up, isn't it?'

Jeannie swallowed hard and nodded. 'Ted's been round to see us,' she said.

Kate stilled, not sure how she felt about that. He hadn't been to see her. She knew she'd told him not to, but then she'd hoped that maybe he still would, because she wasn't sure if she'd done the right thing by turning him down like that. But then again, there was a chance that he'd found that letter she'd written months ago – after all, it might well have fallen out of her bag right in front of him at the asylum. What if he'd read it and decided to leave well alone because he didn't feel the same as she did?

'All right,' she said. 'I suppose it's to be expected that he'd come here. Him and Lucas were pals before the war, weren't they? I expect he wanted to catch up while he's visiting his folks for Christmas. When's he leaving again?'

Louisa came back in with a sleepy Ruby in her arms. 'That's the point,' she said. 'He's not leaving. He's got his discharge from the army and is starting a job as an assistant teacher at a school in Wells in the New Year, so he's staying with his parents.'

'A teacher?' said Kate, frowning. 'But he left school at fourteen, like the rest of us.'

'We know,' said Jeannie, looking excited. 'But you know he liked languages? Well, while he's been away, he's learned to speak French like a native, and he ended up an officer – did you know? He's only twenty-three, but they made him a captain. Anyway, someone recommended him to the school and they've taken him on from the New Year. If he gets on all right, they'll sponsor him to get his teaching certificate to become a full teacher.'

'He said that with a lot of male teachers not coming back, they've got a shortage,' said Louisa. 'The government is looking at ways to get ex-servicemen into teaching even if they don't have formal qualifications, and with Ted's language skills, he'll be perfect as a French teacher.' She wrinkled her nose. 'He says he's got a lot of book learning to do so that he can explain the workings of French grammar, but he's enjoying that well enough.'

Kate didn't know what to say. She hadn't expected any of this. 'But... he said he would never come back.'

Jeannie gave her a sympathetic look. 'I'm not sure he meant it, Kate. He seems happy enough to be home now.'

She nodded, looking down at her hands, which were clenched together. 'Then it must have been me he meant. He didn't intend to come back to me.'

Mrs Musgrove appeared in the doorway. 'That's the kitchen all tidied up,' she said. 'I'm going to take myself off to bed now, girls. It's been a lovely day, but I'm quite worn out.'

They all wished her goodnight and Jeannie escorted her ma up the stairs. Kate had remained silent and Louisa had settled into the armchair and was discreetly feeding Ruby her last feed of the evening with a shawl around her shoulders to shield her bare breast.

'Look, Kate,' said Jeannie as she returned and sat on the settee beside her. 'I don't think Ted meant what he said in that way either. He was asking after you. Wanted to know if you had a sweetheart.'

She barked out a harsh laugh. 'Oh wonderful. Now he knows how pathetic I am. Not a single sweetheart since he walked away from me.'

'We mentioned Gerald,' said Louisa. 'To see if he might get jealous.'

Kate regarded her with narrowed eyes. 'But Gerald's nothing but a friend.'

'We know,' said Jeannie. 'But Ted didn't know that at first, and he looked sick when we talked about how well you got along with him.'

She shook her head. 'Did you tell him he's a conscientious

objector? Yes, well, of course he looked sick. He was probably disgusted with me. It doesn't mean he's jealous.'

Louisa huffed out a breath. 'Of course he was jealous. You didn't see his face when we finally told him you were just friends. I've never seen a man look so relieved and happy in my life.'

Kate sat back with a sigh. Much as she wanted to believe her friends, the facts spoke for themselves. She'd told Ted to stay away and he had. If he really cared for her, especially if he'd found and read her letter, he wouldn't have let anything keep him from coming back to her, would he?

'Look, I know you two are full of the joys of love, but I don't want you thinking everything's going to turn out all right for me and Ted. He left me. I didn't hear a peep from him for years. You can't expect us to just take up where we left off, because, frankly, where we left off was horrible and I can't forget it. Between Ted's treatment of me and everything I had to put up with from my pa, I'm never inclined to want to trust a man with my heart again, and that's that. You're just going to have to accept that I'm going to be one of those fierce spinsters that run their own lives regardless of men's attempts to dominate us.'

Jeannie looked sad, but Louisa simply shrugged as she moved Ruby to her shoulder to burp her. 'Well, that's told us,' she said cheerfully. 'It's up to you, of course, Kate, and we'll love you even if you turn into a cranky old woman who scares the children. But…' Ruby let out an enormous belch that made them all laugh. 'Goodness, Ruby, that wasn't very ladylike!' Louisa giggled. 'Anyway, as I was saying before we were so rudely interrupted by my daughter, I wish you'd at least talk to Ted. I know what he did wasn't right, but I get the impression there's more to it than any of us thought.'

Jeannie nodded. 'I do, too.'

Kate sighed. In truth, she regretted not listening to him when she had the chance. But if, as she suspected, he'd seen and read her letter to him, then his continued silence since then only went to show that he didn't care for her as much as she cared for him. 'I don't know,' she said. 'I think we should let sleeping dogs lie.'

The clock on the mantel chimed the hour.

'I must get Ruby to bed,' said Louisa, standing up with the baby in her arms.

'And I must get off home,' said Kate. She'd had about as much as she could take of this talk about Ted for one day. 'I'll see you in a couple of days.' She had plans to catch up on her laundry and to practice her lessons before Auntie got back from Bristol. 'You can let me know what I can do to help with your wedding dress, Jeannie.'

Jeannie nodded. 'It won't be anything fancy. I rather liked the style that Louisa had, although maybe I'll have a different colour. I know some brides are keen on white these days, but I'd rather have something I can wear again, so I'm thinking of something in a soft shade of pink or blue.'

Kate nodded. 'Either would suit you. Have a think about it, then we can all get to work on it.'

Louisa took the baby upstairs and Jeannie saw her to the door.

'I'm sorry if we've upset you with all this talk about Ted,' said Jeannie softly.

'It's all right,' she sighed. 'I just don't know what to think about it all. Maybe I *should* talk to him, but I'll not make the first move. If he really wants me to know what's what, he'll come to me.' But she doubted he would.

20

Louisa had a mouth full of pins as she knelt on the floor of the parlour, adjusting the hem of the dress Jeannie was wearing. It wasn't her wedding gown, they still had to buy the material for that, but this was a smart, green, woollen dress that Jeannie had made to wear to meet her future in-laws when they arrived the day before the wedding.

'Thanks for doing this, Lou,' said Jeannie as she stood still and tall so that she could get the length of the hem right. 'I couldn't ask Ma. She could never get down on her knees like that, and if she did, she'd never get up again! I know there's months to go yet, so there's no rush,' she went on, her voice becoming breathless. 'But I'm that nervous about everything, so I want to get as much done as possible in advance so I can stop fretting about it. I'll feel better knowing I'll look smart and presentable in this dress.'

'Uhumm,' said Louisa, unable to speak for all the pins she was holding between her lips. She wanted to say that she didn't understand why Jeannie was so worried about meeting Tom's family. His parents and sisters had all written to her and they sounded lovely so she was sure they'd all get along splendidly. But Jeannie was Jeannie, and she would fret because she loved Tom so much and wanted to make a good impression upon his family.

At last, the hem was secured. Louisa sat back on her heels. 'It's a lovely colour,' she said. 'It suits you. You'll do Tom proud with his folks.'

Jeannie's cheeks flushed. 'I hope so. They sound very nice in their letters. I want them to be pleased with Tom's choice of bride this time.'

Louisa chuckled. 'Does Tom know that his sisters have told you they hadn't liked the other one?'

She shrugged. 'He knows. I think he suspected they felt like that, but he was daft in love at the time, so he didn't care to listen.'

'But he wishes he had now, eh? Well, she's gone now and he's marrying you. He might have been daft then, but it's clear to everyone that he's found the true love of his life this time, and thanks to all that money Tom was saving to divorce her, you get to have your very own house. It's all worked out perfectly.'

'Mmm.' Jeannie looked troubled. 'I don't like to think that she had to die so that we could be together; it still makes me feel guilty. But I suppose it was God's will.'

Louisa didn't say anything as she stood up. She'd been told time and again that it was *God's will* that Mattie had died, and her mother had even had the audacity to suggest that it was His will that Mattie's brother was childless and so willing to take on her illegitimate child to cover up her shame. She had decided then that she wanted nothing to do with a god who could be so cruel, deciding everyone's fate and not caring about the hurt and grief it would cause. At the Friends' meetings, she focused on the power of nature, of the strength of human endeavour and the difference between right and wrong. She had no time to contemplate a god she had no respect for. Whether the elders would approve, she didn't know, but that was the benefit of silent worship – no one needed to know what was in her heart.

'You've nothing to feel guilty about,' said Louisa, her tone firm. 'You weren't driving the tram, you didn't push her under it, or wish that fate upon her. It was sheer bad luck on her part. Nothing to do with divine intervention. I mean, if God answered everyone's prayers by killing off folk who stood in their way, there wouldn't be many of us left, would there?'

Jeannie sighed and nodded. 'You're right. I've got to forget the past and concentrate on the future with Tom.'

Her words struck a chord with Louisa. She knew that she was going to have to face her past soon. Peg and Will were due back in Street any day now. For the first time since she'd left Lincolnshire, she would see her son in the flesh. He was two years and ten months old now. Not a baby, but rather a little boy. She knew that he was sturdy and preferred to run rather than walk, that he loved picture books and building blocks. Peg had kept her informed of all of his milestones and had even been kind enough to send her a photograph that they'd had taken in a proper studio on his second birthday. He was so beautiful, so like Mattie, that she had wept with joy and grief over that image for days. Thankfully, she had shared all of Peg's letters and the photograph with Lucas, so he understood. But even his kindness and support couldn't comfort her for a while. Mrs Musgrove had assumed that her tears were the result of her emotions being all over the place in the early stages of her pregnancy with Ruby and they hadn't confessed the truth of it to her. Now, her mother-in-law was in the kitchen, singing to herself as she baked, while Louisa was on tenterhooks, waiting to hear that they had arrived.

As if conjured up by her thoughts, there was a knock on the

door. She opened it to see Kate standing there and she knew from her friend's expression the reason for her visit.

'They're here, aren't they?' she said.

Kate nodded, her expression full of sympathy and compassion. 'They arrived yesterday. I think you should come with me to see them now, love. Get it over with. Don't give yourself time to fret any more over it. What do you think?'

She closed her eyes, afraid and excited at the same time. When she opened her eyes, she felt more determined. She could do this. She'd done right by little Mattie, ensuring he would be brought up in a loving family – his own father's kin. This was her reward – the chance to see him grow and flourish. It might be painful at first, but it was what she wanted. It was far better than never knowing his fate, of always being afraid that he wasn't being treated right.

'All right,' she said. 'Just let me get Ruby up from her nap. I want to take her with me.' She knew that holding her second baby in her arms when she saw her first-born would keep her strong and remind her that she had been lucky to have found sanctuary in her marriage to Lucas.

'What about Lucas?' asked Jeannie from behind her. Louisa turned to face her. She'd changed out of her new dress and was fastening the buttons on her skirt.

'He's helping Tom in his workshop,' she said. 'Will you go and get him for me, please? Ask him to meet me there?'

Jeannie nodded. 'Of course I will.' She hesitated. 'Do you want me to come, too?'

Part of Louisa wanted all of her friends to be there, but she didn't know what sort of a state she'd be in, so it was probably best to keep the gathering small. 'Maybe next time? But thank you for offering, Jeannie. I appreciate it.' She paused. 'I've been thinking. I know you've kept my secret from Tom all this time, and I'm grateful. But, well, he's going to be your husband and Lucas's brother-in-law, isn't he? If you think he'll be all right about it, I don't mind if you tell him now. It might save him asking awkward questions if I act strange around little Mattie.'

Jeannie hugged her and kissed her cheek. 'All right. I'll go now,' she said.

* * *

Louisa pushed the baby carriage up Goswell Road, past the Davis brothers' cottages, although she didn't look at them, instead concentrating on the smiling face of her daughter gazing back at her from her pram. Ruby was delighted by this unexpected outing and showed her approval by displaying her new teeth in a wide grin. She had eight altogether and was enjoying chewing on biscuits and crusts of bread. She took cows' milk from a bottle now as well apart from her last feed at night, so she wasn't quite so dependent on Louisa for nourishment.

Kate touched her arm to slow her as they approached the cottage the Searles were renting. 'Like I said, they arrived yesterday,' she said. 'So they're still unpacking and getting sorted. Everyone's going to be spending Sunday helping them. They'd have all been there now, but Peg told them to give them today to get over the journey.'

'Should I go away and come back another time?' asked Louisa. She was so nervous that she'd welcome the excuse to turn tail and run away.

She shook her head. 'No. Peg asked me to bring you round. She knew you needed to do it sooner rather than later and there's less chance of anyone popping in today.'

'What about Auntie Betty?' Surely Will's ma would want to see them.

'They went round to her as soon as they arrived yesterday and they told her the same thing. They're going to have supper with her this evening, so don't worry.'

Louisa nodded and took a deep breath. 'All right. Let's get Ruby out and go in before I lose my nerve.'

She had just picked up the baby when they heard footsteps running up the road. Lucas joined them at the front door.

'Jeannie told me to come,' he said, catching his breath. He held up a bag. 'I brought a little something for the lad. Me and Tom made him a wooden train to welcome him to Street. I've been waiting to give it to him.'

Louisa smiled at him, even though she felt shaky with anxiety. 'You're a good man, Lucas Musgrove,' she said. 'That was really thoughtful of you.'

'He'll love it, I'm sure,' said Kate. 'I can't wait to see his face when he sees it.'

Before Louisa could catch her breath, her friend had knocked on the front door and immediately opened it. 'Peg?' she called. 'We're here.'

As they entered the cottage, Louisa barely noticed the piles of boxes and sacks in the parlour. She heard the patter of little feet and a toddler with a halo of brown curls appeared. 'Annie Kay!' he squealed and held his hands up to Kate.

She laughed and picked him up. 'That's right, Mattie, I'm Auntie Kate. You remember me telling you last night, don't you? You're such a clever boy.' She kissed his cheek and then turned her smiling face towards Louisa and Lucas.

Louisa froze, hardly daring to breathe as Kate continued to chatter to the boy.

'This is your godmother, Auntie Louisa and her husband Uncle Lucas.'

Little Mattie gazed at them with brown eyes so like his father's that Lucas couldn't hold in a quiet gasp.

'Ooo dat?' he asked, pointing a chubby finger at the baby in Louisa's arms, who was staring at this newcomer with interest.

His question seemed to unfreeze Louisa. She offered him a shaky smile and stepped closer. 'This is Ruby. She's still a baby, not all grown up like you. Will you be her friend?'

He studied the little girl curiously before reaching out a hand towards her. Ruby, who had been watching him just as seriously, grasped his finger and pulled it towards her mouth. Before she could bite him – for that was what she did with anything she could get her new teeth around these days – her mother gently rescued Mattie's hand.

'Woah, Ruby. Don't bite Mattie, love. You mustn't hurt him.'

A movement caught her eye and Louisa looked up to see Peg and Will standing in the doorway.

'Ah, Louisa, lass, she's a beauty. She looks just like you,' said Peg.

She realised she was still holding Mattie's hand only when he tugged it away and leaned towards Peg.

'Mamma,' he said, his tone demanding her attention.

Peg gave her an apologetic look as she reached for him. As she took him in her arms, Louisa was struck by the look of unconditional love on Peg's face. She knew in that moment that she had made the right decision, without a shadow of a doubt, and that everything was going to be all right. She smiled at Peg and as Lucas put his arm around her shoulder, Louisa felt the tension drain from her.

'Thank you, Peg,' she said softly. 'And you've got a bonny lad there.'

Lucas's arm tightened around her as the two women stared at each other. A wave of relief ran over Peg's face and she smiled.

'Aw, come here,' she said, hugging Louisa with her free arm. The two of them embraced, the two children clinging to them. Mattie let out a squeal when Ruby grabbed a fistful of his hair and the women stepped back, both of them laughing as they disentangled the baby's fingers from the little boy's curls.

'Welcome home,' said Lucas, shaking hands with Will. 'It's good to see you.'

Will nodded. 'Didn't think we'd be away so long. It's grand to be back at last.'

Peg kissed Lucas's cheek. 'We're glad you're back safe as well, Lucas. Too many lads never made it back. We give thanks every day that you and my brothers got home, and pray for the souls of those who didn't.'

They were all silent for a moment. Louisa knew they were all thinking of Mattie. Her gaze strayed back to little Mattie and she marvelled again at how like his pa he was. If Will hadn't looked so much like his brother, Louisa might have worried that people would take one look at the child and know the truth of it all. But of course, no one would. He would forever be known as Will and Peg's son.

No one had noticed that Kate had slipped away until she called from the kitchen. 'I've made a fresh pot. Who wants tea?'

They all moved towards her voice, Will, Peg and Mattie leading the way. Lucas touched Louisa's arm, halting her. 'All right, love?' he asked softly.

She took a deep breath and nodded. 'I think I am,' she said. 'Part of me wants to grab him and never let go, but then, I can see how much they love him and how happy he is. It's going to be all right, I'm sure.' She kissed his cheek. 'I'm not saying I won't have a wobble now and again,' she whispered in his ear. 'But with your help, it'll all be all right.'

He kissed her hair and nodded. 'Good. I'm always here when you need me. Now, let's go and have a cuppa.'

Peg had clearly been busy, unpacking her kitchen goods, as the room was already in good order. 'This is the only room that's straight at the moment. We slept on mattresses on the floor last night. But at least we can sit here and chat in comfort for now.'

As Kate poured cups of tea, Mattie wriggled, wanting to be put down. As soon as he was free, he began running around the table and the people standing there. 'Brrrmm, brrrmm,' he said, waving his hands in front of him.

Will laughed. 'He loved riding in the lorry to get back here.' George hadn't been able to drive them, but one of the other men from the haulage firm had. 'I swear he'd have demanded to be able to drive if he could have reached the steering wheel.'

Lucas dropped to his haunches. 'Well, maybe the gift we've brought him will get him interested in a different mode of transport. Here, Mattie. What do you think of this?' He took a brightly painted train out of the bag he carried. 'Have you seen a train before?'

Mattie spotted it and stopped in front of Lucas. 'Choo choo!' he said.

Peg nodded and smiled. 'That's right, love. Like in your picture book.' She turned to Louisa with a cup of tea in her hand. 'Can I have a cuddle of Ruby while you drink your tea?' she asked.

For a moment, Louisa's grip on her baby tightened. Memories of handing another baby to Peg overwhelmed her.

'Peg,' said Will softly.

His gentle warning and Peg's contrite expression were enough to bring Louisa back to her senses. This wasn't the same. It was all right. She forced a smile and nodded. 'Of course,' she said. 'But be warned, she's chewing anything she can get into her mouth at the moment, and she's got a fierce bite.'

They laughed as they juggled baby and tea cup, trying not to drop either. Soon Louisa, Peg and Kate were seated at the table while Lucas and Will sprawled on a rag rug on the floor, playing with Mattie and his new train. Peg cooed over Ruby, who basked in her attention.

'Are you all right, Lou?' Kate asked softly.

She dragged her fascinated gaze away from Mattie to smile at Kate. She suspected her friend would recognise that her smile was tinged with sadness, but she didn't want to dwell on what couldn't be changed.

'I am,' she said. She turned to Peg. 'Welcome home, Peg. It's so good to see you all again. I'll never forget the kindness you showed me.' She glanced at Mattie again. 'He's so happy. Thank you for that. It's all I ever wanted for him.'

Peg reached a hand over the table and touched Louisa's. 'It's us who owe you thanks, Louisa. You gave us the most wonderful gift. We're more grateful than we can ever tell you. Is it going to be very difficult for you with us being here?'

She shook her head as she turned her hand and grasped Peg's fingers, realising the truth of it. 'No,' she said firmly. 'This is what I wanted – to see him grow in a happy, loving family. That's the gift you've given me, Peg.'

She sniffed and wiped at her eyes. 'Oh, you. Don't get me going, or I'll cry buckets. I've been so worried about upsetting you by coming back. But now the war's over, all we could think of was returning to Street and our families.'

'I'm glad you're here,' she said, squeezing Peg's hand before letting go of it and sitting back. 'I hope we'll be able to spend time together with the little ones. Ruby hasn't got any cousins yet, although with Jeannie getting married soon, she might have one in a year or so. In the meantime, we've sort of adopted the Davis children as honorary cousins and Mattie's part of the tribe, isn't he?'

Peg nodded. 'They'll be good friends, I'm sure. Ow!'

While they'd been talking, Ruby had been resting on Peg's lap. But now she had pushed herself onto her feet and grabbed at Peg's hair.

'Ruby!' Louisa cried. 'Don't pull her hair.'

Kate, who sat next to Peg, laughed and untangled the baby's fingers from her sister's hair with practised ease. 'She's always doing that to me,' she told Peg. 'Come here, Little Miss Mischief. Come to Auntie Kate.' She pulled Ruby into her arms and kissed her cheek.

'Annie Kay!' Mattie shouted, a scowl on his face. 'Mine!'

Will laughed and cuddled the boy to his chest. 'It's all right, lad. She's everyone's Auntie Kate. You're going to have to learn to share with others now we're here.' He winked at Louisa. 'He's not used to sharing with anyone yet, but he'll soon learn.'

Lucas chuckled at the boy's disgruntled expression. 'Louisa found it hard to share when she went from the splendid isolation of the Clements' home to ours. She's still not sure about having the twins for brothers, but she's getting used to it, aren't you love?'

'I'll never get used the twins,' Louisa confirmed, rolling her eyes. 'But I do like having Jeannie for a sister.'

'And Lucas for a husband,' said Kate, wriggling her eyebrows and grinning.

She blushed and hushed her friend, suddenly worried that Will would think badly of her, marrying his dead brother's best friend. But Will laughed along with the others.

'At least you picked the best of the Musgrove lads,' he teased before his gaze became warmer. 'Our Mattie would be happy to know he's looking after you, lass. We're pleased for you both.'

They spent another half-hour chatting and playing with the children, until Ruby began to grizzle.

'We'd better get her home,' said Lucas. 'Thanks for having us. I know you're busy unpacking and getting settled. We appreciate it.'

'You're welcome any time,' said Will.

Peg nodded her agreement.

Lucas took Ruby to settle her into her pram while Louisa said her goodbyes. Peg had picked up Mattie and came close to kiss Louisa's cheek.

'Don't be a stranger,' she said softly. 'I mean it.' She kissed her again to emphasise the point.

'Tiss, tiss!' said Mattie, his chubby hands grabbing Louisa's face and making kissy noises against her skin.

Louisa was stunned by the child's spontaneous affection. She had spent the past hour watching him, not daring to imagine what it would be like to touch him beyond that brief hold of his hand. But now he had reached for her as though it was the most natural thing in the world. Her son had kissed her!

She blinked and turned her startled gaze to Peg, who smiled through tears.

'It's going to be all right,' she said.

Louisa nodded, unable to speak. Her own eyes were welling up and she didn't want to upset Mattie or his parents by bursting into tears. Instead, she gave them a watery smile and rushed out of the front door to find Lucas waiting for her, Ruby already dozing in her baby carriage.

Kate followed as they began to walk away. 'Lou!' She flung her arms around her. 'I'm so pleased it went well.'

She nodded, sniffing. 'So am I. Thanks, Kate. You were right. Better to do it without fretting.'

Kate touched her cheek, gently wiping away the tears that flowed freely now. 'I'm going to stay and help with some more unpacking. I'll see you soon, all right?'

Lucas put an arm around Louisa's shoulder. 'I'll take care of her. Thanks, Kate. Tell Will to let me know if he needs any help. He said he's got some furniture to build and stuff to shift.'

'I will do, thank you. Bye.'

They were silent as they walked down the road and turned left into the high street in the direction of West End. Louisa pushed the pram while Lucas strode along at her side. Her tears had dried and she felt lighter than she had in years.

'He's the image of Mattie,' he said eventually.

She was afraid to look at him, suddenly terrified that he would take against her because of what she'd done with his friend, whom he'd loved. 'I know,' she said.

'But I could see a likeness between him and Ruby too,' he said, his tone thoughtful. 'They've got your shape eyes, and even though their colouring is the opposite, their curls are identical.'

She shrugged, still not looking at him. 'Both me and Mattie had curls, so I suppose it was inevitable.' Her own waves were usually hidden in a tight bun or plaited, and Mattie's had been kept under control by the barber. When he didn't respond, she risked a glance at him. 'If you'd rather I didn't go round there, you've only to say,' she blurted out.

He frowned and slowed down, putting a hand on the pram handle to stop her from rushing off. 'Lou, don't be daft. I don't know what's going through that head of yours, love, but I'd never stop you seeing them. I regard Will as a friend as well – I've known him all my life. The only reason I'd suggest you stop would be if it were too upsetting for you.' He touched her cheek gently. 'But I think it went well, don't you? You can see he's happy and loved. That's what you wanted, wasn't it?'

'It is,' she said, taking a deep breath. 'And you're right. It went well. I thought I'd be a sobbing mess, that I'd want to scoop him up and run off with him. But I wasn't and I didn't. Because he's happy. Peg and Will love him so much, that's clear. They're a family and I'm happy for them.' She looked up into his kind, concerned face. 'He kissed me,' she said, smiling through the tears that welled again at the memory. 'When Peg kissed me, he wanted to do the same. He pulled my face towards him and kissed me. I never dared hope something like that might happen.'

He smiled and pulled her into a hug. 'I'm happy for you, love,' he said as he kissed her temple. They stood like that for a moment before stepping back, both suddenly aware that they were in the middle of the street.

'Come on,' she said, relief that the meeting she had dreaded had gone so much better than she'd expected making her feel quite light-headed. 'Everyone will be wondering where we are.'

They walked the rest of the way home in companionable silence.

21

It was a shock to see Ted at Sunday communion at Holy Trinity a few weeks after Kate had bumped into him at the asylum. Even though she'd been told he was staying, she hadn't believed it, especially when he hadn't come to see her as she'd hoped he would. She sat lower in her seat, angry with herself. Why would he come to see her, when she'd told him not to? Yet she hadn't been able to deny to herself that she had been sorely disappointed that he had stayed away.

But here he was now, sitting beside his parents in their usual pew near the front, reminding her of days gone by when she'd sat in her usual pew at the back with her ma, knowing that the Jacksons were far above the Davis family in status, given that his pa was a foreman and her pa was a drunken wastrel. Nothing had changed in that respect, so it was just as well she'd told him to leave her alone, she decided. Nothing could come of it. She'd be forever wondering when he was going to disappear out of her life again, and even if he didn't, his ma would have something to say about him taking up with her again.

She averted her gaze from Ted's back, but not before noticing that he no longer had the sling he'd had when she'd seen him last. He seemed to stand straighter than she remembered and his shoulders were broader. He was a man now, one who'd been to war. He wasn't the lad she'd known.

At her side, her nephew George Junior fidgeted, so she reached into her bag and took out a crayon and a piece of paper. She gave it to him with a wink. He took it with a smile and immediately sat on the stone floor between the pews and began drawing something. Over his head, her sister-in-law sent her a grateful smile. She cradled little Katherine on her lap. The toddler cuddled a rag doll that had become her favourite toy and looked like she was going to doze off. On the other side of Ada sat George. He was still thinner than he had been before the war, on account of living on near starvation rations while being forced to work in the prisoner of war camp, but he was looking better every day. Just thinking about how he'd been treated made Kate angry, given that the German prisoners who'd been brought to England had been treated with respect and had been well-fed. She read somewhere that they had reported that their rations in the British camps were better than they'd received when they were fighting in the trenches. She thought it was shameful that this was so, and even more so the treatment her brother had received. She gave thanks that the Allies had won, otherwise they'd all have been ill-treated, no doubt.

The service began and Kate took comfort in the familiar rituals. There had been a time when they'd been too painful for her to bear, when she'd left the church and gone to the Friends' meetings with Auntie Betty. The silent meetings had soothed her soul once she'd got used to them. The only thing she'd missed had been singing hymns. She'd only come back to help Ada with the children while George was away, but now that he was home, she hadn't thought about leaving again.

Her gaze landed on Ted once more and she wondered whether now was the time to go back to the Friends. It would be easier to do that than to see him here whenever he was in Street. She still didn't believe he would stay. He'd been so adamant that he wouldn't return that she couldn't even believe the evidence of her own eyes that he was here now.

As though feeling her fierce gaze, Ted looked around, immediately spotting her in her usual pew. He raised his chin slightly in acknowledgement, a soft smile on his lips. She looked away before she did something silly like smile back at him.

Kate planned to rush off at the end of the service to avoid him, but she needn't have worried. So many people gathered around him to welcome him home that there was no danger of him catching up with her. So she took her time, chatting to her brother and sister-in-law and a few other folks, before slipping outside to make her usual stop at Ma's grave. She wouldn't stay long, just time enough to kiss the tip of her finger and touch it to Ma's name as she always did.

'Kate.'

She turned, startled that Ted was there. 'I thought you'd be busy,' she said. 'Lots of people wanted to talk to you.'

He shrugged. 'I can talk with them any time. It's you I really want to speak to.' He looked at the headstone. 'I'm glad you managed to get her such a fine stone. It's what she deserved.'

Kate's breath caught in her throat. He remembered how much it had meant to her after her pa had refused to pay for a proper marker. 'Thank you,' she said, turning to leave.

'Will you let me walk you home?' he asked.

'It's hardly worth it,' she said, pointing across the churchyard towards The Mead. 'I'm lodging with Mrs Searle these days.'

He nodded. 'I heard. I'm glad. She's a nice lady. Kind, like your ma. I expect you're relieved your pa's finally dead and buried now as well, eh?'

She couldn't help the harsh laugh that escaped her lips. 'You've got that right. We're all well shot of him, and none of us are inclined to mark his resting place like we have Ma's.' No one had any idea how much it meant to her to know that she could walk the streets of the village without fear of encountering Reggie Davis. She gathered her coat around her, suddenly cold despite the heat in her cheeks. 'Anyway, I must be off.'

He put a hand on her arm. 'Kate, please. God knows I don't deserve it, but hear me out, I beg you. Then if you want nothing more to do with me, I'll have to accept it.'

She gave him a sideways glance. 'Do you honestly think you'll be able to explain all these years of silence in the minute or two it will take for us to walk round the corner?'

He gave her that bashful look he'd used to such effect in days gone by and she had to fight not to soften. 'Of course not,' he said. 'I was kind of hoping that you'd invite me in for a cuppa when we got there.'

'Auntie Betty will be back from her meeting soon,' she lied, knowing full well that her landlady was going home with Peg, Will and little Mattie for Sunday lunch. She'd been invited as well, but she'd been round there a lot since they'd got home and thought it only fair to let Auntie Betty enjoy some time on her own with the family.

'It will be nice to see her. I hear Will's back and working at Clarks again. I must catch up with him soon as well.'

She frowned.

'What?' he asked.

'I thought you might have taken against the men who refused to fight. Your ma certainly did.' She shivered as she remembered being confronted by Mrs Jackson when she was with Gerald at the Clothier's house after his release from prison.

He shook his head. 'We all did what we had to in accordance with our consciences,' he said, a shadow passing over his face. 'I'll not judge any man for fear of being judged myself.' He ran a hand through his hair. 'Lord knows, I'm not proud of some of the things I've done in the name of king and country. I'm just relieved it's all over.'

She wanted to ask him about it. Wanted to know where he'd been all these years and how it had changed him – for she could see with her own eyes that it had. Whether the changes were for the good or not, she had no idea. But, would learning anything about Ted help her get over him? All these years she'd avoided getting involved with another lad, guarding her heart with a fierce distain for men and a growing need for independence so that she didn't need to rely on another one for her happiness. She couldn't help thinking that even talking to him for a few minutes would undo all the hard work she'd done to keep herself safe from heartache. But how could she tell him that without revealing the extent to which he'd hurt her?

When she remained silent, he went on. 'The thing I'm least proud of is how I treated you, Kate. I should have been kinder, told you how much I cared for you. But you walked in moments after I'd been through a tough interview with an officer who'd made it clear that the mission they had in mind for me was one they didn't expect me to come back from and that it would be better for me to cut all ties with home without delay. In that moment, I thought it was better that you went away angry with me than to have you wait for me and then have you grieve when I never came home.'

She closed her eyes. What he said made sense. She'd known

he wasn't cruel by nature. 'Don't you realise I've been grieving anyway?' she whispered.

She felt a shift in the air. When she opened her eyes again, he had stepped closer. He gathered her in his arms, not caring that they were in the middle of the churchyard and people were still standing around outside the church door. She thought she ought to protest and push him away, but she couldn't bring herself to do it.

'I know, sweetheart. I read your letter.'

She gasped. So he *had* found it. But if that was the case, he must not care very much about her, or he'd have come to her weeks ago, wouldn't he?

Unaware of her thoughts, he went on. 'Oh Kate, love. I'm so sorry for what I put you through. I've never forgotten you. I've hated myself for the way I treated you and wanted to write to you to tell you, beg for your forgiveness. But I couldn't. Every day, every damned day, I expected to die. But I swear it was the thought of coming back to you that got me through, helped me survive. Tell me it's not too late, my darling. Tell me I've still got a chance.'

She searched his face, torn between believing him and denying that she trust him again. 'Why have you waited all these weeks to talk to me?' she asked.

He sighed. 'I felt so bad about hurting you; I thought you deserved better than me, that I should leave you in peace. But I've missed you so much and it's been even harder since I got back to Street, knowing that you're here. When I saw you this morning, I knew I couldn't stay away any longer. I had to see if there was a chance you could forgive me.'

'You hurt me so much,' she confessed, tears filling her eyes. 'But I'm glad you're back. I prayed every day that you'd be safe, even if you didn't want me.'

He took her face in his hands and lowered his lips to hers in a gentle kiss. 'I *do* want you,' he whispered. 'I never stopped, I swear. Give me a chance, Kate, and I swear I'll never do anything to hurt you again.'

She stiffened. 'You can't promise that. Don't you dare make promises you'll break.'

He rested his forehead against hers, his hands still holding her face. She felt his gentle strength, his touch warming her. 'All right, I won't promise that. But I *will* swear to be honest and faithful to you if you'll just give me another chance. Do you think you can do that?'

She sighed. 'I want to, but I don't know if I can.' Truth be told, she was scared.

He was silent for a moment, not moving. 'Have you got another sweetheart?'

She shook her head. 'No. You know I haven't. I've not been willing to trust my heart to any man.'

Then he sighed too. 'I understand. I realise you've no reason to want me any more. But I'll not give up, I swear, until I've earned your trust again. I came back for you, Kate, and I'll be here waiting for you when you're ready. In the meantime, I hope you'll still be my friend.'

'We're neither of us the same,' she pointed out.

He kissed her forehead and raised his head. 'I know, love. But we're still the same underneath. Let's take the time to get to know each other again. Now the war's over, there's nothing to stop us, is there?'

Without letting herself think about it, because if she did, she would surely turn tail and run away as fast as she could, she moved closer still until they were in each other's arms, her cheek resting against his broad chest. She took a shaky breath. 'All right,' she agreed. 'But can we just be friends for now? I really don't know you any more, Ted, and I'm not the same girl you left behind.'

He sighed. 'If friends is all you're ready for, then friends is what we'll be. But I won't give up hope that one day, we'll be more than that.'

As he held her and kissed her hair, she prayed he wouldn't hurt her again.

'Come on, then,' she said. 'You can walk me home and have that cuppa.'

* * *

At the cottage on The Mead, Kate got busy brewing the tea while Ted sat at the kitchen table watching her. Her movements were stiff because of her nerves and she nearly spilt a whole pint of milk as she transferred some into a jug, but she caught it in time and carefully placed the jug on the table before she dropped it.

'I expect your ma and pa are glad to have you home,' she said.

'They are,' he agreed with a slight grimace. 'Truth be told, it's getting a bit much, all of Ma's fussing. But... with Albert gone and Stan still not right, I suppose it's to be expected.' He sighed. 'But I've spent the last few years living on my wits, not relying on anyone, especially not for the comforts of home.'

She poured the tea and passed him a cup and saucer. He took it with a nod of thanks and added milk.

'We haven't got any sugar, sorry,' she said. 'With the shortages, we've trained ourselves not to put it in our drinks, and Auntie used the last of what we had to make a cake to take round to Will and Peg. She's so happy they're home at last, it's only natural she wants to spoil them a little. A bit like how your ma is with you, I suppose.'

'That's all right,' he said with a smile. 'I went for months at a time without a decent brew, let alone any sugar.' He took a sip. 'This is perfect.'

They drank their tea in silence for a few minutes, each casting furtive glances at the other, noting the subtle differences that the years had wrought. Eventually, Kate couldn't help but ask the question that had been burning inside her.

'The Howard lad wrote months back and told his ma he'd seen you,' she said. 'Is it true?'

Mrs Howard, a bully of a woman who worked in the Machine Room had delighted in telling Kate that Ted had been seen with a local woman and had pretended to be French. The woman had concluded that Ted had deserted and was a coward. Kate hadn't believed that for a moment and Ted's father had confirmed it by revealing that his son was working in a special unit behind the lines.

He looked down at his drink. 'It is,' he said.

She'd thought it was so, because of what Mrs Howard had said about her lad recognising Ted's laugh. She hadn't heard that since he'd returned and she realised she missed it.

'He said you were with a woman,' she said, wishing she hadn't brought it up when an emotion that looked a lot like pain transformed his expression.

'Paulette,' he said. 'We worked together. She reminded me of you.'

She studied him, trying to work out what that meant. His gaze was clear as he looked back at her, but it was tinged with sadness. 'You were fond of her,' she concluded.

He sighed and scrubbed at his face. 'I was,' he admitted. 'She was brave and fierce and she saved my life more than once.'

Kate felt guilty that she felt hot jealousy of this unknown woman when she also gave thanks that she had helped to keep

Ted alive. 'Will you keep in touch with her now that you're home?'

He looked down at his hands on the table and shook his head. 'She's dead,' he said, his voice flat and defeated. 'Someone betrayed her and she was taken by the Hun. They tortured her but she never told them a thing. In the end, they executed her.'

'Oh God, that's awful,' she whispered, her guilt growing as she thought about Paulette's fate. 'That poor woman. Do you know who betrayed her?'

He nodded, his expression grim. 'I do. And I made sure they paid the price for their treachery.'

He didn't say it, but she knew in her bones that he had killed the traitor. She should be horrified, but she refused to judge him. He had been fighting in a war. Who knew what anyone would do in the circumstances? She sometimes wished she'd had the strength and courage to fight back when the Floozy had attacked her. Maybe if she had, she might have killed her. As it was, the woman's own husband had done that.

'I heard you defended me,' he said, clearly wanting to change the subject.

She huffed. 'Of course I did. Mrs Howard was implying that you'd deserted. I knew you'd never, so I spoke up.'

He nodded. 'I appreciate it, especially after the way I treated you. I wouldn't have blamed you if you'd let her carry on spreading her poison.'

Kate shrugged. He should know that she couldn't abide gossips, and she wasn't about to let her get away with it when Ted hadn't been there to defend himself. But mention of the incident raised more questions in her mind.

'Your pa said you were fighting with a special unit,' she said. 'Can you tell me about it now?'

He put down his cup and laced his fingers together on the

table. She wanted to reach out and hold his hands, but she was still trying to work out whether she could trust him with her heart so she stayed where she was and waited for him to gather his thoughts.

'I can't tell you much, because I had to sign something relating to the Official Secrets Act,' he said eventually. 'So what I do tell you, you'll need to keep under your hat. Is that all right?'

She nodded, even though she wasn't sure he should be telling her anything.

'Do you remember Pierre, the Belgian lad?' he asked.

'Yea, I do. The refugee who was teaching you French and Dutch.' She frowned, remembering. 'He disappeared about the same time you did.'

'That's because we were recruited together.'

'Oh. Did they let refugees enlist, then?'

'Not with the regular British army,' he said. 'But some formed their own platoons under the regulation of our generals; and others, like Pierre and me, were drafted into special units.'

'That man who you met outside the factory – the one you said was Pierre's uncle. Is that who he really was?'

Ted nodded. 'He was, actually. But he was also quite high up in the Belgian government in exile. He was a liaison officer between them and the British authorities. When Pierre told him about me and how quickly I'd been picking up the languages he was teaching me, his uncle thought I'd be just the type of man they were looking for. When he met me, he chatted to me in French, then he'd switch to Dutch, and he would act like he couldn't understand English, so I had to answer him in kind. He was testing to see if I could think on my feet... and whether I could pass muster as a Frenchman or a Belgian.'

'Oh my lord,' she said, covering her mouth with her hand as the realisation hit her. She'd suspected it for a long time, but now she was sure. 'He made you become a spy, didn't he? In return for Stan's life.' She remembered that the poor lad had lost his mind in the trenches after witnessing the death of their older brother, Albert. Ted had told her that there was a chance that the army would execute Stan for cowardice. After Ted had signed up, Stan had been transferred to an asylum rather than face a firing squad.

'Pretty much,' Ted agreed.

'And your parents let him, even after he said it was a suicide mission?' she demanded, outraged.

He shook his head. 'No one mentioned how dangerous it would be to Ma and Pa. I told them not to, although I'm sure Pa worked it out. And anyway, it wasn't Pierre's uncle that told me how dangerous it was. Pierre hinted at it, trying to give the chance to back out. He was set to go because it was his home and his freedom he was fighting for, but he didn't think I should be expected to put my life on the line like that. But the major who came to the house didn't beat about the bush when he spoke to me privately. He said I had a talent for languages that made me valuable to the war effort and they'd teach me the skills I needed for the rest of it. He made it clear I wasn't likely to survive longer than a month or so, but he said my mission might help shorten the war.' He scoffed. 'But, of course, he was wrong on both fronts.'

She closed her eyes, trying in vain to stop the tears that threatened to flow. 'So he was willing to send you to your death, and blackmail you to agree to it by holding your brother's fate over your head?' She opened her eyes and glared at him. 'Oh, Ted! Why didn't you tell me? Why did you let me think you were tired of me?'

He reached across the table for her then, wiping her tears with gentle fingers. 'Don't cry, Katie, love. I'm home now because of you. I had to tell you that back then – the major insisted I break all ties – but I never meant it, not in a million years. But the thought of coming back to you, of getting the chance to explain and maybe be forgiven, that's what's kept me alive all these years.'

She grasped his wrists as he held her face in his hands. 'Was it as awful as we've been told?' she asked.

He closed his eyes and nodded slowly, his expression full of sadness. 'It was. I've seen and done things, Kate, that I'm not sure I can ever forgive or forget. But it's over now. I've left the army, although they asked me to stay on. I'm done with it all. I want to live my life in peace now. If you're willing to give me a chance, I hope we can have a future together.' He sighed as he looked at her again, rubbing his thumbs across her cheekbones, wiping away the tears that continued to flow. 'I'm not the same man I was. I've seen too much, done too much to ever be that daft lad again. But underneath it all, my heart still belongs to you if you want it. Can we take some time to get to know each other again, see how we get along?'

She searched his expression, wanting to trust him, yet afraid. He had more power than he realised. He could hurt her so badly if he decided that he didn't want her after all.

'I'm not the same, either,' she said. 'I've got plans, dreams. I won't be held back or held down by anyone. Can you accept that, Ted? Or will you turn into every other man around here and expect me to give up my dreams to look after home and family while you're following *your* dreams?'

'Yes, Kate, I can accept that. I didn't spend the past years fighting for freedom to come home and take yours away, love. You're taking evening classes, aren't you? Learning the skills to give you a chance of a different job, right?'

She nodded. 'I'm taking my exams in the summer term. If I pass, I could transfer to the office.'

'Well, we're more alike than you think. I'm working as an assistant teacher over in Wells, to see how I get on. That's why I haven't been around much, and they've agreed to take me on and to sponsor me to go to college in the Autumn to get my teaching certificate. But I've got a lot of catching up to do before then. We'll both be studying hard, learning our new jobs, but it will be worth it, won't it? Working at Clarks was fine when I was younger and dafter, but I want something different now. It might not be better, but I've got to give it a try.'

'I don't mind carrying on working at Clarks,' she said. 'But I'd rather work in the offices. The Machine Room's not the same with Louisa already gone and Jeannie finishing when she gets married at Easter.'

He smiled. 'Everyone's getting wed, eh? I never expected Lucas and Louisa to get together, but there they are, married and with a baby already.'

Kate sighed. 'They both missed Mattie so much, it brought them together,' she said. She didn't mention anything else. Now that Peg and Will were back in the village with little Mattie, the fewer people who knew the truth of the little boy's birth, the better. Ted could probably be trusted to keep the secret – after all, he'd been living a whole secret life for the past few years – but she couldn't tell him without permission from the people involved.

He nodded. 'I met Jeannie and her man in the high street. He seems a good sort.'

'He is. They've been through some difficult times, but they're happy now, thank God.'

'And that leaves you and me, doesn't it, Katie? Will you give us a chance to see if we can be happy together?'

He looked so hopeful, his eyes shining as he gazed at her. She was still clinging to his wrists as his hands cradled her face. After the abuse she'd received at her pa's hands, she usually avoided any physical contact with men, but she felt safe with Ted and she relished his touch. Even though she was terrified that he'd break her heart, she was equally afraid that if she turned him away now, she would regret it for the rest of her life.

She took a shaky breath and blew it out. 'All right, Ted. I'll give you a chance. But I want us to be friends first, mind. I won't rush into anything with you because I'm still not sure I can trust you.'

'I swear—'

'Don't!' She pulled her hands away. 'I told you, I can't accept any promises from you, Ted. And anyway, actions speak louder than words, don't they? We'll be friends for now and see how we get along. That's all I can offer you right now. Take it or leave it.'

'I'll take it,' he said without hesitation.

22

'This is the happiest day of my life,' said Jeannie. One she thought she'd never see. She had been so nervous in the days leading up to her Easter wedding, more so yesterday when she'd met Tom's family from Northampton for the first time. But they had been so kind and friendly, welcoming her into the family, that her fears had turned to excitement. Her wedding day had dawned bright and clear, reflecting how she saw her and Tom's future.

Tom held her in his arms, a proud smile on his face as he gazed at his bride. 'You look beautiful,' he said. 'I'm a lucky man. I can hardly believe I'm going to be able to spend the rest of my life with you.'

Jeannie blushed as he kissed her cheek, aware that the eyes of everyone in the Friends' Meeting House were upon them. 'It was lovely, what everyone said, wasn't it?' Like when Lucas and Louisa had married, many of their family and friends had stood and shared their good wishes and reminiscences during the ceremony. 'I know your family aren't used to Quaker weddings, but your pa's words were so nice.'

Her new father-in-law had talked about his family's delight that their beloved son had found love and happiness here in Street after the heartache of the war years. No mention had been made of his previous marriage. Lucas had spoken too, welcoming Tom into the family and wishing them well. Ma had cried happy tears, which had nearly set off Jeannie.

Tom nodded. 'I told them about your brother's wedding, so they knew what to expect.'

Jeannie was relieved that his family hadn't disapproved of his change of faith from Methodist to Quaker when he'd moved to Street. 'We all worship the same God,' his ma had told her. 'The important thing is that he's happy.'

Louisa approached with Ruby on her hip. 'Jeannie, love' – she kissed her cheek – 'have either of you eaten anything? I remember at my wedding, I was so busy talking to people that I forgot and nearly fainted with hunger by the end of the day.'

Jeannie and Tom shared an amused smile. 'We have,' he told her. 'Both Jeannie's ma and mine have brought us plates of sandwiches and cakes.'

'But thank you for thinking of us,' said Jeannie. 'I confess I've been too excited to eat much, but Ma made me.' She felt her cheeks warm again. 'She said we need to keep our strength up.'

Louisa giggled and leaned close to whisper in her ear. 'I heard she gave you the same talk she gave Lucas the night before our wedding. Don't fret about it, love. Tom'll know what to do. Just try to relax and enjoy it.'

That made her whole face flame and she looked away when Tom asked her if she was all right. 'We've been lucky with the weather, haven't we?' she said, her voice pitched a little higher than usual as she tried to change the subject before she died of embarrassment right there in front of everyone. She was equal parts excited and terrified about her wedding night but she wasn't about to discuss it with anyone, not even her new husband, in the middle of the Friends' Meeting House.

Taking pity on her, Louisa nodded. 'Happy the bride that the sun shines on.' She smiled.

Kate joined them and kissed Jeannie on her cheek. 'Congratulations, Jeannie. I wanted to say it earlier, but couldn't get close enough to talk to you. You look beautiful, love.' She looked up at Tom. 'You're a lucky man, you know that, don't you?'

He grinned, his hand squeezing Jeannie's shoulder. 'I am,' he agreed.

'Annie Kay! Annie Lou!' Little Mattie ran up and grabbed onto Kate's skirts.

'There's our big boy,' said Kate, picking him up. 'Oof, have you eaten all the cake? I swear you're growing so fast, I can hardly lift you.' She pretended to scold him. 'No more treats for Mattie.'

'Oh, hush,' said Louisa, reaching out to a plate on the table beside them and picking up two sweet biscuits. She gave one to Mattie and the other to Ruby. 'Here, sweetheart.' She winked at Mattie. 'Don't take any notice of Auntie Kate.'

'Ta.' Mattie beamed. He took a big bite and grinned at Kate, who laughed at his cheek.

The children munched happily on their treats while the grown-ups chatted.

'Where's Ted?' Jeannie asked Kate. She knew that the two of them had come to the wedding together.

Kate inclined her head towards the other side of the meeting room. 'He's talking to Lucas and Peter about Tom's projects. I think he'd like to help if he can.'

Tom looked across at the lads. 'I'm sure we can find something for him to do. We're keeping pretty busy with it these days.'

'It's just as well he's got a workshop at the end of the garden,'

Jeannie said. 'Otherwise I think they'd drive me mad with all the work they're doing.'

'Well, Ted wants to see it, but I've told him and the others they're not to disturb you when you've only just got wed.' Kate rolled her eyes. 'Lads haven't a clue about giving a couple some privacy.'

This time, it was Tom who blushed. 'I'll... er, just pop over and have a chat with them,' he said, kissing Jeannie's cheek. 'And leave you ladies to embarrass my bride a bit more.'

Jeannie laughed and slapped his arm. 'Oh you! Go on then.'

She watched him walk across the room. His limp was hardly noticeable these days. His progress was only slow because people kept stopping him, shaking his hand and congratulating him. He accepted their good wishes politely, smiling the smile of a man well pleased with his life.

Louisa nudged her shoulder with her own and Jeannie looked away, bashful about being caught staring. Her friends laughed.

'Don't be embarrassed, Jeannie,' said Kate. 'He's your husband now. You're entitled to stare at him.'

'You've got yourself a handsome one there, love,' said Louisa. 'Why wouldn't you stare?'

'I know,' she sighed. 'I can't believe my luck.'

'Well, as happy as I am for you,' said Kate, 'I'm not sure I can forgive both of you for leaving me on my own in the Machine Room.'

Mattie wriggled, demanding to be put down. Kate lowered him to his feet and Ruby wailed as the little boy ran off towards Peg and Will.

'Aw, don't cry, Ruby, love,' said Jeannie, taking her from Louisa's arms and spinning her around. 'I know you want to run after him, especially now you've found your feet. But you're still too little to be running around with all these grown-ups wandering around. Someone will be sure to tread on you.'

The child frowned at her aunt, pouting, but stopped wailing as her interest was caught by the sight of Mrs Musgrove, who was sitting nearby, chatting to Tom's ma and pa. She reached out her arms towards her grandmother, nearly pulling Jeannie off balance.

'Go on then,' said Louisa, plucking her from Jeannie's arms and putting her down close to Ma. 'Go and see Nanna.'

Ma looked over as Ruby toddled towards her, her face lighting up with delight at the sight of her granddaughter rushing towards her on wobbly legs. The three friends smiled as she reached her and Ma and Jeannie's new in-laws started to fuss over the little one.

'Aw, bless her,' said Jeannie. 'I can't believe Ruby's nearly a year old already. I'm going to miss not being there every day to see her grow. She's learning something new every day, isn't she?'

Louisa chuckled. 'You'll still be seeing her often enough. If you don't come round to us, we'll be round to see you, you can count on it. We're only a few minutes' walk away, after all.'

'It's going to be strange, not having to go back to work after the Easter weekend,' said Jeannie. 'I know it's what I wanted, but it'll take some getting used to.' Even if she'd wanted to stay on at work, Clarks weren't so keen on employing married women since the war ended. The men had come back to claim their jobs, and most of the married women had been let go. The only ones who kept their jobs were those who had been widowed or abandoned and needed to work to support themselves and their children.

She noticed that Kate was quiet. She felt bad when she realised her friend was probably feeling left out, with both her and Louisa now married. 'I hope you get someone nice taking over my machine,' she told her. The lass who'd taken over from Louisa was pleasant enough, but quite a lot younger than them, so they didn't feel they had a lot in common with her. Jeannie remembered what it had been like when she'd started at Clarks at fourteen. The intervening years, with the losses and hardships of war, seemed like a lifetime.

Kate huffed. 'I'm not bothered. Whoever it is, it won't be the same. I'll concentrate on my evening classes and, with any luck, I'll be able to transfer to the office soon. I've already spoken to personnel and they've noted my interest.'

'Oh, are you still going after another job?' asked Louisa. 'I thought you might be changing your plans now you and Ted are back together.'

Kate rolled her eyes. 'Why does everyone assume I'll give up my dreams, just because I'm letting a lad pay me attention?'

Louisa frowned. 'But I thought you were happy about being with Ted,' she said. 'Don't you want to be with him?'

She sighed. 'Of course I do. It's just... we're still working it out, you know, seeing whether we're a good fit or not. He's not the same lad he used to be, and I'm different as well. We're getting along all right, but... I'm not ready to just throw away everything I'm working for. I mean, what if we get sick of each other one day soon and he goes off again? I'd end up in the Machine Room forever if I place all my faith in him and he lets me down again.'

'Oh Kate, love,' said Jeannie, touching her arm. 'He'll not let you down, I'm sure. You know he didn't want to last time, but he had to, didn't he?'

'He's not going anywhere without you, Kate,' said Louisa. 'He's as smitten with you as he was before, it's plain to see.' She grinned. 'And you're just as bad.'

Rather than argue, Kate chuckled. 'All right, I admit I'm glad he's back. But I hate that everyone assumes that means I'm going to stop trying to do things for myself. I told him I won't tolerate it, and thank God, he's all right about that. After all, he's busy training to be a teacher, so why shouldn't I learn new skills?'

'But, don't you want children?' asked Jeannie.

She shrugged. 'Eventually, I suppose. But we're only friends. We're not even courting.' She huffed out a laugh. 'His ma would be horrified if we were. She's still not forgiven me for being Gerald's friend, even though Ted has no problem with it.' The conscientious objector had finally been released from prison in February, and Kate and Ted had travelled to Bristol for a day with Auntie Betty to see him. The two men, although different, got on quite well. She pulled a face. 'But I suppose the worst thing in her eyes is that I'm Reggie Davis's daughter.'

Jeannie shook her head. 'That's plain daft. You're your ma's daughter, which is far more important. She was the sweetest, kindest lady. You're nothing like your pa.'

Kate gave her a sideways look and smirked. 'I'm hardly regarded as sweet and kind like Ma, either. I'm far too outspoken for that.'

'You're your own person,' said Louisa firmly. 'But you also have your ma's qualities and good heart. Ted can see that. That alone should be enough for his ma.'

Jeannie nodded in agreement, even as Kate shook her head.

'The point is,' said Kate, 'that me and Ted haven't made any plans for the future together, other than getting to know each other again.'

'Yet,' Louisa pointed out.

Kate narrowed her eyes at her. 'Yet,' she agreed. 'But in the meantime, I'm not in any rush to settle down and give up my freedom. Remember, I've spent the past few years determined to remain a spinster, so I need some time to adjust to the idea that me and Ted might end up like the rest of you.'

'It's put poor Peter's nose out of joint, seeing you with Ted,' said Louisa. They looked across the room to see Peter glaring at Ted.

Kate sighed. 'Even if Ted hadn't come back, I wouldn't have been with Peter. If he lets that get in the way of him working with Ted on the projects, then someone needs to have words with him.'

Louisa nodded. 'I'll get Lucas to have a quiet chat with him.'

'Thank you,' said Kate. 'And in the meantime, will you all please stop trying to rush me and Ted into something I'm not ready for? And can we talk about something else now? Like how scrumptious little Ruby is in that sweet little pink dress?' She grinned.

Jeannie could understand why Kate was hesitating, protecting herself by remaining as fiercely independent as possible. But if anyone could change her mind, it would be Ted. It was obvious that he adored her, and she hoped that one day, her friend would realise the strength of his feelings and accept that her future lay with him.

'I can't wait to have a baby,' said Jeannie softly, her gaze on Ruby, who was being fussed over by Ma and Tom's ma. 'But I'm not looking forward to giving birth after seeing what you went through, Lou.'

Kate pulled a face, but Louisa smiled and shook her head. 'I won't lie, it hurts like the devil,' she said, following Jeannie's gaze. 'But it's worth it.' She glanced around before she turned back to her friends and leaned in, the way they always did in the factory to avoid letting anyone lip read what they were saying. 'In fact, I think I'm expecting again,' she whispered.

Jeannie squealed and hugged her sister-in-law. 'Why didn't you say?'

Louisa laughed. 'It's early days yet, and anyway, I didn't want to steal your thunder on your wedding day. Now you and Tom need to get on with it so our babies can grow up together.'

Again, Jeannie felt her cheeks warm at the thought of what she and Tom needed to do to make a baby. She couldn't think about it with so many people around at her wedding breakfast, but she felt her heart flutter at the knowledge that soon, she would be sharing a bed with her husband and finally learning about married love. She wasn't afraid, not really – even though she'd heard that the first time could be painful when the man broke through the woman's barrier. But she would gladly go through that because she was keen to go beyond the toe-curling kisses and caresses she and Tom had shared in recent months.

'Well good luck,' said Kate. 'I'm happy for both of you. But I'll not be rushing to catch up with you. I'll be content to be Auntie Kate to all your babies and I'll think about having my own when I'm good and ready – if I ever am.'

'Fair enough,' said Louisa. 'Motherhood's not for everyone.'

Jeannie wondered whether she was thinking about her own mother's coldness in recent years, or maybe the Floozy, who was the worst example of motherhood any of them had ever come across.

Lucas came to stand beside his wife. 'You told them, didn't you?' he said. 'Even though you insisted you wouldn't today.' He didn't look cross about it.

Lou glanced at him and at Tom and Ted, who stood behind him. 'And you told your friends, didn't you?' she said archly.

He grinned. 'I did.'

'Congratulations, Lou,' said Ted, moving to Kate's side, sliding an arm around her shoulders and kissing her cheek. 'We've got some catching up to do,' he said.

Kate huffed. 'It's not a race, Ted Jackson. You just hold your horses. I'm in no rush, thank you very much.'

The others laughed at his crestfallen expression before he grinned. 'I love a challenge,' he said, winking at her.

'It's great news,' Tom said to Louisa as he claimed his bride again and smiled down at her. He leaned in to whisper, 'We'd better get a move on, eh?'

* * *

Jeannie and Tom left their guests to continue the party, the bride blushing like mad as they took their leave and walked back along the high street. It seemed strange for Jeannie to turn right into Cranhill Road instead of continuing along to West End, although she'd been looking forward to it ever since Tom had told her he'd bought the house.

They didn't speak as they walked, although Jeannie clung to his arm and they exchanged smiles and she giggled a little as they went. Tom didn't seem to mind, covering her hand on his arm with his, his gaze on her so full of longing that she blushed.

'You're not going to pick me up, are you?' she asked as they approached the front door of the house.

He grinned. 'Of course I am. It's the law.'

'It is not,' she laughed, slapping his hand.

He gave an exaggerated sigh and let his shoulders slump as he took the key out of his pocket. 'All right,' he said, sounding disappointed as he unlocked the door and pushed it open. But before Jeannie could step inside, he turned and swooped her up, making her squeal as he carried her over the threshold. By the time he put her down, they were both laughing hard.

'Welcome home, wife,' he said, touching her cheek.

'Welcome home, husband,' she said, smiling up at him before she reached up and kissed him.

23

Even though the weather improved after Easter, and the community's mood was joyful as more men arrived home from the war, there was an underlying worry as some of them came home with nasty coughs and sneezes. Spanish Flu, they called it, although by all accounts it was spreading like wildfire across Europe and beyond as millions of people moved around the globe. It didn't take long for the soldiers' families and friends to catch it from them and for it to spread throughout Street. This influenza seemed stronger than any they'd seen before and it soon began to take its toll.

Clarks struggled to keep up production as more workers fell sick and couldn't work. It hit close to home at the Musgrove cottage when their neighbour Mr Baker fell ill along with his grandson Cyril, who had caught the flu from a child in his class at the board school. Mr Baker's advanced years and Cyril's chronic asthma meant that both of them suffered greatly, but it was still a shock when both men died within days of each other.

Worried, Louisa kept Ruby away from other children and scrubbed the Musgrove cottage with disinfectant in an effort to keep the germs at bay. She didn't want her child or her mother-in-law catching the flu.

'You mustn't overdo it,' said Jeannie, who had come round to help her. 'You've got the new baby to think about.'

Louisa wiped her forehead, hoping that she was hot from working hard rather than the high temperature that accompanied the other symptoms of influenza that had been reported. 'I know. I'm being careful,' she said. 'But I'm more worried about Ruby and your ma. After Mr Baker and Cyril...' She shivered as she remembered how when he'd first become ill, Mr Baker had insisted on sitting in his garden to get some fresh air after the government had issued advice that it was likely to encourage recovery. The poor man had slumped in his garden chair, coughing and wheezing until he could be persuaded to go inside. That had been awful, but it had been worse when he'd stopped coming out of doors, too ill to leave his bed. It had all happened so quickly. From the day Cyril had come home from the school, wheezing and sneezing and red-faced from his high temperature, to the deaths of both men, had been less than a fortnight.

Jeannie nodded, as concerned as Louisa was. 'Let me finish off scrubbing this floor while you put your feet up, love.'

Louisa was thankful to hand over the bucket and scrubbing brush. This pregnancy was exhausting her, especially with Ruby walking now. The whole Musgrove family needed eyes in the back of their heads to keep track of the little minx – she didn't stay still unless she was eating or sleeping. Although she was sleeping through the night now as all that running around wore the little girl out. That meant Louisa got a decent night's rest at least.

She sank into a chair at the kitchen table and chatted to Jeannie as she finished scrubbing the flagstone floor. In the parlour, Ruby was still for a moment while her grandmother showed her a picture book that Louisa had borrowed from the library in Crispin Hall. She could hear Ruby's excited voice as she recognised chickens and pigs and other farmyard animals and she clucked and oinked and made other appropriate noises, just like her uncles had taught her. Louisa smiled to herself. The twins loved to play with Ruby, and delighted in making her giggle or make rude noises.

'There, that's done,' said Jeannie, standing up and rubbing her back. She picked up the bucket and emptied it into the drain outside the kitchen door. 'The twins better not come in with muddy boots after all our hard work.'

'Thanks, Jeannie,' she said. 'I don't know whether it's running after Ruby or this new baby, but I'm like a wet rag these days.'

Jeannie smiled. 'She wears everyone out. It's just as well she likes to sit with Ma with her picture books. It gives us all a break.'

Louisa chuckled. 'I know. Actually, those books have given me an idea. She kicks up such a fuss when it's time for them to go back to the library, that I'm thinking about using my art supplies and making picture books so that she's got some to keep.' They had to watch every penny these days since Louisa gave up work before Ruby was born and then Jeannie had moved out when she married Tom. Lucas was the main bread-winner and the twins handed over some of their wages, but losing two incomes in as many years made it difficult to pay the bills. She realised that having another baby so soon wasn't going to help.

'That's a good idea,' said Jeannie. 'You're so good at art. Tom and I love the painting you did for us as a wedding present.' It was a beautiful view of the Chalice Well gardens near Glastonbury Tor. She tilted her head to one side, looking thoughtful. 'In fact, we've both said that you could sell your art.'

'Funny you should say that,' she said. 'Lucas and I have talked about it. I've got lots of watercolours, mainly local views, some flowers and wildlife. He thought he could frame them and maybe we could take them to a market and see whether people like them.'

It had all started when Mattie had bought her some art supplies for her birthday. During the war, she had sent her small pictures as gifts to Lucas and other lads they knew in the trenches as mementoes of home.

'If you made picture books for children as well, and maybe some greetings cards, you could make a pretty penny without even leaving home.'

'Mmm. It's worth a try, isn't it? If I do as much as I can before this baby arrives, I'll have stock available to sell even when I'm nursing.'

'Me and Ma can help you with the children. You just need some space to work where little fingers won't spoil all your efforts.'

Louisa sighed. 'Do you really think I could do it, Jeannie? I know people like it when I give them drawings or paintings, but maybe they were just being kind. I can't imagine that anyone would be willing to pay for them. But some extra pennies coming in would certainly make a difference.'

'They're not being kind. You're a good artist. It's worth a try, isn't it?' she said. 'Remember how much people appreciated your little postcards of local views that they could send to the soldiers during the war? Everyone loved them, so I'm sure they'd like to buy a bigger version or another view from you now. But maybe the market isn't the place to sell them. Why don't you ask at the shop where you get your art supplies? They might know of a gallery or a shop that might sell them for you. You'd get a better price there.'

Lou had found that the best place to buy her paints and

drawing pencils was a shop in Wells. It meant a bus ride to go and buy them, but she didn't mind that – it was a nice day out.

'Mmm. I haven't been there for months. I've been using up the supplies I have rather than spend more money. But I suppose I could visit and ask them. I know they do display some art for sale, although whether they'd be interested in my little efforts I have no idea. Maybe I should write to them first, see what they say.'

'Good idea. Then if they are, you can take some of your framed pictures to show them.'

Louisa nodded. 'I shall. It doesn't sit well with me, not working and contributing to the family.'

'Of course you contribute,' Jeannie scoffed. 'You run the home, look after Ma and Ruby, feed everyone. Don't ever think you're not doing a valuable job.'

She laughed. 'Now you're sounding like Kate. Are you turning into a suffragette, Jeannie?'

'I may not be as fierce as Kate about a woman's right to vote and decide her own future, but I do agree with a lot of what the women's movement are saying. I'm quite looking forward to being able to vote one day.'

'Me too. Before the war, I never expected it to happen. But now that women over thirty have been granted the vote, maybe the rest of us will get it soon. After all, it was only a few months after parliament finally agreed to allow some women to vote that they passed a law so that women could even become MPs.'

Jeannie pulled a face. 'I wouldn't want to be in government. I'm happy to leave that to the men.'

It had gone quiet in the parlour, so Louisa got up to check. She smiled when she saw her mother-in-law and daughter cuddled up and snoozing on the settee. Jeannie came up behind her in the doorway.

'Aw,' she whispered. 'Bless 'em.'

'Let's leave them to it and have a quiet cuppa,' said Louisa. 'After all, once that little madam wakes up, there'll be no peace for anyone.'

* * *

Ruby was wide awake by the time her pa arrived home from work. He greeted her with a distracted smile before he turned to his wife.

'Will wasn't at work today,' he told her, 'and when I saw Kate just now, she said Peg's got the flu.'

Louisa felt a shiver run down her spine. 'Oh no. I noticed she had a bad cough at the meeting on Sunday. I hope she gets better soon. She'll recover, won't she? I mean, she's healthy, not like Cyril or old like Mr Baker.' She paused. 'But what about Mattie?'

He put an arm around her shoulders. 'I know. Kate's going round to see what she can do to help. Auntie Betty too. They're worried about Will missing work to look after Peg. They've still got to pay the rent. If he misses work, they'll be in trouble.'

'But Kate and Mrs Searle both need to work as well. Maybe I should offer to go and look after Peg while Will's at work?' After everything that she and Will had done to help Louisa when she was desperate, it felt like the least she could do.

Lucas shook his head. 'I don't think that's a good idea, darling. You're expecting and we've got Ma and Ruby to consider.'

She sighed. 'I suppose so. I just want to help. I owe them so much.'

'I know, love. Look, why don't we talk to Kate and arrange to send some food round so that they can have a decent meal? You don't have to be there and put yourself at risk to help them.'

She nodded. 'All right. I can always cook extra, stretch some meals out with more vegetables from the garden so there's plenty for everyone. But if there's anything else we can do, you must tell Will to let us know.'

'I will.'

* * *

Over the weekend, Louisa heard that Auntie Betty had taken little Mattie to stay at her cottage while Kate and her sisters-in-law helped Will to look after Peg. Everyone hoped that she would rally, but on Sunday evening, Lucas opened the door to Mrs Searle, who carried a sleepy Mattie in her arms.

'I'm sorry to bother you,' she said. 'But Katie said you'd offered, and I wondered if you would be kind enough to look after this little man for a while? Poor Peg is proper poorly and they've sent for the doctor. Kate's been there all weekend and I want to be there for them all.'

Lucas stepped back, gesturing for her to come in. 'Of course. I'm sorry Peg's suffering. Let's hope the doctor can help. Here, let me take him.'

She passed the child to him, together with a bag of his clothes and toys. Little Mattie snuggled against Lucas's chest and he felt the pang he always did when he looked at Louisa and Mattie's child. It provoked mixed emotions in him – grief that his beloved friend had missed seeing his son grow up and that Louisa had suffered so, having to give him up, coupled with gratitude and guilt that he had had the chance to make a life with Louisa in Mattie's place.

Louisa came out of the kitchen with Ma and he quietly explained what Mrs Searle had told him.

'Of course we'll look after him,' said Ma. 'Now don't you

worry, Betty. We can keep him here as long as you need. Ruby will be delighted to see him when she wakes up, won't she, Louisa?'

Louisa nodded and gave her a reassuring smile. The poor woman looked so worried.

As Mrs Searle thanked them and took her leave with the Musgrove family's good wishes, Lucas caught Louisa's eye. She had become used to seeing the little boy over the past few months – both at the Friends' Meeting House and on visits between her and Peg with both of the children. But it was still hard for her and this was the first time that the boy had been here without Will and Peg.

'Poor Peg,' said Ma, shaking her head. 'It doesn't sound good, does it?'

'I hope she's all right,' said Louisa, reaching out and putting a gentle hand on Mattie's back. 'This little man needs his ma.'

* * *

Despite being tired, Louisa barely slept, knowing that her son was sleeping under her roof. She couldn't rejoice in it though, as it was only because Peg was so gravely ill that he was here. She loved her like a sister and was forever in her debt for the kindness and generosity she had shown Louisa after her parents had refused to help her.

Peg had proved to be the perfect mother for little Mattie and it worried Louisa that this Spanish Flu, which was taking so many people in the aftermath of the war, might take Peg too. That set Louisa to worrying about whether Will would succumb as well.

Lucas turned over in bed and sighed. 'Have you managed to get any sleep?' he asked softly.

She turned her head to see him looking at her in the moonlight coming in through the window. Lucas liked to leave the curtains open a little so that he awoke when the sun came up. 'No,' she said. 'I'm so worried about Peg. Kate must be beside herself, and I can't imagine how Will's feeling.'

He pulled her into his arms, holding her close. 'Try not to worry, love.' He kissed her temple. 'We'll keep the lad safe so they can concentrate on helping Peg get better.'

'But what if Will gets it as well? Mattie could lose them both. I don't want that for him.' She felt her fear rise; she felt so helpless. 'What would become of him then?'

'Hush now,' he soothed her with his hands and lips. 'Peg will get better, I'm sure. Don't fret so, love. It's not good for the baby, and you don't want to frighten little Mattie when he wakes up, do you?'

She sighed, trying to relax. He was right. She was probably worrying about nothing. But she couldn't stop herself. She buried her face into his neck and clung to him until sleep finally claimed her.

24

The flu epidemic showed no signs of abating as the summer arrived. Millions were dying across the world. It was said that one in four people in Great Britain had caught the disease and thousands were succumbing to it. After a week of debilitating influenza, Peg developed pneumonia and her condition worsened. Will was beside himself, having to rely on others to look after her while he worked all hours to find the money for the medicines prescribed, even after he received an anonymous donation to help through the Elders at the Friends' Meeting House. She remained at home because the doctor said she was safer there – the hospitals and sanitoriums were over-run with influenza sufferers. He likened it to a plague and recommended isolation as the best option for the patient. Peg fought on while others succumbed quickly.

Ada, George's wife, had also had the flu a few weeks before Peg, but had recovered quite quickly, so she left her children with Fred's wife Vi and spent the time when Will had to work looking after Peg. Little Mattie remained with the Musgroves, with regular visits from Will, Betty and Kate to reassure him. It was bittersweet for Louisa, being able to step in and look after him, but it was especially hard when the little boy asked for his ma.

The epidemic also had an effect on the local sporting calendar, even though the government's advice was that everyone should keep as fit as possible and outdoor sports were encouraged. Some local league football matches were being postponed when teams couldn't offer a full squad. But eventually, in an effort to raise morale, a match was finally arranged between Street and Somerton on a Saturday afternoon in early June. Being near the end of the season, both teams were vying for the coveted first place in the local league. Lucas and Tom went along to watch as the twins were playing.

Tom arrived at the football club a few minutes after Lucas.

'Ah, there you are,' said Lucas. 'I was nearly late myself. It's pandemonium in our house this morning. Louisa is baking biscuits with Mattie and Ruby, and the little beggars are both trying to eat the dough before it's cooked.' He smiled at the memory of Ma's laughter as Louisa tried to scold them. The two little monkeys were fast friends now and definite partners in crime.

'Sorry,' said Tom. 'I meant to get here earlier but Jeannie's been a bit poorly.'

Lucas frowned. 'She's not got the flu, has she?'

Tom shook his head, grinning. 'No. We're pretty sure she's expecting. Been sick as a dog every morning for a week now, then she feels all right. She's planning on telling your ma tomorrow.'

Lucas raised his eyebrows. 'That didn't take you long,' he said. 'You've been married less than a couple of months.'

Tom shrugged, unable to wipe the smile from his face. 'Honeymoon baby, I reckon.'

Lucas laughed and shook his hand. 'Congratulations. Our littl'uns will be growing up together. Ma didn't have any brothers and sisters, and Pa's brothers are down in Yeovil somewhere. We never got to know our cousins. It'll be good for ours to be close, won't it?'

'It will.'

'So, apart from being sick, how's Jeannie feeling?'

Tom's smile widened even further. 'She's over the moon.'

'You look pretty pleased with yourself as well,' said Lucas.

He laughed. 'Oh, I am.'

The whistle blew for kick-off and they turned their attention to the match. It was going to be a tense one. There was a lot of rivalry between the two teams and of course, the honour of being top of the league was at stake. Somerton managed to score in the first five minutes, eliciting groans from the home crowd.

'Come on, lads, you can't let 'em get away with that!' someone shouted.

'The Street team's a bit ramshackle today,' Lucas commented. 'Half their regulars are off with the flu.'

'I think it's the same for Somerton,' said Tom. 'But I suppose it gives some of the reserves a chance to show their mettle.' They watched the play as the ball went from one end of the pitch to the other and back, each side fighting for possession.

'I can't see either of the Davis brothers,' said Lucas. 'I thought they'd be here, but I suppose they've got other things on their minds, with Peg being so poorly.'

'Is she no better?'

He shook his head. 'I don't think so. Will comes round to see little Mattie every evening for a bit, but he wants us to keep looking after him so the family can concentrate on getting Peg better. The man looks like he's aged ten years.'

'Understandable. I'd be the same if it were Jeannie.'

Lucas nodded. He knew what he meant. His and Louisa's marriage might have had an unusual start, but he had grown to love his wife and the thought of her getting ill like Peg was didn't bear thinking about.

'Let's hope Peg recovers soon,' said Tom. 'In the meantime, who's that gaggle of girls by the goal line?' he asked, nodding his head towards three lasses who were squealing and cheering every time a Street player got the ball.

Lucas chuckled. 'Peter says they've been coming to all the matches this season. The one with the red hair has got her eye on our John, apparently. Her and her pals are driving Peter round the bend, but John's enjoying the attention.'

Sure enough, when the ball came his way and he managed to score Street's first goal, the girl jumped up and down, shrieking and clapping. John grinned, bowed and then blew her a kiss, which seemed to send the daft lass into raptures. Her friends looked on, envious, while Lucas and Tom laughed at the spectacle. They could see Peter rolling his eyes and shaking his head, although he wore a smile as he congratulated his twin on the goal.

'Ah, young love,' said Tom.

'She'd soon be cured of it if she had to live with him,' said Lucas with a grin. 'Although let's hope someone will put up with him eventually.'

The game seemed to move up a notch after that, with both sides trying their damnedest to break the deadlock. No one wanted a draw. Somerton scored again just before half-time, leaving the home supporters downhearted. During the break, the Street players huddled around their coach, who looked like he was giving them a stiff talking-to. John seemed to be paying more attention to the redhead, but he nodded when the coach addressed him directly and he said something to his twin as they returned to their positions. In the first minute of the second half, Peter got possession and ran the ball the length of the pitch. He kicked the ball over the heads of their opponents towards John, whose left boot connected with it, sending it to the back of the net. The crowd erupted and the girls screamed. John strutted like a peacock until the coach shouted from the touchline.

'Well done, lad. Let's have a hat trick now, eh? We need this win.'

Lucas rubbed his hands together. 'This is turning out to be a good match. If John manages a hat trick and they win the league, he'll be crowing like a cockerel for months. And you know, he might even deserve it!'

'It'll be a miracle he's not distracted, with all the female attention he's getting,' chuckled Tom, nodding his head towards the excited lasses again.

The game recommenced, with the play even fiercer than before. The Somerton players were trying to guard John now to prevent him from getting another chance to shoot, but he was quick and full of himself, laughing as he dodged around them. He got a couple of shots in, but their defence was too good for them. Five minutes before the final whistle, Somerton got the ball and ran it to their end. Only a miraculous save from the Street goalie prevented them from triumphing. The fight went on, with the Street team winning the ball and moving it from man to man until it was close enough for another shot. John ran out from behind the defenders, calling for the ball. The lad who had it kicked it towards him, but it went high.

Lucas groaned. 'He'll never get that in. The angle's all wrong.'

But John had other ideas. As the crowds yelled encouragement, he leapt into the air, heading the ball into the corner of the net above the heads of the defenders and the goalie. But even has he let out a celebratory yell, John's body was still moving towards the goal in a perfect dive. There was a dull thud as his head connected with the post and he dropped to the ground like a sack of potatoes. He lay there, completely still.

'Damned fool's knocked himself out,' said Lucas as the final whistle blew and the rest of the Street team and their supporters erupted in joyful pandemonium.

While all around them celebrated, he and Tom followed Peter across the pitch towards their brother. Lucas was thinking he'd have one heck of a headache when he woke up and that they'd probably have to carry him home. He only hoped Ma didn't get into a state about it. She always fretted so when one of them were hurt.

The redheaded lass reached John first and knelt beside his still form. She touched his shoulder, smiling, leaning in towards him. But then she froze. By the time the brothers reached them, she was screaming.

John's eyes were wide open. His head lay at an odd angle. There was blood coming from his ear.

The Somerton goalkeeper lifted the screaming girl away from John as the others surrounded him. 'I think his neck is broke,' he said, looking as though he was going to vomit as Lucas dropped to his knees beside John. Peter joined him, his hands shaking as he touched his twin's face.

'Stop mucking about, John,' he said. 'Come on, you won the match for us! Get up!'

But John didn't move. Lucas reached out and picked up his hand, feeling for a pulse. There was nothing. He checked his neck. Still nothing. It felt odd, as though it was out of place. He looked up at Tom, unwilling or unable to comprehend what it meant. As Peter continued to admonish his twin to get up, Tom put a hand on his shoulder and Lucas's.

'Here's the first aider. Give him some space, lads,' he said, urging them to their feet so that the man could see to John. He did the same checks that Lucas had, then listened to John's chest. After a few minutes, he sat back on his heels and looked at the brothers. He shook his head.

'I'm so sorry,' he said. 'He's gone.'

Peter ignored him and knelt again, shaking John's shoulder. 'No! Come on! Get up! Stop playing daft!'

Lucas stared at the twins, knowing it was too late, but wishing John would suddenly blink and jump up to celebrate his victory. He could hardly believe it, but as people realised that something awful had happened to the star goal scorer, the crowd around them grew quiet and the only sound was the loud sobbing of the redheaded lass. Lucas had to face the fact that this stupid accident had robbed them of their brother. He reached for Peter, staying his hand. All the shaking in the world wasn't going to help. He felt his throat close as the shock of it took hold of him.

'Peter, lad. Stop it. There's nothing you can do. He's gone.'

* * *

It was a good hour before they arrived back at the cottage in West End. Lucas and Tom held Peter up between them as he sobbed inconsolably, barely able to stand, let alone walk. They each hooked an arm under his and urged him along. Several silent men carried John's body on a stretcher, swathed in a blanket. A constable who had been at the match also accompanied them. He had sent someone to get a doctor, saying they needed to properly certify the death.

Lucas felt sick. He was still in the grip of shock, his mind a whirl of confusion and pain. He looked over Peter's bowed head at Tom, who gazed back, grim-faced. 'How am I going to tell Ma?' he asked.

Tom shook his head. 'I doubt you'll have to say anything,' he said, glancing at the procession following behind them. 'I expect the constable will take charge until the doctor arrives. Let's hope he brings a sedative to give him' – he nodded towards the still sobbing Peter – 'and your ma. This will be an awful shock for her.' He paused. 'It's awful for everyone, you included.'

Lucas nodded, his eyes burning, although he couldn't let himself give in to tears. He needed to be strong for Peter and for Ma. 'Will you go and tell Jeannie? God, I hope the shock isn't too much for her.' If she lost her baby because of this, it would be too awful to contemplate.

Tom nodded. 'As soon as we get you home. I'd better not hang around in case anyone decides to rush round and tell her. Best it comes from me, don't you think? I'll bring her back to West End. She'll want to be with you all.'

He nodded, grateful that it was one task he didn't have to take on. Telling Ma was going to be bad enough. He glanced back at the stretcher again, still trying to come to terms with the fact that John had been full of life one moment, then one risky move to win the match had cost him so dearly. How could he be dead? He should be celebrating, basking in the glory and maybe even kissing his girl. He was a local hero. His hat trick of goals would have become the stuff of legends anyhow, but now all people would remember would be that he had died at the moment the ball hit the back of the net.

He swallowed against the hard lump in his throat as they approached the cottage, his heart filled with dread. The constable joined them.

'How are you bearing up, lads?' he asked. 'Do you want me to tell your ma?'

Peter sobbed again as Lucas sighed. 'I don't know, sir. I feel like I ought to do it, but truth be told, I'm not sure I can find the words. Ma's... delicate. She lost our pa in an accident at the factory and she's never been the same since. I'm not sure how she's going to be able to cope with this.'

The constable nodded. 'Well, I'll do what I can. I've got to stay and deal with the doctor anyway and I'll have to take statements from you about what happened. I'll have to make a report to the coroner and there'll be an inquest.'

Lucas vaguely remembered the same thing happening when Pa had died. He closed his eyes, breathing through his nose in an effort to quell his growing nausea. He'd been a child then and his grandparents had been there to support Ma and all of them through everything. But they were gone now and he was the man of the house. It was up to him to guide everyone through the next few weeks and the coming months as they laid John to rest and came to terms with his stupid, senseless death. He didn't know if he had the strength.

25

Hours later, while Louisa was still reeling from the sight of the men carrying John's lifeless body home, Kate arrived with Mrs Searle.

'We were on our way to see you when we heard about John from one of the lads on the team,' said Kate as soon as Louisa opened the door. 'I can hardly believe it. Is he really gone?'

Louisa nodded and tearfully accepted the hugs of her friend and Auntie Betty. 'It's such a shock. His brothers saw it all and there was nothing anyone could do. He knocked his head against the goalpost so hard, he broke his neck. The doctor said he would have been gone before he hit the ground. I hardly know what to say or do. Lucas and Peter are beside themselves, wondering if they could've prevented it. His ma collapsed when she saw them bring him in and the doctor had to sedate her. Poor Jeannie is upstairs, sitting with her ma, afraid to leave her alone since they took John's body to the mortuary. The constable says it needs to stay there until the coroner is informed. She's so upset about it all and Jeannie's terrified of what this will do to her.' She took a shaky breath. 'Tom's playing with the children in the garden, bless him. He's been a tower of strength. But he's in a state of shock as well – he was at the match with them. I... I don't know what to do!' She began weeping as Auntie Betty took her arm and gently led her into the kitchen.

'Come and sit, lass. We'll put the kettle on, shall we? Where are the brothers?'

She sank into a chair as Kate filled the kettle and set it on the range. 'Lucas is upstairs in the twin's room. He didn't want to leave Peter alone. I've never seen the poor lad in such a state. He thought John was playing a joke on them. Even Lucas thought he'd just knocked himself out and was expecting him to get up once he'd come to his senses.'

'Those poor boys,' sighed Betty, sitting beside her and patting her hand. 'What a terrible thing to witness. And Jeannie and their dear sweet ma, they must be devastated. None of them deserve another terrible loss like this.'

'I know,' she said, tears still streaming down her face. 'We thought that with the war being over, everything would be good and the suffering would be over.' She pulled a damp handkerchief out of her pocket to wipe her face. 'But then this happens, and there's all those people ill with the flu. You know our neighbours died, didn't you?' She paused, remembering how the Searle and Davis families were suffering right now. 'I'm sorry, I shouldn't have said that. Is Peg all right now? Please tell me you were coming here to tell us she's getting better,' she begged.

Kate turned away, staring out of the kitchen window as Auntie Betty sighed and shook her head. 'It's not good news, lass.' She took Louisa's hands in her own work-roughened ones. 'The doctor says there's nothing more they can do. The pneumonia has done so much damage to her lungs that her heart's failing. Will doesn't want to leave her side, but Peg's desperate to see little Mattie one last time. That's why we were coming here when we were stopped in the high street and learned about John. I can't ask you to leave your family at a time like this, so is it all right if we take him back with us?'

Louisa thought this day couldn't get any worse, but the news about Peg and the realisation that Will would now want Mattie back just about broke her heart. She had prayed for Peg to recover, of course she had. But a little part of her had also wished that she could keep the child with her for a little longer, even though she knew it couldn't be forever. This felt just like the first time she had had to give him away, or maybe worse, because she had been able to spend so much time with him lately. She'd seen what a wonderful little boy he was and how well he got on with his half-sister and she'd foolishly allowed herself to pretend that she could keep them together. She felt a flutter in her belly, reminding her that she had another child on the way and could well have more children with Lucas in the coming years, but Peg never would. While she could never forget her first born, or love him any less than she did Ruby and the baby to come, she realised that she mustn't be greedy or selfish.

Peg and Will had been her saviours. If it wasn't for them, she'd have lost Mattie completely. As it was, they'd given her a selfless gift – they were loving parents to her little boy and had still had enough goodness in their hearts to be willing to share him with her, making sure that she would always have a connection to him and know that he was happy and loved. Now, in their time of need, Louisa had to be selfless too.

'Of course,' she said. 'He'll be so happy to see his ma and pa. He misses them.'

Auntie Betty nodded, her expression full of love and sadness that Louisa wanted to weep all over again.

'You must let us know if there's anything else I can do,' said Louisa. 'I think the world of Peg and Will, we all do. I mean it, I'd do anything.'

Kate sniffed, her back still to the room, as the kettle boiled. As she went to make the tea, Louisa rose and went to her friend.

'Leave that, love,' she said, putting an arm around her shoulders. 'You don't need to be wasting time here. I'll get Mattie and you can get back to Peg. Do you want me to get his things, or can we bring them round in a day or two?'

Betty stood. 'There's no rush for his things, lass. Him seeing Peg is what's important right now. They're in the garden, did you say?'

Louisa nodded, glancing out of the window. Tom was lying on the grass at the end of the garden, where she and Lucas liked to sit and talk on lazy summer evenings. The two children were climbing all over him.

'I'll go and get him,' said the older woman, casting a worried glance at Kate. 'I'll just be a minute or two.'

She went out of the back door, closing it behind her as Kate let out a sob. Louisa turned her friend and pulled her into a hug.

'Aw Kate, come here, love. I'm so sorry. God, what a rotten time! I want this to be a bad dream and for us all to wake up, comfy in our beds and start the day all over again.'

'I'm so sorry about John,' she sobbed. 'My heart is breaking at the thought of losing our Peg, and now this. It's not fair! And... and I just realised that we've come to take Mattie away from you all over again, haven't we? I can't begin to imagine how awful that is for you, especially today. I'm so sorry, Lou. But if we don't, Peg will be so sad. She misses him so much and she's desperate to see him one last time.'

Louisa hugged her tighter, her own tears falling again. 'Hush now. It's all right. I understand. I'd never deny her Mattie. She's his mother, not me. She's been so good and kind to me, letting me be part of his life. If it wasn't for Peg, I'd have lost him forever. Of course you must take him to her.'

Through the window, she could see Betty walking slowly back up the path, little Mattie holding his grandmother's hand and talking nineteen to the dozen, oblivious to the sadness that hung over all the adults around him. Louisa kissed Kate's cheek.

'Come on, wipe your tears. We can't upset Mattie. He'll be so happy to see his ma. We can do that much for Peg, can't we? Let her have her baby back, content and smiling. It's what she deserves. Lord knows, the poor little mite is going to have to learn to live without her. We've got to be strong for him and for Will.' She sniffed and blinked against her own tears as Kate scrubbed the wetness from her cheeks. She took a deep breath. 'Now, you go with Auntie Betty and spend what time you can with your sister. I'm here for my family; you'll be there for yours. We're all facing horrible losses, but we have to remember what we still have and concentrate on the people we need to care for as we come to terms with all this.'

Kate returned her kiss and stepped back. 'You're right,' she said, her voice a little scratchy. 'Will you give Jeannie my love, and tell them all how sorry I am?'

Louisa nodded. 'Of course I will. And will you give my love to Peg and Will and tell them if there's anything I can do...?'

Kate sighed. 'Why did we ever think life would just go back to normal after the war when the world's been torn apart? I swear this year has been harder than ever and it shows no sign of getting better.'

Louisa touched her cheek as Betty and Mattie approached the door. 'You've got Ted back, though, haven't you?'

Kate shrugged. 'I suppose. But I'm still not sure I trust it to be real, and right now all I can think of is Peg.'

'Remember how you helped each other when Ted's brother and your ma passed? He understands,' she said softly. 'Let him help you again. You'll need him in the weeks to come.'

'Annie Kay!' Mattie cried, letting go of his grandmother's hand and rushing at Kate.

Kate smiled and bent to pick him up, covering his face with kisses as he giggled. 'Hello, little man. Have you been good?'

He gave her an angelic smile. 'Me berry good,' he declared proudly.

'Right then, young Matthew,' said Betty. 'Let's get you home to see your ma, shall we? Say thank you to Auntie Louisa for looking after you so nicely.'

'Tank oo.' He beamed at Louisa, leaning across from Kate's arms, reaching out with his chubby hands to grab her face. He gave her a wet kiss. Louisa closed her eyes, her heart bursting.

'Bye, my lovely boy,' she said softly, touching his cheek. 'You be good for your ma, now won't you?'

He nodded. 'Me berry good,' he said again.

As Kate carried him out of the house, Betty held back. She put a hand to Louisa's cheek as she had with her son.

'Thank you, sweet girl. God bless you. I know both our families have troubles right now, but we'll all get through this, God willing.'

She nodded. 'One of us will bring Mattie's things round later, when things have settled down here a bit. Will someone let us know if... when...?'

'We shall, lass. Much as I hate to acknowledge it, it will be *when* rather than *if*. It's just a matter of time.'

As she closed the front door behind them, Louisa leaned against it for a moment, her whole body hurting from the sadness of this day. Then she straightened and went back into the kitchen and put the kettle back on the range. She might as well make that tea for everyone, and she'd better think about supper. None of them would want to eat, but they ought to. They needed to keep their strength up for what was to come.

Ruby toddled into the kitchen from the garden, followed immediately by Tom.

'All right, Lou?' he asked gently as she picked up her daughter and cuddled her, nuzzling her neck and reminding herself that she was a lucky woman and that she needed to keep remembering that. 'Betty told me why they'd come.'

She realised that he would have an inkling as to her state of mind over Mattie leaving, given that he now knew about the child's true parentage, but she didn't want to talk about it right now. She nodded. 'I'm going to make a pot of tea. I think we need to try and get them all to have some sustenance, even if it's only tea and biscuits.' Her breath caught as she remembered the fun she'd had with the children baking just a few hours ago.

Ruby tugged on her mother's hair, causing Louisa to wince. She gently untangled the little girl's fingers from her locks. 'Be kind, Ruby, love,' she said. 'No pulling hair.'

As Ruby pouted at her ma before cuddling closer, Tom moved toward the kettle. 'Let me make the tea,' he said. 'I think the princess wants her ma's attention.' He winked. 'I tried to wear her out for you, so she might be ready for her bed soon.'

'Thanks, Tom,' she sighed, sinking into a chair at the table and letting Ruby snuggle on her lap. 'I feel utterly useless at the moment. I don't know what to do.'

'You'll know,' he said as he warmed the pot and spooned in tea leaves. 'You're already doing it – thinking about them and how to make sure they're all right. It's been a terrible shock and they'll not know what to do either. We just need to be here and try to get them to eat and sleep and function until they can do it again for themselves.' He put the cosy over the teapot and let it stand while he got out cups and saucers. 'I've a feeling it's going to be hardest for Mrs Musgrove to get over this. From what Jeannie's told me about her ma's health, this could set her back a lot.'

'I know,' sighed Louisa. 'When Lucas was away fighting, she was in a terrible state and took to her bed. Poor Jeannie had to take everything on her shoulders, especially when the twins started playing up... Oh God!' She squeezed her eyes shut before opening them again to look at him. 'How on earth is Peter going to cope with losing his twin? He's never been without him.'

'He might never get over it,' he sighed. 'Who does when someone close dies? We'll all have to keep an eye on him and help him, though, won't we?'

She nodded. 'He looks up to you.'

'He's a good lad. I hope this doesn't set him back with his apprenticeship. Let's hope work will help take his mind off his loss.'

He poured milk into the cups as Louisa rocked Ruby. The child had her thumb in her mouth and was slowly drifting off to sleep. Louisa thought she ought to at least give her a wash and get her nightclothes on, but then she thought about the day's events and realised it wouldn't hurt if she let her fall asleep as she was and put her straight to bed for once. If she woke in the night, she would change her then.

She looked up to see Tom's gaze on Ruby.

'Jeannie's pregnant,' he said softly.

Louisa gasped, happiness flooding her after the storm of grief and pain that had overwhelmed her today. 'Oh my lord, that's wonderful news. I'm so happy for you both.'

'Thanks. She was all set to tell her ma after the meeting tomorrow but I expect she'll have told her by now. Maybe the prospect of another new child in the family will help her to deal with her loss. I know it won't replace John, but, you know, it might give her something to look forward to. She'll have her grandchildren to fill the gap.'

'I know what you mean,' she said. 'I know how happy she was when Ruby was born and when I announced I was expecting again. With Jeannie having a baby as well, she's got two new grandchildren on the way. Let's hope it will ease her pain a little.' She stroked her baby's head, smiling sadly down at her. 'No mother want's to even think about never seeing their child again. I hope our children can help her through her loss.'

She could see from Tom's expression that he understood that she was thinking about Mattie and everything she'd gone through to make sure she didn't lose him forever to strangers.

'I'm sorry about Kate's sister too,' he said. 'It's bad enough when someone dies suddenly, but to have to watch a loved one suffer through an illness like that...' He shook his head, then turned his attention to the tea. 'Why don't you put Ruby to bed? Then I'll take teas to Jeannie and her ma, and you can see to Lucas and Peter.'

She nodded and stood up, her baby in her arms. 'There's a tin of fresh biscuits on the shelf in the pantry. Ma and I made them with the children earlier. They're a bit misshapen, but they taste all right. We should try to get them to eat something.'

A few minutes later, she came downstairs after leaving Ruby sleeping soundly in her crib. She hadn't been able to bear to look at little Mattie's makeshift bed. Tom was at the open front door. Louisa recognised a couple of women from the Friends' Meeting House. They greeted her quietly as they came in, offering their condolences and baskets of cooked food.

'You'll not be feeling like cooking,' said one of the ladies. 'You must let us know if there's anything else we can do for you at this sad time. Everyone will be holding your family and dear John in the light. May God bless you all.'

Louisa was glad that Tom was there to thank them and to see them out, for she was incapable of saying one single thing as she wept, grateful beyond words for their loving generosity.

26

Peg lingered for another two days, but in the end, she couldn't hold on any longer. The whole family had been with her during that time, those who had to only leaving for work but returning immediately. Like Will, Kate had refused to leave Peg's side, uncaring that she would lose pay. Her sisters-in-law had taken care of Mattie when he wasn't snuggled up beside his ma on her sick bed.

At the end, just Will and Kate were with her in the early hours when she breathed her last breath. In the morning, she and Auntie Betty had the heartbreaking task of laying out the body.

'At least she's with Ma now,' she said softly as she kissed Peg's cold cheek. 'But lord knows, I'm going to miss her. I can't bear to think of the pain poor Will is in right now.'

'I know, lass, it breaks my heart for my poor lad. She was the perfect wife for him and she's gone far too soon. They should have had many years ahead of them and now he's got to go on alone with little Matthew. At least I had my dear William until the boys were old enough to remember him. I can only pray that

Will can find as much solace in the lad as I did from both of my boys. They kept me going when I wanted to just give up and die.'

Kate collapsed onto the pallet bed in Mattie's room a few hours later, too weary to go home or do anything else. Will had taken the little boy for a walk. She thought he was going to try to explain to him that Peg was gone, but she doubted the child would understand. Kate just wanted some time alone. She didn't think she'd sleep, but within minutes, she had slipped into a deep slumber.

'Annie Kay! Annie Kay!' A chubby finger poked at her cheek. 'You in my bed.'

She opened her eyes to meet the twinkling gaze of her nephew. 'Hello, little man,' she said, her voice raspy from sleep.

'Annie Kay go nigh-nights?' he asked, his head turned to one side as he studied her curiously. 'Mamma gone nigh-nights. She no wake up.'

She squeezed her eyes shut tight to stop her tears from falling as she sat up and swung her legs over the edge of the bed. 'I know, sweetheart. But Auntie Kate is awake now. Where's your pa?'

'Right here,' said Will from the doorway. He looked dreadful. His eyes were red-rimmed and he looked as if all the energy had been drained from his body and soul. 'I'm sorry he woke you. I was going to leave you to rest, but the moment my back was turned…'

'It's all right,' she said, trying to give him a reassuring smile.

'The doctor's been and issued the death certificate,' he said. There was no emotion in his voice. 'The undertaker's coming soon.'

She felt a wave of emotion that nearly had her curling up on the bed again. But there was so much to be done. She couldn't leave Will to do it all. She nodded. 'I'll pop down and wait for him.' She stood up, scooping Mattie into her arms. 'Have you had any rest? I can watch Mattie if you want a few hours' sleep.'

He shook his head, reaching for his son. 'I'll wait until the undertaker's been.' He scrubbed a hand down his face. 'I think I'll sit with Peg a while if you can watch Mattie.'

She nodded. 'Of course.' She'd done the same earlier, holding Peg's cold hand until she couldn't bear it any longer.

'There's food in the pantry,' he said. 'Help yourself. Ada and Vi brought some round, so did other neighbours and Friends.'

Her stomach churned at the thought. 'I'm not hungry, thanks. But I'll make something for Mattie. You should eat, too.'

The corner of his mouth turned up and he huffed out a humourless laugh. 'Ma wouldn't leave until I'd some food in my belly. Mattie's eaten as well, but no doubt he'll be happy to have a snack. I wouldn't say no to a cup of tea.'

She nodded, glad of something to do. 'I'll brew a pot. A cuppa sounds nice.'

She went downstairs as Mattie demanded that his pa play with his train with him. 'Choo choo!' he sang, oblivious to the turmoil in his father's heart. She was fiercely glad that the child was too young to fully understand what Peg's death meant, but at the same time, she was heart-sore to think that he probably wouldn't remember the woman who had been a loving mother to him since the moment he was born. Aware that Will wanted time with Peg's body before the undertaker came, she scooped Mattie up.

'Come on, little man. Bring your train and we'll play in the kitchen where it's nice and warm. Let your pa have a rest now.'

Mattie was happily playing under the kitchen table and the tea was in the pot when someone knocked on the door. Expecting it to be the undertaker, she was surprised to see Ted standing there.

'I heard and came as soon as I could,' he said. 'I'm so sorry, love.'

She nodded, unable to say anything. She stepped back, letting him into the house. As soon as the door closed behind him, he took her in his arms, enveloping her in his warmth, his scent. She rested her cheek against his broad chest and immediately felt better. 'I'm glad you came,' she whispered.

'I wouldn't be anywhere else,' he said, kissing the top of her head. She felt his words vibrate through his chest and she let them settle in her heart.

'There's tea brewing,' she said. 'It's all I can get Will to take.'

'Understandable. Where is he?'

'Upstairs with Peg.'

He nodded, solemn. 'I don't suppose he wants to let her go.'

She shook her head. 'None of us do,' she said as her eyes filled again. She dashed away her tears. 'Mattie's playing in the kitchen. I wanted to give Will some privacy.'

'Good. Let's go and see how he is. I don't suppose little Mattie realises what's happening, but he'll be his pa's reason to go on.'

She'd thought that as well, and it comforted her that Ted saw it too. They went into the kitchen and she poured three cups. Leaving Ted fussing over Mattie and his train for a moment, she slipped upstairs to deliver Will's cuppa, then returned to the kitchen. He'd found a fruit cake in the pantry and put a generous slice on a plate.

'You need to eat,' he said, nudging it towards her. Mattie already had some cake in his little fist.

She was going to refuse, but was too weary to argue. Instead, she broke off a mouthful and ate it. 'It's good,' she said. 'But I can't eat all this. Share it with me.'

He nodded and they ate the cake together in companionable

silence while Mattie finished his snack then went back to his game.

'Did you hear about John Musgrove as well?' she asked.

He nodded. 'I could hardly believe it. It's the talk of the village. Such a freak accident. I went round to offer my condolences yesterday. I reckoned they'd be overwhelmed with folk the first day.'

'How are they?' she asked. 'I saw Lou on Saturday when me and Auntie collected Mattie.'

He sighed. 'Not good. Mrs Musgrove hasn't got out of bed. Lucas says it's like she's lost within herself. The doctor sedated her and he's coming back to check on her again today, I think.'

'And the others? Louisa was in bits but I didn't see Jeannie, Lucas or Peter.'

'They all are, really. Peter doesn't seem to know what to do with himself. Lucas says he had to sleep in the twins' room with him the first night because he was so distraught. I don't suppose any of us can imagine what it feels like to have your twin die. It must be like losing part of you.'

Kate rested her elbows on the table and put her chin in her hands. 'Poor lad. Peter rescued me once, you know. Gave Pa a black eye when he grabbed me in the high street.' Ted's eyes widened as she told him the tale. 'He was so fierce and so outraged, he managed to best Pa easily.'

'He must think a lot of you,' he said.

She pulled a face. 'I know. He confessed he was sweet on me. But I told him as gently as I could that I couldn't ever feel the same way about him. He's Jeannie's little brother, for God's sake! But now I feel sorry for him and wish I could help him – all of them. I should go round, but right now I've no energy for anything.'

Ted reached across and stroked her hair. 'I'm sure they'll all be glad to see you when you're ready, but you've your own loss to deal with. They understand that.'

She nodded. 'I asked Ada to let them know about Peg. I haven't left this house for days. I know I'll have to go soon. I should get back to work. But right now, I can't bring myself to care that I'm losing money and I might get into trouble with Mr Briars. Peg was my sister and I loved her with all my heart and I'll not abandon Will to deal with all this on his own.'

'Kate, darling, you can't do it all. Will's got his ma, and your brothers and their wives want to do their bit as well.'

She scrubbed at her tired eyes. 'I know. I've already had this conversation with the rest of them. I just need today here. I'll pull myself together and go back to work tomorrow.'

'There's no rush, love. I'll be here to help you through.'

She gave him a narrow-eyed glance. 'You said that last time and then walked away. How can I believe you now?'

He sighed and nodded. 'I know and I don't blame you for not trusting me. All I can do is stay close and keep on showing you until you finally believe me.' He gave her a sad smile. 'But don't worry, I'll always be here for you, no matter how long it takes. I'm a patient man these days and you're worth the wait. I'll not be leaving without you again.'

She took a sip of her tea, watching him, trying to work out the range of emotions swirling through her at the moment. There was the pain of grief, that gnawing ache of loss of her sister that brought back the same feelings from when she lost her darling Ma. There was the worry about how poor Will and little Mattie would survive without Peg. There was the heartfelt sympathy she felt for her friends and all of the Musgrove family as they dealt with the totally unexpected loss of young John alongside the guilt that she was powerless to help them right now because her own family needed her. Added to that, Louisa must be feeling awful about having had Mattie with her and then having to give him back again. She reached down and ruffled the boy's head. He looked up and gave her a sweet smile before he turned his attention back to his train.

Her emotions were a confused maelstrom and she didn't know what to think or feel. But... as she looked up and Ted gazed back at her, his warm eyes filled with concern and love, she had a moment of clarity. Tying all those emotions together was fear. Fear of being alone. Fear of Ted walking away again. Fear that she'd never be enough to make anyone stay and love her as unconditionally as her ma and sister had. Even though Ted had been back a while and they'd been walking out together, she knew that she'd been holding back, unwilling or unable to trust that this time, it would be all right.

'I'm scared,' she confessed.

'I know, love.' He reached out with both hands and she put hers into his. Their fingers curled together and she felt his strength flood through her.

'All those years you were away, I was always scared that you'd die and no one would tell me. That I'd never see you again and never know why.'

He nodded and squeezed her hands.

'Since you've been back, I've been scared to trust my feelings because, if you leave again, I don't think I'd survive it.' She shook her head to stop him when he would have spoken. 'No, let me say this.' She took a deep breath and blew it out. She could feel the tears that were never far away welling again. 'But, losing Peg and seeing John being taken from the people who love him so suddenly... it's... it's like a light has been switched on in my head. I don't know how to explain it.' She paused, trying to marshal her thoughts.

'Just say what's in your heart,' he said softly.

'All right,' she said, raising her head and staring at the ceiling. 'What I've realised is that none of us knows what God has planned for us. We all expected Peg to survive the Spanish Flu but it turned to pneumonia and destroyed her heart. John Musgrove was a fit young lad, doing something he loved when his life was snuffed out in the blink of an eye. Neither of them were bad people, it wasn't a punishment from God, though I can't even begin to imagine what His plan was to be taking the two of them from the families who love them when they were still so young. Same as with your brothers and Mattie. We couldn't have known their fates, could we?' She gulped in another breath as Ted nodded his agreement. 'So I don't want us to wait. I don't want to carry on thinking that you'll let me down again, because none of us knows what the future holds. I'd rather take what I can now than wrap myself in this cloak of distrust and self-righteousness I've been clinging onto. That won't comfort me if I lost you, would it? But letting myself love you and the two of us creating memories together will at least make me happy now and if, God forbid, we lose each other again, at least I'll have been happy with you for a while and I'll have that to remember.'

Ted squeezed her hands as he sagged with relief. 'Thank God,' he said, then he leaned over the table and kissed her while Mattie played on the floor below them, oblivious to the emotions swirling above him.

27

By the end of June 1919, both John and Peg had been buried in the graveyard at the Friends' Meeting House, along with several flu victims, young and old. It was the same picture all around the world. There were still cases in Somerset, but the disease seemed to be losing its strength and fewer people were dying. It still inspired fear in folk when someone sneezed or coughed, though.

All three of the girls were grieving, but the friendship between them and the love they received from their menfolk helped them through.

Kate came to the Musgroves' cottage in West End after her shift at Clarks one Saturday in early July to see Jeannie and Louisa. Ted was off to visit Stan with his ma and pa. He'd asked her to accompany them, but as Mrs Jackson was still not keen on the idea of Ted and Kate courting, Kate had decided to stay behind. She and Ted would go on their own another time. She'd seen Lucas in the factory yard at the end of their shift and he'd told her he and Tom were working on a project at Jeannie's house in Cranhill Road, so she knew it was a good time to meet with the girls.

'Oh, I miss you two so much at work,' she said as she hugged them both and little Ruby, who giggled with delight when Kate picked her up and rained kisses all over her face.

'Come into the kitchen, Kate,' said Louisa, taking her daughter from her.

She followed them and Jeannie into the room and stared as they both turned towards her after Louisa had settled Ruby into a highchair with a biscuit. She blinked in surprise as she looked at the two of them. 'Goodness, I thought Lou was a couple of months ahead of you, Jeannie, but I swear I can see your bump already.'

Jeannie blushed and Louisa gave her shoulder a sympathetic squeeze.

'Don't you start,' said Jeannie, putting a protective hand over her belly. 'Someone asked Tom the other day if he'd anticipated our wedding night. I was so embarrassed when he told me. We didn't, of course, but I seem to be blowing up like a balloon. I think I must be eating too much.'

'No you're not,' said Louisa. 'You can barely keep anything down. I'm surprised you haven't wasted away.'

Kate frowned. 'Are you all right, Jeannie? Have you seen the doctor?'

She shook her head. 'I haven't had time. But apart from the sickness, I feel fine... well, as fine as I can be after...'

The three friends were silent for a moment, remembering their losses.

'Her ma thinks she might be carrying twins,' said Louisa. 'And she should know.'

Kate clapped her hands together. 'Oh, of course! That makes sense, doesn't it? They run in the family.'

Jeannie nodded. 'In Tom's family as well, apparently. Two of his sisters are twins, and his ma's brothers are twins.'

'You don't look very happy about it, love,' said Kate gently.

She sighed. 'I think I am,' she said. 'But I don't know. The twins came early, and they say that's normal because the babies just run out of room in there.' She pointed at her growing bump. 'But that makes it more likely that they'll be poorly or maybe not even survive. Peter and John were so tiny when they were born, no one thought they'd make old bones.' Her eyes filled with tears. 'That's why we spoiled them so much. And now John won't anyway.'

'Aw, Jeannie, love,' said Kate. 'Try not to worry. Even though they were born small, they both turned out to be great big lads, didn't they?'

She sniffed and nodded. 'I know. I'm being daft. It's not like I can do anything about it, is it? It's in God's hands.'

Kate nodded. 'How's your ma?' She didn't need to ask how her friends were coping; she could see the sadness that surrounded them. She couldn't help but worry that part of Louisa's sadness was that she didn't see so much of Mattie since Peg's passing as the whole Davis family and Auntie Betty were competing to spend time with the little man in order to help Will out.

Jeannie shook her head, blinking away her tears. Louisa put an arm around her sister-in-law.

'Her ma's barely stirred from her bed,' said Louisa.

Kate nodded. She'd seen Mrs Musgrove at John's funeral. She was in a bath chair and almost unresponsive, as though she was hiding away inside herself.

'Some days, she seems all right, but most of the time, she's not. We keep talking to her and trying to get her excited about our babies,' she went on. 'We thought we were succeeding when she mentioned that Jeannie might be carrying twins. But then she's so deep in her grief a lot of the time that I'm not sure she even hears us. The doctor says we've just got to keep on trying and hopefully, she'll come around again.'

'I'm so sorry,' said Kate. At a time when Jeannie and Louisa should be happily anticipating the births of their babies, it must be awful for them to see Mrs Musgrove so mired in her grief.

'She barely notices Ruby at the moment.' She sighed, stroking her daughter's hair. 'The poor little mite can't understand why her nana can't look at picture books with her any more. I take Ruby into Mrs Musgrove's room with me and we sit on the bed and go through the pictures, hoping she will take notice. She does sometimes, but then she gets upset again and sinks back into her darkness.'

'I feel so guilty about not being here all the time,' said Jeannie. 'I should be helping.'

'I'm sure you do what you can,' said Kate.

'She does,' said Louisa, regarding her sister-in-law with affection. 'God bless her, she and Tom have even offered to have Ma live with them in Cranhill Road so we won't be so cramped.' She nudged Jeannie's shoulder with her own. 'But if she's carrying twins, she might need more room than she thinks.'

Jeannie was looking at Kate as Louisa spoke and she must have recognised the wave of loneliness that crossed her expression. 'Enough about us, Kate,' she said. 'How are you?'

She shrugged. 'I'm all right. I've kept myself busy with my evening classes and catching up before the exams, but they're done now and I've got to wait a few weeks before I get the results. I see Ted when I can, but he's studying and working hard as well. Mind you, the lucky beggar will have the long school summer holidays, while I have to carry on working at Clarks until factory fortnight.' Clarks had always closed for two weeks in the summer before the war, but that had been reduced to just one week during the conflict. This was the first year they were going back to giving their workers a fortnight off in the summer.

Her friends gave her sympathetic smiles. 'I miss Peg something terrible. After being separated during the war years, we were really enjoying being close again.' She sighed. 'I take solace in the thought that she's with Ma in heaven, while that old devil is burning in hell.'

'Hell!' said Ruby, banging her hands on the tray of her high chair. She looked so pleased with herself that she'd said a new word that she said it again. 'Hell!'

Kate grimaced. 'Sorry, Lou, I forgot little ears.'

Louisa chuckled. 'Don't worry about it.' She turned to her daughter. 'Hello to you too, Miss Ruby. How are you?'

The little girl looked confused, so Kate and Jeannie both said, 'Hello' to her in exaggerated voices. Soon she was copying them and shouting, 'Hello!' at the top of her lungs, making them all laugh.

'Phew!' said Kate, pretending to wipe her brow. 'Well played, Ma.' She chuckled.

Louisa bowed her head in acknowledgement of her praise. 'I'm learning all sorts of tricks,' she said. 'But tell us what you were saying before we were so rudely interrupted.' She winked while glancing sideways at her daughter, who was now distracted by her knitted teddy bear.

'Not much else to tell. We're all doing what we can to help Will and Mattie.'

'How are they?' she asked. Her voice was soft while her gaze was sharper.

Kate knew that Louisa must be missing Mattie something awful. 'Will's finding it hard, of course. As for Mattie, he asks about Peg sometimes, but he really doesn't understand why she's not there. So long as he's got someone to play with and feed him, he's happy. Will's doing his best to keep his grief away from the little lad, but it's not easy.'

Louisa nodded, looking sad. 'I wish I could do more to help, but...'

'We all do,' said Jeannie.

'I know, and I love you both for it. But you've got so much on your plates right now, haven't you? How about I bring Mattie over here to play with Ruby when I'm looking after him?'

Louisa swallowed hard. 'Would you?' she asked.

'We'd all love to see him,' said Jeannie softly, knowing how much it would mean to her sister-in-law. 'We've missed having him around.'

Ruby started wriggling, trying to get herself out of her high chair. 'Oh, thank goodness we've got these reins Tom fitted to stop her climbing out,' said Louisa, rising to release the child and put her safely on the floor. 'She took a tumble out of there the other day and I just caught her before her head hit the stone flags.'

'Oh my word, you must have had such a fright,' said Kate, examining the leather straps and buckles that served to stop Ruby from doing it again.

Louisa chuckled. 'I've never moved so fast in my life! At least now, thanks to these devices Tom came up with, I can make sure she's stuck fast before I turn away.'

'I'm telling Tom he's got to do the same for our baby or babies,' said Jeannie. 'I've learned from being around Ruby and Mattie that you need eyes in the back of your head to keep little ones safe. If I've got two to watch, I'll be a nervous wreck. I don't know how Ma managed it with four of us.'

'But she did, love,' Kate pointed out. She was going to say *and you all survived,* but it didn't seem appropriate to say it now that John was gone.

Louisa settled Ruby on the rag rug in front of the range with a box of colourful blocks of wood and returned to the table as the little girl began to build a tower.

'How are Lucas and Peter coping?' asked Kate. 'I've seen them and Tom around the factory, but haven't had a chance to speak to them much.'

Both girls sighed.

'Peter's really struggling,' said Jeannie.

'He has nightmares,' said Louisa. 'I think he pushes it all out of his mind when he's awake – he's been working hard at the factory and then going round and helping Tom with his false limb and splint projects in the evenings and weekends. He hasn't been near the football club. I doubt he'll ever play again, although he won't discuss it. It all seems to come out at night when he's sleeping.'

'It's so sad,' said Kate. 'Let's hope the nightmares stop soon.'

'Lucas had nightmares when he first came back from France,' said Jeannie. 'It was awful to hear him crying out. It upset Ma something terrible.'

Louisa nodded. 'He still has them sometimes,' she said. 'More so lately, of course. And yes, Ma does get upset when one or both of them cry out in the night. We both do.'

'I did wonder if Tom would have them,' said Jeannie softly. 'He said he did when he was in the hospital after he lost his leg, but they gradually stopped. He had a bit of trouble sleeping after John... but he seems to be all right. I think he's more worried about me.'

'Of course he is. I worry about Lucas, as well,' said Louisa. 'Apart from the nightmares, he seems to be coping all right most of the time. He gets up and goes to work, helps me with the children and his ma when he's home, makes sure Peter's all right... but I think he feels he has to hide his pain and grief because he's the man of the house, and that worries me. Sometimes, he looks so lost, but when I ask him, he swears he's fine. It's as though he's being strong for everyone and daren't admit to any weakness. I'm concerned because he won't let us be strong for him.'

'Aw, Lou,' said Jeannie. 'I know what you mean, but Lucas has always been like that, ever since Pa died. It's his nature to look after everyone else, but he won't let anyone do the same for him.'

'All you can do is keep an eye on him and let him know you care about him,' said Kate as Ruby's brick tower collapsed. The child laughed and clapped her hands and began building it up again.

Louisa nodded. 'I know.'

It occurred to Kate that the Musgrove household had had its share of upheavals lately. With Louisa giving up work to have Ruby, Jeannie moving out when she married, and now John's passing, they'd lost three wages. Lucas and Peter were the only ones bringing in any regular money, although Louisa had managed to sell a few of her watercolours which brought in a little extra now and again. Yet there were still four adults and Ruby to feed. They'd not asked for any recompense to care for Mattie in the weeks he'd been with them, and by the end of the year, they'd have another mouth to feed and even less space to put everyone. It wasn't as though Peter could share a bed with his Ma like Jeannie had done, was it? She suddenly understood why Jeannie and Tom had offered to have her ma live with them. Tom was on a good wage as an engineer, so even with a little one – or twins – on the way, it would be less of a hardship for him to support his mother-in-law.

'Did Ted tell you he's been round?' Louisa asked, unaware of her thoughts.

'He's been to ours as well,' said Jeannie. 'Helping the lads with the projects.'

'I know,' said Kate, feeling her cheeks warm as she thought about him. 'I expect he's told you we're officially courting now, even though his ma isn't happy about it.'

Louisa smiled. 'He did, but we guessed anyway. He wasn't about to go anywhere now he's found his way back to you. I doubt he's bothered about his ma. Let's face it, the woman's never happy about anything, is she?'

Jeannie shuddered. 'She's a frightening woman.'

Kate laughed. 'Yet you stood up to her all those years ago. It was you who pointed out that she wasn't a bad person, just a scared one.'

'I know. I bet you never dreamt the woman would end up your mother-in-law, though, did you?'

Kate raised her chin and her hands. 'Hold on a minute! We're only courting,' she said. 'And even if she were to become my mother-in-law, I've survived the Floozy, haven't I? Ted's ma doesn't scare me.'

'So long as Ted is sure to make it clear he's on your side if she's being difficult,' said Louisa, frowning. 'I mean, look at Mr Jackson. He's a foreman, used to telling people what to do. Yet he seems to let his wife walk all over him and doesn't complain. Maybe she's expecting Ted to be the same if she starts on you.'

Kate huffed. 'If he ever was, I'd give him his marching orders, and he knows it. But I doubt he will be.' She looked thoughtful. 'I don't think Mr Jackson is quite the pushover you think he is, either. I think he just understands that his wife has been through a lot, losing Albert and all the trouble with Stan, then Ted being away and out of touch for so long… he probably thought he ought to go soft on her. But I reckon him and Ted can handle her just fine. Ted's a man now, anyway, not the daft lad who went away.'

'Speaking of which, did Ted ever tell you what he got up to in the war?' asked Louisa. 'I know Lucas has asked him, but he wouldn't say.'

'Not really, just little hints but no details,' said Kate, not letting on that she knew that Ted had been a spy because she knew he didn't want to talk about it right now. 'If he wants to tell me, he will, but I won't press him about it. I'm sure he just wants to put it all behind him now.'

'We all do,' said Jeannie. 'I know Tom doesn't like to remember it. Although it's hard to do that when he's reminded of it every day as he takes his prosthetic foot off.'

Neither of her friends knew what to say to that. They didn't like to ask about what it was like to live with a man whose foot had been blown off.

The silence that followed was punctuated by another falling tower.

'Uh-oh,' said Ruby looking up at her mother.

'Never mind,' she said gently. 'You can build it up again.'

It seemed to Kate that that was something they should all remember. The war years had brought so much heartache and destruction, but they were still here and, if they worked hard, they could build a new life for themselves in peacetime.

28

Will opened the door of his cottage in Goswell Road to greet his ma. He kissed her on the cheek as she entered.

'There you are, my darling boy. Here, take my basket. I've brought you a lovely rabbit pie. Now, where's our Matthew, eh?'

'Nanna!' Mattie came barrelling out of the kitchen into the parlour and flung himself at Betty's legs.

'Oh, there you are, sweetheart.' She smiled, bending down to hug and kiss him. Will knew that she wouldn't attempt to pick Mattie up because he was a sturdy lad now and a wriggler to boot. She was worried about dropping him these days, although Will knew that the lad would likely bounce just like any other child of his age.

'Nanna's brought us a pie, Mattie,' he said.

The boy rubbed his tummy. 'Yum yum.' He grinned.

Will smiled, his heart contracting. Little Mattie was the shining light in his dark world these days, yet he felt inadequate as a father without Peg at his side. A wave of grief washed over him and he welcomed it. He spent so much time pretending he was all right for Mattie's sake that he felt guilty that he wasn't allowing himself time to properly grieve his darling Peg.

His ma laughed and poked at Mattie's belly. 'Come on then, little man, let's set the table and boil some potatoes and carrots and we can have a feast.'

Will was trying to remember whether they had any potatoes or carrots in the pantry as he followed them into the kitchen. He tried to keep up with everything, and Peg's sisters-in-law helped him a lot, but he still hadn't got the hang of shopping for food so they had run out of a few things in recent weeks. Perhaps Ma realised that, because when he put her basket on the table, she lifted the cloth inside it to reveal not only a perfectly cooked rabbit pie, but also some potatoes and carrots.

He was thankful that Ma took over and insisted that he spend some time playing with Mattie. Peg's brother George had given the lad a toy lorry like the ones he drove for his father-in-law. He'd even painted the company name on the side, telling Mattie it was a magic toy that he had to look after because, when he was old enough, it would transform into a proper lorry like his Uncle George's that Mattie would be able to drive. As soon as Mattie saw his favourite toy, he started making 'brrrmm brrrmm' noises, pushing the toy around in his favourite spot on the floor under the table.

Much as he loved the lorry – and the train that Lucas and Tom had made for him – Mattie liked his food more, so he came out from under the table as soon as Ma said it was time to eat. Will helped cut his food then gave him a spoon and a fork and let him feed himself. Peg had started doing this, saying he was growing up fast and they should let him, even if it meant the table and the floor around it got a bit messy for a while. 'How else is he going to learn?' she'd said.

'This is delicious, Ma,' said Will after he'd taken a couple of bites. His appetite was still poor, nothing tempted him these days, but he ate what was put in front of him and tried to make sure Mattie ate well. He didn't want anyone thinking he wasn't a good father. He'd promised Louisa he'd be the best father he could for little Mattie, and he'd made the same promise again to Peg. While his heart wanted to lie down and die so that he could be reunited with his love, his head reminded him that he had to stay strong and carry on for the boy's sake.

'I know you like a good rabbit pie, son. I'll leave the rest here so you've got something for another meal for the two of you.' They carried on eating, Mattie silent apart from the odd 'Yum yum' to signify his enjoyment of the food.

Will and his ma talked about work, about people they knew and the general goings-on in Street.

'I saw young Peter Musgrove at work on Friday,' he said. 'With everything going on with Peg, I'd forgotten about John's accident.' He'd felt bad that he hadn't sent his condolences; it was the sort of thing that Peg would have done on behalf of both of them, but Kate had assured him that they understood. He suspected she'd done it for him anyway, in Peg's stead. Everyone had been so kind, helping him when he had no clue as to what he should do. No doubt the Musgroves had had a similar experience. 'The poor lad looked so lost.' He'd recognised his grief – that aching loss of a part of you that made you complete. He'd felt it when his pa had died all those years ago and again when his brother had been lost. But neither of those were as bad as the pain he felt at losing Peg. 'I know that feeling all too well.'

His ma patted his hand. 'I know, son. It's early days yet. You'll never forget Peg, nor will young Peter forget his twin. But the pain will ease with time, I promise.'

'I'm not sure I want it to,' he mumbled. The pain meant that Peg was still there in his heart. He might have lost her physical presence, but he never wanted to lose this pain, this proof of his overwhelming love for her.

She nodded, her gaze full of love and understanding as she squeezed his hand. 'Give yourself time, son. You'll be all right. You've got your son to think of. He needs you.'

'Just don't go telling me I should find a new wife,' he said. 'I nearly punched one of the old fellas at work this week when he said that. He had the cheek to suggest I meet his niece, who'd lost her husband in the Somme. If the foreman hadn't told him to shut up, I'd have taken a swing at him.'

'Good grief!' Betty put a hand to her chest. 'Some folk have no sensibility at all, do they? I'm not saying you'll never remarry, but goodness me, it's far too soon for you to be thinking of anything like that.'

He raised his eyes to the ceiling, praying for patience. 'Ma,' he said, keeping his voice calm so as not to distract Mattie from his meal. '*I'm* saying I'll never remarry. Peg was the best, the love of my life, like Pa was for you. I don't want to settle for second best.'

Mattie dropped his fork, distracting both of them as Will retrieved it for him. He deliberately changed the subject, and the conversation turned to other, less painful topics.

After dinner, Mattie went back to playing with his lorry while Will and his ma enjoyed a cup of tea. He told her to leave the washing up, but she ignored him, so he'd grabbed a cloth and wiped up while Ma washed. The kitchen was soon spotless again, so they went out into the garden to enjoy the late-afternoon sunshine. Mattie ran up and down the path, finding abandoned toys under bushes and waving them at his pa and grandmother as though he'd discovered priceless treasures.

'I'm glad I won't have to travel all across the country to Lincolnshire to visit you this factory fortnight,' she said. 'I loved coming to see you, but that journey was a trial I'm glad is no longer necessary.'

He nodded. 'We were always glad to see you, Ma. I'm sorry we couldn't make the journey back to Street.' He and Peg had decided not to, for fear of upsetting Louisa. They'd wanted to give her as much time as possible to adjust to her new life, although they'd made it clear that they would eventually return to Somerset. Hearing she'd married Lucas and then had Ruby had eased their minds. He'd missed Ma, but at least she'd been able to come and see them. 'I'm glad we're home now, though.'

Mattie was sitting on a patch of grass now, his toys lined up in front of him as he chattered away to them in his own sweet world, while Ma talked about Kate and her friends. The child looked up and grinned and he look so like Will's brother that it almost took his breath away.

When Ma mentioned that both Louisa and Jeannie were expecting, Will turned to look at her. 'I'm so pleased for Louisa that she's found happiness with Lucas,' she said. 'They both loved our Mattie so much; it does my heart good to see them together. And with two children soon. I was afraid that both of them would live in the shadow of their grief for Mattie and would never be able to be happy.' She smiled. 'Two babies in two years,' she said.

Will glanced back at little Mattie. He had never intended to say anything to Ma about the boy's true parentage, but at that moment, the need to tell her overwhelmed him – like the spirit did to some Friends in meetings. They would begin to shake inside, feeling the words building inside them, until they burst out and they shared what was in their hearts.

'Three babies, Ma,' he said. 'She's had three babies.'

She held his gaze for a moment before he turned to look at the child playing a few yards away, unaware of the secret Will had just revealed. 'When Mr Clements wouldn't agree to them marrying before Mattie was shipped overseas, him and Louisa...' He shrugged, not wanting to say exactly. 'Then Mattie didn't come back and Louisa realised she was in the family way. Her ma was all set to send her to Exeter to her aunt and have the baby taken away from her. It was Kate who asked us to help her. So Louisa ran away and came to Lincolnshire with us. She never went to Exeter at all, but her ma kept up the pretence until she couldn't any more. Louisa wanted to know that Mattie's child would stay with his family and not go to strangers who might not love him as much as we do.' He paused, taking a deep breath. He should feel guilty telling Ma all this, but he felt at this moment that it was the right thing to do. He felt lighter in his heart. She should know the truth of it. 'Peg and me, we tried for years, Ma. But it wasn't to be. So we agreed to take him and pass him off as our baby. For Mattie. For you. Louisa had wanted to tell you the truth of it right from the start, but her ma forbade it. Said she would be tainting your memories of your son and you would hate her for it.'

Betty gasped at that and shook her head, but she remained silent.

'We promised her that we'd love him as our own. No matter how long we tried, me and Peg just weren't destined to bear our own children. We don't know why.' He shrugged. 'We were just about resigned to the fact that we'd remain childless. But thanks to Louisa, we were given the gift of a son – Mattie's son. My nephew.'

He ran out of words. His mother remained silent as little Mattie carried on playing with his toys in the grass.

Will glanced at her, expecting her to be shocked. But as their eyes met, he realised that she wasn't.

'You knew?' he asked.

She nodded. 'I guessed. The day after Mattie left for the last time, I found spots of blood on his bedsheets. I assumed they'd defied her father. But it was between Mattie and Louisa, no one else. When she left town, my suspicions grew, and then the news that she was with you and that I was going to be a grandmother... well, I'd come to the same conclusion as you had about you and Peg, so I fitted all the pieces of the puzzle together.'

'Why didn't you say something?'

She shook her head. 'It was none of my business and I wasn't about to upset any of you. No matter what, that child is my grandson, and whether he had been yours or Mattie's didn't matter and it still doesn't.'

He took a deep breath and blew it out again, his eyes filled with tears. 'That's what Louisa said. After her own ma and pa rejected the child, it was important to her that his remaining grandparent would love him unconditionally. She knew you would.'

'Ah, God bless her. That poor girl's been through so much. I've wanted to talk to her about it, but I realised she was afraid and maybe a little ashamed.'

'She was. She said she couldn't bear it if you reacted like her ma said you would and hated her for ruining your memories of Mattie.'

Betty huffed. 'Mrs Clements has a lot to answer for. Not everyone will reject their child for loving someone. I would never do that. I still love Louisa like a daughter, same as Peg. They both made my sons happy and that was all that matters to me. That Louisa gave us the gift of little Mattie at such a cost to herself is something I will always be thankful for.'

'So will I.' He sighed. 'I'm so proud to be his pa. Although it breaks my heart that Peg won't be here to see him grow.'

She reached across and kissed his cheek. 'I know, son. Mine

too. But we can take comfort from the fact that Peg had all this time with him and had the joy of being his mother – something she'd never have had were it not for Mattie and Louisa.'

He closed his eyes, trying to control the emotions building in him. 'Do you think Mattie was there when Peg passed, Ma? I prayed and prayed that, if the lord wouldn't let her stay with me, that he would let Mattie meet her on the other side and care for her in heaven.'

'I'm sure he is, son. I'm sure he is, and so is your pa. You're caring for their son and grandson as your own. They'll want to make sure Peg is all right up there in the light.'

29

By the end of July, most of the men had returned to Street from overseas and Jeannie's sickness had eased, although she continued to vomit occasionally and her belly continued to grow fast and folk often thought that she was further along than Louisa was. She was patient, explaining that her baby was due late in January, while Lou's was likely to come in November or early December, but that twins were a possibility for Jeannie.

Now that she was feeling a little better, she was finding her days were slow. She knew that she should relish it, because she'd worked hard at home in West End and in the Machine Room in Clarks for so long. It also occurred to her that she ought to make the most of the peace and quiet because whether she was carrying one or two babies, she was going to be busy and likely exhausted once they arrived. But with all the upset since John's and then Peg's passing, the last thing she wanted was to take the time to sit and think. So she kept busy – cleaning, cooking, knitting and sewing.

When she could do no more, she would walk round to West End to see Ma and Louisa. There she would help in whatever way she could, even if it was only to sit with Ma or play with Ruby to give Lou a break.

She arrived there one warm afternoon to find that Ma had left her bed and was sitting out in the garden, watching Ruby play with her rag doll.

'How did you manage to get her downstairs?' Jeannie asked as she watched them from the kitchen window. She hadn't been out to say hello yet, wanting to talk to Louisa first. She was sitting at the kitchen table, sketching.

Lou smiled and put her pencil down. 'It was Peter, bless him. He promised to come home for his dinner today if she agreed to come down and eat with him at the table. I think he almost feels responsible for her grief, even though he's not and the poor lad's got enough of his own pain to deal with. But it worked and we ate together, then persuaded her to enjoy the garden for a bit.' She grimaced. 'But if she gets tired and wants to go upstairs, I might need your help to get her up there now Peter's gone back to work.'

Jeannie nodded. 'You know I'm happy to help. I'm delighted to see her down here. Can we take it that she's improving, d'you think?'

Louisa shrugged, looking unsure. 'It's early days yet, isn't it? So who knows? I think it's a good sign, though. She seems happy to be out there with Ruby, but I'm keeping a careful eye on them, in case it all gets too much for her.'

'Oh, Lou,' she sighed. 'I'm so grateful. If you hadn't married Lucas and come to live here, I'd probably still be here, with no prospect of getting wed because I wouldn't have been able to leave Ma. As it is, I feel guilty, leaving it all up to you.'

Louisa pulled her into a hug and they watched Ma and Ruby through the window. Both of them were content in the sunshine.

Ma even gave Ruby a brief smile when she picked a buttercup and presented it to her grandmother.

'You've no need to feel guilty, Jeannie,' she said. 'I'm happy to do what I can for your ma. She's been so kind to me, more than my own ma has been ever since Mattie.' She sighed. 'So don't you go fretting about it. You're still round here most days; it's not like you've abandoned us all.'

Jeannie rested her head on Louisa's shoulder. She knew her sister-in-law was thinking of the way Mrs Clements had effectively abandoned her daughter by moving to Exeter when she knew that Louisa didn't want to leave Street.

'I know I've said it before, but I'll keep saying it,' she said. 'Our house is a bit bigger than this and there's only the two of us. Tom doesn't mind. This baby—'

'Or *babies*,' Lou pointed out, patting Jeannie's bump.

Jeannie blew out a breath and narrowed her eyes. She was tired of the speculation. It probably *was* twins, but they wouldn't know until she gave birth, so she couldn't assume. It might just be a big baby. 'All right, *or babies*. The point I'm making is that we've got plenty of space and even with two babies, we've got room for Ma. She could even have a bedroom downstairs. We're happy for her to come and live with us if she'd like. You'd still have Peter, until such time as he finds himself a wife and moves into a home of his own. But at least he's paying his way and you'd have one less mouth to feed and there'd be the other bedroom free for the children as they grow.'

Louisa frowned. 'We couldn't push your ma out of her home, Jeannie,' she said gently. 'We'll manage, I'm sure. I've sold some of my paintings, and the gallery that took them asked if I could design some greetings cards. If they like those, it could be a nice earner for me. But even if they don't, we'll support your ma, I promise.'

'Now I've offended you, haven't I?' said Jeannie, feeling worried. 'I know you'd manage, love, and she loves being with you. But the truth is, I miss having Ma around. That's why I'm always turning up here – and to see you and Ruby, of course. But I can't help worrying about her all the time I'm away from her, especially since we lost John.'

'Aw, bless you. I'm sure you do. You've worried about your family most of your life, haven't you? Especially when Lucas was away fighting.'

She nodded, feeling tears well. She blinked them away, tired of how emotional she was since she'd fallen pregnant. 'I can't get out of the habit. I'll probably be a nervous wreck over my own children.'

Louisa laughed. 'You'll be fine. You're allowed to worry; we all are. In fact, I know you'll be a good ma because you've been a mother hen for your brothers all these years – caring when they need it, patient even when they don't deserve it, and fierce when they push their luck.'

That made Jeannie chuckle as she blushed with pleasure. It was such a lovely thing for Lou to say. 'I try my best,' she said.

'Let's not worry about who has your ma for now, eh? We'll work something out. There's some elderflower cordial in the pantry. Shall we make some cold drinks and go and join them in the garden?'

As they were gathering beakers and pouring drinks, the second post arrived. Jeannie was putting everything on a tray when Louisa came back into the kitchen with an envelope. She was frowning.

'What's that?' asked Jeannie, nodding towards it.

'It's from Ma,' she said. 'I recognise the handwriting.' She turned it over in her hands. 'She rarely bothers writing. I wonder what she wants.'

'Only one way to find out, love. Open it.'

With a sigh, Louisa did just that, scanning the contents. 'I wrote and told her I'm expecting again. She said she'd come and see Ruby, but she never did. Something about being busy with her lodgers and my aunt suffering with lumbago so she had to help her as well. We said she was welcome any time, but she never mentioned it again. Now it seems she's suddenly got this urge to see us.' She pulled a face. 'She's invited me, Lucas and Ruby to Exeter to stay for a few days during the factory closure fortnight.'

'But that's only a week away,' said Jeannie.

'I know. She probably left it until now to invite us, expecting us to refuse. Which we will do.' She read on, her frown deepening before she checked the envelope and pulled out another piece of paper. It was a cheque. 'Mind you, we can't use the expense as an excuse,' she said. 'Look. She's sent us the money for the train fare.'

'She must really want to see you, Lou,' said Jeannie gently, aware of the difficulties between her and her ma. 'Are you sure you don't want to go? It might be nice to have a little holiday.'

She wrinkled her nose, stuffing the papers back into the envelope. 'I'm not keen. What if she spends the whole time criticising us?'

'You could always come home early,' she pointed out.

Lou shrugged. 'We could, but I'm still not keen. I'll have to talk it over with Lucas. He might prefer a quiet fortnight at home.'

'Well,' said Jeannie as she picked up the tray. 'If you do decide to go, Ma can definitely come and stay with us. Peter too, if he wants. The change might do everyone some good.'

'Thanks, Jeannie. But don't say anything to your ma yet. Let me think about it and talk it over with Lucas first.'

* * *

Ma was delighted to see Jeannie, as was Ruby. They all had a pleasant half-hour in the sunshine, until Ruby started to grizzle and Louisa took her upstairs for a nap.

'It's good to see you up and about, Ma,' said Jeannie. 'We've all been worried about you.'

Ma sighed. 'I know, love. I'm sorry. Peter gave me a good talking-to. He said it's horrible that we've lost John, but he reminded me there's still the rest of you and the babies on the way. I need to stop wallowing and count my blessings.'

'He shouldn't be telling you off,' she said, thinking she should have words with her brother. He could have pushed her deeper into her depression.

'Yes he should,' she replied, patting Jeannie's hand. 'He's right, I realise that. It's not fair on all of you if I just give up. Peter needs me, so do the rest of you, especially with you and Louisa expecting.' She sighed and rubbed her temple. Her light-brown hair was shot through with silver now – more so in recent weeks. Her arthritis had caused her to shrink within herself, the lines around her mouth evidence of her constant physical pain. 'I'm so sorry, Jeannie love. He said you've been so sick and I've barely taken any notice.'

She shook her head. 'There wasn't anything you could do, Ma. It's something every woman goes through, isn't it? And you have noticed things, even when you've been really sad.' Ma looked confused and Jeannie smiled. 'It was you that made me realise there's probably two babies in here.' She stroked her belly. 'Remember? You only had to look at me.'

Her expression cleared and she nodded, laying a hand on Jeannie's growing bump. 'I remember. You're carrying all at the front and bigger than you should be. I was like that with the twins. I was quite small and neat with both Lucas and you, like Louisa is with her babies. My ma predicted it was twins when I was barely three months gone.'

Jeannie nodded, covering Ma's hand and keeping it against her. It was such a relief to see Ma taking an interest after weeks of nothing but overwhelming grief. Her biggest fear now was that something would go wrong with her or Lou's pregnancies. That would be more than any of them could bear.

'I can't say I'm happy with Peter taking it upon himself to tell you off,' she said. 'But he's right about one thing – we all need you, Ma. We're none of us going to forget John. But we've got to go on and we need to think about the next generation. Little Ruby has missed being able to play with her nana, and she's far too young for us to be able to explain it to her.'

Ma smiled. 'I know,' she said softly. 'The little love kept coming over to me for a cuddle while we've been out here.'

'Aw, she's been missing you and is making up for lost time. She's such a little sweetheart, isn't she?'

'She certainly is. She's missing little Mattie as well; he's become like a brother to her.'

Jeannie felt herself tremble at how close Ma had come to realising the truth, but she didn't dare say anything. She was relieved when Louisa came back out and joined them and they talked of other things until Ma declared she was tired. The two girls helped her upstairs so that she could have a lie down, then both of them returned to their respective kitchens to prepare supper for their menfolk.

30

News received at the beginning of the factory fortnight was a welcome cause for celebration for Kate. She rushed round to tell Ted.

'I've passed!' she said as soon as he opened the door. 'Shorthand, typewriting and book-keeping. All with distinction!' She laughed with sheer joy. 'I got a note from my teacher with the results to say that I need to see the office manager when the factory opens. She says they'll probably have a job for me as someone's leaving to get married.'

Ted picked her up and swung her round before kissing her soundly right there on his parents' doorstep. 'Well done, love. I'm proud of you.'

'We should celebrate,' she said.

He agreed. 'Just as well I've got something planned, then, isn't it?' He grinned and winked at her.

'What?' she asked. 'You couldn't know I'd pass. I might have been a failure. Especially after Peg...' She'd been so busy helping look after her dying sister that she'd got behind with her studies.

He shook his head. 'You would never have failed, Kate. You

always do your best and I know you worked twice as hard to catch up because you wanted Peg to be proud of you. Of course I knew you'd pass. So I've arranged a little treat. I'm taking you on the train to Weston-super-Mare tomorrow. Just for the day, mind. I'll deliver you back to Mrs Searle's safe and sound before bedtime.' He tapped her nose. 'I know you'll be disappointed by that. But if you want to have your wicked way with me, you'll have to wait until you make an honest man of me.'

She slapped his chest. 'Oh, you daft beggar!' she laughed. 'No one is having their wicked way with anyone, thank you very much. But I'll gladly take a day trip to Weston with you. I've been wanting to go for years, but the girls were never as keen as I was.'

They left the next day, wearing their Sunday best and carrying a picnic basket. Ted promised to hire deckchairs so that they could eat their feast on the beach. 'And we'll have an ice-cream cornet for pudding.'

The sun was shining and the train was full of folk escaping to the seaside for the day. While everyone chattered around them, Kate and Ted sat side by side, his arm around her shoulders, as they both watched the Somerset countryside flash by.

'There were times when I thought I'd never see this again,' Ted said quietly. 'This is a dream come true.'

She reached up and linked her fingers with his on her shoulder. 'It is for me, too.' She felt him kiss her hair, but she kept her gaze on the fields outside the train carriage. She sighed, relaxing against him, letting the feeling of contentment she always felt in Ted's presence grow until it gently pushed aside the ever-present grief she'd been living with for far too long. She couldn't banish it completely, and nor did she want to. She had loved Ma and Peg too much to ever forget them. Their absence from her life would always hurt. But she would be all right. As Auntie Betty had pointed out, the strength of someone's grief was a measure of the power of the love they felt for those they had lost.

The train wheezed into Weston-super-Mare station and the young children in their carriage urged their parents to hurry to disembark. There was much chatter about donkey rides, sticks of rock, and Punch and Judy puppets. Ted shared a smile with Kate as they witnessed their excitement.

Soon everyone was on the platform, jostling with others trying to board the train and disembarking families laden with all the essentials supplies that were required for a day on the beach: buckets, spades, nets, blankets and, of course, picnic baskets. Ted held theirs while Kate had her bag looped over one arm. He held her other hand to make sure they didn't get separated in the crowd as he led her through the throng towards the exit.

They were just outside the station when Kate felt a heavy hand on her shoulder. She glanced to the side to see grubby fingers grasp the strap of her bag. She yelped as her assailant pulled it off her arm. She grabbed it, pulling it back. 'No!' she shouted as she struggled to hang onto it. The man scowled and fought against her for possession, lifting his free hand to smack her. Around them, women and children screamed and scrabbled to get away from the fray.

It all happened in a split second, but his blow never landed. The moment she yelled, Ted dropped her hand and launched himself at the man. There was a grunt and Kate felt the pressure on her bag strap disappear, causing her to fall backwards onto her bottom. Stunned, she watched as Ted soon had the man face down on the floor, his knee on his back holding him in place. His loud protests were quickly subdued as Ted knelt harder and spoke quietly into the man's ear. Kate couldn't hear what he said, but the thief froze and didn't move or speak again.

Ted's bettering of the man and his calm, commanding voice as he asked for assistance spurred other men on the street into action and within moments, someone had produced a belt and the thief's hands were tied with it. The station master had been summoned and he'd telephoned the police. Kate was helped to her feet and fussed over. She assured everyone that she was fine, that he hadn't had a chance to hurt her, but she couldn't stop the trembling in her bones that the man's attack had brought on. She kept glancing at the captive, consciously reminding herself that this was a random thief, a stranger, and not her pa come back to terrorise her. It wasn't until she raised her eyes to meet Ted's steady gaze on her that she began to calm down a little.

Four constables arrived and two of them led the attacker away while the others ushered Kate, Ted and a few other witnesses back into the station where the station master opened his office for the officers to organise the taking of statements. Kate began to shake again, remembering how she'd been questioned in the aftermath of Pa's attack on her. Then, it had taken Peter and Tom to subdue him. But today, Ted had overcome her attacker single-handedly, and without even breaking a sweat. He was calm and polite, recounting what had happened to the police officers, all the while holding her hand, not letting anyone move her away from his side. When he felt her trembling, he simply moved closer, putting his arm around her. She relaxed a little more, taking comfort from his warmth and strength.

After they had both recounted their tales and given the police their addresses, they were finally allowed to leave.

Outside the station again, where it was less busy now between trains, Ted turned to Kate and touched her cheek. 'Would you rather go straight back on the next train, sweetheart?' he asked.

She shook her head. 'No. I don't want to be left with a

horrible memory of our trip to Weston. I won't let him spoil it for us.' She raised her chin, determination filling her. 'I want to have a picnic on the beach and eat an ice cream. Then I want a stroll along the pier.' She shrugged. 'What the heck, I might even slip off my shoes and stockings and have a paddle if the tide's in!'

He chuckled and pulled her into a hug, kissing her hair. 'That's my girl. We'll have a super day and it will be something to tell our grandchildren one day, eh?'

She looked up at him, her eyes narrowed. 'Who says we're going to have grandchildren?'

'A man can hope, can't he?'

'I'm not sure I want to marry at all, let alone have children and grandchildren,' she said. It wasn't entirely true. The more time she spent with Ted, the more often she could imagine doing just that. But she still felt the need to test him.

He sighed. 'All right, if that's what you want.' He kissed her forehead, earning a disapproving look from an elderly lady who walked past them into the station. 'Then I'll just have to be content with being your beau and taking you on day trips until we're too old and frail to manage it any more. Because you're the only girl for me, Kate Davis. No one else will do. So I'll take what I can and that's that.'

They stood there, the picnic basket at their feet, Kate's bag held tight against her side by their entwined arms while people walked around them. Neither cared; they simply looked at each other. After the fright of the attack, Kate felt safe again.

'Thank you for rescuing me.'

He pulled a face. 'I'm only sorry he got his hands on you. I noticed him when we came out of the station but my reactions are a little slower these days.' His lips thinned to a straight line, his jaw tight. 'He's damned lucky I didn't break his neck there and then.'

She realised in that moment that he was perfectly capable of dispatching a man in such a way. There was something in his eyes that confirmed it. As soon as she saw it, he masked it with what looked like regret, as though he hadn't wanted her to see that side of him. She reached up and touched his cheek. He leaned into her hand and closed his eyes.

'You're a good man, Ted Jackson,' she said softly. 'You kept me safe, and when you might have done lasting harm to that man, you held back. It had nothing to do with your reactions being slow, but rather it was because you knew to do what's right.'

He opened his eyes and smiled at her. 'Thank you. That's a nice thing to say.'

'It's the truth,' she assured him. 'I know you've hinted that you've done bad things, but the more I think about it, the more certain I am that you only did what was necessary. You're too honourable to do anything truly wicked.'

'I don't know about that,' he said. 'If he had hurt you, my love, I wouldn't have hesitated. I'd have killed him. And I could've done it and made it look like an accident, even in front of all those people.'

His earnest gaze searched her face. He might have expected that statement to frighten her. But it didn't; it made her feel protected. She knew he meant it and she was sure he could do it, too, in order to save her from harm. But she also knew she need never fear that Ted would ever hurt her physically. He could break her heart, of course. But she was becoming more sure every day that he would never do that to her. Not again.

'I know,' she said. 'But I'm glad you didn't have to.' She smiled, her fears forgotten. 'Now, let's go and find some deckchairs to rent and get on with the rest of our day. I'm starving!'

* * *

The sun continued to shine. Deckchairs were procured and their picnic eaten. They greeted a few people they knew from home who wandered past them on the long beach, none of whom seemed to have heard about the incident outside the station. Kate didn't get her paddle as the tide was too far out into the Severn Estuary and neither of them was keen to walk over the mud and quicksand to reach the water's edge.

'We'll come back another time,' said Ted as they wandered along the pier. 'You'll get your paddle one day.'

Kate wasn't bothered. 'Even without a paddle, I'm still having a lovely time,' she assured him.

'Even though someone tried to rob you as soon as we got here?' he asked, looking askance at her.

She shrugged, feeling surprised at how carefree she felt. 'Yes, even with all that. Because you were there and you protected me. It made me realise that I will always be safe when I'm with you.'

'You will,' he said. 'I swear to you, Kate, I will always keep you safe, but I also promise that I will never stop you from following your dreams. I love you, Kate. I love your strength, I love your courage and sense of right and wrong. I love that you haven't made it easy for me to get close to you again – it's no more than I deserve.'

'I love you too,' she said softly.

He squeezed her hand, his smile telling her how much her words meant to him. 'Enough to make an honest man of me?' he asked.

She gave him a sideways glance. 'Your ma would object.'

His smile widened and he laughed.

'What?' She narrowed her eyes. 'Are you laughing at me?'

He shook his head, still smiling. 'Never, my love. I'm just happy because you didn't say no like you usually do.'

She chuckled. 'I didn't, did I?' And for the first time, she didn't want to say no. 'So... if I did say yes... what about your ma?'

He squeezed her hand. 'She'll learn to love you.'

She huffed. 'I doubt it. I'll always be Reggie Davis's lass to her.'

His smile disappeared. 'You're nothing like your pa, everyone – including Ma – knows that. She's stubborn, but she *will* come round; she'll have to,' he said. 'Because if she won't, she'll be losing another son. I'll not let her make you unhappy.'

Kate felt her heart swell. He was willing to stand up to his ma to keep her happy. 'You can't turn your back on your ma, Ted,' she said. 'It would be too cruel.'

He shrugged. 'I would rather not,' he agreed. 'But I will if I have to, to make sure my Kate is happy.'

'Your Kate?' She raised her eyebrows.

He looked a bit sheepish, but then he raised his chin.

'That's right,' he nodded. 'You're mine and I'm yours.'

She regarded him for a long moment, trying to decide how she felt about that. It didn't take long to realise that he was right. 'I'm yours and you're mine,' she confirmed with a nod.

This time, it was Ted who raised his eyebrows. 'Does that mean you'll marry me?'

She frowned. 'What about my new job?'

'You can keep it if you want to. With me training to be a teacher and studying all hours when I'm not working, you'll want something to keep you occupied.'

It was what she wanted to hear but... 'It's not that simple though, is it?' she said. 'You can say that, but you'll still want your conjugal rights, won't you?'

She blushed as he laughed.

'I would, if that's all right with you,' he agreed, his gaze heated.

It was. She loved his kisses and couldn't wait to get to know what it would be like to give herself to him completely.

'But then I'll get pregnant and have to give up my job.' She glared at him, her cheeks glowing.

His eyes were still warm, full of desire, but he at least had the decency to look serious. 'Kate, love, there are ways to avoid pregnancy until we're ready to have babies. My French and Dutch comrades told me some of them. And there's a book I've heard about that came out last year. It's called *Married Love* by a Mrs Stopes. It's caused a bit of controversy, because she says it's possible to have a healthy physical relationship without the woman always ending up in the family way. It sounds like it's just what we need. I'll order a copy and we can read it together.'

She blushed again. 'Well that won't be embarrassing, will it?'

He laughed out loud at her sarcasm. 'Wouldn't you rather that than being stuck barefoot and pregnant?' He sobered, his expression turning earnest. 'I'm trying to show you that you have a choice, love.'

For a moment, she wanted nothing more than to choose to be barefoot and pregnant, so long as it was with Ted by her side. But she wasn't ready to admit such a thing. After all, she'd worked jolly hard to get the chance of an office job, so she really wanted the chance to enjoy it for a while. She sighed. 'Get the book,' she said, 'and we'll see what it says.'

He took her face in his hands. 'Does that mean we're engaged?' he asked.

She smiled. 'I think it does.'

He let out a whoop before he kissed her soundly.

31

'Happy Birthday, Lou!' said Jeannie as they greeted each other at the Friends' Meeting House on the first Sunday in September. The two of them laughed when they went to hug but were unable to get close to each other on account of their growing bellies. Tom shook hands with Lucas, who was holding Ruby, and both husbands laughed along with their wives. Peter stood with them. He kissed his sister and ruffled Ruby's hair, sending a nod of acknowledgement to his brother-in-law.

'Ma sends her love,' said Jeannie. Mrs Musgrove had gone to stay with her and Tom during the factory fortnight so that Louisa and Lucas could take Ruby down to Exeter to visit Lou's ma. Even though they'd only gone for three nights, Mrs Musgrove still hadn't returned to the cottage in West End, deciding that it was time to give Louisa and Lucas a rest from having to care for her. Louisa also suspected her mother-in-law was worried that she was a financial burden on Lucas, not that he agreed with her. But everyone knew Tom earned a lot more, and he was happy to support his mother-in-law because it pleased Jeannie.

'How is she?' asked Lucas.

'Her arthritis is bothering her now that the weather's beginning to turn,' said Tom. 'She has good days and bad, as always. She didn't feel up to coming today. She'd like you all to come round and see her this afternoon, though,' said Tom.

'Would that be all right?' asked Jeannie. 'She misses you all and wants to catch up with how you are – and to wish Lou a happy birthday.'

'Of course we can,' said Louisa, speaking for all of them. Peter hesitated.

'Is she still in bed?' he asked.

Jeannie shook her head. 'No. I helped her get up this morning and we left her in the parlour, reading her book. She just thought it would be too painful to walk all this way.' She knew Peter found it hard when Ma was depressed, so she sought to reassure him that her problems today were physical rather than mental. 'Tom's offered to get her a bath chair so we can push her and she doesn't have to walk anywhere, but she says she's not ready for that just yet,' said Jeannie.

'Well that's a good sign,' said Lucas as Ruby wriggled and asked to be put down. As soon as her feet touched the ground, she was off, running towards Mattie, who had just arrived with Will. The children were then rounded up with the other little ones and they happily followed their leaders up the stairs to the upper room where they would enjoy Bible stories and activities while the grown-ups had their silent meeting for worship.

'I can't believe how she rushes off without us now,' said Lucas. 'They grow up so fast.'

'Seeing them off to Sunday school won't bother me,' said Tom. 'It's when they want to start courting that I'm already worrying about. I witnessed all the drama when lads started calling for my sisters.'

The four of them laughed. They greeted Will when he

approached. He was still carrying the air of sadness that had enveloped him since Peg had fallen ill. They didn't have much time to chat before they needed to take their places and the congregation fell into silent contemplation.

Louisa sat between her husband and sister-in-law and settled into the peace of the Meeting House. She gave thanks for all the blessings in her life, including this quiet hour when her daughter was being entertained and she could relax without worrying about her disrupting the silent worship. Her unborn child shifted inside her, as though it was settling down just as its ma was. Louisa smiled and rested a hand on her swollen belly. She would be glad when this child arrived. She was tired of being pregnant now and was keen to meet Ruby's new brother or sister.

She opened her eyes and looked up. Across the room, she could see Auntie Betty sitting with Will. The poor man looked awful and she realised how hard he worked when little Mattie was around to hide his grief from the lad. It was as though the moment he was out of sight, Will's energy drained away. It was all credit to him that Mattie had no idea of his pa's suffering and that he was a happy, healthy little boy, even though Kate said he occasionally asked about his ma, wondering where she was. Louisa's heart ached for the two of them. She wished she could do more to help, but knew that she had to let Will decide who would help him. After all, he had Auntie Betty, Kate and the rest of Peg's family close by. She mustn't be greedy. She would continue to be Mattie's godmother and be part of his life. It was more than she ever expected and she was grateful for it. She hoped that Will would begin to feel a little better soon, but she knew from her own experience of grief that it was never easy. She held him up in the light, hoping that Peg and her Mattie in heaven were looking over him and little Mattie. She found it comforting to think of Peg and Mattie being together up there, helping each other and watching over their loved ones left behind on earth.

As she prayed that it was the case, it occurred to her that maybe her pa was there too. Would he have seen Mattie? Or would he have turned his back on him, as he'd done in life, and sought out the souls of Anglicans to help him make the transition from physical to spiritual? After everything Louisa and her father had been through, would Pa be watching over her like she was sure Mattie was? She hoped so, although it would make more sense that he was watching over Ma, wouldn't it? It occurred to her that, from what she'd learned in Bible classes and from listening to the reverend's sermons at Holy Trinity over the years, Pa's spirit might well be capable of watching over all of his loved ones should he choose to do so. Yet she never felt his presence, not like she had with Mattie.

Maybe he decided Ma needs him more than I do, she mused. It made her feel sad, but she could understand it. When she'd told Lucas about Ma's invitation, he'd encouraged her to accept. 'She's still your ma,' he'd said. 'It will be good to build bridges and introduce her to Ruby. And wouldn't you like to see how she's getting on?'

She hadn't been convinced, still holding onto the hurt of the previous years. But then his ma had said she'd like to go and visit with Jeannie and Tom and that they shouldn't worry about her. Peter had agreed. He relished the idea of having the house to himself – although he'd still turned up at Jeannie's for his meals – if only for a few days. So Louisa had compromised. They went for just three nights, because she feared any longer might prove too much. It had been all right.

The large, terraced house that Ma had purchased in a nice area of Exeter was smart and attracted a good quality of lodgers and a comfortable income. Ma had seemed more relaxed and contented than Louisa had seen her in a long time. Ruby had been a little angel, bless her, and Ma had been delighted with her. She'd even been respectful to Lucas. Louisa and her ma had gone out shopping in Exeter, enjoying each other's company for the first time since before Louisa had taken up with Mattie all those years ago. It seemed as though moving away from Street had finally helped her ma to put the past behind her and there was not a single incidence of reproach or argument, much to Louisa's relief. Maybe in the future, things would continue to improve between them. She had promised that they would stay longer next time, and Ma had agreed to visit them in Street after the new baby was born.

Louisa opened her eyes again and once more her gaze landed on Will. She couldn't help but feel a lingering resentment against her ma when she denied little Mattie's existence, yet as Louisa looked at Will and knew how much joy the child had given him and Peg after years of childlessness, she couldn't regret that she'd given him his brother's son to raise as his own. *Maybe that was God's plan. To help Peg and Will. But if that's the case, why has He been so cruel as to take Peg so soon?* None of it made sense to her. Ever since Mattie had died, she had questioned whether there truly was a god, and if there was, whether he was worthy of worship. It was still a puzzle to her, even though she still firmly believed that Mattie and Peg and Pa were all now at peace in heaven, and that Kate's pa and that awful Floozy were suffering for their sins in hell. She sighed, fidgeting a little as the baby shifted again. She wasn't sure if her thoughts were appropriate for silent worship, but they were the things in her heart that had her attention right now.

* * *

At the end of the meeting for worship, Will approached Louisa while his ma and Lucas collected the children.

'Happy Birthday, Louisa,' he said.

'Thank you.' She smiled. 'How are you, Will?'

He sighed and looked away. 'I'm all right,' he said, although he didn't sound very convincing. 'Look, I know you're probably busy on your birthday, but would you and Lucas mind coming round to Ma's cottage for a bit before you go home? There's something I need to talk to you about.'

She frowned. 'You're not ill, are you?'

He shook his head and looked at her, his eyes sad. 'No, lass. I'm fine. Well, as fine as I can be without my Peg. And Mattie is in good health as well, don't worry.' He glanced around. 'I'd rather we discussed what I have to say in private, though. Could you both spare us a little while? Mattie and Ruby could play for a bit while we talk?'

Auntie Betty had clearly mentioned it to Lucas already because he agreed as soon as Louisa mentioned it. After a quick word to Peter and Jeannie, they set off with the Searles. At Betty's cottage, Kate greeted them as she returned from church and then whisked the children off to the parlour to play with the collection of soft toys that she and Auntie Betty had made especially for when little ones came to visit. As she closed the door behind her, Lucas turned to Will.

'What's the matter?' he asked.

While his ma bustled around making tea, Will urged the two of them to sit with him at the table. He was silent for a moment, his head bowed, his hands clasped together in front of him. Louisa got the impression he was praying for strength. She exchanged a glance with Lucas. He looked as confused as she felt.

'Will,' she said softly. 'Are you sure you're all right?'

Auntie Betty placed the teapot on the table and placed a hand on her son's shoulder. 'You're worrying them, son. You need to talk to them.'

He dipped his head and then raised it to look at them. 'I'm sorry. I've been wrestling with what to do for the best. Me and Ma have talked and prayed and I know I have to do what's best for Mattie. I promised Peg I would do whatever was needed to give the lad the best life.' He paused and rubbed a weary hand across his forehead. 'But it's so damned hard.' His voice almost broke.

Louisa's heart went out to him. 'We know how much you love him, Will,' she said.

He took a deep breath, nodding. 'I do. I adore that boy. I want what's best for him,' he repeated.

'We know,' said Lucas. 'And we'll do anything to help you, friend. Just tell us what you need.'

Will looked at his ma. Betty looked sad as she touched his cheek. 'It's all right, son,' she said.

He looked up at the ceiling, blinking hard before looking back at them, and spoke again. 'I've struggled ever since Peg's passing,' he confessed. 'I thought that being here amongst family would help, but... everywhere I turn, I'm reminded of her, of what I've lost.'

'It's only to be expected,' said Louisa gently. 'I was the same after Mattie.' She looked at Lucas. 'It was like that for both of us, wasn't it?'

He nodded. 'We know how hard it is.'

Will looked down at his hands again. 'It's been difficult at work,' he said. 'I'm struggling to concentrate. I thought I'd be glad to be back, but after being away for four years... and then Peg falling ill when we came home... I can't explain it.'

'You don't need to,' said Lucas. 'You just need to give yourself time.'

'That's what I said,' said Auntie Betty. She looked unutterably sad. 'Oh, I forgot to pour the tea!' She went to stand up, but Louisa touched her hand.

'Don't worry, Auntie,' she said. 'We're all right, thank you.'

The older woman subsided into her chair as Will spoke again.

'The thing is, I'm not sure all the time in the world will make any difference. I'm not happy here without my Peg. I think I need a new start. Somewhere fresh.'

Louisa felt dread squeeze her heart. 'You're going away? But who will help you look after little Mattie?' She looked at his ma. 'Are you going with him, Auntie?'

'No, lass,' she said. 'I would if I could, but it's not practical.'

Lucas frowned. 'Where will you go?' he asked Will.

Will rubbed at his eyes. 'The Clarks have got connections in South Africa. I've been offered a job there.'

Louisa gasped and brought a hand to her mouth. 'You're taking Mattie to Africa?'

Will shook his head. 'That's the thing. I don't think I can. This job is to help set up a new factory. The accommodation will be basic at best to start with. I can't risk the boy. Peg would never forgive me. He'll have to stay here.'

'So what's to become of him?' asked Louisa. 'Is he going to stay with you, Auntie? Because we can help look after him if need be. You know we'll help if we can.'

Before she could answer, Lucas spoke. 'Will, my friend. Are you sure about this? Both Louisa and I tried to escape our memories by leaving Street, but it doesn't work you know.'

Louisa nodded, agreeing with him. 'Your memories will always be with you. We both found that coming home and learning to concentrate on the good memories eventually helped us to learn to accept the bad ones.'

'I have to go and try,' he said. 'I… It's been so hard… I've prayed and prayed, and me and Ma have talked and talked, trying to work out what to do for the best.' Betty nodded sadly as he went on. 'I promised Peg I would do what was best for Mattie, and the more I think about it, the more sure I am of my path.' He reached across the table and took both Louisa and Lucas by the hand.

Louisa grasped his hand in both of hers, tears in her eyes. 'But you're his pa, Will. You're what's best for him. He needs you.'

Will took a deep breath and met her gaze. 'Louisa, I love that boy with every fibre of my being, and I'll forever be grateful to you for giving me the opportunity to care for him. But without Peg, I feel like I'm letting him down. He should have a ma *and* a pa.'

She shook her head, horror filling her. 'I don't understand what you're saying. Are you going to give him away?'

He squeezed her hand. 'No, lass. I'm not giving him away. *I'm giving him back.* To you and Lucas. It's only right.'

She stared at him, stunned, unable to think of a single thing to say. She glanced at Auntie Betty, fearful of the woman's reaction. But she looked back at Louisa with understanding.

'It's all right, lass. I know you're little Mattie's ma. I've suspected for a long time, but Will confirmed it a while ago. I'm grateful to you for what you did to make sure I would know my grandson, and I'm only sorry for the pain you've been through.'

Louisa sniffed and nodded, relieved beyond measure that she wasn't judging her as harshly as her own ma had done.

'If he comes to live with you,' Will went on, 'he'll have a ma and a pa again, as well as his little sister and the babe to come. If I keep him, even if I stay in Street, he'll never have any brothers or sisters from me. You see how he loves playing with Ruby and his Davis cousins. With me, he'd be lonely. I don't want that for him. I want him to be surrounded by family who love him. I want you and Lucas to have him.'

Betty patted Louisa's shoulder. 'I'll still be here for you; so will all of Peg's family.'

'And I'll always be his uncle,' said Will, smiling through his tears. 'He'll be my heir as well one day. But he's young enough that he won't remember that I was his pa for his first three years, will he? He might miss me for a little while, like he has with Peg, but he was happy staying with you when she was ill, so he'll soon settle, I'm sure.'

Louisa sobbed as the realisation hit her. He was coming back to her. She would truly be Mattie's ma, and not just his godmother, watching his life from a distance.

Lucas put his free arm around her shoulders and let her cry as he spoke to Will. 'Are you truly sure about this, Will? What if you get to South Africa and change your mind?'

'I won't come home and steal him away from you again, I promise,' he said, his voice firm. 'I know I'll miss him and will wish I could've kept him. But I also know that, in order to fulfil my promise to Peg, I need to do this because it's what's best for the boy. I'm not planning on getting wed again, and anyway, what other woman could love him as much as Louisa? He needs his true ma. He needs Louisa.' He stared at Lucas, his expression suddenly hard. 'But if you don't think you can love another man's child, you must say so now. I'll not expose him to the risk that you won't care for him like you do Ruby and the other children you have.'

Lucas huffed. 'For God's sake, Will. I was Mattie's best friend. I loved him better than my own brothers most of the time. If you think I would turn against his son, then you don't know me very well.'

'I told you that, son,' said Betty softly, stroking Will's back as though storing up memories of the feel of him in her very bones.

Lucas nodded. 'If you need to do this, Will, then rest assured I will love that lad as well as I love my own children. I'll do my best to raise him to be a good man, and there will always be a welcome for you in our house whenever you can visit.'

Will nodded. 'Thank you. I'm sorry I...'

'Don't fret,' he said. 'You needed to ask. I'd have done the same.'

Louisa took out her handkerchief and wiped her face. 'Thank you, Will. For everything. If it weren't for you and Peg, I'd have lost him forever. It breaks my heart to get him back under these circumstances, and like Lucas says, you'll always be welcome in our house and to see Mattie. But I swear to you, we'll look after him. He's already loved and we'll make sure he knows it every single day.'

He nodded. 'I know it, lass. I can see what a good mother you are. I know he'll be happy with you.'

They talked a little longer. Will would likely leave the country by the end of the month. Arrangements were made to gradually move little Mattie to the Musgrove home. Will would see a solicitor and give them official guardianship of the child. He even insisted on settling a little money on them to help them with the extra mouth to feed. Lucas promised that they would send Will news of Mattie as he grew and that Mattie would be told about his Uncle Will.

Eventually, Will collected Mattie from the parlour and took his leave of them. He would keep the lad with him for another week or so and then they would begin to move him into the

Musgrove family so that Will could still be on hand to help him settle in before he left for foreign shores.

Lucas went into the parlour, explaining to Kate what had been agreed while he rocked a sleepy Ruby. Louisa stayed in the kitchen and talked to Auntie Betty.

'I'm so sorry, Auntie,' she said. 'It must be hard for you seeing Will going away again.'

'It is, lass, I'll not deny it,' said the older woman. 'I'd rather he stayed, but it's plain to see he's not happy and he needs to go and see what there is out in the world for him. I worry that I'll never see him again, like with my Mattie. But I worry more that if he stayed here, he'd never be happy. I pray every day that he'll find peace in his heart, wherever he goes.'

'He might not be happy abroad,' said Louisa, feeling sad for both mother and son. 'Even though Will and Peg were so kind to me, I couldn't escape my grief over losing Mattie while I was away, no matter how far I was from Somerset.'

'I know, lass. But you found your way home and you've a good life now. You can give little Mattie all the love he deserves and I'll be blessed to see my beloved grandson grow up. I pray that my boy will find his way home again as well one day. Maybe he'll be lucky like you and find another to love, although I daren't suggest such a thing now, not when his grief is so raw. All I can do is let him go, pray for him and have faith that the good lord will watch over him and bring him peace.'

32

The first anniversary of the armistice was commemorated around the world on the 11 November 1919. The king and queen held a ceremony in Buckingham Palace. In America, the red poppy – the fragile flower that had proved its strength and tenacity when it had grown through the mud and destruction in the fields of Flanders, prompting Canadian soldier John McCrae to write the haunting poem 'In Flanders Fields' – had been declared a symbol of remembrance, and was soon adopted by all English-speaking countries, while the French and Belgians chose the cornflower.

Across the land, there was a two-minute silence at the eleventh hour on the eleventh day of the eleventh month. Fathers, sons, husbands, brothers and sweethearts were remembered, their absences all the more poignant because their last resting places were on those fields where they died. There was talk of memorials to be created to give the bereaved a focal point where they could remember their lost ones. Clarks commissioned a plaque to go on the wall of the factory near the entrance to commemorate the thirty-seven workers who gave their lives in battle.

'It's a damned miracle there weren't a lot more lost from Street,' said Ted after he and Kate left the service at Holy Trinity.

'Well, I'm grateful for that,' said Kate. 'It's awful that you lost your brother and that Mattie never came home either. But I give thanks every day that both of my brothers returned home, even though their suffering has changed them. And Stan's getting better, isn't he?'

Ted sighed. 'He is.' The hospital authority had got him working in the kitchen gardens at the asylum and he seemed much happier now he had something to occupy himself with. 'Although the doctors say they doubt he'll ever be strong enough to come back to the life he knew before the war.'

'Well, considering they said he'd likely never be capable of doing anything at all and now he's gardening, it's got to be a good sign, hasn't it? Who knows what might happen in the future. Now that the peace is established, he could well continue to improve.' She paused as they stopped by her ma's grave as usual, kissing the tips of her fingers and touching the stone. 'Did I tell you? My friend Gerald has taken over as manager at the market garden where he worked after he got out of prison. The owner hates paperwork, whereas Gerald is very good at it – he was a solicitor's clerk before the war. So now he looks after the administration and ordering, leaving the owner more time to grow his business.' She grinned and nudged his shoulder with her own. 'Get it? *Grow* his business?' She giggled when he groaned at her awful play on words. 'Anyway, the reason I brought it up is that if Stan continues to improve, maybe one day, he can leave the asylum. If he does, I think we should ask Gerald to give him a job. I'm sure he would.'

Ted frowned. 'I don't know,' he said. 'What if he had a

relapse? Just a loud bang going off could send him back into his fears again.'

Kate touched his cheek. 'I know that's a risk, love. But Gerald spent time as a stretcher-bearer in an ambulance unit. He understands the hell Stan went through, and I'm sure he'd keep an eye on him and take care of him if needed.'

Ted nodded. Kate had introduced him to Gerald. She knew he'd been prepared to dislike him, on account of his jealousy over how close Gerald and Kate had become during his years of incarceration as a conscientious objector. But he'd soon realised that Kate had spoken the truth when she'd said that the two of them were simply friends and that there was no attraction between them, and the two men had begun to build a mutual respect for each other, though Kate suspected that Ted was still relieved when Gerald had started courting a lass in Bristol.

'Stan's not ready yet,' he said. 'But, as you say, who knows what the future holds for him? We'll bear it in mind and speak to Gerald if it looks like Stan might need a job to support himself one day.'

'Are you going home to your Sunday dinner?' she asked as they reached the churchyard gate. 'Only I said I'd go over to see how Jeannie's getting on.'

He shook his head. 'My folks are going to see my Uncle Ted.'

She frowned. 'The one you're named for? Who took you up Glastonbury Tor to talk to you after Albert died?'

'That's the one. I'm surprised you remember.'

'Of course I remember you telling me about him. It was just after Ma had died and you said he'd told you to find a little bit of joy in every day. You made me think about the blessèd silence when my pa wasn't in the house, the joy in a child's laughter, and...' She laughed as she remembered. 'And the simple pleasure of a boiling kettle and a nice strong cup of tea.'

He grinned. 'That's right.'

'Didn't you want to go with them?' she asked.

He shrugged. 'I saw him a few weeks back. Apparently, he wants to talk to Ma and Pa about something and he said he'll invite me again in a few weeks. Pa said Uncle wants to meet you, so expect to be invited as well, won't you?'

She smiled and nodded. 'I'll look forward to it.'

'Good. You'll like him. He's been a great help to me, starting over again since I got home.' He kissed her cheek, not caring that they were just yards from the church. 'So it looks like we're both heading to Cranhill Road today. Tom's got some new project he wants to talk about. He's getting requests for help from all over now. Word's spreading about his appliances and how they've helped wounded soldiers, so now people who've had accidents, or were born with deformities, are asking if he can help.' Although glad he didn't have to go back to work in the Clicking Room at Clarks, Ted was still utilising the skills he'd learned there to help cut leather for the splints and straps for prosthetics that Tom designed.

'I know,' she said. 'He's manufactured some devices to help Mrs Musgrove with her arthritis. A brace for her back and neck when it's bad, oh, and he made these special stands for the kettle and teapot that tip so that she can still pour from them without the risk of dropping them and scalding herself. She says they're little miracles that have given her a new lease of life.' They began walking towards the high street. 'Which is a miracle in itself, given how poorly she's been over the years, and especially since John died. It's a relief as well, because Jeannie's got enough on her plate right now. You know she's been ordered to have total bed rest, don't you?'

He nodded. 'Tom said. Is she really poorly?'

She shrugged. 'Not ill as such,' she said, a little uncertain even as she said it. 'It's just that both the doctor and the midwife are fairly certain she's carrying twins, given the size of her, bless her. And she had a funny turn the other day – nearly fainted, she did. Her ma was frantic with worry and so was Tom, so the doctor was sent for. He said that if she didn't want to have these babies too early, she would have to have total bed rest to try and hold onto them for as long as she can. While it might leave Jeannie weak, carrying them for the full nine months, they're much safer in the womb for as long as she can manage it than being born too soon.'

'How will they cope with Jeannie confined to bed?' he asked.

'I don't suppose it will be easy,' she sighed. 'I've offered to help when I'm not working – that's why I'm going today, to do whatever chores need doing, then I'll sit with her and keep her occupied so she doesn't get tempted to get out of bed. Lou can't do much either because she's due any time now, and she's got the two children already.'

'Mmm,' said Ted. 'When you told me the truth about little Mattie, you could've knocked me over with a feather. Mind you, once I'd thought about it, it made sense and wondered why I hadn't realised before. But I suppose she's got her hands full right now, with him and Ruby and a new one on the way.'

Kate had checked with Louisa that it was all right for her to tell Ted about the true circumstances of little Mattie's birth after Will had gone abroad.

'She has, but neither she nor Lucas would have it any other way. And my sisters-in-law are doing what they can to help. They weren't fooled when Louisa rushed off to Lincolnshire with Peg and Will, but they knew she was doing something selfless for Peg, so they've never said anything or held it against her. Mattie's still family as far as they're concerned as Peg had loved him so much and he's Will's true nephew, and Louisa is family now on account of her being Mattie's ma. It's all a bit confusing to anyone else, I'm sure, but only the families know the truth of it. To everyone else, Louisa and Lucas have taken on the guardianship of her godson while Will goes off to work in foreign parts. Because it's no one else's business who Mattie's true parents are, so long as the little lad is loved and well cared for, is it?'

'Quite right, sweetheart,' he said as they turned into Cranhill Road. 'It seems that, after all these years of war, and then the chaos of the repatriations and the flu epidemic these past twelve months, there are families that have been fractured and reset into a lot of different shapes all over Europe. Didn't you say that Tom had been married before, as well?'

'He was.' She pulled a face. 'But let's not talk about that now,' she said as they arrived at the house that Tom had bought for his bride and knocked at the door.

Tom answered and welcomed them inside. 'Louisa's upstairs with Jeannie, Kate. Why don't you go on up? Ted can join me, Lucas and Peter in the workshop.'

'Aren't there any chores to do?' she asked.

He shook his head. 'Between Auntie Betty, the Musgroves and the Davises, it's all done.'

She frowned. 'It's mighty quiet. Where are the children? And Mrs Musgrove?'

He smiled. 'Auntie Betty took the little ones with her over to Fred's to play with their cousins, and Ma has a cosy chair by the range in the kitchen where she's reading her book. She says there's a pot of beef stew big enough for us all simmering on the range, so I hope you'll stay for a meal.'

Ted rubbed his hands together. 'I never say no to a good stew.' He grinned.

* * *

Kate left them to it and ran upstairs to find her friends. When she entered the bedroom, she burst out laughing. Jeannie was sitting up in bed, resplendent in a pink bed jacket, while Louisa sat next to her on top of the covers.

'Look at you two,' she said. 'You remind me of Tweedledum and Tweedledee with those bellies of yours.'

Louisa groaned and covered her face. 'Don't mock,' she said. 'This is the most comfortable I've been all day and the first time in ages since I could see my toes.' She wiggled her stockinged feet.

Kate kissed both of them and then settled herself against the board at the other end of the bed, facing her friends. 'So, how are you both?'

Jeannie pulled a face. 'Bored!' she said. 'I've done so much knitting and sewing and reading that I swear I'll go blind if I do much more.'

'Then take some naps while you've got the chance,' said Kate. 'You know you'll be wishing for another hour in bed when you've got two babies to take care of.'

'That's what I said,' Louisa agreed. 'I'm having a lovely time here and I'm determined to make the most of every minute of it. Once Auntie Betty gets back with the children, there'll be no peace for any of us.'

Jeannie poked her in the side. 'Don't pretend you're complaining,' she said. 'You're relishing every moment you have with Mattie and Ruby.'

She chuckled. 'I am. So is Lucas, and even Peter's having fun with them. But that doesn't mean I can't appreciate a quiet hour or two when they're otherwise engaged.'

Kate beamed at her friends. 'Aw, it's so lovely to see the two of you, both married and having babies. And you say Peter's doing all right?'

Louisa shrugged, sobering a little. 'He's still awful sad. We never get over the loss of a loved one, do we?' Jeannie and Kate both nodded, remembering all of the losses they'd suffered. The three friends were silent for a few moments, until Jeannie gasped.

'Ow!' She rubbed the side of her bump and fidgeted, making the edges of her bed jacket fall apart, exposing her nightgown-clad swollen body. Then she yelped and rubbed the other side. 'I swear, if there aren't two babies in here, I'm growing a monster. There seem to be so many feet, knees and elbows, and they always seem to catch me unawares when they shift about.'

Kate watched, fascinated as her friend's belly undulated.

Louisa stroked a hand over Jeannie's belly.

'It's bad enough carrying one at a time,' said Lou. 'I can't imagine what it would be like with two.'

Kate shivered. 'I'm not sure I want anything growing inside me, thank you very much.'

The others stared at her. 'Really?' asked Jeannie. 'But you're so good with the little ones. Don't you want some of your own?'

'Not for a while,' she said.

'Is that why you and Ted haven't set a date?' asked Louisa.

Kate tried to look nonchalant, but couldn't help it when a small smile escaped. 'Actually, we're thinking of next Easter for the wedding. But that doesn't mean I'm going to give up work and rush into having babies,' she went on as they squealed with excitement. 'Ted's still got to finish his teacher training and I'm loving my job in the office, so there'll be no honeymoon babies for us,' she said, pointing at Jeannie's belly.

Louisa shook her head. 'Kate, love. I hate to tell you this, but you do know that if you're married and enjoying conjugal relations, having a baby is almost inevitable.'

'Unless you have problems like dear Peg, bless her heart,' said Jeannie.

'Even if I didn't have Peg's problems,' she replied. She realised it was a possibility, but Ma had had four babies and her brothers were all fathering children at regular intervals – and of course Pa had produced more offspring than he ought to. 'I want to be able to choose if and when I have children.'

'We'd all like some control over that kind of thing,' said Louisa. 'But it's just not possible.' She pulled a face. 'I can tell you, it's far easier to get in the family way than it is to prevent it once you're having regular physical relations.'

This time, Kate's smile widened, even as her cheeks grew warm. 'Not necessarily. Have you heard about the book by Mrs Marie Stopes? It's called *Married Love*. It helps couples to enjoy married life without ending up pregnant if they don't want to.'

'I heard about that,' said Jeannie. 'Aren't some people trying to ban it?'

Kate scoffed. 'Mainly men, I'll wager. But it's been published and my Ted has just managed to obtain a copy.'

The girls' eyes widened. 'Have you read it?' asked Louisa.

'Not yet,' she said. 'We're going to start studying it together.'

'Oh, my,' said Jeannie. 'Some folks are saying it's indecent.'

'Some folks take against anything they've a mind to,' she said. 'But it's mine and Ted's business what we read and what we do. If we want to read this book, then that's what we'll do.' She paused for a moment, her expression earnest. 'If we didn't have it, I doubt I'd agree to marry Ted for another year or two. But, provided it seems sensible when we read it, I'd be willing to get wed soon and we'll use whatever methods it suggests to stop me falling pregnant straight away.'

Lou looked thoughtful as she rubbed her belly. 'Do you really think you can stop it?' she asked.

She nodded. 'Ted says people he met in France and Belgium knew how to put off having babies as well – they didn't want to bring children into a war zone, so they took steps to prevent it. I'm pretty sure that Mrs Stopes's methods – she calls it *family planning* – must work, otherwise folk wouldn't be so against it. I know our vicar is always going on about how we need to produce a new generation to replace the one we lost in the war. He'd be horrified if he knew we had the book.'

'Hmm,' Lou murmured. 'I must confess, much as I love my babies, having three in four years has worn me out. I might want more later, when Mattie, Ruby and this one are a bit older, but I've been worrying about how I can stop falling if we carried on... you know,' she finished, going red.

'Making married love?' Kate grinned.

'Oh you! Yes, all right, making married love,' she laughed, her cheeks still glowing. 'But it's not just that. Lucas works so hard, and the more children we have, the harder it is for him to support us all. I've tried to help by selling my paintings and that's brought in a few extra shillings now and again, but with more babies, I'll have less time to do my art, so I won't have anything to sell.'

'You'll find a way,' Kate assured her. 'Didn't the chap at the gallery in Wells say he knew someone who was looking for designs for greetings cards? You could earn good money from that with just a few paintings.'

'I suppose. I'm still waiting to hear.'

Jeannie was silent, frowning.

'What's got that expression on your face, Jeannie?' asked Kate when she noticed.

Jeannie sighed and shrugged. 'I don't know. I think I've had too much time to think, being stuck in this bed,' she said. 'I've been fretting. I mean... I fell so quickly, and we're likely having twins. I'd barely got used to being married and enjoying personal time with Tom before I was expecting and being so sick. What if that happens every time? And if I have more twins, how will I cope if I have to have bed rest like I am now? Ma does what she can, but she struggles and I can't expect her to do a lot once the babies arrive.' Her eyes filled with tears. 'I really like making married love with Tom; it's much better than I expected. But if I keep ending up like this, we'll never get the chance to enjoy it, will we? What if he ends up wishing he'd never married me?'

'Aw, love.' Louisa put an arm around her shoulders and hugged her. 'Don't fret. Tom will never regret marrying you. That man loves you with all his heart.'

'She's right,' said Kate. 'But if you're that worried, why don't we pass the book onto you once we've read it?'

'I want me and Lucas to read it, as well,' said Louisa. 'In fact, with this baby due first, I think we should get first dibs on it. Then we can pass it to Jeannie and Tom after their babies are born. How does that sound?'

Jeannie nodded, wiping at her eyes.

Kate laughed. 'Then I suppose me and Ted had better read it quick.'

'But if you're not getting married until Easter…' said Louisa.

She smirked. 'Well, we might not have to wait until then to enjoy *making married love* if this book is as good as people say it is.'

Jeannie gasped. 'Kate! What if his ma or Auntie catch you?'

Louisa shook her head. 'Where there's a will, there's a way. Mattie and I certainly didn't worry about it, did we?'

Kate held up a hand. 'I'll not being doing anything I shouldn't in Auntie's cottage, nor at the Jacksons' house. Ted's looking to rent somewhere that will be our home once we're wed.

If he finds somewhere soon, well, we might just do what we want to whether we're wed or not.'

Louisa raised her eyebrows. 'And if you still end up expecting? Only me and Mattie thought it couldn't happen the first time, and look how that turned out.'

Kate gulped. She might be acting cocky, but she wasn't as confident as she made out. If she were honest, if they could prevent pregnancy, then she saw no reason to wed at all until they wanted children. But, just in case, she'd agreed to set a wedding date with Ted. 'Well, then we'll have to face the consequences, won't we?' But with any luck, they wouldn't become parents for a couple of years yet at least. That didn't mean she wanted to wait that long to find out what it was like to be with Ted in the closest sense. His kisses and caresses were getting her mighty excited these days and she didn't see why she had to wait to go all the way.

* * *

While their sweethearts were discussing such intimate things, Tom, Lucas and Ted, plus Peter, had reviewed the projects they had been working on together and decided on the ones they would do next. Every request Lucas received was a plea for help for someone who was in discomfort and needed something to aid them in either their recovery or their rehabilitation. The work they did together wasn't paid, although their anonymous sponsor provided funds to pay for the materials they used and for any extra tools they required in order to complete their projects.

'We might need to slow down a bit once these babies arrive,' said Lucas. 'I know I've been lagging a bit lately with Mattie coming to live with us, and much as I wish I could do more, I'll need to be around to help Lou even more once the next one arrives.'

Tom nodded. 'I know. I'm aware that my life is about to change as well.' He gave them a sheepish grin. 'I can't wait, but I'm also terrified. That's why I think we need to be careful to control the number of requests we accept. I don't want to keep people waiting longer than necessary, nor do I want to let anyone down. But we've all got our paying jobs as well as our families to consider.'

'I can probably do more in the school holidays,' said Ted. 'I'll still be studying, but I'll definitely have more time on my hands.'

'Is that why you decided to become a teacher instead of coming back to the Clicking Room?' asked Lucas with a smirk. 'Short hours and all those holidays?'

Ted laughed. 'Of course. Although don't believe everything you hear about those short hours. I'll still be planning lessons and marking work outside of school hours. If I don't get my students through their exams at the end of the year, I'll be back in the Clicking Room before you know it.'

'You'll be teaching French, right?' asked Peter. 'At the grammar school?'

'I will, God willing. Who'd have thought when I got chatting to Pierre, the Belgian refugee who came to work at Clarks, that I'd end up fluent in French and a schoolmaster to boot?'

'Well, I think it's a grand thing,' said Lucas. 'I always thought you were too clever for your own good. I was sure you'd end up a foreman like your pa.'

'What happened to Pierre?' asked Peter. 'He left when you did.'

Ted was quiet for a moment, his face sombre. 'He died,' he said eventually. 'Such a damned waste.'

'The whole war was a damned waste,' said Tom.

Lucas put a hand on Peter's shoulder. 'All right, lad?'

Ted glanced at the boy and realised his eyes had filled with tears. 'Oh crikey, I'm sorry, Peter. I didn't think. You must miss John.' He deliberately mentioned his dead twin, refusing to be like so many people who would avoid talking about those who'd passed. It wasn't fair to the departed, nor to those who grieved for them.

Peter sniffed and nodded. 'I do. But at least he didn't end up dead in some trench. He was doing what he loved and I reckon he was as happy as he could be when he passed. He was the hero of the match. He saw that ball hit the back of the net. He'd have been well pleased with that.'

'He would,' Ted agreed. 'A hat trick, eh? Must have been quite a match.'

They all fell silent, thinking about it.

'Right,' said Tom after a few moments. 'Are we agreed? There's two prosthetic legs to finish for different people, another arm with hand attachments and some splints all nearly done. I'll work out what materials we need for the next batch of projects and put a request for funds in. Then we can start working on those whenever we have the time.'

Peter nodded. 'I'm happy to do more hours if need be. I know Lucas and Louisa will need my help with the littl'uns, and I've got some studying as well. But I feel better when I'm busy, so you might as well use me. I'm getting better at the engineering side, aren't I?'

'That you are,' said Tom. 'Thanks, Peter.'

33

Everyone but Tom and Jeannie gathered round the kitchen table to enjoy Mrs Musgrove's beef stew. She had sent her son-in-law upstairs with a tray so that the couple could eat their meal together. It was a bit of a squeeze, especially when Auntie Betty came back with Mattie and Ruby, but they managed it.

'They've got room for a proper dining room next door,' Jeannie's ma told Auntie Betty. 'But, bless them, they didn't want me struggling on the stairs, so they made a bedroom for me in the front parlour and what should be the dining room is our parlour now.'

'Ah, that's nice,' said Betty. 'It's good to be comfortable. I know I find my old bones protest more and more on the stairs after a long day's work.'

'You don't need old bones to feel the strain, Auntie,' said Kate. 'I'm so grateful to be working in the office now instead of the Machine Room. The three flights of stairs were bad enough, but I used to come home with aching fingers, a sore back from leaning over the machine all day, and a rotten headache from the noise and smells. At least now, there's less stairs, I sit up straighter at my desk and it's a lot quieter. It makes a big difference to how I feel at the end of the day.' She grinned. 'The better pay packet is nice as well.'

Betty beamed at her. 'I'm so proud of you, lass. I know your ma would be too.'

'Oh yes,' said Mrs Musgrove. 'She would. And now you're getting wed.' She smiled at Ted. 'You must tell us what we can do to help. Just because your ma and pa aren't here, doesn't mean you don't have people who love you, Kate.'

Ted squeezed her hand as Kate welled up. 'Thank you,' she said. She blinked hard against her tears as everyone carried on eating as though it was the most natural thing in the world. She supposed it was for these good folks. They'd never judged her for who her pa was and they'd loved and respected her ma. There might be times when she felt alone, especially after Ma and then Peg had died. But, she realised, she wasn't alone. All these people here today, and Jeannie and Tom upstairs, were as much family to her as her own kin.

Mattie was sitting on Peter's lap, sharing his bowl of stew. Lucas held Ruby and was feeding her chunks of potato and carrot from his own. Ted caught Kate's eye and winked as he took a spoonful of the rich broth. She smiled then looked away before she got too hot under the collar thinking about that book they were going to start reading and everyone saw her blush. Auntie and Mrs Musgrove chatted quietly about people they both knew. Between her mother-in-law and Lucas, Louisa was quiet, frowning down at her food.

'Are you all right, Lou?' Kate asked.

'I think so,' she said, not looking at all convinced as she put a hand to her belly. 'Just a twinge.'

'Try and eat something, sweetheart,' said Lucas. 'You need to keep up your strength.'

She nodded and picked up her spoon and had a few mouthfuls. The chatter carried on around the table, but all eyes were on Lou as she concentrated on her meal. When she dropped her spoon and gasped, Lucas was immediately on his feet. Kate jumped up and took Ruby from him as he knelt by Louisa's chair.

'Do we need to get you home, love?' he asked quietly.

She nodded and tried to stand, but immediately sat again. 'Oh no! I can't!' she said, looking down.

At her feet, Kate could see water dripping onto the stone floor. Mrs Musgrove pushed herself to her feet. 'She's right, Lucas, love. Her waters have broken. You shouldn't try and move her through the streets now. If it's anything like last time, it won't be long. Better get her into my room.'

'What can we do?' asked Auntie as Lucas picked up his wife and carried her out of the room.

'Can you help me get some towels on the bed, Betty, please? Then we'll need to boil some water. Kate, can you and Ted help Peter get Mattie and Ruby back to West End and look after them for the time being? I'll send Lucas round to bring some of Louisa's things from home. Can you sort them out ready for him, please, lass? And don't forget some clothes for the baby.'

Within minutes, Mrs Musgrove had organised everyone. Kate had run upstairs to tell Jeannie and Tom what was going on before she, Ted and Peter whisked the children off to the cottage on West End, leaving the older women to attend to Louisa.

* * *

The children were in bed and the three of them were sitting in the parlour waiting for news. Lucas had arrived not long after them to kiss the children, collect the bag of things Kate had prepared and rush back to Cranhill Road. He said Louisa was calm and wanted to apologise to Jeannie and Tom for giving birth in their house, but they weren't bothered about that. Kate, Ted and Peter settled down to wait for news.

He finally let himself back into the Musgrove cottage at gone ten o'clock.

'It's a boy,' he said, with a tired smile. 'Henry John Musgrove. After Lou's pa and our brother.'

'Is Lou all right?' asked Kate.

'She is.' He nodded. 'A bit tired. But Ma says that was an even quicker labour than when she had Ruby. She reckons we'll have to be careful in future. No outings near her due date.'

Kate laughed. 'Is she going to have to lie-in at Jeannie's now?'

He shook his head. 'No. She'll stay there tonight, but I want her home. I'll pop into the factory first thing and arrange a day off. I can borrow a hand cart and get Lou and the baby home on that.' They'd used such a cart to get Mrs Musgrove to Glastonbury Station when Lucas had come home from the war. She hadn't wanted to wait at home but hadn't been strong enough for the walk. 'We've already arranged for your sisters-in-law to help here while I'm at work, so she'll be able to rest and get to know little Henry John.'

She smiled. With Vi and Ada being close neighbours, they often watched each other's children while one of them had something to do. No doubt they'd take turns watching the combined Davis and Musgrove children while the other spent time making sure Louisa and little Henry had everything they needed. 'Good,' she said. 'I can pop round and let them know before work in the morning. I'm sure one of them will be round straight away to watch the little ones and help Lou while you get things organised.'

'Thanks, Kate. I appreciate it.'

'I can come round when the shift ends every day as well, if

you like?' she said. 'I expect you'll be rushing home every dinner time to check on them.'

'I will,' he agreed. 'But I'm sure she'll be glad to see you after work as well.'

Peter stood up and yawned. 'Right, I'm off to bed.' He paused, then looked at his brother. 'I'm glad John's his middle name. It might've been hard if that had been his first name.'

Lucas nodded. 'I know. And Louisa thought you might want to call a son of your own John one day.'

He shrugged. 'Maybe. Who knows what's going to happen?' He yawned again and headed for the stairs.

Ted congratulated Lucas. 'Get yourself some rest, my friend. You're going to need it. I don't know, I turn my back for a few years and here you are, married with three littl'uns before I've barely got my feet back on the welcome mat.'

Lucas laughed. 'I never thought it would happen, but I'm a happy man. We just need to get you two wed now.'

They said their goodnights and went out into the night. The electric lights along the high street would remain on until eleven o'clock, so their way was illuminated as far as The Cross.

'It's strange, isn't it?' said Kate. 'When the war started, we were all young and daft, working at the factory and having fun. Then everything turned dark. Mattie and your brothers went, then Lucas, then you. Ma got ill and Pa showed his true colours. Louisa lost Mattie and little Mattie and we didn't think she'd ever be happy again. But even that brought a blessing when my sister Peg stepped in to be the boy's ma. It made her so happy.' She sighed. 'I still can't believe God could be so cruel as to take her away from us, but I suppose it brought little Mattie back to Louisa.'

He squeezed her arm but didn't say anything.

'We thought there wasn't any hope for Jeannie when Tom

confessed he already had a wife,' she went on. 'But then the woman died and he was free to wed again. Now she's going to be a ma twice over, and Louisa already has three.'

He held her close as they walked. 'We're all of us changed by the war and this past year has shown us that change will carry on happening, whether we're at war or at peace. Life goes on, but so does death. I'm sorry you lost your ma and sister, that I lost my brothers one way or another, and that Mattie never got to see his son. But I thank God every day that He brought me back to you, Kate. I can't wait for our wedding. I know you're not in any rush to start a family, but that's all right. We'll be careful, I promise. I want you to be happy. That's all that matters to me.'

'Mmm,' she said, looking up at him, a little sheepish. 'About that book you've got. I might have mentioned it to the girls.'

He raised his eyebrows. 'Oh? And what did they have to say about it?'

She giggled. 'That we're to read it quick and then pass it on to them. Jeannie's terrified of having more twins, so she wants as big a gap between pregnancies as she can manage, and Louisa's ready for a break after three babies, so she'd like to find out how to prevent it as well.'

'And what will their husbands think about it?' he asked.

She huffed. 'They're our bodies, you know. It should be up to the wife, who has to carry and birth the babies. Your part is easy. Why should you have a say at all?'

'I'm not arguing with you, sweetheart. But isn't it between a husband and wife to make these sorts of decisions together? I don't want to come between couples, that's all.'

She was silent for a bit, thinking about what he'd said, as they passed the factory entrance. 'This book, *Married Love*,' she said.

'Yeah?'

'It's about couples enjoying a healthy physical relationship in their marriage without having babies if they don't want them, isn't it?'

'Sort of. Mrs Stopes wants couples to enjoy intimate relations and for them to have a choice as to when they have a family. It's not all about preventing pregnancy, but rather about loving relationships.'

She nodded. 'Well, then, I don't think Lucas or Tom can complain, can they? If the book helps them to have more intimacy with their wives, without the burden of more and more children, it's got to be a good thing, hasn't it?'

'I suppose so,' he agreed. 'I'd still feel happier about passing it along if I knew the lads were all right about it.'

'Fair enough. I'll tell the girls to talk to them about it. In the meantime, we get first dibs. When are we going to read it?'

He laughed. 'As soon as you like, sweetheart.'

They passed the Quaker Meeting House and reached The Cross. The street lights ended here, but there was still some light coming from the windows of the Street Inn, and there was a full moon out. Soon they were at the cottage in The Mead. Auntie Betty had obviously arrived home and left a lamp on in the parlour for Kate before she'd gone to bed.

'What a day, eh?' said Ted as he kissed her on the doorstep.

'I know. I can't wait to meet little Henry John tomorrow. Then Jeannie's babies will be here in a few weeks. I'm planning on having lots of cuddles.'

He smiled and touched her cheek. 'When you're ready, you're going to be a good mother. I can't wait to marry you, Kate Davis.'

'I've been blessed to be surrounded by women who are good mothers,' she said. 'My ma, Peg, Auntie Betty, my sisters-in-law, and Louisa. I know Jeannie will be a wonderful ma as well because she's such a caring person. If I can be half as good as any of them, then I'll be content.'

'You will be, and I'll do my best to be as good a man as my pa as well.'

'Then our children will be very lucky indeed,' she said, kissing him again. 'And so will I.'

* * *

After he'd gone home, Kate took the lamp and made her way upstairs. She thought about what he'd said and she knew that Ted would be a good husband and father. Both of her friends had chosen good men as well. She couldn't imagine anyone more perfect for them than Lucas and Tom. She felt a pang of sadness for poor dear Mattie, who'd lost the chance to prove himself as Louisa's husband, but she felt sure he would be looking down on his best friend and wishing him well, knowing that he made Louisa happy and that he had welcomed Mattie's son into their lives and loved him as much as he did his own children.

This first armistice had been a day to remember the dead, but it had also been a symbol of everyone's hopes for the future. For a world at peace, for a brighter future for everyone. Little Henry John's birth was a sign of the joy to come for the Clarks factory girls and Kate looked forward to seeing what further joys were to come for her, Louisa and Jeannie.

EPILOGUE

EASTER 1920

Kate stood before the mirror as Auntie Betty fitted the veil to her hair. Behind her, she could see Jeannie and Louisa, her matrons of honour, both looking pretty in their matching blue dresses.

'You look beautiful, lass,' said the older woman, kissing Kate's cheek. 'Ted's a lucky man.'

'I know.' She grinned. 'I'm going to miss living here with you, though.'

'Ah, don't be daft. You'll be too busy with married life to miss anything. Besides, it's not like you're rushing off to foreign parts, is it? We'll see each other often enough between the factory and family gatherings. And if that's not enough, you know you're always welcome to pop in for a visit.'

Kate nodded. 'I will. Thank you so much, Auntie. You're like a second mother to me.'

Betty sniffed and blinked rapidly. 'Don't make me cry now, Katie, love. I'm just so happy for you.'

'We all are,' said Jeannie.

'Yes,' said Louisa. 'We never thought we'd see the day. You were always so fierce about wanting to remain a spinster.'

She shrugged. 'I probably would have if Ted hadn't come home. He's the only one who will let me be me.'

'So you'll still be working in the factory office once you're married?' asked Betty.

'I will. Ted's got a little while to finish his teacher training, so my wages are coming in handy.' Not least to pay the rent on the little cottage they'd found in Grange Road near The Cross, although Ted's uncle had settled some money on him which would cover his living expenses until he qualified. The alternative had been to move in with Ted's parents and, although Mrs Jackson had softened a little since their engagement, she was still a formidable woman and Kate didn't think living under the same roof as her mother-in-law was a good idea.

Her friends didn't say anything about the possibility of falling pregnant now that she and Ted were finally getting married, because they knew that it was possible these days to enjoy physical relations without it always having to end in pregnancy.

Auntie Betty merely raised her eyebrows and smiled. She'd seen the book, *Married Love* when Kate had forgotten to put it away one day, so Kate suspected she knew more than she was letting on about Kate and Ted's intentions.

'I'll be off to the church now, love. Your brothers are downstairs, ready to walk you there. The little ones are waiting there for you.' Her niece and nephews and Louisa's two eldest were to be bridesmaids and page boys. Kate had expected to have a quiet wedding, with just her best friends standing as her matrons of honour, but Mr Jackson had declared that as she had no parents to do so, then he and his wife were paying for all of the wedding, and that Kate should have as many attendants as she wished. It had left her choked with emotion, knowing her own pa wouldn't have given anything towards her special day.

Auntie Betty turned to the others. 'Are you walking with me, or following on with Kate?'

'We'll walk with Kate, Auntie,' said Louisa.

She nodded and took her leave. 'Don't be long now. Ted will be impatient to see his bride.'

Left alone with her friends, Kate turned back to the mirror for one final check. Her mother-in-law had insisted that she follow the trend of wearing white and a veil, although Kate had felt a little uncomfortable, given that she and Ted had anticipated their wedding day. But Mrs Jackson didn't know that, so they'd agreed that if it pleased her, then Kate would be content to wear white.

'So, your brothers are escorting us to the church, then Fred will walk you down the aisle, right?' said Jeannie, standing next to her to smooth a wrinkle in the fine net of Kate's veil.

'That's right. I'd rather them than anyone else.' She was eternally grateful that Reggie Davis was cold in the ground, unable to turn up and disrupt the day. 'I wish Ma could be here, though.'

Louisa came to stand on the other side of her. She touched the silver cross that Kate wore, the one that Ma had given her. 'She is, I'm sure. She'll be so pleased and proud.'

Kate fanned her face and blinked hard. 'Stop it, you'll make me cry.'

'We'd better go,' said Jeannie. 'Can't keep him waiting any longer.'

The short walk to Holy Trinity was accomplished in a few minutes. Kate stood proud between her two brothers, thankful that they had both survived the war and come home to their families. When they arrived, George kissed her cheek and went into the church where the Davis and Jackson families and all their friends were gathered. Even some of the Clark family were in attendance, marking Mr Jackson's status as a foreman at the factory.

'All right, lass?' asked Fred, offering her his arm.

His voice still rasped with the after-effects of the gas attack, but he was getting stronger all the time. He'd never be as fit as he was before the war, but he was doing well.

'I am,' she agreed. 'I'm ready.'

He escorted her slowly up the aisle as the organ played. Behind her, Jeannie held Kate's niece Catherine's hand and Louisa guided little Ruby. Her nephews, including little Mattie, held hands and walked solemnly together behind the others. Everyone rose and turned to watch her. For a moment, she faltered. She'd never expected so many people to turn up to her wedding, to wish her well. But here they were.

Gerald, his ma and his sweetheart smiled at her from one of the back pews. Ahead of her, she saw Auntie Betty dabbing her eyes as she stood next to Mrs Musgrove, who remained seated due to her arthritis. Baby Henry was held in the arms of his Uncle Peter. Tom stood to the side, rocking the baby carriage that contained his and Jeannie's twin daughters, born in January. They were tiny but perfect.

There were her sisters-in-law and George near the front. Even Mrs Jackson looked pleased as she stood with her husband and Ted's uncle, who both beamed at Kate. There were dozens of other people there, but as she drew nearer to the altar, she had eyes for no one but Ted. He stood, tall and proud in his best suit, waiting for her. She knew that Lucas was standing next to him as his best man, but she couldn't even spare him a glance once her gaze had met Ted's.

At last they reached him and Fred passed her hand to her groom. Ted squeezed her hand and tucked it onto his arm. His eyes blazed with warmth and love. 'You're beautiful,' he whispered. 'I'm the luckiest man in the world.'

The service went by in a haze. Both bride and groom spoke their vows clearly, their gaze not leaving each other, even when little Mattie said loudly, 'That my Annie Kay and Unca Ted,' causing a few chuckles in the congregation.

* * *

The wedding breakfast was held at the Crispin Hall. Mr Jackson had insisted on it, declaring that if only one of his sons was going to wed, he wanted it to be a celebration they would all remember. In the absence of Kate's father, he gave a speech, welcoming Kate into the family.

After a slap-up meal, the speeches and toasts, Kate took a moment to catch her breath. Her matrons of honour joined her in a quiet corner while Ted continued to accept congratulations from all and sundry.

'He's as pleased as punch,' laughed Kate. She was too, but she didn't want to admit it.

'Of course he is,' said Louisa. 'It's been a long, hard journey to get you up the aisle, so he's entitled to be.'

'Look at us,' said Jeannie with a smile. 'All old married women now and with five children between us already.'

'Well don't be looking at me to add to the tally any time soon,' said Kate. 'We agreed we'd wait for a while, until Ted is qualified and settled at least.'

'We know,' said Louisa. 'I'm not planning on any more just yet, either. Although I might try for another girl one day.'

Kate laughed. 'What happens if you have another boy – will you keep trying and end up with a football team of lads?'

Louisa rolled her eyes. 'I don't think so.'

'And what about you, Jeannie? Now the twins are here, are you thinking you'll want more?'

Jeannie blushed. 'I've barely recovered from having the girls, thank you very much. I got so bored, lying in bed all the time for weeks before they were born, that I'm not sure I want to go through that again.' Her cheeks got even redder. 'I do enjoy the intimacy of married love, though, so who knows what might happen?'

The three of them giggled. 'You might have a singleton next time,' said Kate.

'Huh! Knowing my luck, I won't. But so long as we follow the advice in Mrs Stopes's book, we should be all right to enjoy life for a while before we make a decision.'

Louisa smiled. 'Isn't it amazing how life has changed over the past few years? Before the war, we were daft young lasses who only had ourselves to worry about.'

'That we were,' sighed Kate. 'Then we discovered lads.'

Jeannie nodded. 'Not that any of us had any luck at first, did we? It might have been different if not for the war. I doubt if Douglas would have given me a second look, and I know for a fact that Sid Lambert wouldn't have laid a hand on me if Lucas had been home.'

'But then you wouldn't have met Tom,' Kate pointed out. 'Your hero.'

Jeannie smiled. 'Hardly. I'd already bested Sid by the time he arrived. Although he did make Sid think twice about chasing after me. Then we had all those months of dancing around each other when I was sure he didn't fancy me, only to find out about his wife. I thought I'd never get wed after that.'

'Yet, here you are, an old married woman and ma to twins,' said Kate, nudging her shoulder as she grinned at her friend, who grinned back.

'I know! How lucky am I?' she laughed. 'Although I'd feel luckier if the girls would sleep a little longer. I'm exhausted all the time, and so's poor Tom. At least I don't have to work all day like he does. How that man manages his job at the factory and then all the projects that come his way, I'll never know. But he never complains, bless him.'

'You've got a good one, there, Jeannie,' said Kate. She glanced across at Ted as his distinctive laugh rang out as he chatted to some of his old workmates from the factory. 'We all have.'

'Nothing turned out how we expected, did it?' said Louisa. 'I still miss Mattie, but I'm happier than I ever expected to be with Lucas. He's a good man and a wonderful father. What I felt for Mattie was like a moth being attracted to a light. I couldn't keep away from him even when my parents tried to forbid it. But the love I feel for Lucas is steadier. I feel safe and happy with him.' She glanced over to where Lucas was sitting with his ma, rocking baby Henry in his arms as they chatted. Mattie and Ruby sat at his feet, the boy playing with a small car while his sister cuddled her favourite rag doll and watched him. 'I couldn't have chosen a better man, even if it seemed daft at the time. I mean, who gets married just to avoid moving to another place with her ma? It could have ended in total disaster.'

'But it didn't,' said Kate. 'It's worked out perfectly, especially now you've got little Mattie back.'

She sighed. 'I know. But I wish it hadn't been at Peg and Will's expense.' She touched Kate's cheek. 'I pray for both of them every day. I wouldn't have wished Peg's fate on her, no matter what.'

Kate nodded, hugging her friend. 'I know. I miss her like you wouldn't believe, but I know Will did the right thing by all of you rather than take Mattie with him to South Africa.'

'He seems to be doing all right, doesn't he?' said Louisa. 'We write to him regularly with news of little Mattie and he tells us about his new job. He said he wishes I could see the landscape and wildlife over there – it's a painter's paradise.'

'Maybe one day, you can go and visit him,' said Jeannie. 'I know Auntie Betty is hoping she can, maybe when she retires.'

Louisa shrugged. 'We'd love to, but I doubt we'll ever be able to afford it. He promised to get a camera and send us photographs, although we won't be able to see the colours he's described. Maybe I'll try to paint from them.'

'You're doing so well with your artwork, aren't you?' said Jeannie.

Louisa had been astonished by how quickly her watercolours had sold through the gallery in Wells, which had led to her being asked to design postcards and greetings cards. These days, when she could get a free hour or two, she was painting all the time. Thanks to her in-laws and Kate's sisters-in-law, all of whom helped watch the children to give her some time, she was able to keep up with orders. The extra money was a great help, meaning that they could afford a few little extras these days.

Kate sighed, her emotions close to the surface. 'I wish with all my heart that Ma and Peg could be here today,' she said, touching her silver cross. 'But I'm sure they're here in spirit, looking down on us and smiling.' She took a deep breath, blinking away tears. She didn't want to cry on her wedding day. 'And I thank God that Pa isn't around to ruin my day, and that God will forgive me for thinking that.'

'None of us had our pas at our weddings, did we?' said Louisa. 'I still wonder sometimes whether all the trouble I caused was what killed him.'

'Now stop that,' said Kate, giving her a stern look. 'He worked too hard and his heart couldn't stand it. He wouldn't want you thinking you were to blame because you weren't.'

Louisa shrugged. 'Ma thought I was.'

Kate huffed. Mrs Clements had been downright cruel to Louisa. 'It seems to me that if she'd been a bit more loving and caring to you and your pa, things might have been different for both of you.'

'I'm sure she didn't mean it, Lou,' said Jeannie. 'She was grieving when your pa was taken so quickly and wasn't thinking straight. She's trying to make it up to you now, isn't she?'

Louisa looked thoughtful. 'She is. We had a nice visit when she came to see us after Henry was born, and she sent some lovely Christmas presents for all the children. Maybe the distance between Street and Exeter is doing us both good.'

Kate could see that Ted was looking their way and after a moment, he excused himself from the people he was talking to and began to slowly make his way across the hall towards her. His progress was delayed by well-wishers, just as the girls' conversation was interrupted by other guests wishing Kate well and admiring her dress.

'You know,' she said when they were alone again. 'When the war started, none of us had any idea how long and hard it would be.'

'We certainly didn't,' said Jeannie.

'But we got through it, didn't we?' she said. 'I couldn't be happier for all of us.'

'Aw.' Louisa hugged her and Jeannie joined in, so that the three of them were in a huddle, their heads together. 'I couldn't have done it without you. If I'd have had to give up little Mattie completely, I don't think I'd have wanted to go on.'

'You would have,' said Jeannie. 'You're stronger than you think.'

'Only because I have the best friends in the world,' she said.

'That's what we are – the best friends in the world,' said Kate.

'Yes,' said Jeannie. 'We're The Three Musketeers, remember?'

'*All for one and one for all,*' said Kate.

The others grinned at her and joined in. '*United we stand, divided we fall.*'

They were giggling as they broke apart.

'What's the joke?' asked Ted with a smile as he reached them at last. Behind him were Lucas and Tom, both having passed their babies onto doting friends and relatives to watch for the moment. The three husbands of the Clarks factory girls. Each one handsome in body and spirit, who loved their wives without reservation.

Kate beamed at him. 'No joke,' she said as she and her friends moved into their own man's arms. 'Just three friends counting their blessings.'

* * *

MORE FROM MAY ELLIS

ACKNOWLEDGEMENTS

And so the war ends, with each of the friends settled with their loves and looking forward to a future full of hope.

In the course of writing the series, I've encountered so many people who have helped me. First and foremost, I have to thank my dear friend Lizzie Lane for insisting that I write it and cheering me along the way. She didn't let me doubt myself, nor did my lovely writer friends, the Lacock Ladies, especially Jenny Kane, Rachel Brimble, Louise Douglas and Jane Lark.

As ever, I would like to thank my wonderful editor at Boldwood Books, Rachel Faulkner-Willcocks, for helping me to make this book the best it can be; Colin Thomas for the superb cover design; the super marketing team led by Claire Fenby for spreading the word about it, and the family of Team Boldwood and the Boldwood authors who continue to encourage and support me.

Finally, I couldn't have written any of these stories without the inspiration and interest of the many, many lovely people I've met in Street. The community here is still a testament to Clarks Shoes and the Clark family, and it continues to be a welcoming and caring place. I feel privileged to have found it. Special thanks should go to the team at the Alfred Gillett Trust who care for the Clarks archives; all the Friends at Street Quaker Meeting House, including members of the current generation of the Clark family, who have welcomed me into their fold and given me an insight into life as a Quaker – an insight so special that I am now a regular attender there; the retired Clarks workers at the Clarks Social Club for their encouragement as I have written the series; and the ladies of Walton and Street WI for their fun and friendship and stories. There are too many people for me to name, but be assured that I appreciate each and every one of you and value your friendship and encouragement. Thank you.

I hope you've enjoyed these *Clarks Factory Girls* books. Thank you for reading. My next project will also be set in Somerset, but in the Second World War. I hope to have some cameo appearances from one or two characters you've come to know in this series, so watch this space!

ABOUT THE AUTHOR

May Ellis is the author of more than five contemporary romance and YA fiction novels. She lives in Somerset, within sight of Glastonbury Tor. Inspired by her move to the area and her love of social history, she is now writing saga fiction – based on the real-life stories of the Clarks factory girls.

Sign up to May Ellis' newsletter to read an EXCLUSIVE Bonus chapter!

Follow May on social media here:

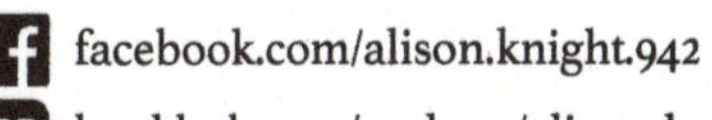

ALSO BY MAY ELLIS

The Clarks Factory Girls

The Clarks Factory Girls at War

Courage for the Clarks Factory Girls

Dark Times for the Clarks Factory Girls

New Hope for the Clarks Factory Girls

Standalone Novels

Lily's Choice

Boldwood

Boldwood Books is an award-winning fiction publishing company seeking out the best stories from around the world.

Find out more at www.boldwoodbooks.com

Join our reader community for brilliant books, competitions and offers!

Follow us
@BoldwoodBooks
@TheBoldBookClub

Sign up to our weekly deals newsletter

https://bit.ly/BoldwoodBNewsletter

www.ingramcontent.com/pod-product-compliance
Ingram Content Group UK Ltd.
Pitfield, Milton Keynes, MK11 3LW, UK
UKHW040421300525
6154UKWH00011B/100

9 781836 339137